**Critical acclaim for Connie Mason's
sensuous Historical Romances:**

Promised Splendor:

"The action never stops in this rip-roaring western.
Ms. Mason's engaging characters and vibrantly
colored backdrop will satisfy fans of sensual, exciting tales set during the wild gold rush days."
—*Romantic Times*

My Lady Vixen:

"MY LADY VIXEN is a delightful 'desire, decep-
tion and disguise romp' in the spirit of
Brandewyne's *Desire in Disguise* and Jude
Deveraux's *The Raider*." —*Romantic Times*

IN THE DESERT NIGHT

"Who are you?" Christa questioned.

No answer was forthcoming as those magic hands continued downward, over full breasts, taut stomach, to thighs that parted naturally at the merest touch. A growl escaped the throat of the man toiling lovingly over her, but Christa felt no fear, only pleasure.

"Are you the Desert Hawk?" she asked fearlessly. "Why won't you show yourself to me?"

"In good time, lady, in good time," he said, his lips and mouth much too occupied for prolonged replies.

"Oh, God," Christa cried out when his mouth found a pouting nipple and he began to suck hungrily.

"You do well to call upon your God, lady," he answered. "For by the time I am finished with you, you will surely think you have gone to heaven."

DESERT ECSTASY

Connie Mason

To Jeri Ann and Lou
Michelle and Rick
Marc and Kari
Heroes and Heroines all

A LEISURE BOOK®

Published by
Dorchester Publishing Co., Inc.
276 Fifth Avenue
New York, NY 10001

The name "Leisure Books" and the stylized "L" with design are trademarks of Dorchester Publishing Co., Inc.

Printed in the United States of America.

1

From that first spellbinding moment when their eyes found each other across the crowded room, defying the barrier of time and space, Christa instinctively knew her life would never be the same. Her breath caught painfully in her throat and she felt her heart skip a beat, unnerved by the intensity of the dark stranger's slow, lazy perusal. Never had she seen a man like him.

He moved with the lithe, sensuous grace of a desert cat, his tall, slim-hipped form exuding a totally masculine aura of confidence, power and authority, hinting strongly of long rapturous nights lost in sensual pleasure, lying in a silken tent cast upon the sands beneath a desert moon. Indecently long lashes, straight and dark, shadowing incredible emerald green eyes; rich, thick hair the color of dark oak; high cheekbones slashed across a bronzed face — a handsome face with lines that would put a Roman statue to shame. His mouth was full and sensuous, carved in strong planes and angles, suggesting an implacable nature. A deep cleft in his chin added to his overall attractiveness.

It was a rugged face, foreign yet familiar in the way it touched a responsive chord in Christa's breast. Expensive, form-fitting clothing molded to sinewy, resilient muscles sheathed by supple skin. His regal bearing commanded instant attention, as Christa, to her chagrin, discovered the moment she set eyes on Lord Mark Carrington, also known as Prince Ahmed, heir to the Berber beylic of Constantine, currently ruled by his father, bey Khalid ibn Selim.

Mark Carrington, grandson and heir to the Duke of Marlboro, coolly surveyed the crowded ballroom, his emerald eyes sparkling with pleasure as they settled on Christa's wide-eyed gaze. He had attended countless functions of this sort during his four years spent in England obtaining an education and becoming acquainted with his noble grandfather, and Mark invariably suffered through them with acute boredom. Though beautiful women intrigued him and were in turn attracted to the virile young prince, a passionate encounter was all that ever came of his association with the fair sex, for according to Berber law a foreign bride was forbidden their bey. And he doubted the pushy mothers of those daughters they deliberately brought to his attention would wish to see them ensconced in a harem at the beck and call of their master. Though his English mother and royal father seemed happy enough with this arrangement, Mark was astute enough to know that, had his mother a choice, she would have much prefered to be Selim's lawful wife instead of merely his concubine.

Mark's gaze lingered caressingly on Christa, wondering who she was and why he had never seen her before. Set under slim, arching brows of tawny gold, cat-slanted sapphire blue eyes dominated her heart-shaped face, a fringe of long, thick golden lashes only increasing their impact. A straight little nose, a full enticingly curved mouth, and a surprisingly firm chin and jaw only served to enhance the delicacy of her features. Waves of glorious hair the rare color of pale silvery-gold were arranged artfully atop a well-shaped head, allowing springy tendrils to brush gently against her cheeks, intensifying the creamy quality of her skin.

"Who is she?" Mark asked crisply of one of the two men flanking him. The Englishman who answered was Peter Trenton, whom Mark had met at the renowned school they both attended at one time. They had become staunch friends and companions and remained so ever since.

The other man standing at Mark's side, a fierce giant whose dark, scowling countenance marked him as foreign, was the bodyguard the bey had insisted accompany his heir everywhere. Not only did Omar possess incredible strength, but he was a desert sheikh from the warlike Tuareg tribe, nomads who roamed the desert of Algeria, and a friend of Selim, chosen expressly for his cunning and strength.

"I assume you're referring to the lovely blonde in the blue gown," Peter said, amusement coloring his words. He had been Mark's constant companion for nearly four years and never had he seen the prince express undue interest in any particular female, no matter how beautiful.

"Why haven't I seen her before?" Mark asked, unable to take his eyes off the woman who moved with sensual grace as she abruptly became aware that she had been staring rudely and moved self-consciously away.

"She hasn't been in London long," Peter revealed in a low voice. "I understand she's been

visiting her aunt in London. Her father is Sir
Wesley Horton, a high-ranking official in the con-
sulate in Tunis." It became obvious that Peter kept
abreast of London gossip as he continued, "Miss
Christa Horton has been in town only two months.
She's due to return to Tunis shortly."

"Christa," murmured Mark, savoring the taste
as he rolled the name around experimentally on his
tongue. "Miss Christa Horton. I want to meet her,"
he asserted with the authority of one born to rule.

Peter eyed Mark narrowly. Could this be the
same man who just last night had unfeelingly
dismissed the beautiful redhead who had been his
mistress for the past six months? Before that it had
been a blonde, then a brunette, and so it went.
Many women tried, but not one had succeeded in
reaching the heart of the formidible Mark
Carrington. They but filled a need that, had he been
in his own country, would have been adequately
assuaged by a bevy of tantalizing harem women.
And now this silver-haired wench had captured his
fancy by a mere glance. Nothing like that had
happened in all the time Peter had known him.

"You're her dinner partner tonight, Mark,"
Peter told him. "I surmised you'd be taken with her
beauty, though I had no idea how much. I hear she
is in London to purchase a trousseau. She's to be
married upon her return to Tunis."

Mark scowled darkly, his brows forming a
continuous slash across his wide forehead. "Married? To whom?"

Peter shrugged. "Don't know, old man. Some
minor official with the government."

"She's not married yet," Mark muttered beneath his breath as he avidly followed Christa's
slim figure, suddenly, unaccountably, jealous of the
man holding her in his arms on the dance floor.

Christa made the appropriate replies to the

smitten young man clinging to her every word. But her thoughts were with the man who had inadvertently captivated her senses: every now and then she dared a sidelong glance at his strong, powerful profile. When their eyes first met across the room, a strange warmth had surged through her veins and her senses had leaped to shimmering life. Not even her fiance had the power to stir her as did the mysterious man she had since learned was not only an English aristocrat but a Berber prince. In the ladies' withdrawing room, where she retired to gather her composure, the women were agog over the heir to the beylic of Constantine.

To twenty-one-year old Christa, the twenty-eight-year-old prince was all she had ever dreamed of in a man but knew she could never have. Already considered past the desirable age for marriage, Christa had finally given in to her parents' urging that she settle down, somewhat reluctantly accepting the proposal of Brian Kent, an official with the government whose career thus far had been likened to a rising star. His gallop to the top was being hastened by Sir Wesley Horton, who would soon become his father-in-law.

Always considered too exacting and independent by her friends and family, Christa was astute enough to realize that Brian wasn't madly in love with her. But he was handsome and ambitious, and he desired her. As for Christa, she was fond of Brian, more than any of her other beaux throughout the years. They would deal well with one another, she thought dispassionately, and that wasn't so bad. Given time, love might grow, as it did for her parents, whose own arranged marriage was a surprisingly happy one. Perhaps, Christa thought idly, she was incapable of love. Mayhap her life was destined to hold no great passion. That only happened in the books she read so assiduously. Though her parents would never force their eldest daughter to marry a man not of her own choosing, Christa had decided there was much she was missing in life by remaining unwed. Thus she had agreed to become Brian's bride.

Then tonight she had met the heated gaze of the handsome prince, who took immediate possession of her senses by the sheer force of his personality, and she hadn't known a moment's peace since.

Air! thought Christa, stumbling through the intricate steps of the dance. She needed fresh air to clear her addled brain. Escaping the moment the music ended, Christa excused herself politely and hastened toward the open door before she could be claimed for another dance by one of the eager young men vying for the privilege of holding her in their arms.

A distinctive sparkle lighting his eyes, Mark watched intently as Christa deftly eluded the crush of people and slipped unobtrusively through the open door and into the moonlit garden. A devious smile curved the corners of his mouth as he parted from Peter and strode purposefully toward the same door through which Christa had passed just moments before, the ever faithful Omar dogging his steps.

The night was balmy and clear, and a full moon hung in a sky filled with myriad twinkling stars. Mark spotted Christa immediately, her blue satin gown a shimmering beacon that made him glaringly aware of her curving form as she walked down a path taking her into a maze of tall evergreens, where few couples ventured for fear of becoming hopelessly lost. But Mark had been to Trenton House countless times in the past and the maze held no mysteries for him. Murmuring a few hasty words to Omar, who nodded and stationed himself at the entrance to the maze, arms crossed over his massive chest, Mark hurried after Christa, content in the knowledge that no one would get by the vigilant Omar to interfere.

Alone at last with her jumbled thoughts, Christa had no idea her steps had taken her into the maze. She had never visited the Trenton estate before, so that when she came to a bench and settled herself comfortably, she wondered idly why she had encountered no couples strolling the romantic, moon-bathed path. But the thought quickly left her mind, to be replaced by the image of a tall, dark man who somehow had captured her fanciful imagination without her ever having spoken to him.

Would she meet him tonight? she asked herself hopefully. If the look in his magnetic green eyes had been any indication, he was just as entranced by her as she was with him. Or was he the kind of man who set out to conquer any attractive woman who placed herself in his path? Was the rich, probably spoiled Berber prince and English nobleman the kind of man to possess women indiscriminately and then cast them aside when he tired of them? Such had been hinted at by the tittering ladies in the withdrawing room, who spoke in whispers of the Duke of Marlboro's heir. But what was a dukedom in comparison to the beylic he was slated to inherit? Obviously nothing, for if gossip could be believed, the prince was soon to leave England for good to return to Constantine.

Christa sighed, closing her eyes and inhaling deeply of the fresh pine scent surrounding her. Soon, she thought, she too would be leaving all this behind. Strange that they should both be going to the same part of the world. Fondly she recalled the soft nights of Tunis, the exotic sea breezes, the people she had grown to love. Suddenly she looked forward to her departure. Not once did the thought that Brian patiently awaited her return influence her eagerness to leave. She missed her parents and younger brother and sister and . . . she wondered if Mark Carrington had any siblings. Scores of them, she assumed, since the bey no doubt adhered to the customs of his country and kept a bevy of beauties in his harem in addition to the four wives allowed him by law.

Did the prince also have a harem? she wondered distractedly. When he left Constantine he must already have been a man. Surely he had a harem as well as a wife or two. For some unexplained reason the thought offered her little comfort, but the reasoning behind her feelings escaped her.

The music wafting across the carefully clipped lawns reminded Christa that it was time to return to the party. By now her Aunt Mary would have noticed her absence and sent someone searching for her. Rising hastily, Christa shook out the folds of her wide blue skirt, which matched exactly the sapphire of her eyes, and glanced to the right. Was that the direction from which she came? She took several steps, then stopped, puzzled. She faced a solid hedge. A frown worried her brow. Turning to the left, she carefully studied the path leading off in that direction. Was that the way out? And then comprehension dawned. Somehow she had wandered into a maze! How in the world would she ever find her way out without causing herself undue embarrassment? It was hardly dignified to stand there and scream for help.

The tall, lithe figure that stepped onto the path, moving on the balls of his feet in the rolling-hip gait of a stalking animal, seemed to materialize out of nowhere. He was slim, yet not thin; muscular, yet deceptively so, for nowhere beneath his costly clothing did he bulge grotesquely with corded muscles. He was all smooth, hard flesh, sleek and controlled, a powerful machine suggesting years of riding a horse across miles of arid desert, the strength of his legs and thighs becoming a part of the power of his mount. Abruptly he stood before her, and her senses reeled from the shock of his nearness.

"Good evening," he said, the deep timbre of his voice smooth and resonant as it rolled off his tongue with a delightful accent. "May I be of assistance?"

"I . . . I'm afraid I've stupidly wandered into the maze, Prince Ahmed," Christa stuttered sheepishly, his royal title coming easily to her lips. "I find I'm unable to make my way back to the party."

"You know my name?" Mark asked, obviously pleased.

"There are few here who don't know your name and titles. After all, this ball is in your honor."

Mark sketched an elegant bow. "And you, lovely lady, are Miss Christa Horton. You are a delightful, exquisite creature and I have been unable to take my eyes off you all evening. I've been waiting for the chance to meet you. And if I'm not mistaken, you share my fascination."

Hot color suffused Christa's pale cheeks. She was unaccustomed to being spoken to in such a forward manner. Had she been so obvious?

"How dare you speak to me in such a familiar manner, my lord!" Christa snapped tartly.

He was too attractive, too sure of himself, and Christa steeled herself to resist the pull of his devastating charm. There was an arrogantly confident look about this swarthy rake, a stamp of wild nobility in his bronzed features, an aura of primitive maleness that drew women like bees to honey. It was difficult not to succumb to his charms. No doubt the stories whispered about him were all too true, she thought distractedly; but she had no intention of becoming another of his conquests.

An imprudent grin hung on one corner of his mouth as he raked Christa's figure with hot green eyes, evidently liking what he saw. "So, I have been cast from my throne and must now settle for a mere lordship," he remarked, highly amused when she addressed him by the English title.

"I hardly know how to address you," Christa argued. "Which are you? An English lord or a Berber prince?"

Mark chuckled, greatly admiring her feisty nature as well as her seductive beauty, which she seemed unaware of. "For your information, my prickly English rose, both titles are correct. Upon the death of my mother's father I will inherit the Marlboro estates, for there are no other male heirs. But an entire beylic will be mine to rule upon my own father's demise."

"Your mother is English," Christa remarked, as if the thought just occurred to her.

"Does that surprise you? Years ago the ship my mother was traveling on was captured by corsairs off the coast of Sicily and eventually she was sold to my father for his harem," Mark revealed, wondering why he was divulging so much of his family history to a woman he had met just moments ago.

"Your mother is a slave?"

"Are you shocked?" Mark laughed, displaying the deep dimple in the cleft of his chin. "Truth to tell, it is doubtful who is slave and who is captor. My father fell deeply in love with my mother and she with him. Though the law of our land forbade their marriage, he elevated her above all his other women, proving his love for her by naming me, their first child, his heir over my older brother, Abdullah, born of one of his wives. I believe my mother is happy with her life. She has been back to England several times to visit her father but she always returns to her—master."

"Her love must be strong for her to choose captivity when freedom awaits her in England," Christa mused thoughtfully.

"Though it may be difficult for you to understand, my mother no longer considers herself a slave. In her heart she is wife to Khalid ibn Selim."

Suddenly a disturbing thought occurred to Christa. "Do . . . do you have many lovely women in your harem?"

"Would it bother you if I did?" he teased her.

"No," Christa was quick to deny. "I was just . . . curious."

"Then rest easy, Miss Horton, for I have no harem. Not yet, anyway," he added cryptically. "I've been away from Constantine for many years and it would be cruel of me to keep a harem when I am not there to . . . to see to their welfare," he faltered, choosing his words carefully. "There is time enough for that when I return. Would you perchance volunteer to become my first acquisition?" Though his tone was light and teasing a chill of forboding ran the length of Christa's spine.

"I'm no man's possession, nor have I the desire to become one," she bristled indignantly. "I will ask you once again, sir, to lead me out of here if you know the way."

"Gladly." He bowed gallantly, his green eyes hinting of deviltry. "Upon two conditions." Christa stiffened but said nothing, waiting.

"My first request is that you call me Mark. It's the name given me by my mother and one I use while in England." Warily, Christa consented, deciding it would do no harm, for in all likelihood she would never see the intriguing prince again. "The second," Mark murmured, his voice low and seductive, "is that you grant me a kiss for my trouble." He advanced a step and automatically Christa withdrew a pace.

"Really, sir, your request is outrageous!" Christa sputtered. Was there no end to this man's audacity? "Addressing a complete stranger by his given name is bad enough, but allowing him liberties goes beyond . . ." Her words died in her throat as Mark, ignoring her protests, reached out and drew her into his arms.

Christa gasped, tiny shards of pleasure racing beneath her skin as his muscular body moved sensuously against her. Her nearness had roused a strange need in him and his body reacted instinctively, allowing her to feel that need in a way that brought a deep flush to her face. But her violent protest never left her lips, for his mouth stole her words as well as her breath.

His kiss was comparable to nothing in her limited experience. Certainly it was nothing like what she felt when she and Brian shared a few innocent kisses. In Mark's arms she was naught but response and instinct; unwillingly she leaned into his embrace, molding her curves into the hard contours of his body. His mouth devoured her; his tongue pushed between her teeth to possess her; and every nerve ending in her body tingled as if exposed, her blood singing with the thrill of danger.

That this man represented danger to her, Christa noted on the fringes of awareness, was all too obvious. Why did he alone possess the power to turn her into quivering feeling and shivering response? In his strong arms she felt as though an invisible hand pressed all the vitality from her body, making movement or protest impossible.

Then his fingers brushed over her breasts, and the sensation was so intense, so exquisite, that she felt she would surely die. In all her twenty-one years no man had touched her so intimately. Suddenly his lips left her mouth to follow the path of his fingers, lingering on the white swell of flesh rising temptingly above her low-cut gown. It was all Christa needed to release her from her frozen stance as she burst into a frenzy of righteous indignation, pushing and shoving against the hard wall of his chest.

"You, sir, are a scoundrel and a rake!" she blurted out furiously. "I don't remember giving you permission to maul me."

Two dark brows peaked in amusement. "Would you have willingly granted me a kiss?"

"Of course not!" Christa sniffed haughtily. "What kind of woman do you take me for?"

"As I said before, you're a beautiful, passionate woman who has yet to be awakened to her own strong appetites. If you doubt my words your response to my kiss should put your mind at ease. Is your fiance aware of your sensual nature? Or has he already sampled your considerable . . . charms?"

Before her mind reacted fully to his words her hand had lashed out, catching Mark hard across one cheek. The brilliant moonlight clearly illuminated the vivid red mark left by her hand. But Mark might have been made of stone for all the emotion he displayed. Only his jewel-like eyes showed the slightest reaction as they glinted dangerously.

"So, the English rose has sharp thorns," he said

tightly. "One day, Christa, you'll belong to me, totally, body and soul. Do you believe in kismet? Our coming together is inevitable; I knew it the moment I looked into your eyes. Our fates are intertwined. You were born to become mine."

"Are you mad?" Christa challenged. "I am to be married soon and you will shortly return to your own country. You are mistaken if you think I would willing occupy a place in your harem with dozens of other hapless women." Shards of blue flame shot from Christa's outraged eyes. This man made her feel and experience things she had heretofore only dreamed about, placing her in jeopardy. Not only must she guard against his powerful charm but against her own weakness where he was concerned. "No, Mark," she demurred hotly. "After tonight we will never see each other again."

"You're wrong, Christa," Mark smiled mysteriously, savoring the way her name fell naturally from his lips. "We will be together again, sooner than you think. In ways you never imagined." His deep voice was filled with unmistakable promise.

Christa searched her numb brain for an appropriate reply, but she was far too annoyed to form a coherent thought. In the end none was necessary; Mark courteously offered his arm, which she hesitantly accepted, and he led her unerringly through the maze to where Omar stood sentinel, a huge immovable force ready to surrender his life for his prince.

Treading lightly beside Mark, Christa seethed inwardly. The man was impossible! He had everything—wealth, a glorious future, looks, all the women he wanted. So why was he toying with her? Kismet indeed! It was highly unlikely they would ever meet again.

When they reached the place where Omar

stood guard, she dropped her hand from Mark's arm, intending to give him a thorough tongue-lashing. But when she turned to confront him he was gone, melting into the shadows just as silently as he had appeared, his words ringing in her ears. Was it truly their fate to meet again?

Upon her return it took considerable effort for Christa to invent a suitable explanation for her long absence that satisfied her aunt. In the end she confessed that she had become lost in the maze, which in truth was what had happened. She made only one glaring omission—the presence of Mark Carrington. That incriminating bit of information she wisely kept to herself. But if Christa thought she had seen the last of her charming rescuer, she was sadly mistaken. A short time later he boldly claimed her for a dance, whirling her onto the floor beneath the noses of a score of more eager swains vying for the privilege.

"Did you think to be rid of me so soon?" Mark asked, smiling in secret mirth. Against her will Christa noted how the dimple in his chin deepened with his smile.

Steeling herself against his masculine allure, Christa replied tartly, "That was my hope."

"If I thought you meant that I'd be deeply hurt," Mark whispered seductively in her ear. "It will avail you naught to fight this strange attraction between us, sweet siren. Your eyes beckoned to me and I answered your call. Now you belong to me."

The audacity! Christa fumed in silent rage. "I neither signaled to you nor gave you a sign of any kind," she denied vehemently. "Your conceit is overwhelming!"

"We will discuss this later," Mark answered smugly. "You are to be my dinner partner."

"Your dinner partner! Have I no choice in

this?" In truth she was giddy with the thought of sitting next to him for several hours.

"I'm afraid not. The Trentons made the arrangements and I couldn't have chosen better myself. They thought . . ." But Christa never learned what they thought, for his words faltered as he spied Omar standing on the sidelines, motioning frantically.

Maneuvering skillfully, Mark soon had them standing before the formidable Omar, whose stony countenance suddenly appeared greatly agitated. His arm still around Christa's slim waist, Mark asked, "What is it, Omar?"

His face set in grim lines, Omar handed Mark a folded sheet of paper. Frowning, Mark read the message, his face paling long before he reached the end. Christa knew the news contained therein must have been grave indeed as she watched Mark crumble the paper in his fist, his face a mask of rage.

"What is it?" she asked, concern coloring her words. Mark looked unseeing into her eyes, as if unaware of her presence. Christa was shocked by the animal fury glazing his handsome features. Suddenly she was vastly relieved that she wasn't the recipient of that implacable rage and felt sorry for the person to whom it was directed. "Mark," she repeated, tugging on his arm to gain his attention.

As if coming out of a trance, Mark directed his gaze at Christa, his features softening. "I'm sorry, Christa, but it looks as if I'll not have the pleasure of your company at dinner after all. I must leave immediately."

"Leave?" Christa asked, confused. "You're returning to Marlboro House tonight?"

"I'm returning to Constantine," Mark revealed, startling her. "I've just received news that changes my plans and compels me to leave immediately. But never fear, sweet siren, we will meet again. It is written in the stars. It is kismet. . . ." His words hung in the air long after he was gone.

2

Two weeks later, Christa's stay in England came to an end when she boarded a three-masted, fore-and aft-rigged schooner in the bustling port of Marseilles, France. Of French registry, *Bon Ami* rode high and proud above the foaming waves slapping against her freshly painted hull. Accompanied by her maid, Marla, and surrounded by mounds of luggage, Christa cast one last look at the busy port city before settling into her cabin.

Situated on the Gulf of Lions on the Mediterranean Sea, Marseilles was a labyrinth of steep, dark, and narrow streets inhabited by a seafaring population. The steeples of the old cathedral were visible in the distance. The center of the old city was marked by the spires of the ancient church of Accoules. On the northern quay stood the Hotel de Ville. The harbor teemed with ships of all sizes and descriptions, from small fishing boats to ships much larger even than the *Bon Ami*.

Two days after the ball given by the Trentons in honor of Mark Carrington, Christa had crossed the English Channel. Her aunt Mary had the sudden inspiration of showing her niece Paris before she departed for Tunis, which was why Christa had chosen to depart from Marseilles rather than retrace her steps to England. She and Marla had taken a coach from Paris to Marseilles in plenty of time to board the *Bon Ami* bound for Algiers and Tunis.

Departure day dawned bright, the cloudless skies predicting a pleasant trip. By the time Christa awoke the following morning, Marseilles and Europe would be scarcely a dot on the horizon.

But to Christa's chagrin, all was not as serene as she would have liked. Perhaps the sea and skies were calm, but the turmoil in her heart allowed her scant rest. The dashing Mark Carrington had captured her romantic fancy and nothing had been the same after their fateful meeting, so quickly had he become an obsession. Where was he now? she wondered, vividly recalling the rapture of his kiss. Had he spoken the truth when he said kismet would bring them together again? What an absurd thought, she chided herself sternly. Their paths took them in different directions—hers to Tunis to become Brian's bride and his to Algeria to one day become ruler of a beylic.

"Excuse me," a haughty voice demanded. Christa started, surprised to find herself inadvertantly blocking the passageway leading to the deck below and most of the passenger cabins.

"I'm sorry," Christa murmured, moving aside to allow a striking redhead room to slide past. She knew there were several passengers other than herself aboard the *Bon Ami*, and obviously this beautiful woman was one of them. But before Christa could satisfy her curiosity as to the woman's identity she had pushed her way through the passageway, followed closely by a stout maid, huffing and puffing from the effort of keeping up with her thoughtless mistress.

Christa's own small cabin wasn't much larger than her dressing room at home in the large rambling house in Tunis, but somehow Christa found space for her trunk, placing some articles of clothing in the small chest beside the bunk. She noted that the chest was bolted to the deck, as were the desk, chair, and small, round table. A lamp swung from the ceiling and a pitcher and bowl rested in a kind of cradle atop the chest to keep them from sliding off. A bright coverlet on the bed dispelled some of the cabin's gloom, as did the curtain of matching material shielding the porthole. As ships went, the *Bon Ami* was better than most in the amenities it offered.

Dispensing with the help of the middle-aged Marla, who served more as companion and chaperone than personal servant, Christa busied herself with her unpacking. She eagerly looked forward to dinner, when she would be afforded a chance to meet her fellow passengers, particularly the brash redhead she had encountered earlier.

As luck would have it, the woman who had piqued Christa's curiosity sat next to her at the long table seating about a dozen fellow travelers, most of them young Frenchmen in military uniform.

"I'm Christa Horton," Christa offered in a friendly manner. "It seems we are the only two unaccompanied females aboard ship."

"How fortunate for us," muttered the redhead

as her lively blackberry eyes traveled the length of the table and back, flitting from one man to another in a flirting manner. "I'm Lady Willow Langtry."

"To which country are you traveling?" Christa questioned curiously. "I'm bound for Tunis. I've been to England visiting my aunt." Christa realized she was babbling, but for some reason the woman made her nervous.

"I'm joining my husband in Algiers," Willow revealed, somewhat reluctantly, Christa thought. "Richard has been there over a year directing shipping for his father's import firm."

"And you're just now joining him?" Christa blurted thoughtlessly, earning a frown from her companion.

Willow bristled indignantly. "Of course, Richard begged me to join him sooner but something always arose to delay me. Besides, certain . . . inducements persuaded me to remain in England as long as I could." A sly smile tilted the corner of her full lips and her eyes assumed a dreamy look, leading Christa to wonder if the "certain inducements" weren't male.

"Your husband must be anxiously awaiting your arrival after all this time," murmured Christa, devoting herself to her excellent meal.

Willow, older than Christa by several years, continued to ogle the male passengers, toying with her food in a distracted manner. She was quick to note that more than a few were casting covetous glances in Christa's direction, ignoring her own considerable charms.

Though considered a great beauty, Willow Langtry guarded that beauty jealously, regarding all women, even those of average looks, as keen competitors. She viewed Christa as more of a rival than most. With hair a flaming red, skin pale and translucent, eyes dark and mysterious, promising pleasure in their fathomless depth and a voluptuous figure flaunted brazenly in revealing gowns, Willow at first viewed Christa as presenting no great threat to her quest to become reigning queen aboard the *Bon Ami*. But upon closer inspection, Willow decided that the younger woman, though pale in comparison to her own vivid beauty, was attractive enough to divert attention to herself.

Unconsciously Willow thought back several weeks to the time she had everything she desired, only to find herself being summarily dismissed as the mistress of a handsome, extremely rich man who had satisfied her in every way, far better than any other man she had ever bedded. In the past year their number was not inconsiderable. Thank God stuffy Richard was in Algiers, where gossip could not reach him. Their marriage had been a mistake right from the beginning. She had accepted his proposal in a moment of weakness when she was between lovers, and at the time his offer seemed attractive. Almost immediately he had left for Algiers and she had promised to follow in a month, but managed to drag it out to a year using one excuse or another.

But somehow Richard's parents had learned of her latest affair and offered an ultimatum. Either she join Richard immediately in Algiers or they would apprise him of her adulterous liaison. Already humiliated over being sent packing by her lover, Willow had acquiesced, deciding to enjoy one last fling in Paris before traveling to Marseilles to board the *Bon Ami*. But deep in her breast she harbored the belief that, given ample time, she could have won her lover back, for in her somewhat fickle heart she fancied herself in love with this prince among men.

After dinner the passengers gathered in the saloon to become better acquainted, and just as Willow feared, Christa soon became the undisputed darling of the group of young military men. Though Willow received her share of adulation, she was far from pleased to find herself sharing the limelight with a washed-out blonde who seemed unaware of her impact upon the opposite sex.

Not only did Christa meet most of the young men taking up posts scattered throughout the Mediterranean, but also several friendly couples. Only Lady Willow remained distant and reserved during most of the pleasant evening, until one by one people began drifting off to their cabins. Christa murmured her own excuses, leaving behind a flurry of protest from disappointed young men who had been monopolizing her time. Truth to tell, she was becoming bored by their constant fawning, much preferring her own solitude where she could allow her thoughts free rein.

Safely tucked in her narrow bed, Christa was unaware of the two shrouded forms who made their secretive way up the gangplank under the darkness of night just scant minutes before the *Bon Ami* unfurled her sails and rode the midnight tide out to sea. The two were met by the captain, who seemed to be expecting them, and immediately escorted to their cabins.

Upon awakening the next morning Christa rushed to the porthole, the rocking of the ship telling her that they were on the open sea long before her eyes encountered nothing but unbroken stretches of vibrant aqua. The distant shores of France had all but disappeared beyond the horizon, but Christa was not sorry to have left and eagerly anticipated a happy reunion with her family. Her future husband commanded less of her thoughts at the moment, for in truth another man had captured her imagination, leaving her little room for another.

Where was Mark now? she wondered as she hurriedly washed and dressed, accepting Marla's help. The maid had entered the cabin while Christa stood gazing out the porthole.

"It's a beautiful day, Miss Horton," Marla chatted breezily.

The middle-aged woman was a Berber by birth and had been with Christa's family since their arrival in Tunis some years ago. With dark hair and snapping black eyes, she was a merry creature, pleasantly plump and practical. She was chosen to accompany Christa to England as chaperone because Sir Wesley trusted the woman to protect his beloved eldest daughter from the unwanted attention he knew Christa's uncommon beauty would attract.

Christa smiled fondly at the older woman bustling about the cramped cabin, laying out clean clothes and gathering up soiled. "It promises to be a pleasant trip," Christa agreed absently, her mind too full of her own thoughts for idle conversation. Noticing of her mistress's preoccupation, Marla lapsed into silence, fastening up the back of Christa's dress before excusing herself to seek her breakfast with the other servants while Christa took hers in the dining saloon.

Willow Langtry was noticeably absent at breakfast when Christa seated herself with the eager assistance of Lieutenant Henri Gervais, one of the young officers traveling to new duty in Tunis aboard the *Bon Ami*. Evidently Willow preferred her bed in the mornings, for in the days that followed the haughty redhead rarely appeared before noon. Which was fine with Christa for they never seemed to reach the camaraderie she had envisioned when she learned they were the only single females aboard a ship whose passengers consisted mainly of young men and married couples.

Almost a week elapsed before Christa became aware of the mysterious passenger who occupied the cabin next to hers. Though she occasionally heard movement and muted voices coming from the other side of the bulkhead, the person or persons did not emerge from seclusion, choosing instead to take his or her meals behind closed doors. Her curiosity was piqued even further by Willow, who had heard talk circulating about the ship concerning the reclusive passenger.

Not a cloud marred the azure sky and the gentle sea breeze kissed Christa's skin as she turned her face to the welcome warmth of the sun. Standing at the high teak railing, she was unaware of the tantalizing picture she made with the wind whipping her lightweight yellow frock about her legs and thighs, capturing more than one pair of eager eyes.

That afternoon Willow, clinging to the arm of handsome Captain Pierre Lefevre, approached Christa. Though Christa had studiously avoided entanglements with any of the French officers, she seemed never to be free of Henri Gervais, who hovered constantly at her elbow. He became so persistent that she took to strolling the deck with Marla in tow, hoping to discourage the young man. But he was undaunted, and this afternoon found him walking at Christa's side, blithely ignoring Marla's disapproving frown.

"We were just talking about the mystery passenger," Willow remarked, halting Christa. "Do you know anything about him? Your cabin is next to his and I thought you might have heard something."

Christa shrugged. "How do you know it's a man? It could be a woman, you know."

"Then you do know something!" Willow pounced on Christa's reply. "Is it a woman? What does she look like? Is she horribly disfigured? Is that why she's in seclusion?"

Christa heaved an exasperated sigh. "I know no more than you, Lady Willow. I've seen nothing of the mysterious passenger. Nor do I care to. If he or she wants to be left alone, then I suggest we cease this speculation."

"Mademoiselle Horton is right," Henri Gervais agreed. "Let us forget that poor devil below deck. Whatever his reason for desiring seclusion, it is of no concern of ours."

"*Mais oui, mon ami*," Pierre Lefevre chimed in. "With two lovely ladies for company, who cares about anyone else?"

Bestowing a radiant smile on Captain Lefevre, Willow nodded to Christa and Henri and guided the smitten officer to a more secluded corner of the ship. As yet, she hadn't taken the young man to her bed, but desperation was driving her to that final step. It had been weeks since her lover had abandoned her and by now her body ached for fulfillment. Soon she'd be with Richard and she was glaringly aware of the inadequacies of his lovemaking. His perfunctory performance was uninspired and dull, leaving her far from satisfied. It was no wonder she was forced to take lovers. With Richard far away in Algiers it had been simple to drift aimlessly from lover to lover, until the one man had come along who possessed all the attributes she had searched all her life to find. Rich, handsome, of noble birth, he was a man who knew how to please a woman, how to tease and tantalize her senses until she begged to be taken, how to fashion and mold her until she became nothing but response and torment in his arms. Willow had wanted it to last forever and was devastated when it had not.

After the evening meal that night, Christa returned immediately to her cabin, having had just about all she could take of Henri, who was becoming more and more persistent as each lengthy day passed without Christa's succumbing to his Gallic charm. Twice during the past few days he had tried to kiss her when Marla's head was turned, and both times was firmly repulsed. Christa's announcement that she had a fiance waiting for her in Tunis had little effect on the amorous Frenchman, especially after he learned how close Lefevre was to bedding Lady Willow.

It was obvious to Henri, displaying an enormous amount of male conceit, that all he had to do to match Lefevre's luck was to press his suite for Christa more forcefully. Perhaps Christa was the type who required more than the usual amount of inducement to succumb to his charm, but he vowed that one way or another Christa Horton would be in his bed before he left the ship.

After dismissing Marla for the night, Christa was far from ready for sleep. A strange, pervasive restlessness destroyed whatever inclination toward sleep she might have harbored earlier. Her body burned all over and a thrill of anticipation set her nerves atingle. She felt as if something was about to happen. Something she had no control over. Kismet? she mocked, laughing at herself.

The cabin was stifling, its tiny confines more a prison than a haven, and the urge to flee drove her to act impulsively. Throwing a concealing cloak over her nightgown, Christa rushed headlong from the cabin, caring little that her feet were bare and pale strands of her silvery hair hung in glorious disarray down her back. It being long past midnight, no one was about except the watch, who paid little heed to the lone passenger taking a late night stroll on the deserted deck.

Inhaling deeply of the tangy, salt-flavored breeze, spindrift collecting on her long, feathery lashes and smooth cheeks, Christa relaxed as all the tension slowly drained from her body, causing her to laugh at the strange panic that had sent her fleeing into the night. Though she had no idea what had caused her fear, she now realized how silly she had been.

"It's a beautiful night, *cherie*, one made for lovers," a smooth voice whispered close to her ear.

Starting violently, Christa whirled, and was more than a little annoyed to find Henri standing beside her. "Wha . . . what are you doing here?"

"The same thing you're doing, I suppose," said the lieutenant, leering openly as the sudden rise of wind molded Christa's cloak against her supple form, outlining every luscious curve. "I couldn't sleep, so took to the deck. Imagine my surprise to find a fairy creature posing as a beautiful woman beneath the moon's glow."

Henri moved closer, and reflexively Christa retreated, caring little for Henri's intimate manner. "It's time I went inside," she muttered warily, poised on the balls of her feet.

"*Non, cherie*, not yet," Henri murmured, his voice a seductive purr. "You have been leading me on for days without so much as a kiss to satisfy my hunger. Lefevre is already enjoying Lady Willow's body and I will not be denied yours."

His shocking words released Christa's anger. "You're—you're despicable!" she cried scathingly. "Get out of my sight! It matters little what Willow chooses to do. I am nothing like that woman." Whirling on her heel, she attempted to leave.

But Henri, determined to have his way, grasped Christa's arm and spun her around, bringing her in painful contact with the hard wall of his chest. Exercising his superior strength, he managed to drag her into a secluded corner well out of view of the watch. Sensing her struggles were having little effect on the determined Frenchman, Christa opened her mouth to scream, willing to awaken the entire ship if need be, only to be silenced when Henri captured her lips, grinding them against his in a forceful display of dominance until Christa tasted the hot spurt of blood in her mouth. His hands groped eagerly beneath her cloak and a silent scream rose in her throat, nearly choking her.

Rage and indignation drove her to renew her struggles, and she finally broke free from Henri's confining arms. But in the process she lost her cloak, leaving Henri momentarily stunned at the sight that met his lusting gaze. Christa's thin lawn nightgown did little to conceal the generous proportions of her lithe body fully revealed in the bright moonlight.

"*Magnifique!*" Henri uttered reverently. "With all that flaxen hair flying about you rival the angels in heaven." Desire inflamed his senses as he stepped forward, fully intending to capture his elusive angel once again. But Christa had other ideas.

"Come one step closer and I'll scream my head off," she declared bravely. "Captain Dubois will have you in irons for this assault upon my person."

Henri was far too aroused to pay heed to

Christa's warning. His one consuming thought was to have this tantalizing minx in his bed, willing or not. Even the vibrant Lady Willow paled in comparison to Christa's ethereal beauty. Throwing caution to the wind he lunged, intending to drag her into his cabin before she gathered her wits and carried out her threat to alert the entire ship.

"If I were you I'd listen to the lady," said a disembodied voice floating through the darkness.

Henri froze, rendered motionless as well as mute by the deep, authoritative voice. "Who's there?" he finally choked out. "I suggest you leave. This is none of your concern."

And then Christa saw him as he stepped from the shadows to peer into her soul with those incredible emerald eyes. Recognition flamed instantly. "You!" she whispered, recalling vividly the strong emotions he had roused in her upon their first meeting, how his touch set her afire, the way his eyes seemed to probe into her mind and heart.

Without taking his eyes from Christa, Mark hinted of dire consequences should Henri ignore his warning. "I'm making it my concern. For your own safety I strongly suggest you leave. And if you approach Miss Horton again, you'll live to regret it."

Nervously, Henri's gaze shifted from the man back to the woman, acutely aware that more than a mere meeting between strangers was taking place here. It was more like a communion of kindred souls, and he was neither needed nor wanted. Besides, something told him he'd be lucky to escape with his skin if he continued his pursuit of Christa at this time. One look into those brittle green eyes would take the starch out of any man. Wisely deciding that a hasty retreat was clearly indicated, Henri nodded to the imposing stranger and melted into the shadows. No woman was worth a beating —or worse.

"You seem surprised to see me," Mark said, his green eyes roaming appreciatively over the contours of Christa's body, clearly revealed beneath the thin nightgown. "Are you hurt? Did he harm you in any way?"

"N—no, I'm fine," Christa assured him, suppressing a shudder at the thought of Henri's hands on her body and what he intended to do with it. She would have hated it. Would she act the same when Brian attempted to claim his rights as her husband? she wondered, certain that she would. Had Mark, by a mere kiss and a touch, spoiled her for other men?

"You're cold," Mark noted as she began to shiver. Plucking her cloak from the deck he draped it over her shoulders, his hands lingering on the soft slopes longer than necessity demanded.

"What are you doing here? On the *Bon Ami*?" Christa questioned once she recovered from the shock of seeing the man of her dreams in the very place she wished him, beside her.

"I'll explain later," Mark said, "but first let me see you back to your cabin." Grasping her arm, he led her to the passageway, down the ladder and the short distance to her cabin. They paused at the door.

"You're the mystery passenger in the next cabin!" she exclaimed perceptively. "Why haven't you shown yourself before now? Were you aware I booked passage aboard the *Bon Ami*?"

It was obvious to Mark that Christa was not going to let him leave without an explanation of sorts. He opened the cabin door, glanced down the deserted passageway, then pushed her gently inside, quickly following and closing the panel noiselessly behind him. When he turned to her, his brilliant eyes darkened with an emotion Christa was at a loss to understand.

"Our destinies are closely woven, sweet siren," he said in a husky drawl. "Perhaps now you will believe me when I say kismet has decreed that we should meet again. Did I not tell you that one day you will be mine?"

The man was impossible! Christa sighed in exasperation. He was always speaking in riddles, and his conceit was monumental. "Let's not go into that again, Mark," she declared crisply. "Just tell me why you are traveling on the *Bon Ami* and your reason for remaining in virtual seclusion all this time."

A pained expression flitted across Mark's swarthy features. "Sit down, Christa, and I'll try to explain. I've no doubt what I say may shock you, but it's all true.

"Down through the ages my country has enjoyed a history of violence. I hoped to change all that with my reign as bey, but now I'm not sure I'll ever get the chance."

Dutifully, Christa settled herself on the bunk, a puzzled frown furrowing her smooth brow. "Whatever are you talking about, Mark?"

"My self-imposed isolation allowed me a brief time for mourning," Mark explained carefully, his voice tight with emotion.

"Mourning?" Christa echoed.

"Yes, the death of my parents. I was informed my father suffered some kind of seizure and died instantly. If you remember, I left the ball somewhat abruptly, shortly after we met. A ship had arrived from Algeria bearing a message for me from the Grand Vizier of Constantine informing me of my father's sudden death and urging me to return home immediately on the same ship."

Christa's blue eyes widened as the mystery deepened. "I don't understand. How did you come to be on the *Bon Ami* if your own ship awaited you in London?"

"Nothing in life is simple," Mark remarked cryptically. "The Grand Vizier's message bore far more distressing news. After my father's death, my half-brother, Abdullah, seized the reins of government, declaring himself bey. As a general in the Janissaries, he had their full support behind him. The coup was easily accomplished because I was not there to defend my right to succeed my father. Nor were Selim's followers successful in their bid to claim leadership in my name. Abdullah then announced himself bey of Constantine."

"Mark, I'm sorry," Christa said. "But that doesn't explain why you didn't take your own ship to Algeria."

"Abdullah found out about the Grand Vizier's message and sent a ship in pursuit. While I was preparing for my journey home, Abdullah's ship sailed into the Thames, boarded my own sloop in the dead of the night, overpowered the crew and attacked me and Omar when we attempted to board. We barely escaped with our lives, but thanks to Omar, whose sixth sense warned us in time, we were able to flee unscathed. Abdullah wants me dead. He won't rest until I am no longer a threat to him. He has placed a price on my head and forbidden me to return to my own country."

"So you crossed over to France and found the *Bon Ami* at Marseilles ready to depart."

"Exactly." Mark smiled grimly. "I am certain we were pursued, but with the help of Allah we made it aboard safely."

"Mark, you said both your parents were dead. What happened to your mother?"

Rage rolled over Mark's face and pain dimmed

his brilliant eyes. His fists clenched at his side and the muscles tensed beneath his expensive coat. Christa was rendered mute by the suppressed violence in Mark's expression. It was as if another person had invaded his body, one capable of great violence.

"Abdullah had my mother—my sweet, beautiful mother—put to death. He feared her influence, feared she might gain support on my behalf. It was all in the Grand Vizier's report. Thank Allah my younger brother, Yazid, was able to escape before Abdullah could order his death as well as my mother's. But it was my mother's misfortune to be trapped in the harem with no means of escape. By now I'm certain the Grand Vizier has suffered the same fate, for he was ever faithful to me."

Too stunned for coherent speech, Christa could only stare at Mark, her eyes a mirror of the compassion she felt for this special man. Abruptly, all vitality drained out of Mark as he sat down on the bed beside Christa, burying his head in his hands. Great waves of tenderness filled her heart, and tentatively she reached out, her hand absently brushing a tendril of dark hair that had fallen across his forehead. Her gentle touch acted as a balm to his tormented mind, and he turned to her in his great need.

Their eyes met, and Christa felt herself drawn into his very soul as their spirits merged on a plane above mere physical attraction. It was as if she had waited her entire life for this man. No longer was there the remotest possibility of her marrying Brian. Whether it was kismet or not, it was just as Mark said—their fates were irrevocably intertwined and it was as if her life began anew the day they met.

Mark's eyes focused on Christa's lips as if they

were the first pair he'd ever seen, as if the sight of
their soft, sensuous curves fascinated him. With
deliberate slowness his head lowered, and his
mouth slanted across hers with such tenderness
that Christa was moved to tears. The kiss was all
she remembered, and more. She nearly swooned
when his tongue parted her lips and entered the
fragrant warmth of her mouth, sipping eagerly of
her special nectar. Withdrawing slightly, he outlined their contour with the tip of his tongue, then
left her mouth as his greedy kisses blazed a searing
path across her shoulder, roughly pushing the cloak
and nightgown aside to reach his coveted goal,
leaving a white-hot fire smoldering in their wake.
She responded eagerly as his touch ignited the torch
of passion in her.

It mattered little that Christa's nightgown lay
twisted about her waist, for Mark's lips were on her
breasts and time shuddered to a halt. Carefully he
pressed her back against the bed, his mouth trailing
a searing path across pale, silken globes before
capturing the pert tingling bud crowning one entrancing sphere and saluting it with the deliciously
tormenting swirl of his tongue. She cried out softly
at the exquisite sensations he evoked in her, grasping the back of his head to keep his mouth firmly in
place.

His hands gently parted her pale, trembling
thighs so that his fingers could pay wonderfully
slow and highly sensual tribute to the budding
flower of womanhood concealed by the triangle of
golden curls. Christa gasped in shock, never having
known the intimate caress of a man. If this was
what it felt like to be loved, she wanted it to go on
forever.

"You have captured my senses, Christa, as no
one ever has before," Mark whispered against her

lips. "Help me forget for the space of an eternity that I have lost all I hold dear. Take me to heaven, sweet siren."

"Oh, Mark, yes," breathed Christa eagerly. "Make me yours. Make love to me."

Her body craved for release, the place where his fingers worked so diligently throbbed with sweet fire. Knowing something of what went on between a man and a woman, Christa was more than willing to surrender herself to Mark. Rising up, he parted her thighs with his knees, and releasing his manhood, touched where his fingers had been only moments before. Christa arched, waiting for the sweet stab of pain her mother told her about—only it never came.

Suddenly he groaned and tore his mouth from hers.

Her senses inflamed and her pulses rushing wildly, Christa looked at him in confusion and hurt. "Have I displeased you? Is something wrong?" she whispered, wanting him against her again, his mouth upon hers and his touch searing her flesh.

"No, never that." His breathing sounded unsure and there was a line of pain around his mouth. "There is nothing more I desire than your lovely body beneath mine, sweet siren," he rasped hoarsely, "your arms around me, the taste and smell of you surrounding me . . . but that will be another time, another place.

"One day you'll be mine, but for now I have no right to take your virginity. I can offer you nothing. I am a hunted man, a man stripped of his heritage and his birthright. Only my pride remains . . . and my quest for revenge."

She caught her breath, barely comprehending the meaning of his words, knowing only that she wanted him, that the wonder he had brought to her was too electrifying to end. But already he was rising to go and she reached out her hand to detain him.

"No, wait! It doesn't matter, Mark." How could he be so cruel? How could he leave her like this? "There is always England. In time a dukedom will be yours for the claiming. What does it matter if you cannot return to Constantine?"

"It matters to me, Christa," Mark claimed bitterly. "I owe it to the memory of my parents to regain the beylic from Abdullah and avenge my mother's death. Abdullah was never meant to rule. I won't rest until he's punished for his deceit and the pain he's caused me."

"Let me help you, Mark!" Christa cried in supplication. "When will we be together? Isn't it our kismet to be together? Or have you already forgotten your words?

"I have forgotten nothing. Kismet, sweet siren, works in mysterious ways. Someday, somehow, we will know happiness."

"Will I be your wife?" she dared to ask.

Mark frowned, staring distantly into space. When his gaze returned to her it appeared as if the weight of the world rested on his brawny shoulders. "Just as my father was forbidden by law to marry my mother, I will be denied the same privilege."

Christa paled, all her beautiful dreams crumbling like ashes beneath her feet. "You . . . you want me for your concubine?"

"If I am fortunate enough to assume my rightful place as bey, then I can never marry you. But you will be more to me than mere concubine, much more. You will be the food of my soul, the center of my existence. If there is a chance for us to be together in the way we both wish, you must trust me to find it."

"Will . . . will you take a wife from among

your own people?" Christa asked, holding her breath.

"My love, we will face that possibility when we come to it. When the time is right we will be together. It is written and so it shall be."

"No, Mark," Christa denied vigorously. "I will never consent to spending my life imprisoned behind the walls of a harem or shrouded by veils. Our lives are too different, despite the fact that you are half-English. My future awaits me in Tunis with Brian, while yours beckons from another direction. If you want me badly enough you will forsake your father's country and adopt your mother's. Surely your grandfather the duke must have urged you to remain in England."

His green eyes assumed a distant look, as if he was already withdrawing from her. "My grandfather would like nothing better than for me to remain in England and inherit the family estate. But Abdullah has destroyed any inclination I might have had toward granting his wish. I won't rest until the beylic has been wrested from Abdullah's greedy hands."

"Even if it means your death?"

"Even so. But I don't foresee death in my immediate future," Mark said cryptically. "I believe I will live long enough to see my children's children."

"Then we have no more to say to each other, Mark. I wish you luck—and happiness."

"No matter what you think, sweet siren, your future lies with me. Heed well my words. You will never marry your fiance. Allah in his wisdom will bring us together. You will be mine sooner than you think."

"Never!" Christa disclaimed. "There's no room for me in your world. Leave me in peace."

Mark rose slowly, raking the delicious curves

of her nude body regretfully. Any other man would have been only too happy to fulfill her wish and make love to her. Though he truly believed they would be together one day, his future was still too uncertain to take her heedlessly, then abandon her while he pursued his destiny.

3

The following day Christa was shocked to find Mark joining the usual group who gathered for breakfast. Evidently his self-imposed exile had come to an end. He was introduced by Captain DuBois, who like Mark himself offered no explanation for Mark's strange preference for seclusion. He greeted Christa with the cryptic words, "Miss Horton and I have already met." Henri Gervais muttered a sour greeting, then turned away. As was her custom, Lady Willow had yet to make an appearance.

To Christa's credit she managed to choke down her breakfast, aware that Mark's jewel-like gaze rested on her more often than she would have liked. Finishing quickly, she excused herself and made a hasty departure, thankful that Henri didn't rise also and insist on accompanying her on her morning stroll as he so often did. From Henri's downcast eyes as he intently studied his plate of congealing food, Christa surmised that Mark had succeeded admirably in cooling the Frenchman's ardor. His encounter with Henri the night before must have impressed the Frenchman, and Christa was grateful for Mark's timely intervention. But not grateful enough to forgive him for humiliating her.

It was another beautiful afternoon, Christa thought as she gazed appreciatively at the brilliant blueness of the sky, relieved only by white fluffy clouds scudding before the wind. Her waist-length silver hair floated free in the brisk breeze, framing delicate features and sun-kissed skin sporting a healthy glow from long days spent strolling the deck. Her lightweight dress of violet voile outlined the gentle curves of her supple form, defining the slimness of her miniscule waist, the high rise of her breasts and the hint of shapely thighs and legs beneath her billowing skirt. It was a sight that totally captivated Mark as he came up beside her, succumbing easily to her feminine allure. The attraction that existed between them was far too powerful to resist, too magical to deny. Though his life was in a turmoil, his senses spoke loud and clear. He wanted Christa Horton. And not just in his bed. She was his life and he was her kismet.

"Good afternoon," he said, failing miserably in his effort to control the surge of joy her nearness brought him. He knew Christa was angry with him and respected her motives, but her beauty drew him further and further into the web of sensual desire. How long could he resist the love she so unstingingly offered? Not long, he fretted, if last night was any indication. She was as necessary to him as food and water.

Christa whirled, frowning into Mark's sparkling green eyes. "It was—until you showed up," she declared crisply, meaning none of it.

A lazy smile hung on one corner of Mark's full lips. God, why did he have to be so appealing? Christa asked herself glumly. It was obvious from their first meeting that this man wasn't for her. His destiny was to rule and hers was to live free.

"You don't mean that, Christa," Mark murmured in a seductive purr. "When we are finally together in the way we both wish, you will respect the decision I made last night. Suffice it to say I want you more than any woman I've ever known."

"You assume too much, my lord," Christa sniffed disdainfully. "I assure you that once I'm married to Brian you will be naught but a vague memory." Good Lord! How could she tell such lies? After meeting Mark there was no question of her marrying Brian. Even if she never saw Mark again she could not live out her life with Brian Kent. It would not be fair to either of them. No living man could measure up to Mark.

"Christa, let's—"

But whatever Mark intended to say was lost in a high-pitched squeal that drowned out his words. "Mark—Mark Carrington! Is it really you?"

Mark swallowed a groan of dismay as Willow shrugged off Pierre Lefevre's possessive grasp and hurled herself at him. Willow Langtry was the last person in the world he expected or wanted to see. It had taken him weeks to convince her that their affair had run its course. He had taken his fill of Lady Willow, though the woman adamantly refused to accept his departure in good grace. To Mark she was just another woman in a long succession of mistresses who had made his time in England extremely pleasurable. Not one of them meant a fig to him. Only Christa had stolen his heart.

Suppressing a grimace, Mark disentangled himself from Willow, saying, "What a surprise,

Lady Willow. I had no idea you were abroad the *Bon Ami*. Are you finally off to join your dear husband?''

Willow smiled obliquely. The moment she saw Mark she felt certain he had somehow learned she was sailing from Marseilles and followed. To a self-centered woman like Willow, Mark's presence served only to reinforce her belief that her instincts had been correct and Mark had second thoughts about severing their relationship. She yearned desperately for them to be alone so they might talk privately. The reason behind Mark's long days in seclusion had puzzled her, for she realized he was the mystery man who had steadfastly sought the privacy of his cabin. Why hadn't he shown himself sooner?

"So you're the person who refused to leave the cabin!" Willow crowed gleefully. Then her full lips turned downward into a pout. "Why did you waste so much time, darling? Think of all those days and nights we could have . . .'' Suddenly she became aware of Lefevre, who hung on her every word, and of Christa, who wished she could have turned into smoke and blown away.

"You'll excuse us, won't you?" she smiled sweetly to Lefevre. "Mark Carrington and I are old—and dear   friends. There is much for us to discuss.''

Consumed with jealousy, Lefevre slanted Mark a dark glance, then bowed to Willow. "As you wish, *cherie*.'' Seething inwardly, he whirled on his heel and stomped away.

Without waiting for a dismissal, Christa made as if to follow. She was astute enough to realize that Mark and Willow were more than just casual friends. Despite the pained expression on Mark's face, it was all too obvious that Willow fully intended to renew their relationship, whatever it might be. Far be it for Christa to come between lovers. How naive Mark must think her! She had almost believed his false words about their being together one day. Kismet! Bah! It was obvious that Mark had a talent for flattery and a vivid imagination, as well as a hunter's instinct for the fair sex.

"Christa! Don't go," Mark begged when he became aware of her intention to leave.

"You two don't need me," Christa informed him curtly.

"You and Christa know each other?" Willow asked, her eyes narrowing speculatively.

"I had the pleasure of meeting Christa at the Trenton ball not long ago," Mark responded, bestowing a fond look at the woman who had captured his heart.

"Oh, yes," Willow acknowledged shortly. "For some reason I wasn't invited. An oversight, I assume."

Mark suppressed an amused grin. He had expressly forbidden Peter to invite Willow. He had meant what he said when he told her their liaison had ended, and he was extremely gratified to learn that she had left to join her husband, though astounded to find her aboard the *Bon Ami*. It was as if all the fates had conspired against him.

"You must excuse me, Willow," Mark said. "I was about to offer my escort to Christa." His abrupt dismissal couldn't have been more blunt or explicit, but stubbornly Willow refused to accept it. No milksop miss was going to steal Mark's affections while she was around.

Christa recognized Willow's fierce possessiveness and decided to leave her to her feminine wiles no matter what Mark said. "I've had enough air for today," she announced rather pointedly. "I believe I'll go below and read." Without waiting for a response, she wheeled and hastily retreated from the unpleasant situation, an unaccustomed ache orginating somewhere in the vicinity of her heart. It was a strange and unwelcome feeling.

"Up to your old tricks, aren't you, darling?" Willow snapped the moment Christa had disappeared from sight.

Highly agitated, Mark slanted Willow a frosty glare. "What are you talking about, Willow?"

"Why, seducing virgins," she said scornfully. "When will you learn they aren't worth the trouble? Besides, now that I'm available you won't need to pursue your subtle game with that innocent little twit. You know what I can do for you." Her voice grew husky with desire just thinking about experiencing again this man's special brand of love. Captain Lefevre was a novice compared to Mark Carrington, who was a prince in more ways than one.

"You're the one who's playing games, Willow," Mark responded evenly, though he burned with indignation at Willow's assumption that he was merely toying with Christa. "It was over between us weeks ago, and I don't intend to discuss it further."

Willow bristled angrily. "A dead issue, am I! At one time you couldn't get enough of me."

"Perhaps so," Mark agreed. "But that no longer holds true. Be satisfied that you'll soon be with your husband. Try making him happy for a change."

"That inept twirp! You know how I feel about him, Mark."

"Then find another lover. Lefevre, for instance. He seemed more than agreeable from what little I saw of him."

"I've already tried him and he's not half the man you are," Willow admitted with unabashed candor.

Mark's eyebrows rose as hearty laughter rolled from his throat. "You flatter me, Willow!" He grinned roguishly. "But I'm certain I'm not the only man in the world who can please you."

"Maybe not, Mark, but you're the only man I want," Willow admitted in a petulant voice.

Wanting desperately to rid himself of Willow and her unsubtle attempts at seduction, Mark heaved an exasperated sigh. "I've no time for this, Willow. I have something important to attend to."

"Can we get together later, Mark?" Willow pressed, eager for a commitment before he slipped away.

By now thoroughly disgruntled, Mark grew reckless, nodding distractedly in answer to Willow's request before making good his escape.

"Take care of your business, Mark," Willow called to his rapidly departing back. "I'll see you after supper—in your cabin."

"Yes, yes," Mark acquiesced, barely hearing her words as he disappeared into the passageway. Nothing mattered but finding Christa and explaining about Willow and their past relationship.

But much to his chagrin, Christa steadfastly refused to open her door to him. Rather than make a scene, he stood outside the cabin fuming, and the longer he thought about it the angrier he became, deciding it was beneath him to try to explain something that was really of no concern to Christa. They were not married, or even engaged. Yet something compelled him to make Christa understand that Willow Langtry meant nothing to him.

Christa did not go to supper that night, instructing Marla to bring her a tray. After refusing to listen to what Mark had to say earlier, she was not eager to face him with a lot of strangers looking on. But the longer she sat by herself and brooded, the more she became aware of just how unfair she

had been to Mark. Obviously Willow had meant
something to him in the past, but that didn't
necessarily still hold true. She owed him an explanation. Besides, perhaps if she saw him in private
she might yet persuade him not to go to Constantine, where he would be placing his life in danger. If
there was to be a future for them, it lay in England.
Only in England would they be free to love and live
their lives in peace.

That thought moved Christa to act as she
cracked open the door to her cabin, intending to
confront Mark and convince him to listen to reason. But she never passed the threshold. From
somewhere nearby Willow's sultry voice drifted to
her. "Mark, it's Willow, let me in. You told me to
come to your cabin tonight, darling, and I could
wait no longer."

Quietly closing the door, Christa leaned
against the panel, chiding herself for stupidly assuming Mark meant what he said about their
belonging together. It was nothing but nonsensical
mouthings. Perhaps he had meant it, but only until
Willow reentered his life. Christa was glad she
learned just how fickle he was before it was too late.
Her thoughts in a turmoil, she made ready for bed,
wondering at the absolute silence coming from the
other side of the bulkhead. Were Mark and Willow
already making passionate love? she wondered
bleakly.

Little did Christa know that Willow never
gained entry to Mark's cabin. She was turned away
by a dour Omar, who curtly informed the fuming
redhead that his master was sleeping. Willow departed in a huff.

In the days that followed, Christa was hard put
to behave in a civil manner toward Mark. In fact,
she rarely saw him alone, for invariably Willow
trailed in his wake. Nor was she bothered by Henri,

though from time to time he slanted her looks dripping with resentment. Obviously he blamed her for the embarrassment he had suffered at Mark's capable hands.

Then one day, the perfect weather they had been experiencing since the *Bon Ami* left Marseilles gave way to leaden skies, howling wind and lowering clouds, turning the sea into a froth-whipped angry monster, spuming salt-spray and foam. Christa grasped the rail, unable to tear herself from the awesome sight that filled her with terror.

"The captain ordered all passengers to their cabins," a low voice rumbled in her ear. The howl of the wind stripped the words from Mark's throat and flung them back to Christa. "Christa, did you hear me?" he insisted. "All the other passengers have already gone below."

Slowly Christa turned to gaze at Mark. "Will there be a storm?" she gulped, half in fear, half in awe. Never had she seen a more magnificent sight than an angry sea before a storm.

"It's highly likely," he said, fighting the wind to make himself heard. "Come along, I'll see you to your cabin."

Christa nodded, but when she tired to uncurl her fingers from around the railing, they refused to obey. Sensing her fear as well as her fascination with the approaching storm, Mark grasped her hands, uncoiling each finger in turn. His touch was the catalyst that released her from her frozen stance. Her skin burned where their flesh came in contact, and Christa could not help but stare longingly into his jewel-like eyes, baring her soul to the only man who possessed the power to render her mute with desire.

Mark was far from immune to her silent appeal, wondering if she realized what she was asking with those expressive blue eyes. Suddenly it no longer mattered what his heart told him was right or wrong, as his fierce need took possession of his senses.

Releasing a string of curses that were quickly swallowed by the wind, Mark surrendered to the emotions that had been plaguing him since the first moment he set eyes on the tempting minx. His staunch resolve and all his admirable intentions vanished, blown helter-skelter with the fierce squall as he slipped a hand beneath Christa's quaking knees and lifted her high in his arms, her head resting against his wildly thudding heart.

She might have been a feather, so easily did he carry her across the rolling deck, now awash with waves breaking fore and aft. Icy rain began pelting them long before they reached the shelter of the passageway, but neither noticed the slight discomfort, more aware of each other than the raging elements. By the time they reached Christa's cabin, both were thoroughly drenched and shaking violently, although their trembling had little to do with the weather or the condition of their clothing.

Carefully setting her on her feet, Mark moved his shaking fingers to the fastenings on the front of her dress. A lamp, purposely left burning by Marla for her mistress, swung crazily from the ceiling, creating a diffused glow.

"Allah help me, for I cannot help myself," he groaned, as if in pain. "I can no longer resist you, though I know this is the wrong time, the wrong place."

An obstruction in Christa's throat rendered her mute; only his hands fumbling with her clothing held any reality.

"I want to see you the first time I make love to you," Mark whispered huskily. "All of you. If you want me to leave, tell me now, for in another breath it will be too late. I don't mean this to be a frantic coupling, sweet siren. I intend for this to be a night you will remember. It was not my intention that this should happen now, but I can fight this uncontrollable need for you no longer."

An involuntary gasp escaped Christa's lips when his hands made a slow survey of the soft curves of her breasts, looking up at him all the while from beneath tawny lashes. A tremor of arousal shuddered through her, and she couldn't have uttered a word in protest had she wanted to. With tantalizing slowness Mark lowered the bodice of her gown, bringing her chemise with it until her breasts were bared, round and glowing. Rose-hued nipples sprang to life beneath the intensity of his gaze and Mark bent his dark head to lingeringly kiss each one in turn, until Christa moaned in mindless rapture.

"Do you want me, Christa?" Mark asked in a husky growl. "Will you send me away? I will not think any less of you if you do." Though he spoke the words he wasn't certain he could turn and leave should she demand it.

"No! Yes!" cried Christa. "I mean, yes, I want you and, no, I don't want you to leave."

"Then I shan't, sweet siren. I will teach you to love, to accept and give pleasure." His hoarse words vibrated on her skin moments before his firm mouth parted her lips to drink deeply of a kiss that contained undeniable hunger and impatient need.

With a will of their own, her hands roamed his chest and shoulders, loving the feel of him beneath her fingertips. He was all male, hard, brown, and extremely attractive. And she wanted him. A surprised protest bubbled from her lips as he effortlessly lifted her and deposited her on the bunk, the deck rolling beneath his feet hindering him not at all. The rising storm was all but forgot-

ten in their desperate need to quench the hunger
burning within.

With loving gentleness he removed the rest of
her clothing, setting back on his heels to stare
appreciatively at the delightful contrasts of hills
and curves he had bared. "You're beautiful," he
whispered reverently. "Lovelier than any woman
has a right to be."

He removed his coat and shirt, then his boots,
slanting a questioning glance at Christa before
shrugging out of his pants. Christa's eyes opened
wide, and though she tried not to look, her gaze was
drawn helplessly to his erect manhood springing
from the dark forest between his thighs. How
delightfully he is made! she thought, yearning to
touch him. When he smiled at her, she melted
inwardly, blushing as she wondered how it would
feel to have the hard length of him pressed intimately against her soft flesh. Reading her thoughts,
Mark obliged by stretching out beside her, hips and
thighs meshing, legs entwined.

He knew exactly where and how to touch her
to bring her the most pleasure. His mouth found
the sensitive nape of her neck, the bend of her arm,
the curve of her waist, then lingered lovingly over
her breasts before blazing a trail of fire down her
belly to the insides of her thighs. Christa writhed
against him as sheer passion burned away all in-
truding thoughts of guilt or wrongdoing. When he
slipped his fingers between her thighs, she parted
her legs in a mindless rush of desire. His stroking
spiraled her higher and higher, to a place she had
never been before, or knew existed.

Her hands sketched the taut muscles of his
thighs and followed the hard tendons that ascended
his back. She marveled at the strength beneath her
fingertips, loving the feel of his sinewy body. His
kisses trailed along her collarbone to hover over

each pink nipple while his bold caresses below stroked her to a fever pitch. She could not think, she could only respond.

"I'm sorry I must hurt you, my love, but the pain will last only a moment," Mark murmured against her lips as his manhood probed delicately into her moist warmth. A soft moan slid between his parted lips at the feel of hot, wet flesh against his swollen staff.

Flexing his hips he thrust sharply forward, impaling himself in the welcoming heat of her, groaning in agonized ecstasy as her tightness gripped him and held him.

Christa cried out softly at the exquisite invasion of his manhood, the brief, sharp pain quickly replaced by the most acute pleasure she had ever known. Deliberately he resisted the urge to move, remaining motionless until she grew accustomed to the feel of him inside her. Only when she sighed and relaxed did he push his full, extended length into her until he was deeply embedded.

The world spun slowly, time seeming to halt as he rolled his hips and moved within her, offering her his love in physical ways that her flesh understood, whispering his devotion in words that came from the heart. Christa quickly picked up the rhythm, and they rocked in the cradle of each other's arms as they rode out the storm, unaware of the dazzling lightning blazing across the blackness of the night sky, the deep thunder rolling over the sea, or the fierce wind buffeting the ship and tearing at the sails. When it broke, the storm within them far surpassed the wild tempest created by nature, as together they produced their own blinding display of celestial fireworks.

Christa opened her eyes to find Mark staring at her. Unconsciously her hands moved to shield her nudity, a bright flush suffusing her features. An amused smile tilted one corner of his lips as he reached out, capturing her fluttering hands. "There's nothing to be ashamed of, my love," he chided lovingly. "Your body is beautiful. You were made to be loved. One day I will know it as intimately as my own." With one tapered finger he lovingly traced a path from the high ridge of a cheekbone, down her chin to her slightly parted lips.

"Your body is beautiful, too," Christa said, looking at him shyly through a finge of tawny lashes.

A deep chuckle rumbled through his chest. "Men aren't beautiful, sweet siren."

"You are," she insisted adoringly. "I had no idea the . . . the act of love could be so wonderful."

"It was wonderful because love was involved," Mark revealed wonderingly, as if the idea had just occurred to him. "You believe that I love you, don't you, Christa?"

"I . . . I suppose," agreed Christa hesitantly. "Everything that's happened since we met has been so spontaneous . . . so explosive. I suppose tonight was inevitable."

"Kismet." Mark nodded sagely.

"What about Willow, Mark?" she dared to ask.

"What does Willow have to do with us?" Mark replied shortly. "What happened in the past has nothing to do with my feelings for you."

"But I'm not entirely convinced it's over between you and Willow."

"I am, though I freely admit to my affair with Willow. But it ended long before you and I met. Willow is a persistent woman," he allowed with a touch of irony, "who doesn't let go so easily."

"Do you usually sleep with women once you've ended an affair?" she asked quietly.

"What are you talking about?"

"Have you forgotten? My cabin is next to yours. I heard Willow at your door the other night."

"Is that what this is all about? If you had listened a moment longer, you'd have heard Omar turn her away."

A look of total amazement puckered her features. "Truly?"

"Truly."

"Oh, Mark, I'm sorry I misjudged you so. What will happen to us now? Do you really think there is a future for us?"

"Our future lies in our loving each other."

Translating his words to suit her own purposes, Christa seemed satisfied with his response as she snuggled deeper into his arms. This led them into a passionate embrace with Mark once again weaving a spell around her senses as his hands and lips began a slow arousal of her warm, tingling flesh. "Again?" she asked, amazed. "Is it possible?"

"Not only possible, but highly desirable. I could make love to you all night long without tiring." And then there was time for no more talk, as Mark drove all conscious thought from her mind, making her aware of nothing but the play of his hands and lips on her body.

4

Shortly before dawn Mark reluctantly left Christa's cabin, allowing her a few uninterupted hours of much needed sleep. A dull, gray sky greeted her when she awakened later; an opaque mist hung over a sea still angry from the night's tempest. Though the worst of the storm had passed, its memory lingered. When she went on deck, Christa saw immediately that the *Bon Ami* had sustained considerable damage. One mast had snapped in two and the rudder had been rendered nearly inoperable. It was nothing that couldn't be repaired, a confident Captain Dubois assured his concerned passengers. All would be in working order once again in no more than a day or two.

The delay bothered Christa not at all, for she spent those days eagerly anticipating the nights when Mark would creep undetected into her room and make love to her. In the short time since their first meeting she had come to accept the deep, abiding love she felt for him. And in her heart she knew Mark cared for her. He consistently ignored Willow, despite the redhead's machinations to corner him alone in order to throw herself at him. But to Christa's delight, he paid little heed to Willow's outrageous attempts at seduction, preferring instead to spend his time with Christa.

One night, after making love, Christa idly began speculating about their future. "On the morrow the rudder will be repaired, Mark, and we'll be on our way again. In a day or two the ship will reach port. I know my family will love you. Will we be married in Tunis, do you think?"

A look of total amazement swept over Mark's features. "Christa, I thought you understood."

"Understood what?"

"Nothing has changed, my love, except that we have consummated our feelings for each other. We can't marry. Not now. Maybe not ever. I am a hunted man, a man forbidden entry to his own country. There is a price on my head. Danger stalks me no matter where I choose to live, and until I dispose of this threat hanging over my head we cannot be together. Your life means too much to me to purposely place you in harm's way. Until all my problems are resolved and my future is clear, I can think of nothing but Abdullah's betrayal and avenging my mother's death."

"You want me to go home and marry Brian?"

"No! God no! I want you with your family where you'll be safe, but never to marry Brian. Surely you can hold him off until I return for you?"

"And when you do return for me, what then? What if you're successful and regain your right to rule the beylic? Where will I fit into your life?"

"Don't ask me those questions now, Christa. When the time comes we will find the answer."

"I thought you'd changed!" Christa cried, her

words laced with anguish. "I thought you cared for me. Does revenge mean more to you than I do?"

"Don't, Christa. Don't press for a commitment I'm not at liberty to offer. Let the love we share speak for itself. Be patient and wait for me."

"That's not good enough, Mark," Christa insisted bitterly, her chin tilted at a defiant angle. "If you truly loved me, you'd give up this insane quest for vengeance."

"Have you forgotten that Abdullah put my innocent mother to death and would have killed my younger brother if he hadn't escaped? For the love of Allah, allow me a shred of pride! I gave you my heart—do you demand my soul as well?"

"I demand nothing that you aren't willing to give," responded Christa with a hint of sadness.

"Then you understand why I can't be with you for some time?"

"No, I don't understand," she contended stubbornly. "Either you love me and want to be with me or you don't."

"It's not that simple," Mark countered, his temper rising. Other than his step-father, he had never been compelled to answer to another human being for his actions. And he was too old to begin now.

"Until you come to your senses, we have nothing more to say to each other," Christa returned hotly. For his own sake as well as hers, she wanted him to give up this foolish need to plunge headlong into danger.

Red dots of rage exploded behind Mark's brain, causing him to utter careless words without thinking, wrapping them around his tongue and flinging them at her like stones. "Perhaps my countrymen are right in assuming women have but one purpose in life. Keeping them behind high walls and using them for objects of pleasure has much to commend it. Allow them too much freedom and they only complicate your life."

"Why you—you conceited ass!" flung out Christa, rising to her knees, unmindful of her nudity. "How dare you compare me to those poor creatures forced to exist in the shadow of their masters and be used as playthings for men like you."

Mark's green eyes gleamed with wolfish delight as he raked Christa's supple form displayed before him in all its glorious nudity. "All women come with the same accoutrements," he insinuated crudely. "Most of them enjoy what I can do for them."

"You're revolting! Get out of my room!"

A crooked grin twisted his lips and Christa whirled, presenting her back to him. Mark thought the sight of her quivering buttocks adorable, and he told her so. An indignant gasp escaped her lips as she felt his hands knead the twin mounds, molding them to the contours of his palms.

Twisting from his grasp, Christa jumped to her feet, facing him with her fury, blue eyes blazing, breath heaving in short pants. A slow smile spread across his handsome features, and against her will Christa found herself responding to the arrogantly confident rake facing her. There was a stamp of wild nobility in his bronzed features, an aura of primitive maleness about him that moved her deeply.

"I'm going to make love to you again, sweet siren." His eyes tempted her beyond mortal endurance and his voice was so hauntingly seductive that every nerve in her tense body began twitching. He fully intended to have his way and Christa's objections presented no obstacle.

One delicate brow arched in question as Christa surveyed his masculine stance, hands on slim hips, long sturdy legs wide apart, his aroused manhood thick and impressive springing from the dark triangle between his thighs. "I suddenly find myself bored by your lovemaking," she declared insultingly.

Deep, rich laughter rolled over her like thunder as Mark tilted back his head and roared. Though he seemed amused by her remark, Christa took careful note of the violence contained within the smoldering depths of his green eyes. She retreated until her back came in contact with the wall. Grinning with devilish delight, Mark advanced, pouncing on her before she could react.

"Let's see if you're truly as bored with my lovemaking as you imply, or are just pretending indifference," he growled with wicked amusement, his strong fingers biting into the soft flesh of her arms.

She started to speak but held her tongue in the wake of his determination, deciding her best response was no response at all. But Mark would not allow her the luxury of remaining passive as he held her captive, forcing her to accept his caresses though her mind was screaming defiance. A deliciously mischievous smile caught the corners of his lips.

"You want me," he insisted.

"No," she denied.

"Sweet siren, let me take you to paradise."

Then he threw her on the bed and launched an assault so devastating that Christa felt the hard kernel of denial wither and die within her. The man was a sorcerer sent to earth for no other reason than to torment her. Marshaling every ounce of willpower available in her petite body, her chin tilted to a defiant angle as she flung irate words at him. "I don't want you!" She might as well have spoken to the wind for all the good it did her.

His lips latched onto a pink nipple and he sucked vigorously as his fingers slid through the soft curls between her thighs, finding the yielding spot as gently, insistently he brought her to the brink of total surrender. Upward his mouth moved to her lips, his tongue working between her teeth to sip the necter therein. Exhaling a small sob, she savagely bit his tongue, tasting blood.

He howled in pain and his face took on a mutinous expression, losing all semblance of tenderness or amusement. Christa swallowed a gasp as something hard and hot probed at the softness between her legs. As she struggled it managed to wedge itself a little way inside, and she squirmed, trying to escape it. It poked her again, harder, relentlessly, and this time found the passage, burying itself nearly to the hilt.

Abruptly his anger seemed to die inside him, replaced by an enormous hunger, his desire a savage beast that ruled him utterly. A terrible sense of defeat began to destroy her urge to continue this wretched resistence, and while she still made every attempt to curtail her response, it was a losing battle. He filled her fully, completely, and she ached from his sheer size, but it was such a potently sweet ache that it soon turned to pleasure. In a surprisingly short time, this man sent her resolutions into desperate disarray. And then she was soaring, no longer aware of time or place, arching in response to her body's needs and the magic aura of this special man. Only when he felt Christa's body contract sweetly around him did Mark allow his own senses full reign.

The silence between them was overwhelming. Though he had proved his mastery over her body, Christa's anger had not subsided, and her eyes held his in silent combat for a long, tense moment.

"What did you hope to gain by forcing my response?" she asked accusingly. "Certainly not my respect. Or did it salve your pride?"

"Pride is a strange thing," Mark reflected thoughtfully. "Having it trampled on serves little purpose. Next time you criticize my masculinity, be prepared to accept responsibility for my reactions."

"There will be no next time," Christa declared resolutely.

An enigmatic smile curved his mouth as Mark sprang lightly to his feet, looming over her in a blatant display of manly power. "You're wrong, my love. Your siren's song will call to me again and again, and I, like a lovestruck fool, will answer. Allah has fashioned you expressly for my pleasure, and no other man has the power to reach your soul."

"Your arrogance knows no limits," Christa replied sourly. Oh, God, why did he have to be so right? she silently entreated, swallowing convulsively. Instinctively she knew no other man could stir her as Mark did. She loved him, this prince, but he didn't love her enough to follow his heart instead of this urgency for revenge that drove him. It hurt, hurt terribly, to know she served no purpose in his life but to ease his male needs, which any woman could easily do.

Through a feathery pool of golden lashes spiked with bitter tears she watched him dress, some sixth sense telling her it would be the last time she would see him like this. Her sigh of regret drew his attention. For several tense minutes he studied her nude beauty, openly admiring the twin peaks, still flushed from his loving, her narrow waist, the slim columns of perfectly proportioned legs, the swell of her hips.

"I know you're angry, Christa, but one day

you'll realize just how precious your life is to me. Too precious to be placed in danger. If only you'll trust me and be patient, I promise we will be together soon."

"As your concubine?" challenged Christa.

His mouth moved convulsively but no words of denial issued forth. Helplessly, he shrugged, then turned to let himself out of the cabin. His parting words echoed through the darkness, words that would haunt her dreams for all those empty nights ahead. "Kismet, sweet siren. Destiny wills, man fulfills."

The fair skies and soft breezes held a bright promise but Christa's mood was anything but sunny the following day. Mark was nowhere in sight as she stood by the rail watching members of the crew affixing the repaired rudder to the ship's stern. On the bridge Captain Dubois paced nervously, watching the process while keeping a wary eye on the wide expanse of sea surrounding the *Bon Ami*.

Christa's brooding solitude was rudely interrupted when Willow sidled up beside her, for once without the usual escort of Pierre Lefevre. The fierce look she bestowed on Christa was anything but friendly. "You're not fooling anyone, you know," she remarked bitingly.

Startled, Christa whirled to face her adversary. "I have no idea what you're talking about."

"Henri Gervais hinted that you and Mark are sharing more than mere friendship. I know him well and he's not a man accustomed to long periods without a woman. He's not bedding me, so Henri's words certainly make sense. By now it's all over the ship that you and Mark are lovers."

"Henri is not a man to be believed," Christa retorted coolly. "Did he also tell you that he attacked me one night, and only Mark's timely intervention saved me? If I were you I'd pay little heed to what Henri says."

"I care little what happened between you and Henri," Willow said carelessly. "But I am interested in the relationship between you and Mark. Were you lovers in England? Are you the reason he broke off our relationship? Did he follow you to France and take passage on the *Bon Ami* to be with you?"

Her rapid-fire quiz set Christa's blood to boiling. "If you're so anxious for answers, ask Mark," she flung back huffily.

"Ask me what?" a deep voice interjected. So engrossed were the two women in their conversation that neither noticed Mark's approach.

"Darling!" Willow gushed, slanting what she assumed to be a beguiling smile at him. But to her annoyance Mark seemed to have eyes only for Christa.

"What did you wish to ask me, ladies?" he repeated.

"Let Lady Willow explain," Christa flung over her shoulder as she turned on her heel and walked rapidly away. After the angry words they had exchanged the night before, her emotions were far too raw for verbal combat with the only man she could ever love.

Mark's exasperation was evident by the single slash of dark brows meeting in the center of his forehead. When he had finally met the one woman capable of fulfilling his every need, one he could love totally and without reservation, his muddled life rendered him helpless to follow his heart and claim her for all time. Strange as it was, there was no doubt in Mark's mind that he loved Christa, probably from the first moment their eyes met at the Trenton ball.

But the drastic turn of events these past weeks placed his future in jeopardy. True, he could always

return to England and take up his life as his grandfather's heir, but that was the coward's way. If only
Christa would be reasonable and try to understand
that he couldn't allow Abdullah to go unpunished
for killing his mother and usurping what was
rightfully his. Once he resumed the reins of power
nothing could keep him and Christa apart. He
would work tirelessly to change the law so that he
could make Christa his wife.

All these disturbing thoughts and more passed
through his mind as he watched Christa flounce off,
quickly joined by two of the Frenchmen waiting for
just such an opportunity. Reluctantly, Mark turned
his attentions to Willow, who looped her arm in his
and began pulling him off in the opposite direction.

"What is going on between you two?" she
asked archly. "It's obvious Christa is not as innocent as she seems," Willow added with a hint of
malice. "Have you bedded her yet? Is she as good as
I am?"

"Really, Willow, you amaze me." Mark shook
his head. "What will it take to discourage you? You
hold all the young men aboard the *Bon Ami* in
thrall and have a doting husband waiting for you in
Algiers. Why do you insist in pretending there was
anything more than physical attraction between us?
It was pleasant while it lasted, but our affair ran its
course. What I do now is certainly no concern of
yours."

"My God! You do love her!" Willow's riotous
laughter attracted the curious stares of several people lingering nearby. "You've finally fallen in love
—for all the good it will do you. You told me
yourself you are forbidden marriage to a foreigner,
and I know for a fact Christa is soon to be wed. It
does my heart good to see you suffer rejection. Now
you know how it feels and perhaps will show pity

on the countless women who've suffered the same fate at your hands.''

"You don't know what you're talking about, Willow. I—'' His words died in his throat as Mark's eyes flew skyward to the watch clinging to the ropes high above them, the man's warning striking terror in the hearts of those standing below.

"Sail ho! Coming up fast astern!"

Even without a spyglass Mark, could make out the billowing sails clearly visible in the distance. In these waters all ships posed a threat, for Barbary pirates were still a force to be reckoned with. Often they could be found hiding on the island of Sardinia, where a colony of seagoing thieves thrived in caves strewn along the rocky coast, and plied their trade in the Mediterranean and along the Barbary coast. Since the *Bon Ami* had become disabled not far from that infamous pirate haven, Captain Dubois had been expecting just such a calamity. He had hoped desperately that it wouldn't happen until his ship was repaired and in full sail.

Glancing worriedly at the work in progress on the rudder, the astute captain realized that his ship could not possibly hope to escape unscathed, damaged as she was. Of course, it wasn't certain the approaching ship belonged to pirates, but being realistic as well as practical, he wisely prepared for the worst.

"Battle stations!" he bellowed, watching as men converged from every nook and cranny to assume their assigned positions.

Captain Dubois left nothing to chance. Conscious of the dangerous waters he sailed, his ship was equiped with eighteen guns—two twelve-pounders, eight eighteen-pounders and an equal number of twenty-four pounders—and a crew of fifty armed men fully capable of repulsing any pirate ship afloat. Except when their maneuverability and efficiency were hampered by a damaged rudder.

"I suggest you go below, Willow," Mark said tightly as he hurried off to ask the captain what he could do to help. Told that his services would best be utilized by organizing the French soldiers into a fighting unit, Mark hastened to obey.

While Omar saw to their weapons, Mark hurried off to warn Christa of the impending danger. "Christa!" he called through the closed door. "A ship has been sighted. Stay in your cabin until identification is made."

The door flung open. "Mark, is it pirates?" The threat of pirates was nothing new to Christa from her life in Tunis.

"We don't know yet, but until we find out, it's best you remain below. I'll come to you as soon as I can."

When he turned to leave, Christa cried out, "Mark, be careful!"

A look of such tenderness and love came over his face that Christa's eyes grew misty with unshed tears. With a low growl he reached out and pulled her into his arms, lowering his head to kiss her fiercely, as if to remind her that no matter what happened, she belonged to him. A swift shaft of pleasure clawed at her senses as she responded to his kiss, making her glaringly aware of the power this man held over her.

Reluctantly, Mark broke off the kiss, his mind already alert to the danger bearing down on them, despite his body's reaction to the woman in his arms. "Mark, wait!" Christa called as he backed away.

"Don't worry, my love, I'll protect you. Stay

below until the danger is over. Captain Dubois seems a competent seaman accustomed to dealing with all kinds of emergencies. If we are attacked by pirates I'm certain he'll prove a fierce foe. There are over fifty trained men aboard the *Bon Ami*." Then he was gone.

While Christa paced the confines of her small cabin, the crew of the *Bon Ami* prepared for battle, loading and priming the cannon on the gundeck and quarterdeck. A brace of pistols and cutlasses were strapped about each man's waist in anticipation of hand-to-hand combat, since flight was all but impossible for a ship cursed with an inoperable rudder.

Mark turned his attention to the group of young soldiers and discovered that Captain Lefevre had the situation well in hand, freeing Mark to make his own preparations. He glanced to the quarterdeck where Captain Dubois paced, from time to time raising the glass to chart the approaching ship's progress. Suddenly a violent curse spewed forth from his lips.

"Pirates!" he spat, whirling about to issue orders to his first mate.

Training his eyes on the billowing masts filled to capacity and creeping closer by the minute, Mark saw the pirate banner flying proudly from the tallest mast. Omar sidled up beside him, "You are well known in this part of the world, Prince Ahmed. I suggest you remain hidden if we are boarded. According to the Grand Vizier's message, Abdullah has placed a price on your head and the brotherhood is bound to have heard of it."

Mark snorted derisively. "Do you expect me to cringe at the first sign of danger? I am my father's son and will act as a man should. You shame me by suggesting otherwise, Omar."

"Your father entrusted me with your safety and I think only of you, my prince. But if you must charge heedlessly into battle, I will be at your side."

"I would have it no other way, my friend." Mark smiled. "May Allah protect us."

The first volley of shots fell short of the *Bon Ami*, as the pirate ship closed in swiftly. Light and fast, the *Red Witch* sailed rings around the heavier *Bon Ami*. Though the *Bon Ami*'s big guns boomed a constant barrage at the enemy, it was obvious from the onset that the battle was one-sided. The French ship was like a sitting duck, unable to tack either left or right to escape the *Red Witch*'s guns, while the pirate ship easily maneuvered out of harm's way.

From his vantage point, Mark could see the huge hulking form of the corsair captain strutting about the bridge of his ship issuing orders, confident of his conquest. In short order two direct hits added to the *Bon Ami*'s woes. Their only hope now lay in their ability to defeat the pirates once they were boarded. Captain Dubois, recognizing certain defeat, instructed his men as the *Red Witch* hove to and flung its grapling hooks, anchoring the two ships together. Within minutes, boarding planks were run out as men surged over the side, some using the narrow boards while those who couldn't wait their turn flew across the small distance with the aid of lines hanging from the rigging.

The first wave of corsairs was admirably repulsed by the crew of the *Bon Ami*, aware that they were fighting for their own lives as well as those of their passengers. Mark charged fearlessly into the foray, the acrid odor of smoke and sulfur burning his eyes and nostrils. His own safety meant little to him. It was Christa's life he fought for, all too aware what she would suffer if left to the tender mercies of pirates. If their abuse didn't destroy her, she would be sold in the slave markets of one of the Barbary states. Better she were dead than suffer such degradation. Not once did he consider Willow, or that the same fate awaited her should the pirates prove victorious. Only his innocent love consumed his thoughts.

Huddled together on the narrow bunk, Christa and Marla clutched each other in terror as the sounds of the fierce battle being waged above filtered down to them. Exploding cannon, the smell of smoke, and the cries of the wounded were frightening enough, but worse were visions of their fate at the hands of pirates should the *Bon Ami* fall victim to them.

Then another, more terrifying thought replaced the fear she felt for herself. What if Mark was wounded—or worse yet, killed? What if he went to his death believing the angry words she had flung at him the night before? What if he died without knowing just how much she really cared for him? Dear Lord, she couldn't let that happen!

Shrugging off Marla's clinging hands, Christa rose on shaking legs and started for the door. "Miss Horton! Where are you going?" the terrified woman cried out.

"I have to find out what's going on, Marla. I have to know what's going to happen to us."

"No, please don't go, miss! Something terrible might happen to you. I promised your father I'd keep you safe."

"Don't worry, Marla," Christa soothed the maid. But her mind was already made up. "I'll be careful. I promise to remain concealed in the passageway only long enough to learn for myself how the battle is going. If the *Bon Ami* is captured, it will matter little whether or not I am seen, for sooner or later we will be found by the pirates."

"Oh, Miss!" Marla wailed, Christa's dire warning bringing on a fresh round of terror.

Lacking the words of comfort she knew Marla wanted to hear, Christa unlocked the door and stepped into the passageway, calling to her maid to lock the door behind her. Judging from the sounds of mayhem coming from above, Christa knew the battle being waged was a fierce one, and that the pirates were too occupied thus far to search the passenger cabins.

Christa stifled a scream when she stumbled upon a body sprawled on the deck at the bottom of the ladder. Freezing in her tracks, she waited, and when the body did not move she braved a closer look. The odd assortment of clothing the dead man wore was a clear indication that he was one of the pirate crew. His throat had been slashed and she swallowed convulsively in an effort to choke back the nausea threatening to spew forth. Carefully averting her eyes she stepped over the corpse and clutched her way up the ladder, gingerly poking her head up through the opening. The carnage that met her eyes made her wish she had remained with Marla.

The deck was slippery with blood; the sound of clashing swords and pistol shots was deafening. Everywhere she looked men were engaged in hand-to-hand combat. Not far from where she stood the ship's wounded had been pulled behind some crates and were being treated by the ship's surgeon, who appeared to have been wounded himself. The moans and cries coming from those pitiful wretches covered in blood and blackened by smoke tore at Christa's soft heart, and she could no more have ignored them than she could have stopped breathing.

Completely disregarding her own safety, as well as Mark's warning, she emerged on deck, scooting out of the way of two combatants who had taken a stance directly in her path. A quick glance told her neither man was Mark, and she swiftly made her way to the wounded men, offering her help to the shocked doctor.

"*Mon Dieu*, Mademoiselle Horton, what are you doing here?"

Upon closer inspection Christa's assumption that Doctor Tremaine was wounded proved correct. He was bleeding profusely from an ugly gash on his left arm. "I've come to help," she said tersely. "Allow me to dress your wound. If I don't, you'll not be able to continue."

Doctor Tremaine offered no objection as Christa carefully began picking the pieces of shredded material from the slash wound, applying a salve she found in the doctor's supplies and binding it up tightly. When she finished, he managed a grateful but weary smile.

"*Merci, mademoiselle*. I'm grateful for what you've done for me, but this is no place for a lady. Please go below. Weren't you warned to remain out of sight?"

"I was warned," Christa admitted, "but I'm staying. You need help."

Refusing to budge, Christa turned to one of the wounded, using a bandage she found nearby to bind the head of a boy who looked barely old enough to leave home, let alone fight pirates. Tremaine shrugged uncertainly, fearing for Christa's safety, yet grateful for whatever help she could give him.

They worked side by side for several minutes before Christa dared to ask, "How do our chances look, doctor?" Once she had stepped behind the crates, she could no longer see what was taking place a scant few feet away. But the doctor had made several furtive forays into the heat of battle to rescue wounded men and was qualified to answer.

"It doesn't look good, *mademoiselle*," he said evasively. Though he recognized the fact that they were swiftly losing ground to the corsairs, he refrained from telling her the truth for fear of what it would do to her. Tremaine pitied any woman who fell in the hands of the scurvy lot who roamed the Barbary coast.

"I don't see Mark Carrington among the wounded," she said, her voice cracking. "Did you perchance notice if he . . . if he was among those fighting?"

Looking up from his work, the doctor eyed her curiously before answering. "*Oui*, I saw him. Fighting as fiercely as the pirate he so handily dispatched, his man Omar protecting his back."

A trembling sigh and a silent prayer tumbled from her lips as Christa pictured in her mind's eye Mark's bronzed torso glistening with sweat, and his muscled arm wielding a sword in defense of the beleaguered ship. Anxious for just one glimpse of the man who occupied her mind and her heart, Christa abandoned her nursing duties long enough to sidle to the edge of the crates shielding her and peep cautiously around the corner. It was an act Christa would regret the rest of her life.

Wide blue eyes sweeping the deck from bow to stern, Christa's startled gaze fell on the most frigtening man she had ever seen. A veritable giant with flaming red hair and beard to match focused red-rimmed eyes on her and chortled with wicked delight. Standing over six and a half feet tall, hair and beard wild and unkempt, his bare chest and arms glistening with sweat and blood, the ferocious giant spied Christa the moment she poked her head into full view, whooping with glee at his discovery.

Quailing in fright, Christa flattened herself against the crate in an effort to make herself as inconspicuous as possible, but failed miserably. He stood on legs as thick as tree trunks, bared to the waist, a forest of red, curly hair shielding his incredibly broad chest. His arms were thickly muscled and corded, his neck as big around as Christa's waist. Slim hipped and surprisingly agile for his size, the pirate easily dispatched his opponent in a single stroke of his enormous cutlass, grinning wickedly as he mowed down anything unfortunate enough to stand in his path as he fought his way toward Christa.

Sheer black terror seized Christa, and she clutched at her throat, her mouth working convulsively. The fearsome pirate had seen her! He was coming after her! Panic-stricken, she turned to flee. Daring a fleeting glance toward the hatch leading to the deck, from which she had emerged earlier, she discovered her way blocked by two burly corsairs. She whirled, searching for and finding an unobstructed path in the opposite direction. Frighteningly aware that there was little hope of escape, Christa nevertheless launched herself across the deck, slipping and sliding all the way.

From the corner of his eye, Mark saw a streak of frothy blue flash before his line of vision, and his mind screamed in protest. Christa! No! But when he attempted to go to her aid, he found himself challenged by three determined pirates, and his immediate attention was diverted to saving his own skin. In a space of a breath, Omar's skilled blade joined in the one-sided battle as the two men combined forces.

Gritting his teeth in frustration, bleeding from several minor wounds, Mark astutely realized the crew of the *Bon Ami* was slowly but decisively being defeated by the Barbary pirates. For himself he wasn't concerned. If he wasn't killed in battle, he'd be sold as a slave or ransomed back to Abdullah for the reward. If that happened, his death was assured. It was Christa he fretted over. Having lived most of his life in this part of the world, he instinctively knew the fate that awaited her, and it wouldn't be pleasant. He would rather die a thousand deaths himself than see her suffer abuse and defilement.

5

Redbeard stalked Christa as a fox goes after a rabbit, all the while grinning from ear to ear. The sun reflecting off her flaxen tresses had immediately captured his attention, and he knew instantly that he wanted the woman. Leering wickedly, he knew she hadn't a chance in hell of escaping him. With only small pockets of resistence remaining, the ship was as good as his. From his first glimpse of the woman peeking out from behind a crate, Redbeard was stunned by her ethereal beauty, but he was still able to craftily calculate her worth in the slave market. Perhaps the dey of Algiers would want this priceless jewel for his collection. He reportedly had an eye for fair women. Or mayhap she would find a place in the harem of the great Ottoman sultan. Never had Redbeard seen hair that particular shade, neither yellow nor gold, but more like silver touched by moonbeams. Incredible!

Sobbing hysterically, Christa fled across the

deck, panic lending her feet wings. If need be, she vowed grimly, she'd throw herself overboard before she'd allow the red-bearded giant to lay hands on her. Searching frantically for Mark, she saw him backed against the teak railing, fighting for his life. Refraining from screaming out his name lest she disturb his concentration and inadvertently cause his death, she zigzagged across the deck, deftly dodging fighting men and the grasping hands of those who sought to restrain her. Panting for breath, shaking from exhaustion, Christa heard Redbeard's mocking laughter close on her heels and realized he was but toying with her. The final outcome was inevitable.

Suddenly the railing loomed up before her, and without a moment's hesitation Christa scrambled upward, poised to jump. With a roar of outrage, Redbeard realized he was about to lose his prize to a watery grave and his massive legs ate up the distance between them. One huge paw reached out to grasp a hank of long hair whipped to a silver froth by the wind, and yanked her sharply backwards. Christa's scream of agony and despair alerted Mark, who had finally managed to fight free of the corsairs who had kept him from rushing to her aid.

Christa fell to the deck, sprawled beneath Redbeard's outstretched legs. "Did you think to escape Redbeard so easily, my beauty?" he roared with amusement. "I have plans for you and they don't include using yourself as fishbait. The sharks won't appreciate your half as much as I will." His deep, rumbling voice sent cold chills racing up her spine.

"Let her go, you cur!" Wielding his sword with great skill, Mark fought his way to Christa's side. His challenge was met with a stare of incredulity from the huge pirate leader. Though Mark was no lightweight, Redbeard stood several inches taller and pounds heavier, and Christa was consumed by a terrible fear for her prince.

The pressure on Christa's skull intensified as Redbeard's grip on her hair tightened, and he dragged her to her feet. "Is this your woman?" Redbeard roared, eyeing Mark narrowly.

"Yes," Mark replied, his look warning Christa to silence. "Take your filthy hands off her." Gripping his sword firmly, he fearlessly challenged Redbeard, knowing there was virtually no hope of defeating the giant and gaining Christa's freedom.

"The ship is mine," Redbeard growled fiercely. "And so is this woman. Look around you. You'll see that all fighting has ceased and my men are in control. Lay down your sword."

Her eyes pleading with him to do nothing rash, Christa cringed as Redbeard curved a huge arm around her waist, pulling her close in an outward display of ownership. Two of his men sidled up beside him to lend their support should he need it.

"Drop your sword," Redbeard repeated when his previous words seemed to produce no result.

"I'll strike a bargain with you," Mark offered, desperation riding him.

Redbeard's whoop of laughter caught the attention of his crew. Immediately all eyes focused on the young man openly defying their formidable leader. "Why should I bargain with you?" he demanded, astounded. "All you own is mine, including this woman."

"Let me run him through, Barbarossa!" shouted one of the men at his side. Named for the fierce Khair-ed-Din, the first Barbarossa who ruled the seas in the sixteenth century, Redbeard had earned the name from his fiery beard and hair as well as his daring exploits.

"Aye," agreed his companion, "let's finish off the braggart." Both men advanced, and finding himself cornered, Mark leaped high, balancing precariously atop the railing, swinging his sword in a wide arc.

"Wait!" he cried out. "Listen to me. Leave the ship and all its passengers unharmed and I'll go along with you willingly."

"What makes you so valuable?" scoffed Redbeard derisively. "I can get more for the woman than you and all the others combined."

"I think not," Mark returned calmly. "You've heard of Prince Abdullah, have you not?"

"Of course. Who hasn't heard of the bey of Constantine?" Redbeard replied, his massive features wearing a frown.

"And Prince Ahmed? You've heard of him?" Redbeard nodded, a hint of comprehension dawning in his amber eyes, which reminded Mark of great cat's eyes. He dared a glance at Christa and saw that all the color had drained from her face.

"Mark! No!" she screamed, knowing exactly what he was about to reveal.

Ignoring her plea, Mark repeated. "What do you know of Prince Ahmed?"

"I know that Abdullah bey has offered a huge reward for the capture of his half-brother, who is said to be a traitor to his country. Abdullah seized the reins of power from Ahmed after his father's death," Redbeard revealed shrewdly. "What does all this have to do with you?"

"I am Prince Ahmed, rightful heir to Khalid ibn Selim and chosen leader of my people. Abdullah is a liar and a murderer."

From his stance atop the railing, Mark now had the undivided attention of the corsairs, who had herded the surviving members and passengers of the *Bon Ami* into the hold and were now milling nearby. Outwardly calm, he surveyed the motley group representing nearly every nation. "Is there none among you who recognizes me?"

"Aye, he speaks the truth," one man spoke out, stepping forward. "I claim Constantine as my home, and I saw Prince Ahmed many times before I joined the brotherhood. The prince often accompanied his father in the streets. He rode with the Tuaregs and is said to be a fierce fighter."

Rubbing his flaming beard, Redbeard narrowed his eyes thoughtfully as they rested on the brash young man poised before him. He looked every bit the prince he claimed to be—sleek and muscular, with intelligent, compelling green eyes that challenged him defiantly. No wonder Abdullah placed a price on his brother's head. Ahmed definitely wasn't a man to be crossed. Once he set foot in Constantine, he was bound to rally sufficient support to oust Abdullah and gain the seat of power. It was said Abdullah had the support of the Janissaries, but how many among them would remain faithful once Ahmed returned to his native land?

"So, you wish to bargain your life for that of the woman," Redbeard contended. "You are a fool. I will have both of you. Abdullah will pay well when I deliver you to him, and once I finish with your woman she will bring a handsome price in the slave market. Perhaps I will offer her to your brother," he added slyly. "It might amuse him to possess a woman you obviously care for. The wench must have pleased you greatly. I can hardly wait to sample her myself."

Red dots of rage exploded behind Mark's brain, blinding him to all but the knowledge that he had failed Christa. He could not bear the thought of her suffering at the hands of Redbeard and his corsairs, for the pirate leader made it clear he meant to have both Christa and the reward offered by Abdullah. The urge to destroy the red-haired devil was so great that Mark could no more stop it than he could halt the wheels of destiny upon which he traveled.

Balancing on oak-sturdy limbs, clutching Christa about the waist, Redbeard was ill-prepared for Mark's act of bravery as he lunged, his sword aimed directly at the bearded giant's throat. Then everything began happening at once.

Christa screamed a warning when she saw one of Redbeard's men raise a primed pistol, aim and shoot, acting instinctively to the threat to his leader. Mark's body recoiled under the impact, a patch of red blooming on his chest and spreading outward. Where moments before he was plunging downward, now he was reeling backwards, his feet sliding from beneath him as his body pitched over the rail into the murky water below. Christa fainted seconds before one of Redbeard's men cupped his hands to his mouth and shouted, "Sail ho!"

Nor did she notice one of the wounded men lying nearby rise unsteadily to his knees and slip undetected over the side, the splash barely heard in the mad rush across the deck to identify the approaching ship.

Shoving Christa rudely aside, Redbeard snatched the glass from the lookout and focused on the distant set of sails. "Damnation!" he growled, cursing his foul luck. Not only had he lost Prince Ahmed, but it looked as if he was in for another battle. "It's a French frigate, and heavily armed from the looks of her."

"Look to the starboard, Redbeard!" a warning shout rang in his ears. Whirling to view this new threat, Redbeard let loose a steady stream of curses. A second frigate, almost identical to the first, flew before the wind, her gunports open and her guns being rolled into full view.

The choice to stand and fight or flee was taken from Redbeard's hands. One ship he could easily defeat, but two posed too great a challenge, one he preferred not to face. He was no fool. "Over the side, men!" he bellowed, his decision instantaneous. "Back to the *Red Witch*! Bring the wench," he snapped to his lieutenant, who immediately scooped up Christa's limp form and threw her over his shoulder. Redbeard may have lost the *Bon Ami*'s cargo but he still had the woman to make up for the loss.

Gathering up their wounded and dead, the corsairs swarmed over the side in the same manner in which they arrived, using the boarding planks and lines. Issuing orders in a crisp, decisive manner, Redbeard watched with satisfaction as his men sprang into action, hauling away at the braces to trip the yards. There was a thunderous clapping as the canvas sheets and tacking were taken up, until each white sail filled and became taut, easing away from the *Bon Ami*. A loud cheer echoed aloft as the *Red Witch* gathered speed and scudded before the wind to elude their French pursuers.

Christa awoke with reluctance from the dark depths of unconsciousness. Something terrifying lurked at the edges of her mind—but what? As she felt the deep black clouds begin to lift, she sought to pull them back around herself, to sink once again into the dark oblivion of unawareness. She wanted to escape the awful thing that awaited her when she awoke, but she couldn't remember what it was. She clung to the shadows, but finally that brief respite fell away and reality intruded.

Then she remembered. Panic gripped her and

her entire body stiffened. Mark! With her own eyes she had seen him pitch headlong into the sea after being gravely wounded by one of the corsairs. Was he dead? Or had he somehow managed to survive?

Abruptly, an eerie feeling came over her and she knew she wasn't alone. With fear in her heart she remembered the red-bearded giant and opened her eyes. Glancing furtively about, she became painfully aware that this wasn't the cramped cabin she had occupied aboard the *Bon Ami* for the past two weeks. This cabin was magnificent in its proportions and as sumptuously appointed. The bed she lay in was three times the size of her own narrow bunk and covered with the softest velvet, in a rich, deep scarlet color. She noted also that the cabin was not below the water line, for long, velvet-draped windows looked out over the stern of the ship.

Then she saw him. The red-haired pirate leaned above a long table, poring over a set of maps spread out across the smooth teak top. Sensing movement from the bed, he glanced over at Christa, his amber eyes raking her appraisingly.

"So, you're awake." He spoke with an Irish brogue that was still discernible despite the years he had spent in the brotherhood.

"Where am I?" Christa asked, gulping back her fear.

"Aboard the *Red Witch*, wench. I am called Redbeard and you are my prisoner."

"Where is—Mark Carrington?"

"If you're speaking of Prince Ahmed, consigned to the deep, I suppose. I didn't wait around long enough to find out."

"You killed him!" accused Christa hotly. "You're a murderer and—and a despicable pirate!"

"Of course," agreed Redbeard affably. "Quite a spitfire, aren't you? Some lucky man will pay well to tame you. Too bad you're not a virgin. Or are you? Was Prince Ahmed your lover?"

Christa froze. How did he know she wasn't a virgin? Did he . . . did he rape her while she lay unconscious and helpless?

Redbeard's laughter, low and deep, rumbled from his massive chest. "No, wench, I didn't ravish you while you were out," he said, reading her mind. "When I take you, you'll know it. I prefer my women with a spark of life in them. If you please me well, I'll keep you exclusively for my own pleasure until I sell you in the slave market."

Dear God, not that! Christa silently implored. "My father will gladly ransom me," she hastened to inform him. "He holds a government post in Tunis. Send word to him, I beg you."

"If your father is but a mere government official, I seriously doubt he has the kind of wealth I can demand for you in the slave market. You're exquisite. Your hair, your eyes, a figure beyond compare—you'll make me rich, wench."

"No!" cried Christa, denying his words.

"Aye," nodded Redbeard. "What are you called, wench?"

His terrible threats rendered Christa mute and she could only stare at the ferocious pirate, her mouth filled with the bile rising from her throat.

"I asked you a question, wench. What is your name?"

When no answer was forthcoming he launched himself at Christa, grasping her arms and dragging her from the bed. "Answer me, wench! What is your name?" he roared in a voice that shook the rafters.

"C . . . Christa. Christa Horton," she gasped, swallowing the constriction in her throat.

"That's better, wench," Redbeard nodded, obviously pleased. "You'll soon learn to obey me when I speak. You never replied when I asked if you and Prince Ahmed were lovers, although he freely admitted as much.''

His huge hands were still biting the soft flesh of her upper arms, forcing her to acknowledge his question. ''I . . . yes,'' she admitted in a low voice. ''I loved him.'' Dear God, why was she speaking of him in the past tense? Even the odious Redbeard had no idea if Mark had survived the shooting— and the sharks.

''Take off your clothes!'' Redbeard ordered, bringing Christa abruptly to her senses.

''What!''

''You heard me, wench. I want to see if there are any blemishes on your body. If there are, I might reconsider and turn you over to my crew after I finish with you. Should I find you flawed in any way, your value will be greatly diminished. I would rather have found you a virgin, but your beauty is such that it probably won't matter.''

Christa stood as if rooted to the spot. ''No,'' she gasped, quietly defiant.

With an angry roar, Redbeard began tearing at her clothing, holding her with one hand and ripping with the other until it lay in tatters on the thick Turkish carpet covering the teak deck. Only then did he release his hold on her bruised flesh, stepping back to take full advantage of the nude loveliness he had unbared before his lustful eyes.

''Enchanting! Exquisite! Sublime!'' Redbeard chortled gleefully as he slowly rotated Christa so that he could scrutinize her from every possible angle. His choice of words puzzled Christa, for she hardly expected to hear flowery terms spew forth from the mouth of a common pirate.

Mortified, Christa cringed beneath his impersonal perusal, as his eyes swept her supple form from head to toe, eagerly calculating her worth in terms of personal gain. "Your skin is like satin," he remarked idly, running one thick finger along her collarbone, over the rise of her right breast to the impudent thrust of its pink tip. "You're near perfect, wench," he gloated, eyes gleaming greedily. "I've a mind to offer you to Prince Abdullah. It might amuse him to possess his brother's woman. Aye," he laughed raucously. "That's exactly what I'll do. I'll send word to the bey the moment we reach Algiers. If he wants you badly enough, it will make little difference whether or not you're a virgin. Nor will he be able to tell if I've sampled your charms myself."

Rudely, he shoved her aside, sending her sprawling across the wide bed scaled to accommodate a man of his gigantic proportions. "I've no time for you now, wench, I've a ship to run," he growled, reverting to his gruff manner. "When I return I expect to learn for myself just how much Prince Ahmed taught you about pleasing your master." Then he was gone, charging from the cabin with a long-legged stride.

Christa was amazed at how much he resembled a Celtic warlord and shuddered at the thought of being slowly crushed to death beneath his huge body, impaled by his great weapon, which doubtlessly would tear her apart. "I'll kill myself first," she muttered aloud, sifting through the remnants of her clothing scattered beneath her feet. Finding nothing intact or decent enough to wear, she turned her attention elsewhere. She cared little what she found as long as it covered her nudity. Her eyes fell to the sea chest sitting at the foot of the bed, and without a moment's hesitation she set out to investigate.

The chest proved to be a clothes press holding clean articles of clothing, from the size of them obviously belonging to Redbeard. The pants were impossible, but she gladly donned an oversized shirt which reached well below her knees. A few turns of the long sleeves and Christa was ready to focus her attention in another direction. She desperately needed a weapon if she hoped to defend herself.

At the bottom of the chest lay a pistol, but regretfully Christa passed it by. She had no idea how to load and prime it. Further inspection uncovered nothing else that remotely resembled a weapon. Disappointed, she snapped the lid shut and took her search elsewhere in the cabin, keeping a wary eye on the door, should Redbeard return.

The desk seemed the next likely place to search, and Christa hastily scrabbled through the drawers. A satisfied smile creased her face as her fingers closed on a slim blade resting at the back of one of the compartments. Though the knife could hardly be considered a deadly weapon, it was better than nothing, Christa thought as she snatched it up.

Feeling not quite so helpless, Christa crept to the door, noting that there was no lock, and inched it open. Stationed outside but looking the other way, a fierce-looking pirate stood guard. There was no escape, Christa realized with a surge of panic. Even if she did manage to leave the cabin, where could she go? Disheartened, she returned to the bed, perching gingerly on the edge and shoving the blade out of sight beneath the pillow but handy enough when she needed it.

Abruptly, the door flung open and was filled by the amazing bulk of Redbeard. The sight of Christa demurely clad in his best shirt brought a ferocious scowl to his face. "Take it off," he boomed in a voice that brooked no argument.

Her chin tilted at a defiant angle, Christa shook her head, regarding him warily. How different he appeared, she thought curiously, than he had when she first saw him leading his men into battle. Since he left the cabin he had cleaned up; his hair was less wild, and his beard was combed into some semblance of order. A spark of hope flamed in her breast. Perhaps there was a shred of decency left in this barbarian that she could appeal to.

Slamming the door behind him, Redbeard slowly advanced into the room, pausing to light the lantern swinging from the ceiling, for it had grown dark during the time it took him to see to his dead and wounded. Now there was nothing to keep him from the lovely wench he had captured. He had all night to sate himself with her enticing body, willing or not. Though admiring her show of spunk and defiance, it had little effect on his determination to have his way with her.

"I would hate ruining my best shirt," Redbeard growled lustily, "but I will if you don't remove it this instant." He leaned forward, menacingly, and Christa's hand slipped beneath the pillow, her fingers closing on the hilt of the blade, providing a modicum of comfort.

"You'll have to kill me first," Christa defied bravely.

Redbeard's amber eyes crinkled with amusement. "That can be arranged, though I much prefer to have you alive." His large hand moved to the neckline of the shirt and Christa's hand whipped forward, brandishing the small, ineffectual blade as if it were three times its actual size and twice as deadly.

For an instant Redbeard looked stunned, then he broke into thunderous laughter. "Did you think to wound me with that pig-sticker? I could disarm you in a trice and never feel the strain."

A deep flush staining her cheeks, Christa realized he spoke the truth. She was foolish to think such a tiny weapon in the hands of an amateur could deter him from his salacious intent. But defeat was not a word she readily accepted. She had nothing but her own cunning and guile to rely upon and would not give up so easily.

"Redbeard, ransom me back to my father," Christa pleaded. "Think of me as one of your sisters. Would you want them sold and ravished? I can tell by your speech that you are an educated man. Somewhere in that huge body of yours lurks a hint of refinement. You weren't always a pirate. I'd recognize that Irish brogue anywhere."

Hands on wide hips, Redbeard flung back his leonine head and roared. "You think you have me all figured out, don't you, my lady? Well, you're wrong. Aye, I'm Irish," he freely admitted. "But that was a lifetime ago. There is no longer a place for me in the civilized world. Nor do I have a sister. She starved to death when still a child.

"I am a pirate, a man with a price on his head," he continued. "I escaped from an English prison the night before I was to be hanged for participating in a rebellion against the Crown. Hah! Participating in a rebellion is hardly the right choice of words. I masterminded the uprising. The bloody English were too stupid to recognize a leader when they saw one."

Despite her fear of the giant, Christa found herself listening raptly to his words. "How. . . how did you come to be a pirate?"

Christa's question startled Redbeard. No one had ever expressed interest in his life before, and he soon warmed to the subject. "I was unlucky enough to be caught by a press gang and forced to serve aboard an English ship. I spent two miserable years roaming the sea under a cruel master who took special delight in breaking men, especially men of my size and strength. Most of those years were spent in irons when I wasn't performing tasks at sea, and I swore that if ever I became a free man I'd never wear another manacle or suffer the lash again."

"Yet you escaped the hell you just described," Christa remarked, picturing in her mind the Irish renegade fighting for his freedom.

"We were attacked by corsairs, and when offered the choice I willingly joined their ranks. I've been with them ever since. When we captured the *Red Witch*, I was elected captain. My exploits in these waters are legend. I've murdered, sacked, raped and committed every heinous crime known to man.

"So, my feisty wench, I'll feel no remorse over ravishing one more woman, or taking another life. I don't want to harm you, for you are worth far more to me than merely a vessel to slake my lust. You will bring a high price in Algiers, and I'd rather your silken skin remained unmarked. It's not as if you're a virgin. But mark me well, I want you. Defy me in this and you'll suffer. There are ways to force your compliance, none of them pleasant. And put that little toothpick away before you hurt yourself."

Given the seriousness of her situation, Christa decided she had nothing to lose by brazening it out, for there was no way in God's domain that she would allow Redbeard to have his way with her. Not after experiencing Mark's gentle love. She'd kill herself first. That sober thought inspired her to act as she did, surprising herself by her bold words. But as she uttered them she realized she would not hesitate to carry them out.

Before Redbeard could react, Christa brought the blade upward until it pressed into the soft flesh at the base of her throat, grasping it with both hands when she found herself shaking uncontrollably. "Stand back," she challenged him. "One step closer and you'll be bringing back a corpse for your bloody slave auction."

Abruptly Redbeard stepped back, annoyed to think that a mere woman had the gall to oppose him. Any other woman would have swooned the moment he walked into the room. But not this brazen bit of fluff. What a mate she'd make! He grinned appreciatively. If one had such an inclination. Still, he couldn't help but think what beautiful, strong sons they would produce. But Redbeard was too practical a man to dwell long on the improbable or the ridiculous. He took women when he wanted them, used them for his pleasure and then sold them for profit. No other fate was possible for the golden wench so openly defying him.

Yet, he couldn't help but admire her for her sheer audacity. Beneath her penetrating blue gaze, he could feel layers of his rough exterior peel away, and he liked it not at all. It had taken Ewan McGlenn too many years to forget his name and heritage and the lessons in gentility learned at his mother's knee, God assoil her soul, to become the ferocious Redbeard, the most feared pirate of the Barbary coast. And no beguiling wench was going to unman him or destroy his reputation with the brotherhood.

His face beneath the fiery beard set in a scowl, Redbeard reached for Christa, only to halt abruptly as a drop of blood appeared at the base of her neck. He was more than a little startled to learn she intended to make good her threat to kill herself rather than submit to him. Little did he realize it made no difference to Christa if she lived or died. In all likelihood Mark was already dead, and even if by some miracle she should escape, there wasn't the slightest possibility she would marry Brian Kent. Without Mark her life held no meaning.

"I meant what I said, Redbeard," Christa

warned in a strangled voice. "Is your desire for me so great you'd ignore your need for riches? According to your own words, you and your men stand to gain much from my sale in the slave market. Why risk such a valuable commodity? You could try to disarm me, but not before I do myself irreparable harm."

"You'd do it, wouldn't you, wench?" Redbeard growled angrily. "You'd harm yourself just to spite me."

"Gladly," came Christa's calm reply. Never had she felt stronger or more sure of herself.

Eyes narrowed thoughtfully, Redbeard stared at Christa. Their attack upon the *Bon Ami* had been costly. The crew and passengers of the French ship had waged a valiant battle, killing or wounding many of his best men. To complicate matters, they had been forced to flee before relieving the ship of its cargo or the passengers of their valuables. Losing Prince Ahmed had been another stroke of incredibly bad luck, which he might still be able to salvage if Abdullah was in a generous mood. He had been fortunate to escape with Ahmed's woman, who proved to be a flawless beauty, and he was correct in assuming he could profit greatly from her sale. Already his men were calculating their share of the booty, cautioning him to go easy on her lest her worth be diminished in the eyes of the buyer.

Of course there were also those who demanded he share the wench, but the grumbling soon subsided, for he was a fair captain who wielded authority and demanded instant obedience. His sheer size and strength intimidated all but the bravest, and they soon discovered it gained them naught to rebel. But in this Redbeard knew he dare not disappoint his men. The irritating wench had to be kept alive and healthy until he turned her over to a new master. A very rich one, he thought as he grinned greedily.

Christa read capitulation in Redbeard's amber eyes, and exulted. She had won! By sheer dint of will and determination, she had tamed the savage beast by making him aware of her worth to the entire crew. She dared not think ahead to what awaited her in Algiers; she would cross that bridge when she came to it. Perhaps she could persuade the man who bought her to ransom her back to her father. Pray God it wouldn't be Abdullah.

"You have won this time, you blue-eyed witch, but I'll have the last laugh when your new master leads you off. Perhaps a brothel keeper will buy you, and I'll purchase your services." Of course he deemed it highly unlikely that a brothel keeper could afford such a glorious creature, but it salved his wounded pride to taunt her with such a ignominious fate. "I've a mind to put your show of courage to the test."

"You'll not find my courage lacking," Christa retorted glibly, her hands steady on the blade despite her frayed nerves and crumbling composure. If Redbeard forced her, could she actually have plunged home the knife? It was something Christa would never learn, for abruptly he turned and stormed out the door, his vile curses scorching her ears.

Redbeard's foul language continued all the way to the quarterdeck, where he paced back and forth angrily, shaking the timbers beneath his feet. As far back as his memory reached, he could not remember allowing a woman to best him. Suddenly it occurred to him that had he chosen, he could have easily disarmed Christa before she could do herself bodily harm. Why in God's name hadn't he? Because he had never met a woman like Christa

Horton before and more than likely would never meet another. Somehow she had struck a responsive chord in his huge body, rendering him unable or unwilling to hurt her. What other woman would think to protect her virtue with a weapon so ineffectual it bordered on the ridiculous?

Foolish though she might be, he couldn't help but admire her show of courage. Though he had all but forgotten his origins, Christa reminded him of the life he had lived before embracing piracy, a life that had robbed him of his conscience and sense of decency. Growling in frustration and cursing the fates that sent Christa Horton to spark his memory, the ferocious Redbeard decided for once in his life to do something completely out of character. He'd leave the enticing wench with her virtue intact—until he sold her in Algiers. The sooner he rid himself of her the better. If he wasn't careful, she'd have him purring like a kitten. Hell and damnation! He might agree to keep his mighty tool in his breeches, but he wasn't so stupid as to consider letting her go. He had been Redbeard the scourge of the Barbary coast far too long to change his ways.

Christa had no idea she had fallen asleep until she awoke abruptly to find the red-bearded giant standing over her, his boot-clad legs planted firmly on the deck and a mocking grin curling his lips. In one large, hairy hand he held the knife that must have fallen from her grasp when she dozed off. She caught her breath on a grasp, despair and regret forming a hard lump in her throat. How had she fallen asleep? she agonized. All her earlier bravado had been for naught and brought her once again to the mercy of Redbeard and his corsairs.

"What are you going to do?" Christa asked,

gulping back her fear. The thought of being raped by this giant was totally repugnant. Even death was preferrable to what Redbeard intended.

"It wasn't this little pig-sticker that stopped me before," Redbeard scoffed disdainfully, tossing the blade across the cabin. "I could have disarmed you any time I chose."

"Not before I did myself serious damage," Christa declared stoutly.

Throwing back his great shaggy head, Redbeard roared with laughter. "You flatter yourself, little girl. You were never in danger of doing yourself bodily harm." With a start, Redbeard realized the truth of his words.

"As for my intentions," he continued, his strange yellow eyes gleaming ferally, "you may as well know what I have planned for you. I haven't changed my mind about selling you in the slave market. But before I do, I'll send word to Abdullah. If he is interested and his offer is a generous one, I will deal directly with him instead."

"Why would Abdullah want me? There must be dozens of women more beautiful than I in his harem."

Redbeard's eyes gleamed wickedly. "None but you have the distinction of being Prince Ahmed's woman. It might tickle his fancy to possess you. And if by some miracle Ahmed still lives, you will become a bargaining tool."

"You're a—a heartless bastard!" flung out Christa, searching for and finding the right word. Never could she recall using such language, but never had she been in a situation as desperate as this.

"I've been called worse," grinned Redbeard, raking her ill-clad figure insolently. She still wore his shirt, which left most of her legs bare. Christa noted the direction of his gaze and cringed inwardly. Would it come now? she wondered fearfully. His brutal attack?

Watching her through slitted yellow eyes, Redbeard considered slaking his lust on the silver-haired wench, then reconsidered. She was so tiny he could easily break her in two, or crush her with his bulk. What if he seriously damaged her, which was highly probable if she put up a fight? Neither Abdullah nor any other prospective buyer would find much worth in a woman rendered incapable of performing the one function she was fashioned for.

Pickings of late had been slim indeed, with both the English and French decrying piracy and using their impressive fleets to rid the Mediterranean of their presence. Even the newly formed American states had joined in the battle to destroy their way of life. The wench represented more than a body to be used and discarded; she was an investment. His crew needed the feel of gold in their palms to keep them content. Of late there had been little enough to satisfy them.

No, Redbeard grumbled silently, he wouldn't use the girl as he longed to do. Nor would he allow his men to abuse her. She wasn't meant for the likes of them. What he gained from her sale would buy him plenty of willing, lusty women built on a grander scale and better able to satisfy him than the tiny bit of fluff opposing him so fiercely.

To Christa's intense delight and gratification Redbeard issued a snort of disgust and turned away. "Rest easy, wench," he growled, scowling darkly. "No matter how badly I want to poke it in you, I'll not force you. You'd do well to thank your lucky stars you're worth more to me than a lusty lay, else you'd have been sprawled beneath me long ago. Unlike others of my kind, my brains aren't contained inside my britches."

Christa flushed a bright red, his crude language

shocking her but his words instilling in her a new hope. By surmounting one hurdle at a time, she might yet survive intact.

"I . . . I thank you," she managed to choke out, not wanting to sound ungrateful.

"Don't thank me," Redbeard snarled. "You may have cause yet for cursing me when your new master attempts to tame you. I'm but protecting an investment. The days of piracy are numbered, and I must think of lining my pockets against the time I'll be forced to retire. You'll be left alone until we reach Algiers, which should be in two days, barring storms or the like. We have already sailed past Sardinia and soon the north coast of Africa will be in sight."

Christa watched in dismay as he bent her an austere stare and stomped from the cabin, shaking the furniture with the sheer bulk of him.

6

Standing before the long windows overlooking the stern, Christa gazed at the sparkling white city of Algiers rising above the harbor, her mind in a turmoil, her thoughts so morose that had she the courage, she'd have thrown herself into the shark-infested sea. If Mark still lived, going on wouldn't be nearly so pointless. But the prospect of a lifetime of slavery with no hope for escape, no Mark waiting in the shadows to rescue her, was far too painful to contemplate.

Dawn was breaking, and before Christa's start-led eyes the sun came up in a sudden blaze of light from behind distant purple mountains set against a bright blue bay, gilding the spires and minarets and turning to mellowed ivory the whitewashed buildings rising, tier on tier, from the water's edge to the kasbah crowning the lofty hill on which the city stood. From where she watched, Christa could see a sea-front promenade that formed a great balcony, nearly a mile in length, overhanging the Mediterranean.

The harbor itself was a renowned shelter for the corsair fleets that terrorized the shores of the Mediterranean. For centuries the Barbary states had been anarchical pirate republics which chose their own rulers and supported themselves by plunder. Only since the year 1819 had Tunisia renounced piracy and made the taking of slaves unlawful. But Morocco and Algeria still clung to the old ways seven years later.

The door flung open, interrupting Christa's silent revery, and Redbeard's imposing bulk appeared in the portal. It was the first time she had seen him in two days. Her meals had been delivered by the surly cook, who appeared much too old to do her harm had he any inclinations in that direction. At least the bearded pirate leader had lived up to his word and kept her safe not only from himself but from his men. If only he would change his mind about selling her and send her back to her father! But in that he refused to be swayed.

Redbeard pushed into the cabin, surprisingly light on his feet despite his great size. "Ready yourself, wench," he ordered curtly. We go ashore in an hour."

Christa eyed him with barely disguised contempt. "You've torn to shreds the only dress I owned. I've not had a decent bath in days and since I haven't even a comb my hair is positively indecent."

Redbeard's brow puckered in amazement. Not having seen Christa for two days, he expected to find her in tears, or at least subdued by the thought of her unpredictable future. But not this feisty, silver-haired witch, who was instead calmly upbraiding him for her lack of amenities. What manner of woman was she? Perhaps he should claim her for himself after all, he considered thoughtfully. But no—a woman had no place on a pirate ship unless she was one of his own kind. Which Miss Christa Horton certainly was not.

"Here, put these on," he demanded brusquely. "The rest of your needs will be taken care of in Algiers."

"What are they?" Christa asked, holding up the two articles of clothing Redbeard had tossed in her direction. Extended in one hand was a soft, silken cape with an attached hood the color of the sky. In the other she held a heavy, dark robe, also hooded. Both concealing garments were large enough to cover her from head to toe.

"The silken garment," Redbeard indicated, "is called a djellaba. It is worn against the skin. The heavier cloak is a yashmak and goes over the djellaba. The veil is called a haik. You will wear these garments when we leave the ship. It is the standard covering for women in this part of the world."

He waited long enough to make certain Christa understood, and when she nodded he turned abruptly and left.

Grateful that she was still in possession of her shoes, Christa stumbled after Redbeard along the narrow, winding path leading through the city. The hood of the yashmak completely covered her eyebrows and its attached veil, or haik, drawn across her face concealed her lower features. Beneath the yashmak and djellaba Christa's skin was bedewed with perspiration, even though the brilliant sun barely pierced through the overhanging balconies to the snaking street below.

They walked single file through the dusty, crowded streets, first Redbeard, then Christa, followed by two fierce pirates, armed and dangerous. It was no wonder they were given a wide berth as they traveled the steep path upwards to the kasbah, or central city, entering through one of the babs, or gates. Christa noted that the streets were like staircases, leading from the harbor to the kasbah, and that all transportation was by foot or donkey.

Suddenly Redbeard disappeared through a narrow archway and the two corsairs bringing up the rear rudely pushed her through when she hesitated before the portal. Stumbling against Redbeard, Christa quickly righted herself when he made a disgusted sound deep in his throat. Though the courtyard in which Christa found herself was small, it was like an oasis in the midst of an arid desert. Date trees and blooming plants in brilliant colors surrounded a small pond of sparkling blue water in which swam several large, golden fish. Christa was amazed at the serenity of the place nestled amidst the squalor of the kasbah.

"Inside," Redbeard ordered shortly, motioning toward an arched doorway. When she stood frozen in place, Redbeard grasped her shoulder and propelled her forward. The door opened noiselessly and, given no other choice, she stepped inside.

A man with skin the color of polished ebony bowed low in obeisance, saying, "My master awaits. Please follow me." Though Christa did not understand the flowing Arabic spoken by the servant, his meaning was apparent.

The house was not overly large, but the rooms were high and lofty, the ceilings supported by marble pillars and the floors carpeted with the beautifully woven and dyed rugs referred to in England as Turkey carpets. It was obvious to Christa that the owner of the house was a man of means, and she wondered about his relationship to Redbeard. All too soon her curiosity was appeased.

Sitting cross-legged on a thick cushion and clad in a colorful silk caftan beneath a spotless white burnous, was a man somewhere in his middle years. His features were dark and stern and his figure beneath his robe appeared well-developed, almost athletic. Most arresting were his avid black eyes beneath straight bushy brows, and his hawklike nose. The mouth was finely chiseled, his lips full and sensuous above a neatly clipped black beard. His strange headgear consisted of a cloth wound turban style into an elaborate affair rising several inches at its peak. He greeted Redbeard in Arabic, smiling warmly.

"It is good to see you, my giant friend."

"And I you, Kalim," replied Redbeard.

"What brings you to my humble home?" Though Kalim addressed his words to Redbeard, not once did his piercing eyes leave the small, veiled figure standing beside the corsair. "Do you find my hospitality so lacking that you must bring your own woman for your pleasure?"

"The wench is a valuable commodity I intend to sell for profit," Redbeard revealed, capturing Kalim's immediate attention. "I have reason to believe the new bey of Constantine will be greatly interested in my goods."

"Abdullah? What makes you think he'd want the woman? I've heard his harem is quite satisfactory."

"From what I know of Abdullah, he is a man constantly seeking new pleasure and exotic women. Besides, I think he'll find this wench highly . . . amusing."

"How so?" asked Kalim curiously.

"On my last voyage, I engaged in battle a French ship carrying Prince Ahmed, brother to

Abdullah and Khalid ibn Selim's designated heir. This woman was traveling with him as his concubine. During the fierce fighting that ensued, Ahmed revealed his identity and offered himself for the woman's freedom. He seemed extraodinarily fond of the wench, a feisty little thing who fought like the very devil.''

"Prince Ahmed, where is he now?" Kalim questioned sharply. "It is common knowledge up and down the Barbary coast that Abdullah has seized power in the beylic and placed a price on Ahmed's head should he be foolish enough to return."

Redbeard shook his shaggy head in consternation. "One of my men became overzealous and shot the wretch. He fell into the sea, and when I would have sent my crew over the side after him, we found ourselves the target of two French frigates heeling before the wind and closing in fast. We had no choice but to flee in the face of such overwhelming odds, and more than likely Ahmed is dead. I managed to bring his wench along with me, so all is not completely lost."

Once again Christa found herself the recipient of Kalim's bold perusal. He rapped out a few curt words to a servant standing nearby and she was swiftly divested of both yashmak and djellaba, leaving her clothed before the two grinning men in nothing but Redbeard's overlarge shirt.

"Exquisite!" breathed Kalim, awed by the sight of slim, straight limbs as pale as the finest alabaster. "What hair! A prize indeed! I won't insult you by offering to buy her for myself, my gigantic friend, for though I am wealthy I do not possess the riches to purchase such a one as she. I would consider it an honor, though, to be able to view the young woman without that—er, garment she is wearing."

"I would have no objections," said Redbeard, grinning, "but I'm afraid the wench might. She has a mind of her own, and stripping for us is something she would strongly protest."

"I thought you said she was Ahmed's concubine. Why should she object? What is one man more or less?"

"During my brief association with Christa, which by the way is the wench's name, I learned she fancies herself in love with Ahmed. She is a lady born and bred and places herself on a plane above mere concubine."

As the conversation flew fast and furious over her head, Christa fumed inwardly, finding herself unwilling to stand idly by while her fate was being decided, or to provide amusement for the two men, who obviously held her in little regard.

"What are you talking about?" Christa's anger drove her to ask as she bravely conquered the fear gnawing at her. "Why are you staring at me? I demand to know!"

"Didn't I warn you?" Redbeard asked, reverting to English. His great leonine head tilted backwards as laughter ripped from his throat. "She's like nothing you've ever encountered before."

Kalim's piercing eyes gleamed excitedly as he answered in broken but understandable English. "A jewel, a prize beyond compare! I'd gladly give all I possess to be the one to tame her." Then he sighed regretfully. "What is it you want of me, Barbarossa?"

"A few weeks' lodging for the wench while I await word from Abdullah bey. A messenger has already been dispatched to Constantine."

"She is welcome to lodge here as long as it pleases you," offered Kalim grandly, lapsing into Arabic. "But should Abdullah decide against making the woman his concubine, I suggest you offer her to the dey of Algiers. He is a man of great appetites and ever eager for new and lovely acquisitions to his harem. He is especially fond of blondes. His wealth is legend and you'll find dealing with him profitable.''

"Thank you, my friend," Redbeard acknowledged thoughtfully. "I'll keep your advice in mind should Abdullah decline. And now I must leave you. I am anxious to return to sea. Pickings have been lean these past months and the grumbling from my men loud and boisterous. Taking the wench partly made up for losing the *Bon Ami* and her cargo, but not enough to content them for long. I will see you in a month when I return for Abdullah's answer."

"Leave the woman, I will see that no harm—"

"What is he saying?" Christa demanded to know. "Who is this man and why was I brought here? Are you going to contact my father?"

Annoyed by Christa's outburst, Redbeard turned his glittering gaze on her. "Quiet, wench! You have no say in what happens to you. You are my prisoner to do with as I choose."

Silently applauding Redbeard's harsh reprimand, Kalim said in English, "The woman is too bold. Do you wish me to instruct her in obedience while you are gone?"

"You're leaving me here with this man? I demand you tell me what is going on."

"You demand!" Redbeard raged, embarrassed at having his authority questioned before his friend by a mere woman. "You are in no position to demand anything. I will be obeyed! And in my absence you will obey Kalim."

"I obey no man!" retorted Christa. "Not even my father expected total obedience. You're nothing but a dispicable ba—"

Unaware of the growing fury in Redbeard, Christa earned by her outburst a reward she was little prepared for, as she reeled beneath the force of his blow, his heavy hand leaving a vivid imprint across her face. She dropped to the floor with a thud, struggling to remain conscious as darkness began to claim her. Staring into Redbeard's furious features she wished she had possessed the courage to use the knife on herself while she had the choice. And then she knew no more.

"Take her to the women's quarters," Kalim ordered the servant hovering at his elbow. The man obeyed instantly. "Tell Selima to look after our guest. Impress upon Selima that no harm is to come to her."

"I leave the wench in your hands, Kalim," Redbeard said, eyeing him shrewdly. "When I return, I trust I'll find her in the same condition in which I left her."

"Depend on me, Barbarossa. You are far too large to risk offending."

"Then I'll take my leave."

"Will you not remain long enough to share a meal and later partake of more exotic fare? My Selima would deem it an honor to pleasure you."

"Another time, Kalim," Redbeard sighed regretfully. In truth, Christa had created a need in him he longed to assuage, but his men expected him back shortly. With the French and English as well as the Americans hounding him, no ship was safe for long in any port along the Barbary coast. "When I return I'll gladly accept your hospitality as well as Selima's tender ministrations."

Christa stirred, savoring the coolness of the fragrant breeze caressing her heated flesh. Her eyes opened slowly, reacting instantly to the concerned face peering down at her as she blinked several times in rapid succession.

"Oh, they're blue," a soft, lilting voice announced with obvious satisfaction. "I was certain they would be." Christa had to listen carefully in order to understand the halting English spoken by the extraordinarily beautiful woman bending over her. "I am called Selima."

"Selima," Christa repeated, rising to a sitting position on the couch upon which she had been placed. "Where am I?"

"You are in the serai in the home of Kalim."

"Serai?"

"Women's quarters," explained Selima, searching for the right word.

Staring almost rudely, Christa thought Selima the most beautiful woman she had ever seen. Her dark sloe eyes, outlined in kohl, seemed to eat up her entire face. Above full, extremely sensual lips, her nose was small and straight, emphasizing high cheekbones and a long, swan-like neck. Her bare arms and long slender fingers moved with a natural grace Christa couldn't help but envy. Her small, voluptuous body was clearly defined beneath the revealing clothes she wore, causing Christa to catch her breath in dismay. Though she had lived in Tunis several years, most of the women she had come in contact with were always decently swathed in concealing robes and caftans. The costume worn by Selima was something one would expect to see only in a harem.

"Are you Kalim's wife?" Christa asked innocently.

A tinkling laugh filled the confines of the small room. "I am one of Kalim's concubines. There are four of us in the serai, all of whom you'll soon meet. Kalim has taken no wife."

Christa flushed, lowering her eyes in embarrassment. No matter how long she lived in the east, she would never understand their customs. "I'm sorry," she murmured uncertainly.

"There is nothing to be sorry about." Selima

smiled kindly. "We are happy. Kalim is not a cruel master and is an excellent lover. We in his household consider ourselves lucky. We could have been sent to one of his other houses."

"He has more than one household?" questioned Christa, confused.

"Kalim is a whoremaster. He owns many houses where men go to slake their lusts upon the bodies of beautiful women purchased just for that purpose."

Christa blanched, gulping back her revulsion. Had Redbeard sold her to Kalim? Was she to be sent off to one of his bordellos? She knew blondes were highly favored by both Berbers and Arabs, and the thought of submitting to their wild desires sent her spirits plummeting.

Selima seemed to sense her thoughts and immediately put her worst fears to rest. "You are not meant to spend your days in such an appalling place as a whorehouse. Barbarossa has other plans for you. Far grander than whore or concubine to some minor sheikh. What are you called?"

"My name is Christa. Christa Horton."

"You are very beautiful, Christa," Selima said. "Your hair—I've never seen anything quite like it. Neither silver nor gold, yet somewhere in between."

Christa could not help but smile at Selima's obvious sincerity. "You are lovely, too, Selima. Kalim is a lucky man. Are his other—er, women as appealing as you?"

"You will soon meet them and judge for yourself," Selima said warmly.

"Where did you learn to speak English?" Christa asked, rising to her feet.

"Some time ago, an Englishwoman was brought to the serai by Kalim. She was blond, though not so blond as you, and beautiful. She was on a ship taken by pirates. Kalim bought her for his own concubine, but she refused to accept her fate. In the months she was here, she taught me what little English I speak."

"What—what happened to her?" Christa dared to ask, yet fearing the answer.

"Kalim soon tired of her tantrums and had her removed to one of his bordellos. I've not seen her since."

A shiver of dread slithered down Christa's spine. "How cruel!"

"Not so," Selima said, shaking her head vigorously. "Anna was given a chance to remain with Kalim. She would have been cosseted and protected for the rest of her days. Is that so terrible a fate? What better life can a woman hope for?"

Did Selima really believe what she was saying? Christa asked herself wonderingly. "Obviously you don't understand English women," she said, careful not to offend. "We were not born to be kept secluded from the rest of the world. Where I come from, women have only one man and men have one woman."

"Truly? Anna hinted as much, but I didn't believe her. How could a man be content with one woman? It takes four of us to keep Kalim happy. And I'm certain from the way he looked at you that he would happily add you to our ranks. But Barbarossa made it clear no one was to touch you during your stay here. You are to be our guest. Tell me," she asked in a confidential tone, "is Barbarossa a tireless lover? His size frightens me, but should Kalim offer me to him I know he would make me ecstatically happy."

Selima's frank musings startled Christa. Did the women in this part of the world think of nothing but passion and personal gratification? Her answer was quick in coming.

"Algerian women are taught from an early age how to please men. We learn every aspect of erotic pleasure. The happier we make our master, the better we are treated. My father sold me to Kalim for his whorehouse when I was but twelve. Kalim, in his wisdom, saw potential in my face and still undeveloped figure, and kept me for himself. Unlike some men, who like their women young and immature, he waited until I was fifteen before taking me to his bed."

"Your father sold you?" gasped Christa, horrified.

Selima shrugged carelessly. "It's done all the time. We were a poor family with many mouths to feed. I showed the most promise of growing up to be beautiful."

"I'm sorry," Christa sympathized.

"I'm not. What did I have to look forward to in my small village? The life of a drudge? Caring for a cruel husband and many children? I am far luckier than any of my brothers and sisters."

"I see," was all Christa could manage. But in truth she understood little of Selima's explanation. Sharing her man with other women was not Christa's idea of happiness. Neither was languishing behind high walls and being used solely for pleasure.

"Come, Christa," Selima said, taking her hand. "Kalim left strict orders that you are to be cared for and kept happy until Barbarossa's return. Would you like a bath? The other women are anxious to meet you."

Christa nodded, thinking a bath would be divine as she followed Selima from the small, pleasant room to a large open area with a sparkling pool in its center. Around the pool lounged three lovely women in various stages of undress, being attended by several older women. The moment

Christa intruded upon the peaceful scene, all chatter skittered to an abrupt halt as three pair of curious eyes turned in her direction. Christa hesitated, studying the three women as intently as they were scrutinizing her, listening carefully as Selima named each in turn.

Jade was an oriental, as lovely and fragile as an orchid. Her tiny form was perfect in every way. Her huge, dark eyes slanted upwards at the outer corners and her skin, as creamy as a magnolia blossom, was enhanced by the long stream of jet black hair falling to her waist in a straight, sleek line.

Baba was African, as black and shiny as polished ebony. Short curly hair formed a cap about an arresting face unlike any Christa had ever seen. She had eyes like black velvet, and a flaring nose above a wide mouth with slightly fleshy lips; her tall, lissome form moved with the utmost grace.

A Circassian named Alita was the fourth member of Kalim's household. Gold hair fell in fluffy waves about her almost childlike features. Christa was shocked to learn Alita was but fifteen years old and already wise in the ways of women. Her figure, just beginning to ripen, promised a voluptuousness none of the other three possessed. None but Selima could speak English, but all communicated friendliness by their signs and smiles. They had already been told by Selima that Christa posed no threat to their place in Kalim's life, for she was not meant for their master's bed.

Christa delighted in the bath more than she cared to admit, willingly submitting to a massage by one of the serving women. It felt wonderful when fragrant oils were rubbed into her skin, rendering it smooth and supple. She even took pleasure in the meal carried in a short time later, sampling and enjoying each dish offered. They all ate together, Selima translating all questions and answers as they became acquainted during the meal.

Christa balked, though, when given clothes much like those worn by Selima and the others. When it became obvious that she would be offered nothing else, she donned the meager garments with great reluctance. The sheer pantaloons were a gossamer blush-colored silk shot through with silver threads. The ankle bands and hip band were embroidered in pink glass beads and silver thread. Above the hip band Christa was nude, save for a sleeveless, open bolero of blush-colored silk edged in silver trim, which just barely clung to the soft swelling of her lovely breasts. As an added touch, her silvery hair was gathered and tied back with a pink ribbon. Amidst much clapping and sighing, she was admired by one and all.

When it was time to retire to her room, a servant approached little Alita, whispered in her ear, then quietly left. Christa knew from her giggles and wide smile that Alita had been chosen to grace Kalim's bed that night. Idly, Christa wondered if Kalim merely drew straws to see which of his women he'd bed or perhaps employed some other method.

Though Christa did not want for company during the following days, boredom dogged her steps. After all, how many hours could one spend on grooming and idle pursuits? Countless hours were already wasted sitting in the bathing room gossiping with the other women and frolicking in the pool. Sitting around unclothed made Christa uncomfortable, for she had an uncanny feeling that invisible eyes were watching her. Yet try as she might she could see no one but Kalim's women and their servants, usually hags too old for anything but tending to the needs of the young concubines. It was an eerie sensation, one that Christa strived to ignore, never quite succeeding.

It was Selima who delighted Christa by suggesting a way to assuage the dreadful boredom. She began teaching Christa Arabic, at the same time perfecting her own English. Soon the others joined in, and before long both English and Arabic began flowing between the women, all of whom were intelligent but had never been given the opportunity to use their brains.

Somehow the weeks sped by, but in all that time Christa never ceased plotting her escape, hoping that one day the opportunity would present itself. Sadly, it never did. She might well have been in prison, so zealously were the women's quarters guarded. Only when she slept was she left unattended.

At the end of a month, Christa found herself becoming quite proficient in Arabic—and beset by a strange malady over which she had little control.

7

One day Christa awoke to brilliant sunshine and a queasy feeling deep in the pit of her stomach. Thinking it would soon pass, she decided against mentioning it to Selima. Her assumption proved correct, for within a few hours she was feeling her old self again. The next day much the same thing happened, only this time she was vomiting into a basin when Selima hurried into the room, hastily summoned by a servant who heard the retching sounds.

"What is it, Christa, are you ill?" she asked, concern coloring her words. "How long has this been going on?"

"Only a day or two," Christa said, not overly concerned. "It quickly passes, so I'm sure it's nothing to worry about."

Selima's dark eyes narrowed thoughtfully, and she carefully scrutinized Christa's slim form. "Will you let me know if your illness persists?" she asked, a glimmer of suspicion beginning in the back of her brain.

"Of course," Christa agreed, "but it's nothing serious. Truly."

But when the malady continued each morning for a week, even Christa became troubled, confiding her fears to Selima, who promptly reported it to Kalim.

"The girl is ill?" asked Kalim sharply when Selima stood before him. "Have you summoned my physician? I placed the girl in your care, Selima, and I expected nothing to happen to her." His displeasure was obvious.

"What ails Christa is none of my doing, master," Selima returned quickly. "I come from a large family and this particular illness is not new to me. I believe the girl is carrying a child."

A long string of curses escaped Kalim's lips, causing Selima to cringe in fear. Was Kalim angry at her? Would he punish her? Was the child Barbarossa's?

"Barbarossa will be enraged when he returns and finds the girl with child," Kalim said when his anger was expended. "Is she aware of her condition?"

"No, master, the girl is rather naive in such things."

"Good! I will do what I think best for Barbarossa. He expects to earn great wealth from the slave and her swelling with child will not be in his best interest," he mused thoughtfully. "Once the physician confirms her condition, he will be instructed to concoct a potion that will rid her of her burden. She is too valuable to allow any seed but that of her new master to nurture and grow."

"Perhaps the child is from Barbarossa's loins. Shouldn't he decide what's to be done?" Selima dared to ask.

"You presume too much!" Kalim bellowed, backhanding her across the face, one of the few times he had struck her. "Your only concern is caring for the girl. Perhaps a taste of the bastinado will teach you obedience."

"No, master, please, not the bastinado," begged Selima, throwing herself at Kalim's feet. Surely that instrument of punishment was created by the devil himself.

Used judiciously, the bastinado inflicted extreme pain without marring the tender and beautiful skin of recalcitrant concubines or the tough hides of valuable slaves. It consisted of a thick wooden rod and was applied to the soles of the feet. The pain was excruciating, often rendering the recipient unable to walk for several days while leaving the skin essentially undamaged. Selima harbored a terrible fear of the weapon, having felt its devastating effect on more than one occasion.

"Go, then," ordered Kalim imperiously, "before I lose my temper. Report to me after the doctor has seen to the girl."

Wasting no time, Selima hurried away, breathing a sigh of relief. Though she knew Kalim was quite fond of her, he felt no remorse when it came to inflicting punishment when his authority was questioned.

Christa submitted to the embarrassing examination performed by Kalim's physician, an elderly man whose stoic expression revealed nothing. When he finished, he asked several questions that Christa thought were none of his business but answered rather than cause trouble. Finally finished, he assured her she was suffering from no serious or permanent illness and left. Christa snorted in disgust. That much she knew herself.

That night, Christa was served a particularly tasty fruit sherbet while Selima sat by with downcast eyes. The delicious drink was so refreshing that Christa drained the cup without urging, commenting on its piquant flavor to Selima, who managed a nod and half-hearted smile.

When Christa retired later, she found herself unable to sleep. For some unexplained reason, her dreams were haunted by thoughts of Mark—how it felt to be held in his arms, the way his kisses aroused her, the surge of pleasure through her body when he was inside her, the ecstasy he never failed to give her. Are you alive, my love? she whispered in the darkness. Are you even now searching for me? Deep in her heart she knew he wasn't dead and one day he would find her. It was that thought that kept her sane and gave her the courage to face each day no matter what indignities were visited upon her. More than once Mark had told her they would live out their lives together, and she clung to that slim hope. On that comforting thought she fell asleep.

Sometime during the night, Christa was awakened by a searing jolt deep in the pit of her stomach. The tearing, burning pain ripped through her gut in cramp-like sensations, causing her to cry out in agony. What was happening to her? she wondered, writhing beneath the throbbing assault. Had she been poisoned? Was she to die an ignominious death in Kalim's serai without the benefit of her loved ones to comfort her in her last hours?

Christa's cries brought immediate attention as Selima entered the room, followed by the physician and a bevy of serving women. Later, Christa was to think that they must have been hovering outside her door to arrive so quickly. But at the time she was only too happy to see them, gratefully accepting a draught mixed by the doctor to relieve her pain. It also made her sleep—the deep, dreamless sleep of the drugged.

* * *

Sunlight grazed her eyelids and Christa moved her head to escape the relentless stab of light. She groaned, struggling through layers of gray, misty cobwebs that threatened to ensnare her as she fought to break free of the silken trap.

"Christa, wake up," urged a gentle voice somewhere nearby.

Reluctantly, unwilling to give up the protective cocoon in which she lay, Christa opened her eyes, focusing with difficulty on the face swimming into view. "Selima," she croaked, finding her voice strangely hoarse. "What happened to me?"

Selima hesitated. At length, she said, "You were ill. Very ill. But thank Allah you are recovering nicely. Kalim's physician has said so and he is a very learned man."

"What was wrong with me? Was I poisoned?"

"You were not poisoned, Christa. But because I do not understand medical terms, I do not know what your illness is called," Selima shrugged evasively. "What does it matter when you're going to be fine?"

"I . . . I suppose you're right, Selima, for I do feel much better. How long was I sick?"

"Three days." She did not add that for most of those three days Christa had been kept sedated.

"My god! I must have been terribly ill. Are you certain I will recover?"

Selima nodded gravely. "The doctor has said so. Are you hungry? I think you should rise and move around a bit to restore your strength. Can you walk as far as the bathing room?"

"I do feel hungry," Christa admitted, groaning from the effort of moving her legs. She felt as if her entire body were bruised and battered.

Gratefully accepting help from Selima and a servant, Christa managed to totter to the bathing room, where she was thoroughly scrubbed, soaked and laid out nude on a table while another servant prepared to administer a relaxing massage. Suddenly Christa tensed, once again assailed by the eerie sensation that she was being watched. Casting a furtive glance in all directions, Christa saw that save for Selima and the servants, she was alone. Still, the feeling persisted, making her decidedly uncomfortable. Evidently Selima did not suffer the same apprehension, for she was happily cavorting in a pool without a care or concern. Then the old woman began her soothing ministrations, and Christa relaxed, allowing her mind to go blank and enjoy the welcome stimulation to her tortured muscles.

"Why is she so pale?" Redbeard asked as he and Kalim secretly observed the goings-on in the bathing room below. Nearly four months had elapsed since he left Christa with Kalim, and she seemed thinner than he remembered.

From below, the decorative paneling gave no hint that it concealed a small room where Kalim could watch his women as they lounged nude or cavorted in the pool. The women knew of its existence, of course, which resulted in much posturing and posing meant to captivate their master and aid him in making his decision as to who would share his bed that night. But no one had bothered to tell Christa about it, or to inform her that each day she had been secretly observed by Kalim in all stages of undress.

"The girl has been ill," Kalim remarked casually, his eyes feasting on the slim, white body stretched out enticingly before him.

Redbeard's eyes narrowed dangerously. "I left the wench in your care, Kalim. How did this happen? Besides appearing wan, she looks as if she has lost weight. Abdullah will not be pleased. He paid a king's ransom for the right to possess his brother's concubine. What ails her?"

"A sickness to which all women succumb sooner or later," remarked Kalim wryly. "The girl was with child."

"What!" exploded Redbeard angrily. "She can't be pregnant! We must do something about it immediately. Abdullah has sent his Janissaries with a caravan to escort her to Constantine. Even now they are camped just beyond the city gates, waiting for their master's latest acquisition. I'm not certain I can delay them. Nor do I wish to incur Abdullah's wrath by sending a woman expecting another man's child."

"There is no need to delay departure, Barbarossa," Kalim was quick to reply. "I anticipated your wishes and saw to it that the girl was relieved of her burden."

"You had her aborted?"

Kalim nodded. "That was your wish, was it not? The doctor has pronounced her fully recovered and you can see for yourself how well she looks."

A pang of some strange, long-forgotten emotion assailed Redbeard, but it quickly passed. "You did exactly right, Kalim, my friend. I could not allow the pregnancy to continue. Does the wench know?"

"Only that she has been ill. Selima tells me she is amazingly naive for one her age."

"It's just as well," muttered Redbeard beneath his breath. "Perhaps she will bear a son for Abdullah. She is still capable, isn't she?" Redbeard asked sharply.

"She will have no difficulty conceiving and has already proved a quick breeder," Kalim assured him. "My physician is one of the best and knows what he is about. No doubt the girl will bear many children for her master."

Redbeard studied Christa intently, his yellow gaze roaming hungrily over her nude form, searching for blemishes but finding none. He cursed himself roundly for denying himself the pleasure of her body when the choice was still his. But in a moment of unaccustomed weakness, she had struck a responsive chord in his huge body and he had allowed her her way. Not that it prevented him from carrying out his original plans for Christa. Not only was Abdullah ecstatic to learn that Ahmed was more than likely dead and thus no longer a threat to him, but he was anxious to possess the woman who had captured his brother's fancy.

Redbeard earned a generous reward for claiming responsibility for Ahmed's death, as well as collecting a hefty sum for the wench. His men would be well pleased with their share, although his sudden wealth did little to stop him from regretting his decision to forego the pleasure of her body. But, alas, Christa now belonged to Abdullah bey and Captain Hadji of the Janissaries awaited outside the city gates with a purse to be put directly into Redbeard's hands upon delivery of the wench.

"Does Selima please you?" Kalim asked, directing his gaze to the small, dark woman stepping from the pool like a budding Venus.

Reluctantly sliding his eyes from Christa's fair loveliness, Redbeard turned his rapt perusal to Selima. Though small, her voluptuous form was nearly perfect. Lazy droplets of water dripped from breasts the exact size to fill his hands, their large, deep rose nipples jutting impudently forward, begging for attention. The triangle between her legs was smooth and clean shaven, causing Redbeard to lick his lips in avid anticipation.

"She is enchanting," Redbeard acknowledged

sincerely. "You are a lucky man. Such a woman would please Allah himself."

Kalim beamed, aware of his reputation as a gracious host. "Selima is well versed in the art of love. Though she is small, her size will present no problem to one of your—er, magnificent proportions. She is yours for the night to enjoy in any way you desire. Unless, of course, you'd prefer to bed the slave, Christa. No doubt you enjoyed her many times before you brought her to me and would like one last time with her."

Redbeard flushed beneath his swarthy skin. He had no intention of telling Kalim that he had not bedded Christa, though he yearned to do so. It wouldn't do to destroy his reputation as a cold blooded despoiler of women as well as a fierce corsair feared by all who sailed the Mediterranean and beyond. "I will leave the wench for Abdullah to tame," he said gruffly. "Besides, she appears much too weak to satisfy my voracious needs. I want a woman whose lusty appetites match my own."

"Then Selima is the woman for you," said Kalim knowingly. "I will send her to you tonight. Now we will share a meal, and you can tell me about Abdullah and what your messenger learned on his journey to Constantine. One hears that there is much unrest in the hills and desert surrounding the city."

"My man Ramir heard talk in the villages he passed through of a great sheikh aptly called the Desert Hawk by his followers. He recently appeared from nowhere to lead a group of tribesmen who are fierce fighters and renowned raiders. They are Tuaregs who travel on sleek racing camels and are feared by all. Of late they have concentrated mainly on rich caravans laden with goods bound for Constantine and Abdullah's court."

Their conversation continued over dinner, as Redbeard regaled Kalim with stories he had heard of the elusive sheikh whose antics cost Abdullah much in the way of goods and men. The bey sent his Janissaries into the surrounding hills and desert to flush out the Desert Hawk and his cohorts, but found the bandits more than a match for his fearless army. It was said that the Tuaregs were the most warlike nomads in all the great Sahara, for years kept under control by Abdullah's father Khalid ibn Selim, with whom the fierce raiders had negotiated a truce, learning to respect the wise bey. But after Khalid's death and the subsequent seizure of authority by Abdullah in Ahmed's absence, the unwritten treaty was no longer honored. And during the past month Abdullah had suddenly found his caravans no longer safe from attack.

"Did your man see this great sheikh?" asked Kalim avidly. "Is he as fierce as they say?"

"From a distance Ramir saw the Tuaregs cresting a hill as they watched the caravan in which he was traveling, but they did not attack—aware, no doubt, that the caravan was not a rich one."

"Did Ramir see their alleged leader?" he asked excitedly.

"No," Redbeard mused thoughtfully, "though Ramir did say that one man stood out from the rest. His face was swathed in the distinctive dark blue scarf of the Tuareg tribe and he was mounted on a wild Arabian stallion. He wore not the dark, drab robes of the Tuareg but pristine white that flowed on the breeze. Then, according to Ramir, he disappeared as silently as he had appeared, followed by his men. I wish I could have been there to see him."

Kalim grunted, certain he wanted nothing to do with this Desert Hawk, or with the Tuaregs. Those bloodthirsty desert raiders were known to destroy whole oasis towns, riding racing camels known as mehari. Skilled in tracking, extremely cruel, they terrorized desert towns and caravans alike, wielding long, two-edged swords with a skill surpassed by none.

After their meal, Kalim and Redbeard were entertained by six sinuous dancing girls clad in flowing sheer veils that did little to conceal their considerable charms. By the time the entertainment was brought to an exciting conclusion, in which the girls threw off their last filmy garments to reveal their sweat-slicked bodies, Redbeard was more than ready for Sclima.

From the moment Christa awakened, she knew that day would be different from the others. A dreadful premonition crept along her spine until it possessed her mind, filling her with unspeakable terror. It couldn't be her illness, for she no longer felt any effects from that strange malady. Evidently her sickness was to have no lasting effects, she decided gratefully.

Selima did not join her until much later than usual that morning, appearing blurry-eyed and dreamy when she did. Christa wondered idly if Kalim had called her to his bed last night and worn her out with his exuberant loving. Selima's full lips were swollen, and her lithe body moved with a sinuous slowness that suggested long hours of sexual fulfillment. But whatever Selima had experienced during the night was not revealed by the sloe-eyed beauty when she joined Christa for lunch.

"You are to appear before Kalim," Selima said when she was seated on the cushion at Christa's side.

"Wha . . . what does he want?"

"Barbarossa has returned," came her cryptic reply.

After finishing the meal, which consisted of

goat's cheese, dates and cakes made of sticky sweet almond paste, Christa was painstakingly groomed and robed by Kalim's servants. Her pantaloons were fashioned of transparent turquoise silk. Bands of gold rode her slim hips and adorned her shapely ankles. A short turquoise bolero embroidered in gold and barely covering her breasts left her torso bare. She had been given no jewelry, so wore none, her beauty needing no artifice to enhance it. Only after she was carefully scrutinized by Selima, Jade, Baba and Alita, was she taken before Kalim and Redbeard.

Once again Redbeard was captivated by Christa's beauty, easily falling under her spell. Her long silvery hair skimmed her shapely body like a cloak, for it was unbound and allowed to float free, and her costume was revealing enough to tantalize while adding an air of mystery about that which was concealed.

"How have you fared in my absence, wench?" Redbeard asked, his voice made gruff by desire. He was beginning to rue the day he came upon the silver-haired witch.

"Well enough," Christa conceded ungraciously. "Have you notified my father? When may I leave?"

"You well know I had no intention of collecting a meager ransom from your family," Redbeard growled menacingly. "Nor will you be offered for sale in the slave market. I have struck a private deal with Abdullah bey who was . . . most anxious to add you to his harem after my messenger described your beauty and intelligence. Not to mention the fact that Ahmed thought highly of you. Evidently you piqued Abdullah's curiosity, for he would allow no other to have you."

"You're a bastard, Redbeard!" Christa lashed out, shocking Kalim.

Redbeard roared with laughter. "You are truly a gem, Christa. I swear I am tempted to keep you for myself. But luckily my lust is surpassed only by my greed. Abdullah was willing to part with a fortune to make you his."

"Go to hell!" she spat scathingly. "Rest assured, Abdullah will never lay hands on me."

"You are a patient man," Kalim observed admiringly. "The woman is in dire need of discipline. Should I have Abdul bring the bastinado? In the long run, Abdullah will thank you. I can't imagine him allowing a slave to speak to him in such a disrespectful manner."

Redbeard eyed Christa narrowly, secretly admiring her show of spirit but aware that he should not allow it to flourish lest his reputation suffer in Kalim's eyes. To Christa's horror, he nodded agreement to Kalim's outrageous suggestion. Within minutes Kalim's servant Abdul returned with a short wooden rod, which he extended to Redbeard.

"Lie on the floor, wench," Redbeard ordered curtly. When Christa did not respond, he seized her and rudely threw her down on a mat of cushions. Then he nodded to Abdul, who seized her ankles, extending them upward and out. When Christa struggled, Kalim moved forward, sitting across her hips to hold her in place.

"Proceed, my huge friend," Kalim smiled, "but do not get carried away. Abdullah bey will expect her in good condition. Five strokes should dampen her spirit sufficiently."

Looking down at Christa, Redbeard knew he hadn't the heart to mar her lovely skin, not even the soles of her feet. Somewhere in the dark chambers of his heart dwelt tender feelings for the beautiful blonde, and punishing her so severely held little pleasure for him. If need be, he would find another way to tame her, but not with the bastinado.

"Let her up," he said, shocking Kalim. "There is no need to proceed with the punishment. I believe she has learned her lesson.

"And remember," roared Redbeard at Christa. "this isn't England. A woman in this part of the world is mere chattel and lives or dies at the whim of her master. Direct your energies to pleasing Abdullah lest you find yourself flung over the walls of the city. I hear the bey is cruel and a difficult man to please.

"Leave now and prepare yourself to depart at first light tomorrow. Abdullah has sent an escort to transport you to Constantine. They await outside the city gates."

Seething with frustration and consumed with indignation, Christa was forced to obey, leaving the room with the dignity at her disposal.

"You are lucky," Selima said. "Barbarossa must hold a fondness for you."

"He's a monster!" Christa hissed from between clenched teeth. "This entire country is an abomination. I want to go home. I want my family."

"You must forget your former life," Selima advised, "if you are to survive. You'd do well to please Abdullah bey. It is a great honor to be chosen for the harem of so great a man."

"Abdullah is no better than Barbarossa. He's a cruel man who murdered Ahmed's mother because she stood in his way. Ahmed is the rightful ruler of Constantine."

Selima shrugged. "I know nothing of such things. I know only what goes on inside these walls."

Appalled by Selima's ignorance, Christa did not respond, aware that the woman led a totally sheltered life entirely at the disposal of her master. She would rather die than live under such restrictions. And if she had her way she'd never reach

Abdullah's harem. God willing, she would escape long before she reached Constantine. One day, she solemnly vowed, Redbeard would pay for what he did to her.

Christa offered no protest the next morning when she was dressed in a rose silk hooded djellaba, her face covered by a haik and then draped in a dark, encompassing yashmak. She had time for only a brief good-bye and hug for Selima, Jade, Baba and Alita before being whisked off to where Redbeard awaited, impatient to have her off his hands. Being on dry land too long made him decidedly uncomfortable.

Christa was led along Rue Marengo, one of the two roads through the teeming old city, which formed a triangle with the kasbah at the apex, its tall minarets and turreted ramparts stark against the blue sky. Passage on foot through the narrow streets was difficult, but the only travel possible in such tight quarters. Escorted by Redbeard and four of his fierce corsairs, Christa was taken to the south bab, or gate, where they passed through unnoticed among the throngs of people coming and going.

The first thing Christa noticed was a group of small black tents erected just beyond the bab, and white-robed men scurrying about in the process of dismantling and packing them on the backs of sturdy donkeys and surly, mangy camels with moth-eaten coats. At least two dozen Janissaries lounged nearby, overseeing the process. One of the soldiers noticed their approach and immediately detached himself from the others to await their arrival.

"Is this the woman?" he asked in Arabic when they drew near. By now Christa understood enough of the language to follow the conversation without difficulty.

"Aye," Redbeard replied, thrusting Christa forward. "This is the Christian slave, Christa, who is to be escorted to Constantine, Captain Hadji. See that she arrives safely or Abdullah bey will have your head."

"I've no doubt one could achieve heaven between her white thighs," remarked Hadji, grinning lewdly, "but I value my skin too highly to offend Abdullah. I will see that no harm comes to the woman, Barbarossa. I have been instructed by my master to give you this." From beneath his cloak he extracted a weighted bag that jangled enticingly.

Pretending ignorance of the language, Christa kept her eyes trained on the dusty ground while Redbeard opened the sack and carefully examined the contents, nodding his head in obvious contentment as he pulled the drawstrings and slipped it beneath his belt. From the conversation she gathered that she was to be protected from the lusts of the men until she reached Constantine and Abdullah's palace. The knowledge was welcome, if not entirely comforting. Then she became aware that Captain Hadji had left and she was alone with Redbeard.

"Well, wench, this is good-bye. If you're clever, you'll direct your energies to making Abdullah happy. If I hadn't gone soft-hearted for the first time in my life, I'd have sampled you myself. I'll never know what I missed, for now you belong to Abdullah."

"Never!" Christa declared vehemently. "I have no intention of becoming Abdullah's slave, or his concubine."

Redbeard smiled wistfully. "Ah, lass, there's never a dull moment with you around. Did you think to escape in the desert? If the elements didn't kill you, one of fierce desert tribes would find you and make you wish for Abdullah's tender ministrations."

"I'll take my chances," spat Christa defiantly.

Redbeard's answer was forestalled when Hadji returned, informing them, "We are ready to leave, Barbarossa."

Redbeard nodded. "Guard her well, Hadji, the wench thinks to escape her fate." Christa had no difficulty following the rapid Arabic and blessed Selima for her patient teaching.

"With my life," assured Hadji, salaaming deeply. Then he grasped Christa by the arm and literally dragged her toward the group of camels milling nearby. One of the native handlers urged a particularly ugly specimen to its knees while Hadji forced Christa into the strange conveyance perched atop the camel's humped back.

Warily she eyed the striped, hooped, baloon-like tent called a bassourab arranged atop the camel's hump. She knew it was designed exclusively for travel by women, but never had she ridden in one. It would protect her from the burning rays of the sun, but it looked hot and uncomfortable. Despite her feeble protests, however, she soon found herself seated in the cane chair inside the tent-like contraption and hanging on for dear life when the camel tottered to its feet. The side-to-side motion once they were under way was reminiscent of a ship's tossing in a turbulent sea. At least she was able to peek through a slit in the tent from time to time to watch scenery pass by.

For nearly two weeks they traveled southward through rugged mountains, fertile valleys, numerous streams and rich forests of red juniper and pine. At night, hastily erected gitun were erected to provide shelter. Christa was surprised to learn from conversation among the Janissaries that the mountains abounded with lions, panthers and boar.

The first night, an old woman hastened to her tent bearing a meal of dates, olives, cheese, goat's milk and fresh fruit, which was later varied by the welcome addition of roasted lamb. Not only was Christa surprised to see another woman traveling with the caravan, but she was more than a little startled to find the woman spoke English. Upon closer inspection, she saw that though the woman's skin was browned and wrinkled from exposure to the sun, she had vivid blue eyes and the features of a foreigner.

"I am Lenore," said the woman, placing the tray of food before Christa. "Abdullah sent me along to see to your needs."

"You speak English!" gasped Christa, delighted. "How wonderful. You're not Arab," she added astutely.

"I was English," Lenore admitted, busying herself with the food she sat before Christa. "I am a captive, just like you."

"If you were born English, nothing has changed," Christa said, puzzled by Lenore's peculiar phrasing. "You're still English."

"Long ago I embraced Islam. Allah is my God. I was not beautiful like you, mistress, not even in my youth. I did what I must to survive. The old bey bought me as a companion for his favorite concubine. It was a good life as long as they lived, but now I belong to Abdullah and circumstances have altered." Abruptly she changed the subject. "Until we enter the desert there is plenty of water for bathing. Would you like a bath?"

"Oh, yes," Christa said eagerly. "That would be lovely." She watched the old woman for a few minutes before coming to a decision and asking, "Have you ever tried to escape, Lenore?"

Lenore turned startled eyes on Christa. "Escape? Where would I go? And for what purpose? No, mistress, at least with Abdullah I know what to expect."

"Please, call me Christa," Christa insisted, for the woman reminded her much of Marla, whom she was forced to leave aboard the *Bon Ami*.

Christa did not pursue the subject of escape with the obviously frightened Lenore, but it was never far from her mind. Somehow, when the right moment arrived, she would enlist Lenore's help and make her way to her parents.

The days tumbled into one another with a sameness that was frustrating as well as boring. At times the going was rough, especially when they traveled over the area called the Tell, after the Arabic word for hill. Often she spotted the Tell's shifting population of nomads following their flocks and camping in gurbi, portable dwellings made of branches and clay.

Christa had been aware for days that they were traveling west, for the terrain was much like that of Algiers—mountains from three to four thousand feet high, fertile valleys and rivers. At the end of the second week they came down into a dusty plain of grain fields and olive trees surrounded by low, wooded hills. The excitement among the natives and Janissaries mounted, and Christa's heart sank, for it meant they were nearing the end of their journey. That night Lenore confirmed her suspicions.

So far Christa had been offered little chance for escape. True to his word, Captain Hadji proved a vigilant watchdog, posting a guard at her tent each night. Ever mindful of the terrible fate that awaited her once she reached Constantine, Christa decided she could wait no longer to make good her escape. Throwing caution to the wind, she reluctantly confided in Lenore.

"It's not possible!" gasped the old woman when told of Christa's desire to flee.

"It is if you help me," Christa pleaded desperately. "We can leave together. Don't you want to be free?"

"Free?" Lenore repeated vacantly. "I . . . it's been so long." A lengthy pause ensued while Christa allowed the idea of freedom to take hold and blossom in Lenore's brain. Lenore's next words not only shocked but disappointed her. "No, freedom is but a state of mind. A woman is never free."

"But what about your family? Is there no one who would be happy to see you return?"

"No one," Lenore insisted. "I was a ladies' maid, traveling with my mistress to Sicily, when we were captured by pirates. My family all died years before in an epidemic. I was the only survivor. No, mistress, I've nothing and no one to return to."

"Then you'll come with me to my home," Christa persisted.

Again Lenore shook her head, confounding Christa. "How long do you think we'll last on our own in these mountains? Besides, Captain Hadji would not be so careless as to allow you to escape. It could well mean his death—and mine."

"Please, Lenore, help me. You can come and go as you please. Together we'll figure out something. We can go to Tunis, where slavery is outlawed. My family lives there and would welcome you."

"I'm sorry, mistress, I'm too old to change my way of life."

"At least help me, if you won't go with me."

"Do you know what would happen if we returned to Constantine without you?" Lenore asked tightly. Christa shook her head uncertainly. Nothing in this cruel country would shock her.

"Captain Hadji and the Janissaries would be horribly tortured before being put to death. Their heads would be displayed on wooden spikes at the high walls surrounding the city. And I," she said, lowering her voice to a hoarse whisper, "would be forced to endure the same cruel justice. And once you were caught, and you most assuredly would be, you'd wish many times over for death." With that terrifying prophesy, the old woman shuffled away, leaving Christa to ponder her words.

8

After spending a sleepless night alternately weeping and railing at the God who had abandoned her, Christa came to the inevitable conclusion that she could not accept responsibility for the torture and death of so many people, especially an innocent like Lenore who had already experienced too much horror and abuse in her life. If she must face Abdullah, she would do so with courage and fortitude. But once inside his harem, she would search tirelessly for some means of escape that would not bring death to innocent victims.

As they continued their journey the next morning, Christa fought the dust that rose up around the camel's hooves in billowing clouds of yellow grit, noting that it seemed much hotter since they came down from the Tell. Everywhere she looked were groves of olive trees or waving grain fields bowing beneath the relentless sun. Yet she was surprised at how cold were the nights. The Barbary states were indeed a land of contrasts.

That night Lenore was quieter than usual when she brought supper in to her charge. "Are you angry with me, mistress?" she asked timidly. "Please forgive an old lady who no longer possesses the courage to defy her master."

"There's nothing to forgive." Christa smiled sadly. "You were right all along. There is no place for us to go, nowhere to hide. If by some miracle we did manage to escape, we would be found and punished. Please leave me, Lenore, I . . . I want to be alone."

Bowing to Christa's wishes, Lenore silently left the small confines of the tent.

Christa retired with a heavy heart, knowing they were within a day or two of reaching Constantine. Almost absently she donned the sheer, pale pink caftan she wore nightly to bed. Kalim's women had presented her with an attractive array of caftans which she had put to good use during the journey. They even gave her a small carved chest in which to pack her meager wardrobe. As she drifted off to sleep she thought of Mark and his words concerning their kismet.

"You were wrong, Mark, very wrong!" she cried aloud, pounding her fists into the pillow. "Kismet is but a myth and your words a cruel jest. If the Gods meant us to be together, where are you now?"

The stillness of the night exploded with sound, the frightening sounds of staccato bursts of gunfire, the clash of swords, shouts of warning and screams of agony. Christa bolted upright, sheer black terror rendering her mute as a scream died in her throat. What was happening? Was she awakening from a bad dream? But no, this was no dream, she decided, as violence erupted outside her tent. What was taking place in the camp was very real. Willing her legs into motion, Christa swung them to the edge of the makeshift bed of cushions and lambswool robes. But before she could investigate further, the tent flap flew open, revealing a man nearly as large as Redbeard the pirate. All she could see of his face were dark, fierce eyes and black brows that met in a straight line across his forehead, for his face and body were swathed in the blue veils of the Tuareg tribe. Suddenly a terrifying thought jolted through her.

For days she heard talk of nothing but the fierce desert sheikh they called the Desert Hawk. Her knowledge of Arabic made her privy to the Janissaries' gossip about this desert chieftain who seemed to bear a grudge against Abduldlah bey and attacked his caravans almost exclusively. Was it this very same man who had burst in upon them in the middle of the night, killing and sacking?

Cowering against the cushions, Christa was no match for the superior strength of the desert raider as he easily overpowered her, lifting her high in his arms and carrying her out of the tent into the savage night. For as long as she lived, Christa would remember the appalling sight that met her eyes then.

Clearly illuminated by the flames of the dying campfire, men were either engaged in hand-to-hand combat or riding swift racing camels through the camp, cutting down Captain Hadji's men, who had been surprised by the ambush nearly within sight of the crenellated walls of Constantine. The screams of the dying and wounded told a story of death and destruction, causing Christa a pang of remorse for the hapless Janissaries, despite the fact that they were Abdullah's elite fighters.

Picking his way around bodies strewn about the perimeter of the camp, Christa's huge captor carried her effortlessly to where the camels were hobbled at the foot of a low hill. Glancing upward, Christa caught her breath at the sight of a white-clad figure stark against the inky sky, mounted regally atop a midnight black Arab stallion. Majestic was the only word that came to Christa's mind. Was this, then, the desert sheikh called the Hawk? That fierce, feared raider of the Sahara? While Christa watched with bated breath, the raider started down the hill leading another horse, this one pure white and obviously belonging to the man holding her. All the other Tuaregs, it appeared, rode swift, sleek camels, absolutely nothing like the mangy creatures used for transportation.

Dawn was breaking over the hills and mauve streaks colored the eastern sky as the coal-black horse carrying the white-robed sheikh reached them. He was completely covered but for his eyes, which he kept carefully hooded with long dark lashes, and when he reached out, Christa shivered in trepidation. She was shifted into his arms and seated in front of him, embarrassingly conscious of the hard contours of his body, as well as of her own ill-clad form. The last embarrassment was relieved when the other man sprinted back to her tent and returned with her yashmak, which she donned with a sigh of relief and a nod of thanks, though grudgingly given.

Wheeling, the powerful sheikh urged his mount into a gallop. Behind him his chieftain shouted an order and the fighting immediately ceased as the raiders regrouped, collected their dead and wounded, and rode off after their leader, their blood-curdling shouts sending a chill racing down Christa's spine. When they reached the edge of the camp, several men broke from the group and

drove Abdullah's heavily laden camels before them.
The scourge of the desert had struck again.

Two days later, survivors reached Constantine
bearing news that drove Abdullah into a frenzy. He
learned that not only had his newest concubine
been stolen from him, but so had goods worth a
fortune in gold and silver. Immediately he ordered
his remaining army out to locate and destroy the
Desert Hawk and return to him his stolen goods.
The angry bey made it all too clear that they were
not to return without the latest acquisition to his
harem, for failure was rewarded by death.

For long days and endless nights Christa was
aware of nothing but her aching body and the
terrible pain radiating from between her thighs,
caused by riding countless hours in the saddle.
Soon after they left the camp, she was given a horse
of her own to ride, its reins tightly held in the
capable hands of the bandit leader. Because speed
was essential, Christa was not transported in the
tent-like bassourab she had traveled in with the
caravan. Instead, she rode astride, with her yashmak flying around her bare legs. Christa knew she
would not have survived but for their infrequent
stops to snatch an hour or two of sleep. They ate on
the go, drinking from the girba, or water skin, slung
over the saddle horn.

To Christa's chagrin, her barrage of questions
and pleas went unheeded. Little attention was given
her by either the leader or his chieftain. If the
sheikh had a name, she did not hear it spoken for he
was referred to mostly in words Christa loosely
translated to mean "great sheikh." She did note
that his chieftain and companion called him prince,
a title that obviously was honorary, for this warlike
desert raider held little resemblence to royalty.

On the fifth day, after traveling steadily south-

ward, they came out of the Tell to the barrier
formed by the Great Atlas, a region of lofty tablelands, which provided grazing lands for nomadic
tribes. A familiar sight in passing was a slim,
dark-eyed Bedouin girl tending her flock of sheep
grazing on a nearby slope. Beyond the tableland lay
the great Sahara; the very name sent shivers of fear
down Christa's spine.

For the first time since she had been abducted
from Abdullah's caravan, the Tuaregs met another
tribe of desert nomads—lean, hawk-nosed, their
mouths and nostrils swathed in blue veils against
the suffocating dust. Riding atop sleek camels, they
drove before them a herd of animals destined for
market in one of the large cities, probably Constantine or Algiers.

The sheikh rode out to speak with them, but
evidently the Tuaregs meant them no harm for
after a brief discussion they were allowed to proceed with their lives and their herd intact. Did the
Desert Hawk only attack caravans of the wealthy?
Christa wondered curiously as she watched the
nomads disappear in a cloud of dust.

Then one day they came abruptly onto a great
oasis, generating great excitement among the raiders. Christa had seen the tall palm and date trees
and rolling green hills from a distance but thought
she was seeing a mirage, a vision she had heard
much about but never experienced. Now she could
see it was very real as well as vast, watered by a river
rising from beneath the sands and running through
its center before disappearing again.

"The city of Biskra." While Christa had been
staring at the welcome sight, the chieftain rode up
beside her, speaking in halting English. "Beyond
Biskra stretches the great Sahara." It was the most
anyone had spoken to her in five days. "We will
camp here and rest." Then he spurred his mount

and joined his leader, that mysterious white-clad savage whose brooding gaze rested on her more often than she would have liked.

Why did he never speak to her? Christa wondered with a sense of awe. What did he plan to do with her? So far he had made no move to do her any harm, but how long would it last? Did he mean to hold her for ransom? Nothing made sense except that instinctively she felt no menace in his formidable presence. She had not been threatened or abused by any of these fierce warriors. In fact, from the impression given her, the sheikh and his men existed only to protect her.

Their pace was less hectic as they approached Biskra. Now Christa could see native houses, earth-brown, thick-walled and flat-roofed. On the edge of the oasis, tent-dwelling nomads camped in large numbers in their black gitun. She was surprised when the sheikh and his tribe did not enter the city but joined those nomads camped outside the gates. Helped down from her mount, Christa was led to rest beneath a palm tree while the raiders began erecting tents, the first time they had done so since she left Abdullah's caravan.

Relaxing beneath the tree, Christa fell immediately to sleep, having been deprived of that luxury for several days. Her body slumped in exhaustion, totally drained of will and energy. She felt filthy; her hair was matted with grime and hung in lank strands down her back. Beneath her robes fine particles of sand irritated her tender skin and her mouth was as arid as the vast Sahara. But still Christa slept, unaware of the two men who stood over her.

"It was wrong to bring her here," the chieftain dared to reprimand his leader. "The journey is difficult and she is not accustomed to the harshness of our land." His words were laced with pity.

"What do you expect of me, Omar?" His white-clad leader shrugged. "I could not allow Abdullah to lay hands on her. Suffering Barbarossa's abuse was bad enough, but Abdullah is an abomination I would not have her endure. I praise Allah that our agent in Constantine learned about Christa in time for me to act."

"You could provide escort for her to Tunis," suggested Omar, voicing his disapproval. "Her family would welcome her return. It is far too dangerous for the little one here, my prince."

"I still make the decisions, Omar," the prince replied, his face set in stubborn lines. "Besides, who but you could I trust to take her to her family? And we both know I need you here with me. No, Omar, Christa stays. Carry her into my tent once it is erected and set a guard to see that no harm comes to her." His imperious tone left Omar no choice but to obey.

Christa awoke slowly to the muezzin's call to evening prayer. She lay there, listening, too comfortable to move. For the first time in days she felt rested and wondered who had carried her from her resting place beneath the palm—the mysterious sheikh or his chieftain? She shivered, daydreaming about the white-clad man with the brooding eyes heavily lashed to conceal his emotions. What did he look like? she wondered. Did he resemble Mark, her own handsome prince? Or were his features cruel? Disfigured? So engrossed was she in her ruminations that she failed to notice the slim, veiled figure step through the flap and gingerly approach the bed of cushions and woolly lamb-skins.

"Awake, lady," a soft feminine voice demanded, vigorously shaking Christa's shoulder. The words were spoken in Arabic, and without thinking

Christa answered in kind, still lost somewhere in her dream world.

"*Emshi!* Go away!"

"You speak Arabic, lady," the soft voice noted. "You must wake up. Our master bids you rise."

Master? "Who is this master you speak of?" Christa asked, rising to a sitting position. Since she had already given herself away by speaking Arabic, she no longer felt the need for pretense.

"The great sheikh, of course," the girl importantly informed her. "Up, lady. You have slept the night away and now it is night again. The master says you are to have a bath and food before he comes to you. But why he desires a scrawny little thing like you when he can have a woman trained from birth to please men is a mystery to me."

Christa stared dumbly at the woman glaring down on her, hands on ample hips, beautiful face assuming a look of disdain. No, woman was not the correct word, Christa discovered. Child was more like it, for despite being amply endowed, she could not have been more than fourteen or fifteen. Her full red lips pouted elegantly as she raked Christa's bedraggled figure with barely concealed contempt. Judging from the girl's light tan skin and reddish hair, Christa surmised she was a Berber. What was she to the sheikh? One of his women? Somehow the thought was not comforting.

"Who are you?" Christa challenged.

"I am Elissa," replied the girl. "My father is chieftain to the great sheikh. When I was no more than a child he bestowed great honor on my father by accepting me as his concubine."

Christa snorted in disbelief. Elissa was little more than a child now. At what age was she given to the sheikh?

Sensing the direction of her thoughts, Elissa

remarked, "I am a woman fully grown. Like all the daughters in the village of Biskra, I have been trained from birth to take my place in the brothels that line the streets. My mother, as her mother did before her, taught me to dance the traditional dances of our women. Our homes are in the mountains, but when we are well-versed in the ancient art of pleasuring men, we are brought to Biskra to ply our trade."

"You are taught to be a . . . a harlot?" gasped Christa, stunned.

Solemnly, Elissa nodded. "It is our way. Later, after that part of our life is fulfilled, we return to our villages to marry and raise our children. It is a good life," she declared defensively. "Don't scoff at that of which you have no knowledge."

"You . . . you have already been a . . . a harlot?"

"Before I was old enough to go to one of the brothels, my esteemed parent gave me to my master. Our fathers had been friends for many years. But because I was still too young and my master was gone, I continued my lessons with my mother, waiting for his call. It finally came yesterday. Only I had no idea it was to play nursemaid to a foreign unbeliever."

Christa's reply was forestalled by a gruff voice outside the tent asking admittance. When it was granted, two men entered, wrestling a large brass tub between them, which they deposited in the center of the cramped space. Next came a succession of men, each bearing ewers of hot and cold water, until finally the tub was brimful of water the proper temperature for bathing. Suddenly the tent was fragrant with the odor of flowers as Elissa poured liquid from several small vials she had brought with her, and Christa could hardly wait to enjoy the luxury of soaking in the perfumed water. She hadn't had a tub bath since leaving Kalim's serai.

"Come, lady," Elissa gestured impatiently.

Eager to comply, Christa quickly stripped off her caftan, now soiled and wrinkled beyond repair, and sank gratefully into the tub. The warm water lapped around her pink-tipped breasts, soothing and relaxing the weary muscles grown taut from riding days on end without respite. She sighed in delight as Elissa scrubbed her with a large sponge and scented soap. Next the beautiful Berber attacked the long mane of pale blond hair, grudgingly admitting that it was lovely. Using ewers of fresh water left for that purpose, she rinsed Christa's shining tresses until they resembled strands of shimmering silk.

"Rest, lady," Elissa ordered curtly. "I will be back shortly to give you a massage." Then she departed, taking Christa's soiled garments with her.

Truth to tell, Elissa cared little for the role of maid that she was forced to assume. She knew why her master had taken the golden woman, and it did not sit well with her. Why should the great sheikh want to bed this woman when he had yet to partake of her own considerable charms? She was the only fifteen-year-old in the village still a virgin, and all because her master had been gone for so many years. Once he returned she had expected, nay yearned, to be called to his bed. But when the summons finally came, it was not what she expected. Why did her handsome master prefer the pale, skinny woman when her own dark beauty was his for the taking? The woman was old—at least eighteen or twenty, surmised Elissa, wrinkling her nose distastefully. Her one consolation was the thought that when he had his fill of the foreigner's white body he would turn to her for his comfort.

Elissa remained away so long the water in the tub grew cold, as did the night air. Stepping from the tub Christa dried herself with a soft white cloth left for that purpose and stretched out nude on the soft cushions, flopping over on her stomach as she waited for Elissa to return. What in the world was keeping the sullen girl? Christa wondered idly as a languorous feeling took hold of her senses. The bath had so relaxed her that she could barely keep her eyes open, and she drifted lazily toward sleep.

Floating on a cloud of slumber, Christa's erotic dreams took her to a world where no one but she and Mark existed. She ached for his gentle hands, his lips, his lean body next to hers, caressing her, whispering love words in lilting Arabic in that low, seductive voice she so loved. She wanted to feel him, run her hands and lips over the supple muscles and thick hair of his chest and arms. She wanted him inside her, filling her, loving her as only he was capable of doing.

Suddenly she was aware of a draft as the tent flap opened, and the single lamp Elissa had left burning was abruptly extinguished, pitching the tent into blackness. But not before the intruder caught an enticing glimpse of twin mounds of soft white flesh rising between slim waist and shapely thighs. Vaguely, Christa was aware of the change of light, but she was too caught up in her visions to do little more than grunt in pleasure as she felt the soothing touch of oil to her skin and gentle hands working magic on her tortured muscles. Elissa certainly knew what she was about, she thought dreamily, relaxing beneath the slightly roughened palms kneading her flesh so skillfully. Not once did she stop to wonder why Elissa's palms should be so rough, or larger than she recalled.

"You are skilled in the art of massage, Elissa," Christa murmured in fluent Arabic.

Those gentle hands paused, then resumed their sensuous journey with renewed effort, traveling over the slim expanse of white shoulders and back, paying special attention to the miniscule waist and curved hips before moving down to the long supple thighs and legs, deliberately bypassing those soft quivering mounds begging for attention.

Each toe was gently massaged, then each foot, moving to ankles and calves. Christa groaned, the pleasure so intense she blushed, suddenly fully awake. Upwards those educated hands stroked, over the highly sensitive skin of her inner thighs, carefully avoiding that tender slit that began to ache and throb unbearably.

"Elissa, I think you'd better . . ." Her words faltered, then died when those highly skilled hands, slick with fragrant oil, grasped the twin soft hills of her buttocks, kneading in an intimate manner that sent Christa's pulses racing, more than a little shocked by Elissa's bold caresses. When probing fingertips invaded the crease separating those sweetly curved mounds, Christa gasped aloud, highly incensed as the aching, sensitive flesh between her thighs was finally broached.

"Elissa! How dare you!"

"Roll over," a masculine voice whispered in her ear. "Do these hands feel like those of a woman?"

Christa blinked, bewildered and too stunned to offer more than token resistance when her body was gently but firmly turned so that she lay on her back. Then she felt the coolness of the sweet oil being lavished on her breasts and belly by hands moving in a manner so erotic it left her panting and gasping for breath.

"Who are you?" Christa questioned raggedly as

her hands moved with a will of their own to broad shoulders clad in some kind of silky material.

No answer was forthcoming as those magic hands continued downward, over full breasts, taut stomach, to thighs that parted naturally at the merest touch. Something like a growl escaped the throat of the man toiling lovingly over her, but Christa felt no fear, only pleasure.

"Are you the Desert Hawk?" she asked fearlessly. "Why won't you show yourself to me?"

"In good time, lady, in good time," he answered at length, his lips and mouth much too occupied for prolonged replies.

"Oh, God," Christa cried out when his mouth found a pouting nipple and he began to suck hungrily, taking gentle, nipping bites before lavishing the same loving attention to the other.

"You do well to call upon your God, lady," he moaned into her mouth as his lips finally found hers. His deep kiss sent her senses reeling. "For by the time I am finished with you, you will surely think you have gone to heaven."

Her mouth opened to protest but she found it filled with his tongue, the taste and essence of him vaguely familiar in a disturbing way. The kiss went on, and on, demanding surrender, which Christa freely gave. His hands worked magic on her breasts, his fingers stroking her nipples, molding the soft mounds to fit his palms. At length he broke off the kiss, running his mouth down her stomach with feathery touches, tracing her navel with his probing tongue, then burying his face against the tight blond curls between her thighs. She trembled beneath him as he probed with his tongue between her legs, tasting the sweetness of her most secret places. A scream of pleasure and shame ripped upward through her throat.

"Oh, please," she begged, uncertain whether

she was pleading with him to desist or give her the relief she sought.

But he did not stop, straining over her writhing form with renewed vigor, his tongue parting the tender folds, licking greedily at the sensitive bud of her womanhood before sliding into her moist fragrance. Holding her thrashing hips in place he probed hungrily, her moans of ecstasy creating a desperate need in him that had been weeks in building.

Caught in the throes of a pleasure so intense that she felt her sanity slipping away, she clung to the sheikh in desperation, tearing away his headgear in a moment of madness. Higher and higher his probing lips and tongue drove her as she wound her fingers through thick, wavy locks. Then suddenly she was there, her shriek of joy causing those within earshot to smile knowingly.

Small tremors shook Christa as her body continued to explode in wave after wave of sublime bliss. He held her, whispering words she paid scarce attention to until she calmed, then drawing away. Christa protested feebly until she heard the whisper of silk and he rejoined her, the hairy roughness of his nude body highly erotic against her sensitive flesh. Once again he began the art of slow arousal at which he had proved so adept only moments before, deliberately holding his own passion in tight rein until she began to respond. Moving her hips restlessly beneath him, Christa whimpered, then reached for him: his huge shaft pulsed with savage strength beneath her fingertips—so strong, so smooth, like steel sheathed in silk, she thought, reveling in his hoarse cries of ecstasy.

"Temptress," he groaned hoarsely. "Seductress."

His hand covered her mound, his fingers invading the sweet slit he yearned to possess, ached to bury himself into so deeply he would become part of her forever. Suddenly Christa could take no more of this torture, no matter how delicious, and she guided him to that silken portal. With a guttural sob of surrender, he grasped her hips, abruptly changing their positions. Lifting her effortlessly until she hovered above him, he lowered her onto his huge erection, and his penetration was swift and sure. Straddling his slim flanks, Christa met his bold thrusts with vigorous thrusts of her own, finding herself in control as he let her dictate their tempo.

Christa felt the tension slowly build as she dominated their loving. She could hear his panting and knew he was nearing the place from which there was no pulling back. Her own ragged breathing matched his, gasp for gasp. Then, like a candle consuming itself, she burst into flame, burning out of control, blazing a path skyward as she disintegrated into a thousand pieces. Assured of Christa's pleasure, he allowed his own passion free rein as the force of his climax nearly ripped him apart.

Slowly descending from those lofty plateaus where only lovers dwell, Christa clung desperately to the strong arms holding her, marveling at her response to a man she barely knew. A pang of regret smote her heart, knowing she was betraying Mark but puzzled as to why it felt so right to be loved by this man. She closed her eyes, feeling herself drifting off into a peacefulness she hadn't experienced since those blissful nights aboard the *Bon Ami* after Mark had made love to her.

On the wings of a dream, Mark's voice drifted through the darkness, the same low rumble with a hint of humor she had grown to love. "Did I not say we would meet again, sweet siren? Can you deny kismet when it is our fate to love?"

Was she conjuring up Mark's voice out of desperation or was it her desert sheikh speaking those words? Sleep claimed her long before the answer became clear.

9

Dusty sunlight, trickling in warm, molten streams of gold through the open tent flap drifted across Christa's face in a soft whisper, jolting her awake. She lay still for a moment, remembering detail for detail all that had taken place the night before. She had given herself freely and without reservation to her captor, the Desert Hawk, feeling no shame or remorse. What kind of woman was she? She loved Mark with all her heart, yet responded wantonly to a mysterious stranger who might well be a fiend. Certainly he was an outlaw and killer from all she had seen and heard of him. He was the leader of a savage desert tribe who derived great pleasure from raiding and plundering.

Abruptly Christa became aware of a figure standing in the opening, letting in the morning sun. "Well, lady," Elissa sneered jealously, "did you have a good night? Is not our master a vigorous lover? When I am in his bed, I have scarce energy to rise the next morning. But I have no need to tell you this. I can tell by your contented expression that he pleased you well."

Christa gasped, shocked at Elissa's bold words. Had the sheikh already taken this—this child to his bed? Had her plump, voluptuous body responded to his expert caresses just as hers had? The sudden thought of her body writhing beneath his brought a flush to her face, which did not go unnoticed by Elissa.

"I don't believe you," Christa taunted. "I don't think the sheikh would find pleasure in a child's body."

Christa's careless words created a furor of anger in Elissa as she reacted viciously, grasping a handful of lustrous strands of blond hair and yanking Christa from the bed. "You are nothing to him but a whore!" she shrieked in outrage. "A foreign whore into whose body he expends his lust."

Gloriously nude, Christa jerked her head, freeing her tresses from Elissa's fingers. Then she whirled to face the jealous girl. "If you came to trade insults, then you may as well leave, for I refuse to indulge in childish displays of temper."

Her words served only to further enrage Elissa. Elissa prided herself on being chosen as concubine to a prince, even though he had yet to establish a harem. Still, as his first acquisition, she would preside over those chosen later.

Giving full vent to her anger, Elissa flung herself at Christa, spouting insults. Unprepared for another attack, Christa fell beneath her, feeling the spitfire's long nails viciously raking her skin.

"What is the meaning of this?" boomed a voice Christa recognized as belonging to the sheikh's chieftain, and since identified as Elissa's father.

Scrambling to her feet, Elissa faced her irate

parent, well aware of what to expect. Embarrassed by her nudity, Christa scooted to the bed, using the silken cover to shield her body. But Omar seemed not to notice as his cold, disapproving eyes settled on his disobedient daughter.

"The foreign whore insulted me, father," Elissa lied, lowering her eyes respectfully.

"Watch your tongue, woman!" Omar scowled darkly. "It is not your place to give titles to your master's women."

Briefly, Omar's gaze flickered to Christa, then returned to regard Elissa sternly. "I know you well, daughter. You have a willful nature and because of my frequent absences your discipline is long over-due. I do not believe the foreign woman insulted you. More than likely your jealous nature will be your undoing. Your master will thank me for seeing to your punishment."

"No, father, please," Elissa pleaded, seized by fear. "I promise to behave as my master directs. If he wishes me to serve his whore, then I shall do so gladly."

Christa's outraged gasp drew little attention.

"Lie on the cushions, Elissa!" Omar ordered, his voice brooking no argument. Elissa hastened to obey, knowing full well it would go harder on her should she be stupid enough to defy her father.

"The right to punish me belongs solely to my master," she challenged in a final effort to dissuade him.

"You are right," allowed Omar grudgingly. "I will summon him immediately." Elissa's reprieve was short-lived, for Omar went only as far as the tent flap and spoke in hushed tones to the guard. The poisonous look Elissa flung Christa gave her little comfort.

Perhaps ten minutes elapsed before the tent flap parted, admitting the powerful form of the

Desert Hawk. When his hooded gaze found her, Christa dropped her eyes, blushing furiously as she vividly recalled all that had happened between them the night before. He spoke privately to Omar for a few minutes before scowling darkly at Elissa, whose obsidian eyes registered uncertainty. Then his gaze slid again to Christa.

"Are you hurt?" he asked gruffly in Arabic, having already learned she spoke his language fluently. Beyond speech, Christa slowly shook her head.

"Why have you disobeyed my orders?" he addressed Elissa crossly. "You were to serve my woman and see that no harm comes to her. And yet I am told you have ruthlessly attacked and vilified her."

"I . . . I'm sorry, master," Elissa said, her voice quivering. "How was I to know this whore meant so much to you?"

Christa bristled indignantly. Not only had the arrogant sheikh declared her to be his woman, but Elissa kept referring to her as a whore.

"You will do my bidding, Elissa, and show the lady the respect she deserves. It is not for you to pass judgement. Your father insists you must be punished in order to teach you a lesson and I am inclined to agree."

"The bastinado, my prince?" Omar suggested.

"No, Father, not that! I'll behave," Elissa cried, fear coloring her words.

"Twenty strokes," Omar continued, reaching beneath his robes for the stout rod he carried at his belt.

The sheikh slid a surprised glance at Omar and decided his friend was far too stern a parent. Though Elissa had become difficult of late and was deserving of chastisement, Omar was being much too harsh on her. Her sleek, shapely body might suggest otherwise, but to the sheikh she was still a child of fifteen.

He opened his mouth to voice a protest, but before he could make his wishes known, Elissa began screeching, certain she was about to receive twenty strokes of the bastinado. Reacting instinctively, Christa wrapped the silken cover around her nakedness and flung herself at the sheikh's feet, crying out in supplication, "No! Please! Before God, I beg you to reconsider. She is only a child."

Through a mist of tears, Elissa's jealousy raged unabated despite Christa's plea in her defense. She neither needed nor wanted a foreign whore begging in her behalf. She was on the verge of spitting out those very words when the sight of the bastinado hanging between her father's strong fingers brought on second thoughts. She knew she could never endure twenty strokes of that terrible weapon.

"I'm sorry, lady," she sobbed brokenly. "I meant you no harm. I will serve you gladly." Though the words fell effortlessly from her lips, they held no meaning. For in her heart dwelled the wish to rid her master of the silver-haired foreign whore. Only next time she would be more cautious in how she went about it.

A smile hovering at the corner of his mouth, the sheikh signaled Omar to replace the stick he had little use for in the first place. "You can thank your mistress for sparing you," he said sternly. "Now go, bring food. I'm sure the lady is hungry."

There was a hint of humor in his voice and Christa flushed a rosy red, aware that she had good reason to feel hunger. Scrambling hurriedly from the tent, Elissa made a hasty exit after a jerkily executed bow in the sheikh's direction. When the young girl was gone, he reached down, lifting Christa to her feet. He turned to dismiss Omar, but the huge man had already passed unnoticed from the tent.

For the first time since she had been in his presence, he looked at her with his eyes unhooded, his soul laid bare before her. Green! The clear, vivid green of precious emeralds. The same color as . . .

"Mark!" So intense were her thoughts that she failed to realize she had spoken the beloved name aloud. But never was she more certain of anything in her life. She would know those distinctive eyes anywhere. He was alive! Not only alive, but he had made beautiful, tender love to her last night!

Before the sheikh could respond to Christa's sudden insight, Elissa returned, carrying a tray laden with food, her eyes properly downcast. But inside she was a seething cauldron of bubbling anger. That her master cared for the foreign woman was all too obvious. In the beginning she had hoped Christa was but a passing fancy to be used and discarded in swift order, but she realized now just how wrong she had been.

The sheikh's arms dropped from Christa's shoulders. "Eat and bathe," he said, his voice lowered to an intimate purr. "We will talk later." Then he slipped silently through the narrow opening of the tent.

Christa thoroughly enjoyed the delicious meal served by a sullen Elissa. It consisted of couscous, lamb stuffed with almonds and raisins and roasted whole, sweet cakes made of sticky almond paste, a variety of fresh fruits, including oranges, peaches, dates, and coconut, and a sweet fruit drink. She ate ravenously, consuming every morsel while Elissa busied herself preparing Christa's bath.

Though her body was immersed in the mundane acts of eating and bathing, Christa's mind raced furiously. Mark was alive! He had appeared when she thought all was lost, literally plucking her from Abdullah's clutches. Never again would she doubt his love for her. Now that he had found her, she was certain they would return to England together after a stop in Tunis to reassure her family of her safety. They would leave this horrid country where women were mere chattel and men their cruel masters.

Mark entered the tent while Christa lolled lazily in the tub, and grinned wickedly as Elissa wielded the soapy sponge with more vigor than necessary. Christa's eyes were closed so she did not see him when he silently took the sponge from Elissa's hands and motion her from the tent with a curt nod. The dark scowl Elissa aimed in Christa's direction was lost on both of them.

"Ummm . . . that feels wonderful, Elissa," Christa sighed contentedly. Gentle hands suddenly dipped beneath the water to slide deliciously over her breasts and stomach. When a bare hand reached between her legs to stroke the pale forest growing there, Christa's blue eyes flew open to see Mark kneeling before her, swatched in white, green eyes dancing merrily.

"Where did you learn Arabic?" he asked, his fingers roaming restlessly through the silken strands, parting them, finding the tender slit he searched for.

"From Kalim's women," she answered on a breathless gasp.

One slim finger worked its way inside her and she clutched his shoulders convulsively. "I wanted to save you from Barbarossa," he confided sadly. "I'm sorry for what you suffered at his hands. It couldn't have been pleasant." A second finger slid beside the first and Christa's hips gave an involuntary jerk.

"It wasn't pleasant," she readily concurred, "but it's not what you think. Redbeard didn't touch me."

His fingers stilled, and Christa groaned in frustration. "He . . . didn't rape you?"

"He didn't touch me," she repeated.

"What about this Kalim you spoke of?"

"I spent several weeks in the serai with his women while Redbeard awaited word from Constantine. Kalim was instructed to protect me. Except for a short illness, nothing serious befell me during my stay in his home."

"It sounds quite miraculous," he said, astounded. "And I want to hear all about it, but first I have more pressing matters on my mind."

With consummate skill his fingers resumed their fascinating rhythm inside her and she moaned softly. With a cry of impatience, his headdress and veil were thrown aside and he captured her lips, kissing her deeply, his tongue pillaging her mouth as his hand continued to work its magic below. Unable to contain her rising passion Christa thrashed about wildly, splashing water on the floor of the tent as well as on Mark's spotless white burnous.

Suddenly she felt herself being lifted from the cooling tub and set on her feet, her arms locked around his neck. He rubbed his hands up and down her back. She arched her body to his and he grasped her buttocks and held her tightly in position.

"You drive me mad, sweet siren," he groaned hoarsely. "Making love to you all night did little more than wet my appetite."

In a frenzy of wild kisses, he managed to throw off his clothes until he stood as nude as Christa, his skin surprisingly pale where the sun did not touch it. Taking her hands in his, Mark kissed each palm. They stood facing each other, naked in the dim light of the tent. Slowly he knelt before her, gripping her hips in his hands, kissing her breasts, her stomach, and then that enticing mound of golden fleece. When his lips and tongue continued their caressing probe, she reeled in pleasure, panting in sudden and explosive need. Clinging to his shoulders, assailed by waves of dizzing rapture, Christa cried out, begging for fulfillment.

Then she was on her back, soft cushions beneath her, Mark kneeling between her legs, continuing the exquisite torture. Her thighs spread wider and her hands tangled in the dense, dark hair, urging him on with hoarse words of encouragement. And when she thought she'd go insane with pleasure, he lifted his head and smiled with devilish enjoyment. Well aware of her discomfort, he held her thrashing legs wide apart with his hands and once again buried his head against the small pale mound. She arched and writhed in pleasure, coming to a sudden, explosive climax. He continued to hold her thus for a minute and then again began to stroke the tender flesh until she began to respond once more.

Through a haze of renewed sensations she saw his engorged, pulsing staff and of its own accord her hand reached out, curling about the towering pillar. Gently she stroked up and down as a great shudder of pleasure rippled through him. It felt velvety soft, yet hard and indestructible. His sharp intake of breath indicated to her how good it felt. And then he was looming above her, filling her, thrilling her, unable to deny himself a moment longer. Their coupling was swift, urgent as that of wild creatures. He rode her with a fierce, savage joy until one splendorous sensation after another cascaded over her. Feeling her pleasure rip through her in waves of fierce contractions, Mark unleashed his own passion, racing with her to their own private world.

The earth finally stopped spinning and Christa sighed contentedly, finding herself firmly enclosed in a pair of strong arms. "Ah, sweet siren, you please me so well." His voice sounded hoarse, still drugged by passion.

"Mark, I . . ."

"No, not Mark," he corrected gently. "I am Ahmed sheikh. I may no longer be a prince, but I am still a great sheikh to the Tuaregs who have given unstintingly of their loyalty. With their help, perhaps I will still rule Constantine one day."

"Ahmed, I'm truly sorry your life has been turned upside down," Christa said gravely.

"I am the one who should bear the heavy weight of sorrow, my love," Ahmed replied remorsefully. "I was unable to protect you from Barbarossa. Did . . . did he harm you? Were you dreadfully abused by him or his men?"

Christa shook her head. "It's true what I said before. Redbeard left me alone, as did his men."

"Why?" Ahmed asked in disbelief. "The man is a reputed villain. He has no conscience where murder or rape are concerned."

"I . . . I can't say, exactly," Christa theorized. "At first rape is exactly what he intended. Thank God I talked him out of it."

Ahmed laughed, shaking his head in amazement. "How did you manage that, my prickly English rose? I can't imagine anyone talking Barbarossa out of anything he had his mind set on."

Christa flushed, recalling vividly those desperate moments. "I . . . I threatened to kill myself if he touched me. And I would have, too," she added, her chin tilted defiantly.

"Yes, I believe you would have," Ahmed agreed with more than a hint of admiration. "But I also believe there is more to it than that."

"I . . . we talked. About many things. Including his life before becoming Barbarossa. Perhaps I touched a responsive chord in him. I don't know for sure. Whatever it was, he decided to leave me untouched. But his good will ended there. He refused to grant me freedom. Nor would he contact my father. He insisted Abdullah would pay more for me than my family. Undoubtedly he was right, for my father does not possesses the kind of wealth Redbeard demanded."

"Abdullah will never lay hands on you," Ahmed growled with fierce determination. "You are mine."

"How did you know where to find me?" Christa asked, idly stroking his chest. She loved the feel of his bare flesh beneath her fingertips, still warm with the flush of passion. "What happened after Redbeard's man shot you? I know you were hit, for I saw the blood with my own eyes. I . . . I thought you drowned."

Something deep and tender sparked the depths of Ahmed's green eyes. "As you can see, I am very much alive, little one," he murmured. "Thanks to Omar. He promised my father to protect me and he took his vow seriously. The moment I plunged into the sea, Omar slipped unseen over the side and kept me afloat. After the French frigates chased Barbarossa away, I was pulled aboard and treated for my chest wound.

"Though it was serious, the bullet did not pierce any vital organs and I mended swiftly. As soon as I was able to travel, I left Algiers, where I had been given shelter by friends. Omar's tribe, the Tuaregs, have reason to hate Abdullah and they have banded together under my leadership. Together we hope to defeat my half-brother."

"How did you learn about me?" Christa interrupted.

"I'm coming to that, my love," said Ahmed.

"Have patience. I knew Barbarossa's reputation and realized he would try to sell you to Abdullah first before offering you in the slave market. I sent a spy to Constantine and when he reported that a caravan was setting out to escort a woman from Algiers to Abdullah's harem in Constantine, I put two and two together.

"Despite the company of Janissaries sent as escort, they were no match for my Tuaregs. And so, my sweet, that's how you came to be in my arms." As if to emphasize his words, he squeezed tightly, eliciting a small gasp.

"What will you do now, Ahmed?" Christa asked, gazing at him worriedly.

"Do? Why, I intend to make love to you again. That is if you're—" His words died in his throat as Elissa burst into the tent without asking permission, her dark eyes automatically drawn to Christa's nude body held so lovingly in Ahmed's strong arms.

"Master! I—"

"What is the meaning of this?" Ahmed growled angrily, pulling the silken cover upward to shield Christa's nakedness.

"Forgive me," Elissa begged, "but it could not wait. I was bidden by my father to tell you that one of the men has just returned from Constantine with distressing news. He asks to see you without delay." She bowed her head submissively, but not before Christa saw the malicious gleam in her obsidian eyes. Obviously the girl was only too happy to break up what she knew was a romantic interlude.

Muttering an oath, Ahmed disentangled himself from Christa and jumped to his feet, apparently unconcerned that he was blatantly displayed in all his nude glory before a gaping Elissa, whose avid perusal of his male attributes brought a blush to

Christa's pale cheeks. Caught up in his own thoughts, Ahmed quickly donned the baggy trousers, high black boots and white robes that made up his costume, departing without a backward glance.

Once Ahmed was gone, Elissa regarded Christa with cool contempt. "How quickly he forgets. Had I been in his bed he wouldn't be so anxious to leave."

"You can go, Elissa," directed Christa haughtly. "I won't require your help."

"Can't you see Ahmed sheikh cares nothing for you? He is but taken with the whiteness of your skin. You are a novelty he will soon tire of. I pleased our master once and will continue to do so long after you're gone."

"You . . . are you telling me Ahmed has. . . that you and he . . ."

"I am a woman," Elissa said cunningly, "created for the express purpose of pleasing my master. Did you think he would not make use of me?"

"You are still a child! Surely Ahmed knows you aren't ready yet to—"

Harsh laughter greeted her words. "I am long past the age where girls of my tribe are introduced to pleasures of the flesh. Ahmed sheikh has firsthand knowledge of my ability to bring him tremendous joy," Elissa lied slyly. Though she had yet to experience Ahmed's lovemaking, she knew it wouldn't be long before he made his desires known to her. If not, she was prepared to take matters into her own hands before she became the laughing stock of her tribe.

Elissa's announcement stunned Christa. Was Ahmed making love to both of them? How many others shared his bed? Then, as quickly as the thought was born, it was discarded. Elissa was naught but a jealous child, whose words held little truth. Though Ahmed hadn't actually said he loved her, his actions spoke eloquently of his affection. He couldn't make love to her so tenderly if he didn't care for her a great deal, could he? He had risked his life to rescue her from Abdullah and she had no business listening to Elissa's web of false-hoods.

"What have you learned, Ibrahim?" Ahmed asked, pacing back and forth before an obviously weary tribesman whose dusty, begrimed robes suggested a long trek across arid expanses.

"Abdullah dispatched his army of Janissaries the moment word of the looted caravan reached his ears," Ibrahim reported breathlessly. "Talk is that he was livid when told his newest concubine had been abducted by the Desert Hawk. She represents over two hundred ducats in gold. A great deal by any standard.

"A reward has been posted for information leading to the identity of the Desert Hawk. In the meantime, his army has instructions not to return without the raider of the desert. I'm sorry to say, Ahmed sheikh, that they are hard on my heels. We must break camp immediately or suffer their swift justice. Perhaps we should . . ." His words trailed off and he looked decidedly uncomfortable, refusing to meet Ahmed's eyes.

"What are you trying to say?" Ahmed asked sharply.

"Perhaps if we leave the foreign woman behind, Abdullah will be appeased and—"

"No!" roared Ahmed, whipping around to face the cowering Ibrahim. "The woman remains with me. We will leave immediately for our camp in the desert and if we must fight the Janissaries again, it will be on our own territory. You are dismissed!" Bowing respectfully, Ibrahim left before his leader's anger exploded in his direction.

"Omar, you heard?" Ahmed asked his second-in-command, who was never far from his side.

"Shall I advise the men?" asked Omar, anticipating Ahmed's order.

"It's definitely not in our best interest to wait here for Abdullah's army," Ahmed decided. "In the desert we have a far better chance of eluding them. See that camp is broken immediately. We ride within the hour."

"What of the women?"

"Christa goes with me," Ahmed declared defensively. "Elissa, too. She can see to Christa's needs and provide company."

Omar nodded, turned smartly and hurried off. There were tents to be dismantled, supplies to be purchased and men to be gathered from all corners of the city, particularly from the brothels—and all within an hour.

"Come, lady, we must hurry," Elissa said as she bustled into the tent, startling Christa, who was beginning to wonder about all the activity taking place outside.

"Where are we going?" she questioned as Elissa helped her into the silken djellaba and the shroud-like yashmak, carefully attaching the haik in place so that her face was completely covered. Though Elissa was similarly robed, she had not yet drawn the veil across her face and Christa was quick to note her excitement.

"We are to accompany our master into the Sahara," Elissa replied animatedly. "We leave within the hour."

"I must talk to Ahmed first," Christa insisted, leaving the tent with a greatly agitated Elissa trailing in her wake.

"There is no time, lady," Elissa replied, grasping her arm to halt her progress.

"But I must know his plans," pleaded Christa,

searching for the tall, white-robed form amid the sea of blue-clad nomads.

"Ahmed's plans are not for you to know," Elissa declared crossly. "You have only to obey. We will wait here. My father is bringing a horse for you."

And then she spied him, deeply engrossed in talk with one of his men. She started forward, calling his name, but froze in her tracks when he directed an icy stare at her advancing form. Without a word of explanation, he turned abruptly and strode off in the opposite direction. Having no experience in the workings of men's minds in this part of the world, Christa had no idea that, should Ahmed allow a mere woman to rule his actions, he would face ridicule and rejection. His fierce followers held women in low esteem and would not understand his devotion to Christa. Thus he was forced to ignore her until such time as he could fully explain his actions.

No one was happier than Elissa to see Ahmed's apparent lack of concern for his concubine. Obviously he already was tiring of the foreigner and her turn was near at hand. Before long she would be in his bed, she rejoiced gleefully. She yearned to put into practice all she had learned from her mother. Then her thoughts were rudely interrupted when Omar rode up leading two horses.

"It is time," he said curtly, lifting Christa easily into the beautiful red saddle embroidered with shapes and symbols in silken thread. Tossing her the reins, he turned to assist his daughter, but found the agile young girl had already leaped astride the Arabian mare. Mounting his own stallion, Omar motioned for them to follow, then sprinted off after the wildly cheering group of men riding their swift camels into the shimmering yellow sands of the great Sahara.

Ahmed set the gruelling pace, his fierce follow-ers -matching his speed. Lagging a short distance behind came Christa and Elissa, guarded by Omar and a dozen armed men. They stopped briefly for a light repast at midday, and when the night began to grow chill, they made camp in a shallow valley formed by two dunes. Ahmed did not come to Christa that night, nor any of the following nights as they rode deeper into the desert.

Though saddle-sore, weary and exhausted be-yond endurance, Christa was constantly amazed by the desert. Previously she had thought the desert to be a flat, arid expanse of nothing but sand. She couldn't have been more wrong.

The Sahara, in fact, was mountains, valleys and plains broken by deep depressions, lofty tablelands, massive buttes and crags, seas of shifting yellow sands, and oases of green with forests and fruit trees. Christa learned that the Berber word for sand dunes meant sandy oceans. Some of the dunes rose to sixty feet high, while others exceeded three hundred.

During their journey southward, they camped at oases along the way, ranging from a few acres to hundreds of square miles supporting an entire city. Even on the smallest of these grew an abundance of apples, peaches, oranges, lemons, figs, pomegran-ates and grapes. Water was available as well, afford-ing Christa welcome baths along the way.

In the early morning, Christa soon discovered, the desert was a dirty bluish gray. But when the sun rose, it turned a dazzling white, almost like drifting snow. At nightfall the colors were spectacular, changing from white to vivid orange, to blue, to amethyst, to deep purple. When the stars came out, the sky became a soft and misty gray, like smoky chiffon over silver tissue. On those nights, Christa lay on her lonely pallet of cushions longing for

Ahmed, his hands, his lips, the feel of him inside her, filling her, driving her to the edge of ecstasy.

By the fifth day, Christa's head ached beneath the relentless sun. Early that morning, a great silence fell on the desert. Then a howling wind began to blow, and she was certain the entire landscape was in motion. Before her eyes the dunes were changing shape, drifting, melting, walking. Whipped by the roaring wind, sand rose in suffocating clouds, obscuring the sun. And then a terrifying phenomenon took place.

The sky changed from a hot blue to a murky red, then to an angry purple, completely blotting out the landscape. A sullen twilight descended upon the land, enshrouding it in gloom; the dunes heaved and crumbled. All around her, Christa was aware of frantic activity as men and animals ground to a halt, their shouts lost in the rising wind. Like a spectre, Omar rode through the gloom beside her, motioning her to a halt.

"What is it?" she asked anxiously.

"Sandstorm," he informed her tersely. "Dismount." Then he rode off. Bewildered, Christa stared after him, noticing that Elissa had already dismounted and was staggering against the wind.

Flying particles cut her face like driving sleet, and Christa ducked her head. Her skin beneath the yashmak felt as though it were rubbed by emery paper. Dust filled her eyes, ears and nostrils, making her feel as if she were being suffocated. Earth and sky seemed to mingle in a chaos of confusion, a pandemonium of sound.

Abruptly, Ahmed appeared at her side, grasping her elbow as he led her off toward a narrow gully where several camels were made to kneel on the ground, their legs folded beneath them, eyes shuttered tightly against the stinging sand. Quickly guiding her behind one of the reclining animals,

Ahmed pushed her to the ground, pausing only to retrieve a blanket from the camel's pack before joining her. Then he drew the blanket over them, forming a sort of protective tent.

"Are you all right, my love?" he asked anxiously as Christa began coughing in an effort to remove the clogging dust from her raw throat.

"I . . . I think so," she replied hoarsely, grateful for the protection provided by the sturdy camel as well as the blanket. "The storm came up so suddenly. How long will it last?"

"It is often so with sandstorms," Ahmed rasped, his voice harsh and grainy. "Rest in my arms. It will soon pass."

Sighing wearily, Christa allowed herself to relax, enjoying the feel of Ahmed's muscular arms holding her. Thinking back over the past few days, she couldn't help but ask, "Why have you ignored me since we left Biskra? I don't belong here, Ahmed. You should have sent me to my father in Tunis. It has been so long I know he thinks me dead."

"You must trust me, Christa," Ahmed chided gently. "You must know I can't let you go. It is our kismet to be together."

"Why did we leave Biskra so abruptly and why have you all but ignored me since?" She could have bit her tongue to keep from voicing her hurt, but Ahmed seemed to sense her feelings.

"I received word that Abdullah's army was hard on our heels," he explained. "It was best for all concerned to leave as we did. Abdullah will not have you. You're mine."

"You have a strange way of showing your feelings," Christa complained, her words nearly lost to the howling wind.

Beneath the dark folds of the stifling blanket, Ahmed smiled. "Have you felt neglected, my love?"

he teased lightly. Then abruptly he turned serious. "Christa, I don't want my men to know just how important you have become to me. Most of them are loyal, but the Tuaregs are the fiercest of men— treacherous, bloodthirsty, without honor. They have willingly pledged themselves to my cause, but if I show a softness or weakening, especially toward a concubine born solely to please, they will abandon me without a moment's hesitation. I need them, Christa, if I am to defeat Abdullah. So if I seem deliberately harsh at times, it's because I don't wish to lose their respect. Can you understand that and forgive me?"

Greatly relieved, Christa did understand, and she told him so, feeling his arms tighten around her. Removing her veil, she lifted her head, hoping to see his face in the encompassing gloom, only to find her lips seized in the kind of passionate kiss she had only dared dream about these past nights. Sighing in surrender, she melted into his embrace as his hands roamed at will beneath her robes, cupping the soft, unfettered breasts. His thumbs moved sensuously back and forth across the hardening tips, filling his palms.

"Ahmed, stop!" she begged, breathing heavily. "Why are you doing this to me?"

"I want only to pleasure you, my love, until we can be together in the way we both wish," he whispered raggedly. If it were possible, he would take her on the sand in the midst of the raging storm. "Your body is so beautifully responsive, I want to feel your joy, though my own must necessarily wait. Come, my love, give yourself to me. Let me feel the pleasure ripple through you."

Encouraged by Ahmed's arousing words, Christa surrendered to the passion turning her body into molten lava, moving in rhythm to his fingers. Her response brought a smile of delight to his face. The thrust of his tongue in her mouth matched exactly the thrust of his fingers below as she met his kisses with new-found ardor. Lost in a sea of undulating waves, Christa vibrated to the pleasure that burst within her. Only when she had nothing more to give did he cease his tender assault upon her body and cradle her lovingly in his arms, allowing peace to descend.

As the storm within her slowly subsided, Christa become aware that the howling wind outside had ceased as suddenly as it had arisen. Tossing the blanket aside, Ahmed rose to his feet, sniffing the air. Christa blinked, astonished. The air had become fresh and clear again, and the sun was a bright red ball in the sky. Peace and utter silence reigned.

10

That night they camped at a small oasis deep in the Sahara. It looked to Christa like a green island set in the middle of a vast sea of yellow wasteland. Date palm and fruit trees grew in abundance in a glorious tropical setting. There was even a stream of clear, fresh water wandering through the green paradise. Christa dropped to her knees and drank deeply, longing to plunge into the cool water and wash off the gritty sand that irritated the tender skin beneath her hot robes.

Suddenly she realized she was not alone and looked up to see Ahmed towering over her, his eyes tender with a look that sent her senses reeling.

"Come," he said, reaching out his hand. Without a second thought she grasped his outstretched fingers, allowing him to lead her where he would. Behind him trailed a sullen Elissa, bearing a basket containing several items Ahmed had had her gather.

"Where are we going?" Christa dared to ask as they drew farther and farther away from the activity.

"My men are occupied with setting up camp," Ahmed explained, "and I know a bath would please you after your experience with the sandstorm yesterday. I am taking you and Elissa to a secluded spot where you both may bathe while I keep watch."

Only then did Christa see Elissa, who had come up to walk beside her. She was panting slightly from her burden and looked hot and sweaty. "I for one will welcome a bath," she declared, slanting a sidelong glance at Ahmed. "How much further, master?"

"We are nearly there, Elissa."

He led them around a clump of bushes and Christa gasped at the lovely sight that met her weary eyes. The small pool was an incredible deep blue surrounded by a profusion of flowers of every color and description, and Christa couldn't wait to immerse herself in the placid coolness.

Elissa squealed in delight and began tearing off her clothes, stretching languidly before walking with maddening slowness into the water. These past weeks she had longed for the opportunity to display her womanly charms before Ahmed and was grateful for the chance to do so now. She knew Christa's slim proportions paled in comparison to her own generous curves, and she wished Ahmed to note the difference for himself. While Christa stared in dismay, Elissa paraded without shame before the man who owned her but had yet to possess her eager body.

Ahmed sat on the bank, a slight frown puckering his brow as Elissa pranced and cavorted in the shallow water, blatantly displaying her charms. Not only was she blithely unconcerned but inordinately proud of her womanly attributes. Until this minute he had thought her still a child, but now he recognized her as a mature young woman ripe for bedding. And wanting it, judging from her sultry looks and artful posturing. Somewhat reluctantly, he tore his eyes from the enticing nude figure to look at Christa, who stood still as a statue, making no outward move to join Elissa.

"I thought you wanted a bath," he said with a hint of amusement.

"Are . . . are you going to sit there and watch?" Christa stuttered shyly.

A roguish smile curved his full lips. "Unless you'd prefer one of my men to stand guard."

An angry flush crawled up her neck. "You could turn your head."

"I know what an unclothed female form looks like," he reminded her, grinning. "Go on, Christa, have your bath. Elissa seems to be enjoying herself."

"And you seem to be enjoying Elissa," Christa returned tartly.

A burst of laughter erupted from Ahmed's throat. "Are you jealous, my sweet?"

"Certainly not!" she declared hotly. Even if she was, she'd never admit it. It was obvious women came easy to him. And oh, how she thrilled to his lovemaking! Did Elissa enjoy him also? Dejectedly, Christa shook her head, deliberately ridding herself of that thought.

Suddenly she came to a decision. A bath was a luxury she could hardly afford to turn down. Besides, she was grateful to Ahmed for caring enough to bring her here when obviously he had more important duties awaiting him. They had shared too much, come too far, for her to act the prude now. With a natural grace she slowly began undressing, until she stepped out of her last piece of clothing, a silken caftan the color of rich honey. Then she walked slowly to the water's edge.

Ahmed caught his breath in wonder as Christa emerged nude from her tangle of robes, clothed in nothing but the pale blond veil of her long hair. He had viewed her nakedness many times in the dark and near dark but never in the splendor of the diminishing rays of the setting sun, turning her body all gilt and ivory. The sway of her white buttocks bouncing with each step mesmerized him and he longed to grasp those rounded mounds in his hands and pull her into the hardness of his body. He wanted to bury his lips in the pale forest shielding her womanhood, then thrust himself into her tight warmth until pleasure finally claimed them. But now was not the time, he chided himself sternly. Even though he might send Elissa ahead, duty had prior claim on his time. Christa would have to wait until later. And after their passionate interlude with the sandstorm raging around them, Ahmed's need rode him ruthlessly.

Dressed in a sheer silk caftan, Christa paced the narrow confines of the tent. Since returning from the pool earlier, she had not seen Ahmed, though she waited expectantly for him to come to her. From the smoldering look he bestowed upon her when they parted, Christa knew he was counting the minutes until they could be together. Elissa had made her desires for her master potently apparent, but her machinations seemed to have little effect on him, making Christa love him all the more.

She was finally comfortable with the fact that she loved the Berber prince and knew her love was returned. He loved her enough to want no other woman. She hugged herself, recalling the ecstasy she found in his arms and the special light in his eyes when he claimed her. No other woman had ever felt so adored.

If only she could ignore Elissa's words earlier, when she brought her supper. The girl had placed the tray carelessly on the low table at Christa's feet and studied her almost critically before announcing smugly, "Ahmed Sheikh seemed most pleased with me today. Did you see desire flare when he looked upon me?"

"You dream childish dreams," Christa declared stoutly, although she couldn't deny the spark of interest in Ahmed's eye when he gazed at Elissa's nude body. Did he truly find her desirable? "He but glanced at you casually."

"I am a woman wise in the art of love," revealed Elissa confidently, "though I turned fifteen but two days ago. Tonight Ahmed will experience again the delights of my body. You were naught but a passing fancy."

"You lie!" Christa gasped. "Ahmed thinks of you as a child. Of course he looked at you. He is a man," she added, as if that explained everything.

"I am to share his bed tonight," Elissa lied smoothly. "Ahmed is a powerful sheikh, a great prince, strong, vigorous, with needs lusty enough to please many women. When he becomes bey, he will have countless concubines to keep him happy, and more than likely you will occupy a low place in his serai."

Surely Elissa was merely taunting her with lies, Christa told herself with an uncharacteristic lack of confidence. After the girl left, she pondered long and hard on her future, should there be one, with Ahmed. True, he demonstrated by both word and deed that he loved her, and he had told her often enough that they were meant to be together. But in what way? He had already admitted he couldn't marry her despite the fact that he wanted her with him always. She refused to be his concubine. If that's what he had in mind, he must be persuaded to let her go. She would die imprisoned in a harem, no matter how often Ahmed declared his love for her. Tonight she was determined to confront him and demand to know his plans where she was concerned.

The hour had grown very late, and when Ahmed still failed to appear, Christa could no longer wait to receive his answer regarding her future and decided to take matters into her own hands. Swiftly donning her djellaba, she stepped outside the tent, shivering as the cool night air fanned her skin. There was no guard standing nearby, for no longer was there a need for such caution. From earlier observation she knew which tent Ahmed occupied and turned resolutely in that direction, noticing as she did that the camp had settled down for the night and no one was about.

Still in conference with Omar, Ahmed groaned in frustration as the hour grew late and duty still claimed him. He knew Christa awaited him, and he counted the minutes until he was free to hold her in his arms. At last Omar left his tent and the camp grew quiet as one by one his men sought their beds. Only then did duty release him to seek his own pleasure. Thinking of Christa and their hours together before dawn drew them apart, Ahmed gathered up clean clothes and set out for the pool, unwilling to go to his love with the stink of sweat still upon his body. He did not notice the small form detach itself from the shadows and follow.

Elissa watched avidly as Ahmed undressed beneath the brilliant moonlight and plunged into the water now grown cold in the chill night. He bathed swiftly, thoughts of Christa's slim white body as well as the cold water encouraging him to hurry. Drying himself with his soiled clothing, he shrugged into clean robes, strapping the scimitar, which seldom left his side, about his slim hips. Then he stooped to pick up his dirty clothes and retraced his steps back to camp.

Suddenly Ahmed tensed, the hair on the nape of his neck standing up on end. He felt, rather than saw, danger lurking near. Some sixth sense warned him that he was being followed, and all his instincts sharpened. Were Abdullah's men so close that they had invaded the oasis undetected? His steps slowed, as he waited cautiously for the unseen menace to come within striking distance, his right hand poised on the hilt of his sword.

Elissa noted gleefully that Ahmed deliberately tarried. She smiled a secret smile, thinking that he had seen her concealed in the bushes and paused so she might approach. She had waited and schemed a long time for this night. She had seen how Ahmed had looked upon her with desire and lust and knew he wanted her. Nothing but the foreign woman stood in her way of her becoming his favorite. And once he became bey, he would honor her by taking her to wife. In her mind she had it all planned. But first she had to win him from Christa. She was convinced that once Ahmed bedded her, he would have little desire for his pale-skinned concubine. This was her chance, while she had him all to herself, to make him want her enough to abandon the foreign whore.

Ahmed could feel the heat of the body long before he heard the telltale footfall behind him. Whirling, he drew the sword from its scabbard, nearly finding its mark in the throat of the shrouded figure following him, actually slicing through the robe to nick tender skin.

Elissa opened her mouth to scream, but nothing came out except a long sigh as she collasped at Ahmed's feet, frightened nearly out of her wits. Dropping to one knee, Ahmed peered closely into the face of the small figure lying on the ground, gasping in dismay as recognition finally dawned.

"Allah protect me!" he muttered crossly when he realized he had nearly killed a young, defenseless girl. She would be dead now if some instinct hadn't warned him to withhold the killing blow. "Whatever possessed you to sneak up on me like that, Elissa?"

Of course Elissa was beyond hearing, nor did she rouse when Ahmed shook her gently. She must be scared senseless, he thought distractedly as he gathered her limp form in his arms. She looked so young and vulnerable that he cursed himself for frightening her so thoroughly. But why was she following him? Eager to get to the bottom of her secret midnight wanderings, Ahmed turned in the direction of his tent, the lamp glow from the open flap guiding his steps.

Coming to in Ahmed's strong arms, Elissa smiled to herself, willing her body to remain boneless. No need for Ahmed to know she was fully conscious and gloriously aware of the way his hard body felt against her own softness, she thought slyly. If she was forced in the end to seduce him, it was imperative that she be alone with him, away from prying eyes.

A muted light glowed from the open flap of Ahmed's tent and Christa smiled to herself, picturing him standing with bronze chest bared, readying himself for the bed. Anticipation hurried her steps.

Just as they were nearing Ahmed's tent, Elissa

caught a glimpse from the corner of her eye of a feminine form in a flowing robe. She knew at first glance that the woman was Christa, no doubt coming to pleasure her master. Well, this was one night Ahmed would have no need of the foreign concubine's services, she gloated happily. As if to add insult to injury, she slipped both her shapely arms about Ahmed's shoulders, burying her face in the curve of his neck.

As Christa stepped out into full view, she absently wondered if Ahmed would be surprised to see her. Would he welcome her? It was something she would never learn, as Ahmed's towering form appeared as if from nowhere, striding purposefully to his tent carrying a small bundle in his arms. Puzzled, Christa watched in amazement as a pair of slim arms emerged from the bundle to wrap themselves around Ahmed's neck and long black hair swung free over a masculine shoulder.

Immediately Christa stepped back into the shadows, her face a study in abject misery. "Elissa," she groaned softly, the pain of betrayal like a blow to the heart.

Hadn't Elissa told her she would share Ahmed's bed this night? What a fool she had been to think she lied! Evidently Ahmed had wanted Elissa badly enough to go after her and carry her to his tent. She felt as if a knife had been plunged into her heart and twisted for good measure. Why did she have to fall in love with a man whose culture allowed—no, encouraged—multiple matings? Why must her love need a bevy of women at his beck and call? She wanted no part of a life where women were forced to do men's bidding or be punished. Even a lifetime of marriage to Brian seemed preferable to becoming Ahmed's whore. Whirling on her heel she fled back to her tent to rethink her future—a future that no longer included Ahmed.

Ahmed realized Elissa had gained her senses the moment her soft arms crept around his shoulders and he felt her warm breath tickle his neck. Carrying her inside, he carefully set her on her feet. "Are you all right?" he asked, glowering sternly. "Whatever possessed you to follow me like that?"

Quailing beneath his anger, Elissa breathed deeply in an effort to marshal her courage. This was definitely not the time to cower in fear. Not when she was so close to obtaining her heart's desire. "I . . . I was hoping for a moment alone with you," she admitted, lowering her eyes submissively. Long black lashes lay upon her pale cheeks like twin butterfly wings of fringed lace, and for the first time Ahmed was struck by her ripe beauty.

"What was so important that you waited until darkness to accost me? Didn't you realize I could have killed you?"

"N—no, that is, I didn't think. Please, master, don't be angry with me."

"Call me Ahmed sheikh," Ahmed growled, his years in England making him uncomfortable with a term that implied total submission. "And now that you're here, you may as well tell me what you wanted. I'm afraid it's too late now for what I intended anyway."

Elissa gloated, secretely elated. Ahmed would not be visiting his concubine this night, and more than likely would turn to her for bodily comfort. "Did you know I just recently turned fifteen?" she began hesitantly.

"So great an age?" Ahmed teased with exaggerated shock. "I see no gray hairs."

Elissa blushed, taking advantage of his good humor by sidling closer until the tips of her full breasts grazed his chest. Disregarding his warning frown, she asked coyly, "Am I not pleasant to look upon, Ahmed sheikh?"

Ahmed's frown deepened. "You know you are a beautiful child, Elissa. What are you hinting at?"

"I am no longer a child!" she bristled hotly. "I am a woman full grown. Look at me and tell me I am not desirable."

With those words she threw off her djellaba, revealing that she was naked beneath her robe. Ahmed tensed, his eyes traveling lingeringly over the full curves and deep valleys displayed proudly before his eyes. A stirring in his loins caused him to shift uncomfortably. Elissa recognized the act for what it was and was gratified by his reaction.

To admit that the arousing sight of Elissa's young, glowing flesh didn't stir him would be lying, Ahmed recognized instantly. But giving in to those urges would prove him less than honorable. Though he didn't want her sexually, he could not stop his eyes from shifting to the thickly forested vee between her shapely legs, then upward to her thrusting breasts tipped with dark ruby nipples growing erect beneath his smoldering gaze. Exerting all his willpower, Ahmed tore his eyes from her woman's body.

"Robe yourself!" he ordered in a tight voice.

"Ahmed sheikh, I know you want me," Elissa persisted. "Your eyes tell me I am desirable. Take me, Ahmed sheikh. From the moment of my birth I've been trained for this occasion. I can make you happier than that pale-skinned whore you've been bedding. Love me, Ahmed sheikh, let me prove my worth to you. Use me for the purpose for which I was created."

Ahmed stiffened, Elissa's disparaging remark about Christa bringing him abruptly to his senses.

Though his body might yearn to pierce Elissa's virginity, he was committed heart and soul to Christa.

"Elissa"—he sought to explain his feelings as gently as possible—"you are a beautiful woman. Any man would look upon you with desire. And certainly I am no different." At the leap of joy in her eyes, he hastily amended, "But I am not the man for you. I have pledged my heart to one woman. Though I freely admit you present a challenge to my senses, I would only be using you if I took you now."

Elissa's face puckered in puzzlement. What in the world was Ahmed talking about? Had he learned these strange ideas in far-away England? Surely it must be a land without comfort to allow a man only one woman. "A man is meant to possess many women," she explained carefully. "His nature is such that he cannot be faithful to any one woman. My mother taught me it has been thus down through the ages. Perhaps it would have been better had your father kept you in your own country so as not to fill your mind with foreign ways."

"Perhaps," Ahmed mused thoughtfully, "but I did go away. And I did learn lessons not taught in this country. Even though I may become bey one day, I doubt I could ever keep a harem."

As he said this, he realized the truth of his words, words he had never before dared voice. Christa's love gave him the courage to defy generations of tradition, decreeing that men of his culture had little use for women except as receptacles for their lust. If he had his way such intolerable injustice would stop with his reign. When he made Christa his mate, she would share every aspect of his life.

Stubbornly, Elissa refused to believe Ahmed's

words declaring his love and devotion to one woman. Her vanity led her to think she could break down his defenses and rid him of the strange customs he had learned during his years under foreign influence by enticing him beyond human endurance. With a cry of surrender she hurled herself into the curve of Ahmed's hard body, curling her arms about his neck to hold him captive.

"Ahmed sheikh, would you deny me the right to become a woman in your arms? You are humiliating my father by refusing to use me for the purpose for which I was intended. He gave me to you in good faith."

Ahmed grew thoughtful, startled that he hadn't considered Omar's feelings before. True, Elissa was given to him with the intention that one day she would warm his bed. It was an honor to present one's daughter to a bey or even a future bey, and Ahmed had accepted her with that thought in mind. Even from an early age, Elissa had the potential for great beauty, and Ahmed was not averse to accepting Omar's gift. But that was before he met Christa. He would speak to Omar at the first opportunity.

"I will speak to your father and explain the circumstances, Elissa," he promised aloud. "Perhaps we can find you a good husband. Or if you prefer, you can return to Biskra."

"No," Elissa protested, pouting sullenly. "I want no other man. All others pale in comparison to you, great sheikh."

"Allah deliver me from unreasonable women," Ahmed muttered crossly, directing a prayer heavenward. Stooping, he picked up her djellaba and wrapped it around her nude body. "Go, Elissa, before I lose patience and beat you. I grow weary of your senseless drivel. You will have a man, and

soon, that I promise. Serve Christa well, and I will
provide you with a husband and enough gold to
keep you both happy." Then, none too gently, he
shoved her through the narrow opening of the tent
into the blackness of the night.

11

"Ahmed is truly magnificent," Elissa sighed contentedly. "Strong, handsome, virile . . ." She had no need to put into words what she was hinting at, for Christa knew exactly what she meant.

"I'm glad he made you happy," she snapped irritably.

"You should have believed me when I told you Ahmed wanted to bed me last night. He is a wonderful lover," Elissa remarked slyly, casting a sidelong glance at Christa from beneath long, sooty lashes. She thanked Allah that Christa had not still been standing outside Ahmed's tent when she had been ignominiously evicted by her irate master. She did not want Christa to know that Ahmed had scorned her offer of bodily solace. Let her think Ahmed was bedding both of them.

"It matters little to me what Ahmed does or whom he beds," Christa declared unconvincingly.

"Then come, lady, let us go to the pool for our

bath. My father told me we can linger here but another day before we must depart."

Silently, feeling betrayed and as unhappy as she had ever been, Christa followed Elissa to the clear pool where they had bathed the day before. Her frame of mind did not allow her to see the beauty of setting nor even to appreciate the cool, sparkling water caressing her skin. Elissa finished bathing first and stood on the bank, tapping her foot impatiently. "Are you ready to leave, lady?"

"Go on," Christa replied curtly. "I'll come along later. I have yet to wash my hair." Elissa shrugged, tossed her black mane, and strode off toward the camp, leaving Christa to fend for herself.

Christa appreciated the opportunity to be alone. She had a lot of thinking to do and wanted to do it without Elissa around to remind her that Ahmed obviously preferred Elissa's voluptuous body to her own slimness. Though Elissa neither looked nor acted like a child, Christa couldn't forget that the girl had barely reached her fifteenth year. She had thought she was secure in Ahmed's love, but evidently the sultry charms of the younger woman had proved too great a temptation.

Ahmed stood on the opposite bank watching Christa, green eyes narrowed appreciatively, the sudden swelling in his groin too painful to be ignored. He had seen Elissa return from the pool alone and knew Christa must still be there, and with a will of their own his feet carried him in that direction. It was so late by the time he had put Elissa from his tent last night that he had decided not to disturb Christa. And duty had kept him from her this morning. Now, unwittingly, Elissa's hasty departure had afforded him the opportunity for a brief respite with his love.

She stood in water up to her waist, her head

thrown back, long neck arched as she rinsed the soap from the pale gold strands of her hair. The upper part of her body appeared white as the purest alabaster, silky smooth and delicately veined. The coral tips of her breasts, deliciously puckered and pert as ripe cheeries, just begged for his attention, and Ahmed kept his eyes on them as he began divesting himself of his constricting clothing. Since the two women had taken the pool for their own use he had issued strict orders to his men that no one was to come near this place, so he was certain they would not be disturbed.

So engrossed was Christa with her dismal thoughts that she failed to see Ahmed slip noiselessly into the pool from the opposite bank and swim slowly toward her. She had just squeezed the excess water from her hair and was in the process of wading from the pool when something beneath the surface of the water seized her legs, and she screamed. All she got for her efforts was a mouthful of water as she was dragged under, only to come up sputtering when a laughing Ahmed lifted her high in the air, then slowly lowered her, her body making a leisurely path along his.

"I missed you last night, sweet siren," he murmured huskily.

"I seriously doubt that," Christa sniffed disdainfully.

Ahmed's brow quirked in amusement. "Do I detect a note of skepticism, little one? I wanted to come to you, believe me, but was unavoidably detained. And then it was too late. But I'm here now, and I want you."

Christa squirmed uncomfortably when one hand slipped beneath the water to rest on her silken mound. Tossing her wet head, she vowed that Ahmed would never know just how much his touch affected her, or how jealous she was of Elissa.

"Find your pleasure elsewhere, master," she emphasized in a derisive manner.

Ahmed frowned uncertainly. "What is it, Christa? Have I done something to anger you?"

Never would she admit that she had been on her way to him when she saw him with Elissa. She'd be damned if she'd give him that satisfaction. "Why should anything you do anger me?"

"For the love of Allah, Christa, why are you acting like this? I need you, my love. Don't deny me when our times together are so few."

Christa stood unyielding as Ahmed tasted her lips, prying them apart with his tongue and boldly thrusting inside. She whimpered, determined to remain unmoved, but her senses reeled when his mouth slid to her nipples, nipping and licking at the sensitive buds.

"You want me, Christa," Ahmed rasped harshly. "Your body speaks to me with a language all its own."

"No!" denied Christa vehemently. "I won't be your whore!"

Startled, Ahmed drew back sharply. "Is that what this is all about? You think I'm just using you? I love you, Christa. I've told you so time and again. I thought you returned my love."

"You don't know the meaning of the word," Christa spat defiantly. "You confuse lust with love. Any woman could satisfy your needs, perhaps far better than I."

Suddenly Ahmed's formidable temper exploded. "Mayhap you're right, but at this moment it's you I want, and by the beard of the prophet it's you I'll have! What do you want from me, Christa? You have my love; I saved you from Abdullah and have defied everyone to keep you by my side. I own you. If I have to command you to make love to me, I will!"

Ahmed was not a man given to patience. From an early age his every whim had been catered to; rarely was there a need to do more than voice his wishes before they were instantly granted. In his anger he had disregarded Christa's proud English upbringing and stubborn nature. His one consuming thought was that she was denying him what he desperately desired. Though he loved her truly and completely, his upbringing demanded total obedience.

His words succeeded only in further enraging Christa as she fought to escape his confining embrace, his drugging kisses. "I won't be bullied, you arrogant bastard!"

"Open your legs, Christa," Ahmed laughed, delighting in, yet at the same time annoyed at her sudden opposition. Beneath the water he grasped her buttocks, lifting her slightly. Still she refused to obey, until he lost patience and, spreading her thighs and wrapping them about his hips, he thrust easily into her. A quiver of repressed desire jolted through her and a smug smile curved Ahmed's lips when he felt her resistance melt.

Thrusting, withdrawing, thrusting again, Ahmed thought his heart would burst with wanting. Never had a woman excited him like Christa. His fingers dug into the tender skin of her buttocks as he plunged into her velvet warmth, his mouth traveling frenziedly between her pouting breasts and softly parted mouth. When he moved one hand between their straining bodies to find the bud of her desire, she went wild, moaning and grinding her hips in a crazy rhythm that drove him to attempt still greater heights. In wonder, he watched her expressive face as she exploded in climax, head thrown back, mouth slightly parted, blue eyes soft and glazed with passion. Then all thought vanished as he lost himself to his own release.

Christa felt herself being lifted out of the water and carried to the bank, where she was gently stretched out on the mossy ground. "Do you want to tell me about it, sweet?" Ahmed asked as he settled down beside her.

"I—I don't know what you are talking about," she said sullenly.

"What must I do to prove my love for you?"

Don't take other women to your bed! she wanted to scream. But of course she didn't. Her pride would not allow him the satisfaction of knowing she was spying on him. His upbringing and the culture in which he was raised condoned and encouraged taking and using any woman available to him for sexual gratification. Was it enough for her to have his love but not his fidelity? she asked herself dismally. It was something she would have to face one day if she was to remain with Ahmed.

At length, she replied, "If you really loved me, you would need no other woman."

"What makes you think I do?" he asked, his green eyes darkening with desire. As they lay there, he idly began stroking her breasts, her flanks, until the fire kindled once more in his loins. "You have always been enough for me."

You lie! she silently lamented. You took Elissa to your bed. "If you loved me as you say, you wouldn't force me."

"Force you?" he asked, astounded. "You were a little reluctant to begin with, but there was never any force involved. Just mutual need. Do you truly believe another woman could please me as well as you?"

"N . . . no," she whispered uncertainly, for she knew what they experienced was unique. But obviously that wasn't enough to prevent him from taking Elissa when the mood struck him. "But I want to be more than just your concubine, Ahmed."

"You are more, much more than mere concubine," Ahmed insisted, highly incensed. "Haven't you heard a word I've said?"

"Yes, I heard," Christa replied in a subdued voice. But you never asked me to be your wife! her heart cried out. You never said you'd take no other woman!

"Come then, my love," he said, as if everything between them was settled. "Let's go back to camp. There is much to do before we leave. Abdullah's army can't be far behind, and I would lure them farther into the Sahara before I allow them to find us." He placed a gentle kiss on her breasts, then rose reluctantly to find her clothes.

Once they were dressed, he turned to her and said, "Our hectic pace for the next few days will leave me little time for you, my love. Remember that not a minute of the day goes by that I am not thinking of you or needing you."

He sounded so sincere that Christa was inclined to believe him, if not forgive him, for bedding Elissa—so long as he didn't do it again.

The following days were gruelling ones for Christa. A caravan traveling to Fez stopped at the oasis shortly before they left, and Ahmed purchased from a merchant two bassourab, the chairlike contraptions that enabled her and Elissa to travel in a modicum of comfort atop a camel. Though the bassourab offered some relief from the blazing sun, the deeper they went into the great Sahara the more unbearable it became. Beneath her yashmak, her skin felt dry and withered, more arid than the vast sandy expanses over which they traveled. Though she drank from her girba as often as she dared, the inside of her mouth seemed filled with cotton.

When they stopped for the night, only one tent—which Christa was expected to share with Elissa—was erected. As Ahmed predicted, Christa saw little of him in the days that followed. What distressed her more than anything was that Elissa would often disappear for hours during the darkest part of the night, and the thought that the girl might have gone to Ahmed nearly destroyed her. But her stubborn pride kept her from questioning Elissa, whose smoldering looks of late were anything but comforting.

Had Christa but known Elissa's purpose in sneaking out at night, she would have been saved a great deal of heartache. In the face of Ahmed's continued indifference and driven by desperation, Elissa had taken a lover. A young Tuareg named Ishmail, whose attraction lay in his muscular body and arrogant good looks, reminding her much of Ahmed sheikh. Since her own master had no use for her, she became determined to taste fully of love's potion and to fulfill the role for which she was created. In Elissa's arms, Ishmail attained a paradise he had only dared dream about, though he realized he could be put to death for touching one of the sheikh's women. But even death held no fear for him once he experienced the forbidden rapture Elissa's charms offered.

One morning Ahmed deliberately sought out Christa, taking her aside while his men were busy dismantling their camp. "My love," he said, his face lined with fatigue and his voice harsh with exhaustion. "I know all this hasn't been easy for you. The Sahara is a cruel place for one not born to its hardships. We are nearing the Tunisian border and I have come to a painful decision."

Christa stirred uneasily. What was he hinting at? "Tunisia?" she repeated stupidly.

"Yes," he acknowledged solemnly. "I'm taking you to Tunis, to your family. The Tuaregs will wait for my return at the edge of the desert."

"You're taking me back?" Why was she sounding like an idiot?

"I've no other choice, Christa. Once we're over the border you'll be safe from Abdullah. Dragging you from place to place because I am too selfish to part with you is no kind of life for you. Time and again I have placed you in great danger, and I could no longer live with myself should something happen to you. I must keep you safe from Abdullah."

"I'm not complaining, Ahmed. If you truly love me, don't send me away."

"It's because I love you that you must go."

"Will you stay with me?" she asked hopefully, anticipating his negative reply long before it came.

At length, Ahmed replied, "You know I can't, my love. I'm a man with a mission. When I have completed what I set out to do, I will come for you."

"Wha—what if Abdullah succeeds in killing you?"

"He won't."

"What if I decide not to wait for you?"

"You will wait," Ahmed returned, regarding her sternly.

"What about Elissa?"

"Elissa? What has she to do with us? I promised her a husband if she served you well."

Will you be the husband she has been promised? her mind shrieked in outrage. According to custom, he could marry Elissa but not take a foreigner to wife. "I wish you both happiness," she intoned dryly, her sarcasm completely lost on

Ahmed, who had no idea what she was talking about.

"I'll see that Elissa is made happy," he assured her, thinking she had grown fond of the girl and wanted to see her future settled.

"I'm sure you will," she remarked wryly.

"Forget Elissa, my love. We'll have many nights, just you and I, before we reach Tunis. Nights to make up for all those when we shall be parted. Once this business with Abdullah is over, I'll never let you out of my sight."

"Will you keep me captive in your harem?" Christa questioned indignantly. "Will we draw straws to see who will pleasure you each night?"

Completely disregarding the fact that Christa might be serious, Ahmed answered flippantly, "You can be certain your straw will be the short one on most of those nights, sweet. Only when I have thoroughly worn you out would I choose another."

Seeing her downcast look, he continued in a more serious vein. "Come, my love, why the sad face? When I return for you we will be together always."

Let him think what he wants, Christa thought with a pang of remorse, for she wouldn't be there when—or if—he returned. She would share these last precious nights with him, but only to provide her with enough memories to last the rest of her life. Didn't he realize she would not be satisfied to occupy so small a place in his heart? That she could not share him with other women? Once he abandoned her in Tunis, she would return to England and live with her aunt. Marrying Brian was no longer an option. After experiencing Ahmed's love, no other man held any appeal for her.

They parted shortly afterward, when Omar appeared to tell them all was ready for their departure. After a smoldering look, conveying passionate promise, Ahmed turned and strode off. His leaving left a void nothing or no one could ever fill. It was as if the sun had just left her universe, and she shivered, a strange forboding bringing a sudden and implacable chill. Some strange premonition told her she had just seen Ahmed for the last time.

12

Christa stirred restlessly, her sleep interrupted by disturbing thoughts. As had become their custom, Elissa shared her tent while the men slept curled up beside their camels. At her side, the younger woman sighed and turned in her sleep. Was she dreaming of Ahmed and their passionate encounters on those nights when she slipped out of the tent to join him? Distractedly, she wondered if the girl would go to him again tonight.

Suddenly Christa tensed, as a commotion outside jarred her fully awake. The thunder of many hoofbeats drummed in her ears at the same time that she became aware of shouts of warning, followed by bloodcurdling screams of agony. Elissa jolted up with a start as Christa scrambled to her feet, rushing to peer out the tent flap, Elissa close on her heels. What she saw could have been a scene straight from the depths of hell.

Dozens of armed men carrying torches and wielding sinister scimitars rode swift camels through the sleeping camp, hacking and killing without discrimination. "Abdullah's Janissaries," breathed Elissa, her eyes rolling with fear.

Dear God, how could this happen? Christa pondered as she watched the carnage all around her. Some of the Tuaregs managed to reach their feet and were waging a fierce battle, admirably fulfilling their reputation as men of courage. But from where Christa stood, she could see the fight was lost before it really began, for the tribesmen were outnumbered, as well as taken totally by surprise.

"Ahmed! Where is Ahmed?" Christa asked anxiously, searching the moonlit camp.

"Over there!" Elissa pointed to a man whose white robes were slashed and stained with blood. Horrified, she watched him valiantly defend himself against two Janissaries determined to destroy him. Nearby, Omar struggled to come to Ahmed's aid, but he was fully occupied with protecting himself against two more members of Abdullah's highly skilled army.

Terror-stricken, Christa stood helplessly by as Ahmed was slowly being defeated. But then, spying a sword in the hand of a dying man sprawled nearby, she darted from the tent, completely disregarding her own safety. Swallowing her revulsion, she pried the sword from the man's hand, finding it surprisingly heavy. Dragging it behind her until she reached Ahmed, then raising it over her head with both hands, she fully intended to handily dispatch at least one of Ahmed's burly opponents.

But her efforts were in vain when the unwieldly weapon was snatched from her hand and she felt herself grasped from behind. "Hawk!" she cried out, remembering not to use his real name in front of Abdullah's men.

The huge man holding Christa's wildly struggling body froze, studying intently the man fighting for his life. Though nothing was visible but dark, angry eyes, his white robes and commanding presence brought instant recognition. It was the one they call "Desert Hawk"—the man responsible for his embarrassment, who had nearly brought about his death. In his mercy, Abdullah had given him another chance to redeem himself by capturing this desert sheikh who had caused the bey much anguish as well as great loss of property. Captain Hadji had led his men over vast stretches of wasteland in search of the elusive Desert Hawk.

"Hold!" he ordered. Instantly the two men swiftly closing in on Ahmed stayed their hand, looking askance at their leader. "It is the Desert Hawk, the man we seek. Seize him, but do not kill him. Abdullah wants that pleasure for himself. He will suffer a slow death for daring to lay hands on our master's foreign concubine and making off with valuable property."

When several of the Janissaries jumped to obey, they found themselves facing the sharp end of Ahmed's sword.

"Lay down your weapon, Hawk," Captain Hadji ordered brusquely. "I have the woman. Fighting will gain you naught but the loss of both of your lives."

Ahmed recognized the captain from their previous encounter. Hadn't he stolen Christa away from the caravan weeks ago under the captain's very nose in nearly the same manner? Now it looked as if Captain Hadji would have his revenge.

"Be reasonable, Hawk," Hadji cajoled. "The woman will not be harmed. She is to be returned to Abdullah. He will be more than happy to learn we have captured the fierce Desert Hawk."

Sword poised and ready, Ahmed considered his

options. He could fight until death claimed him, which no doubt would not be long in coming, or he could surrender and trust fate to show him a way to save himself as well as Christa. He was no good to her dead. As long a breath remained in him there was a chance, albeit a remote one, that he could save them both, although he had little doubt that once his identity was revealed his brother would order his death in order to preserve the beylic for himself and his heirs. Christa's desperate plea made up his mind.

"Give up, Hawk, I beg you! Don't let them kill you! I love you!"

"You will not harm the woman?" Ahmed asked, his eyes filled with anguish, his voice ripe with despair.

"She will not be harmed," promised Hadji.

"What of my men?"

"It is you Abdullah wants. Without their leader they are nothing and easily controlled. In view of their bravery, the survivors will be left in the desert to fend for themselves. We will take their camels, weapons and supplies. Their survival will depend on Allah's will."

Ahmed nodded. He could ask no more. Knowing the cunning of the Tuaregs, he was convinced most would somehow manage to survive. He laid down his scimitar and was immediately seized.

"Bind him and guard him well," Hadji ordered curtly. "We will be well rewarded for this night's work."

With a grimace of distaste, Hadji vividly recalled Abdullah's insane rage when informed that his caravan had been attacked by the Desert Hawk and his woman stolen. He had screamed and ranted until he fell to the floor in a fit and had to be calmed by his physician. Afterwards he had dispatched his army, led by Captain Hadji, into the Sahara in pursuit of the fugitive sheikh with orders not to return without the Desert Hawk or the foreign concubine.

Abruptly, Hadji became aware of the woman struggling in his arms and started dragging her toward the tent that had surprisingly been left standing. But before they reached it one of his men emerged carrying a screeching Elissa, whose clothes hung in tatters from her nearly nude form.

"This woman belongs to Desert Hawk, Captain, what should I do with her?" asked the man when he spied his leader approaching. From the condition of Elissa's clothing it was obvious the man had already had his way with her.

"Our orders are only to bring the foreign concubine and the sheikh back to Constantine," Hadji shrugged. "Give her to the men or leave her in the desert with the others. I care not."

"The men will be grateful for the diversion," smirked the Janissary. "It has been a long gruelling chase to capture this desert sheikh, and the heat of battle has sharpened their lust for woman's flesh as well as for blood." He turned and strode off, paying little heed to Elissa's anguished screams of protest.

"No!" shrieked Christa, finally finding her voice. "You can't take her! She is only a child."

"A child!" scoffed Hadji with a nasty laugh. "In Biskra children like her and even younger populate the brothels that line the streets. Never fear, this one will survive."

Christa spent what was left of the night huddling in abject terror as she imagined all kinds of horrors being inflicted on Elissa. Though the girl had exhibited little friendship toward her, Christa wouldn't wish her fate on an animal. No one should be treated in such a vile manner. She could only thank God that Elissa's fate was not hers.

Then there was Ahmed to worry and fret over.

Had his life been spared only to be snuffed out by Abdullah once he learned the desert raider was his own half-brother? From all she'd heard, the man was vicious and obsessed with power. Thinking of the bey made her wonder what role she was to play in his harem. Would she dwell there in relative obscurity, or would she occupy a more prominent place—in his bed? She could only hope it was the former. Sometimes near dawn, exhaustion finally claimed her.

What seemed like only moments later, Christa was rudely awakened by soft whimpering sounds coming from nearby. Her eyes widened in horror when she saw Elissa, totally nude, limping into the tent. He body bore numerous bruises, and her face was ashen with pain as she collapsed in a boneless heap at Christa's feet.

"Oh my God, Elissa? What did they do to you?"

Turning stricken eyes on Christa, Elissa moaned through bloodless lips, her throat working convulsively in mute appeal.

"No, don't talk," Christa urged gently as she reached for the water skin nearby. First she helped the girl to drink, then she used the remainder of the water to wash the cuts and bruises purpling nearly every part of her body. Tears of pity sprang to her blue eyes as she tenderly cleansed the blood congealing between her thighs.

"Dear Lord, it must have been terrible!" Christa gasped brokenly.

"Terrible?" croaked Elissa, consumed by pain and nearly hysterical. "Can you name anything worse than having twenty or more sweating men rutting between your thighs, all in the space of a few hours? There would have been more, but they feared I would die and deprive them of another night's pleasure. What would you do, lady?"

"I would not be nearly so brave as you, Elissa,"

Christa admitted, choking on the lump that clogged her throat. "I'm certain I would be long dead by now. You are an extraordinarily brave woman, Elissa. I envy you."

"You envy me?" Elissa laughed, shedding bitter tears. Solemnly, Christa nodded.

Taking quick note of Elissa's exhaustion, she pulled a robe over the girl and said, "Go to sleep, Elissa. I'll not let them take you again."

Too tired to protest, yet fully aware that Christa could not keep her from the soldiers should they want her again, Elissa allowed sleep to drag her into unconsciousness. As she slept, Christa kept close watch, once again amazed at the fortitude and courage displayed by the young girl. And in her compassion she made herself a promise, one she had no idea how she would keep. She vowed that none of Captain Hadji's men would lay a hand on Elissa during the rest of their long journey to Constantine.

Elissa slept all that day, rousing only when Christa tried to force some food into her as twilight approached. Captain Hadji had informed her earlier that they would remain one more night to bury their dead and rest before starting north to Constantine. During their conversation, his eyes fell on the sleeping Elissa, his face devoid of all emotion. To Christa, he appeared a man without compassion, and that frightened her. When she dared ask about Ahmed, she was coldly informed that the sheikh was alive and would remain so until Abdullah decided his fate. His words offered her little comfort.

Later that evening Elissa roused sufficiently to dress and move listlessly about the tent, every motion obviously painful. Her dark eyes focused bleakly on the tent flap, as if she expected to be dragged out at any moment, flung on her back and mounted. She knew that one more night like the previous one and she could not possibly survive. And when the summons did come, she was too petrified to move or even to acknowledge it.

The tent flap was rudely ripped aside, admitting the same rough soldier who had carried Elissa away the night before. He eyed the young girl greedily, then slowly advanced, his lust vividly apparent. Cowering against Christa, Elissa began to sob. "You promised, lady! You promised they wouldn't have me again. I cannot bear it."

"They will not have you," Christa replied, eyes blazing defiantly as she placed a supporting arm around the girl's quaking shoulders.

"Step aside, lady," the soldier said, shoving her roughly out of the way and reaching for Elissa.

"No! Have you no mercy? No compassion? The girl has been badly used. She can't possibly survive another night of vile abuse."

"Janissaries aren't noted for their gentleness, lady," the man smirked. "Nor do they like to be denied when there is a woman available to slake their lust. Come," he ordered sternly, turning his attention to Elissa. "The men tend to get impatient when kept waiting, and in the end you will suffer for it."

"Lady, lady, please," implored Elissa, her luminous black eyes wide with horror as she begged for protection.

"You can't have her!" Christa insisted, her chin tilted obstinately as she rose bravely to the defense of the girl who had previously treated her with nothing but contempt.

Ignoring the vigorous but futile protests, the soldier began dragging Elissa from the tent. Suddenly something in Christa snapped, and finding no other outlet for her frustration, she opened her mouth and screamed. Screamed like a banshee, alerting everyone in camp, including Captain Hadji, who came rushing into the tent.

"What is going on, Harun?" Hadji thundered, breathing a quick sigh of relief when he saw Christa was unharmed.

"I have not touched the foreign concubine, Captain," Harun insisted, slanting Christa a quelling look. "I want only the girl, Elissa. The men have need of her services again."

"Then why the ruckus? Take the whore and leave."

"No!" Christa protested, rushing to Elissa's side. "This girl has been badly abused. She is my—my servant, and I insist you leave her alone."

For a moment Hadji looked thoroughly confused. Finally, he shrugged and said, "I have already given her to my men. She is of little consequence."

Leering gleefully, Harun took Hadji's answer as confirmation to his claim on Elissa and continued his efforts to remove her from the tent. Even Elissa took the captain's words as final judgment, for she seemed to collapse inwardly, lowering her head submissively, prepared to follow Harun meekly. She reminded Christa of a lamb being led to slaughter.

"Captain Hadji," Christa said, summoning all the hauteur she could muster. Desperation rode her now, and the awareness that a young girl's life was at stake. "Should I become Abdullah's favorite, and it's entirely likely, you know, I'll see you punished for the pain and abuse suffered by my servant. I will personally hold you responsible for your men's actions. If I have my way, I'll see you stripped of your command and banished from Constantine. Do you want to risk all you have worked for? Think hard on it, Captain, before you allow this girl to leave with your man."

Captain Hadji was no fool. Abdullah was more than likely to become obsessed with a woman possessing the foreign concubine's beauty and courage. Especially if the lady offered herself willing. It was a known fact that Abdullah favored blondes and this one was particularly lovely to look upon. He could ill afford her hostility, for should she one day hold a prominent place in Abdullah's esteem, he preferred her as an ally, not an enemy. Men had been made or broken in the harem, though few women ever left those sumptuous confines.

"Well, Captain, what is your decision?" Christa demanded, cursing the slight tremor in her voice.

Granting her the grudging respect due her mettle, Hadji came to a quick judgment. "Release the girl, Harun. The men can slake their lusts in Biskra."

"But, Captain," pleaded Harun angrily, disappointment riding him. "Would you go back on your word? The woman is a whore. She is accustomed to harsh usage."

"Enough!" barked Hadji sharply. "You have your orders. The girl is not to be touched. Go!"

When he had stomped from the tent, Hadji whirled in Christa, eyes narrowed consideringly. "Remember me, lady, when you rise in favor. Do not forget that it was Hadji who openly defied his men and granted your wish. See that you are sufficiently grateful when I demand payment."

Then he was gone, leaving Christa shaken but elated. For the time being she had saved a young girl's life.

"Lady," Elissa cried softly, falling to her knees. "How can I repay you? You have saved my life even after I was openly hostile to you. Forgive me."

Embarrassed, Christa gently raised Elissa to her

feet. "I ask nothing in return, Elissa, save that you be my friend. We go to Constantine, where an uncertain fate awaits us. It would be comforting to face this together, as friends."

"Lady, I don't deserve your kindness," sobbed Elissa. "I—I have done you a grave injustice."

"If you're talking about Ahmed, I can understand his need for you. You are young and very lovely. What man could resist you?"

"A man such as Ahmed, lady. He scorned me and sent me away. He wanted only you. He loves you greatly, lady."

Incredible joy let up Christa's features. "Are . . . are you certain, Elissa? Or are you only telling me this because of what I did for you?"

"It is the truth, lady. I lied to you when I said Ahmed—bedded me. I was jealous because he preferred you."

Suddenly Christa recalled the night she saw Ahmed carrying Elissa to his tent. "But I saw him carry you to his tent!"

"Nothing happened," Elissa assured her, lowering her head in shame. "I craftily planned the whole thing but Ahmed would have none of me. Forgive me, lady."

"You are forgiven, Elissa," Christa smiled, hugging the girl to her. "And please call me Christa. I should have never doubted Ahmed's love. I only hope it's not too late. Neither of us know what the future will bring. We must band together, Elissa, and in so doing perhaps we can yet help Ahmed escape Abdullah's sword."

"I am your servant, Christa," Elissa said fervently. "As well as your friend. I will serve you to the best of my ability, do whatever is required of me to prove my loyalty and earn your trust."

Later, lying sleepless on her pallet, Christa

thought of Ahmed and how she had misjudged him. If only I could go to him, she silently lamented, and tell him how sorry I am for spurning his love. Somehow, someday, the time would come for her to prove the strength of her own love. Until that day arrived, she had to believe in kismet and trust that eventually they would be together.

13

The towering walls of Constantine rose to view
long before they reached the ancient city. It was an
awesome sight, guarded by crenellated walls a thousand feet high and encircled on three sides by a
natural chasm formed by a river. The city's fourth
side was connected to the surrounding countryside
by a narrow isthmus. The whole city was perched
atop a lofty plateau a thousand yards wide. Even
from where Christa stood, she could see the houses
crowded one upon the other, many overhanging the
brink of the giddy abyss, their hold on the rocky
sides so tenuous it appeared a heavy wind could
blow them off. It seemed nearly impossible that the
pedestal of limestone rock could support the city,
but evidently it had done so for many centuries.

Surrounding the amazing city were fields of
waving grain, olive groves and wooded hills. The
River Rummel swept around three sides of the city
through a deep and narrow gorge, creating four

natural arches of stone through which the city was entered.

Under a blinding African sun, they entered the city through one of the stone arches, Captain Hadji leading the way, with the women following. Behind them plodded four armed guards. Ahmed did not travel with them, but Christa knew he was not far behind with his own cadre of guards.

Immediately Christa noted that the towering heights were jammed with palaces, temples, villas and arches, all a gleaming white under the dazzling sun. They soon moved into the central part of the teeming city, moving steadily upward. After a time winding through streets packed with humanity, they entered the kasbah, where the bey's palace was located.

As they passed through the serpentine paths, Christa idly remarked to Elissa on the strange mode of dress worn by many of the citizens. Some, Elissa told her, were marahouts, or holy men begging for their daily food. When she pointed out women wearing ridiculously small highheeled slippers only half the size of their feet, with old-fashioned pointed headdresses shaped like a dunce cap, from which suspended a white silk veil which enveloped the whole figure, Elissa explained that they were Jewish women. Constantine supported a very large Jewish population.

There was no time for further conversation as Christa and Elissa were led through a small side gate in the palace walls and found themselves standing in a sun-drenched courtyard flagged with marble and filled with orange and lemon trees. The central plaza was surrounded by cloisters, their arches supported by fluted columns in many colors, where Christa supposed the bey and his concubines passed the heat of the day. The lofty walls of this garden paradise completely shut out the dust and turmoil of the narrow, twisted streets they had just traversed. The only sound to reach their ears was the splash of the fountain and the stirring of the trees. Captain Hadji and the guards seemed to have deserted the two women once they entered the courtyard and they stood alone now, uncertain and more than a little frightened of what was to come.

From beneath one of the white marble columns emerged the enormous form of a man, whose skin was as black and shiny as polished ebony. His eyes were mere slits in his fat face, and his tremendous girth caused his breath to come in labored pants. His flesh seemed to hang in rolls about his huge body, which shook and gyrated with each step he took. He wore a turban-like affair twisted about his head, adding several inches to his already above-average height, and he was clad ridiculously in billowing pantaloons of shiny satin and a vest that left most of his chest and waist exposed. He wore a scimitar at his middle and his large feet were bare.

The two women clung to each other as Elissa whispered in a strangled voice, "He's a eunuch, Christa. Probably master of the harem."

He motioned them toward the door through which he had just appeared, but uttered not one word. When the women did little more than gape at him, he shook his head in disgust and opened his jaws. The gaping hole where his tongue had been appeared as a red chasm in his wide, grinning mouth.

"Oh, no!" gasped Christa, clasping a hand to her mouth to stem the acid gush that threatened to spew forth.

"Allah help us!" echoed Elissa, turning her face from the gory sight.

Having made his point, the man again motioned toward the arched doorway, giving them a shove to add emphasis to his direction. Left with no other choice, Christa grasped Elissa's small hand and together they entered the door to Abdullah's harem.

They traversed long marble-columned hall-ways, rooms richly carpeted with Turkish rugs whose walls were tiled in multi-hued squares, into a bathing room much like those she had become accustomed to in Kalim's serai, only twice the size. Stone benches surrounded a sparkling blue pool that was conspicuously deserted. Certainly a beylic the size of Constantine produced countless women beautiful enough to satisfy Abdullah, Christa mused thoughtfully. Yet the entire harem seemed barren, and a certain sadness hung over the place. There were no happy voices drifting through the halls or the chatter of women's gossip. The silence gave Christa an eerie feeling.

"I'm frightened," Elissa whispered, giving voice to Christa's sentiments. "Something isn't right here."

"I was thinking the same thing," Christa agreed slowly.

"Perhaps Abdullah isn't the kind who likes women," Elissa offered hopefully. "I've heard of such men."

"Perhaps," replied Christa doubtfully. From talk drifting through the ranks of the Janissaries, she had the impression that though Abdullah held women in little esteem, he made regular use of them for sexual purposes.

The huge eunuch motioned them to a bench, intimating that they were to sit. Christa obeyed reluctantly, by now her courage reasserting itself as curiosity overcame fear. Elissa quickly followed suit. Then the man turned and strode from the room, his large feet making loud slapping noises on the marble floor.

* * *

While Christa and Elissa were left in solitude to contemplate their fate, Ahmed was being roughly dragged into the palace and flung at Abdullah's feet. It was ludicrous that he should be brought back a prisoner to the country he was meant to rule, and he struggled against the bonds that held him captive.

His once-white robes were now filthy and in tatters; only the blue veil concealing his face remained reasonably intact. Remarkably, Captain Hadji hadn't insisted on removing the one piece of clothing that kept his identity a secret. The formidable commander seemed more concerned with getting Christa to Constantine safely than with unmasking the Desert Hawk, satisfied to leave the raider to Abdullah's mercy.

Grudgingly provided with barely enough food and water to sustain him these past days, Ahmed lifted dark eyes to his brother and struggled to rise to his feet. Remorselessly, Abdullah glared down at the man who had cost him a small fortune over the past months. At a nod of his dark head, two men stepped forward and jerked Ahmed to his feet by his bound wrists, the rope cutting cruelly into his flesh.

"So you are the man called Desert Hawk," Abdullah sneered contemptuously. "Surely you knew it was only a matter of time before you were apprehended. My army is one of the best, and Captain Hadji has special reason to seek your capture."

Ahmed said nothing, glowering sullenly at his brother. Undaunted, Abdullah continued. "I have my concubine back and your men have undoubtedly perished in the desert. What have you to say in your defense, Hawk? Why have you singled out my caravans for your raids? Who are you and what have I done to deserve your hatred? Speak, man! I would have your answer before I order your torture and death."

"Do you not recognize your own brother, Abdullah?" Ahmed snarled, straining against the ropes binding him.

"Ahmed!" Abdullah gasped, motioning for one of his Janissaries to tear off Ahmed's concealing headdress. "Barbarossa assured me you were dead, but against all odds you have returned to taunt and rob me. Captain Hadji will be amply rewarded for performing a great service. Not only are you now in my power, but your woman is as well."

"If you harm Christa, I'll—"

"You'll what?" Abdullah laughed cruelly. "I have yet to see my new concubine, but I can assure you I'll enjoy her all the more knowing you cherish her. Tell me, Ahmed, have you trained her well? Is she obedient as well as passionate?"

"Bastard!" bit out Ahmed. "I love Christa, and if you hurt her I'll kill you with my two hands."

"Hurt her? She'll not be harmed. But I might let you watch while I bed her. It would be interesting, don't you think, to compare how she responds to each of us?"

"Let her go, Abdullah. Do with me what you will, but release Christa."

"You are in no position to bargain. Besides, I want to see for myself what makes her so special to you. Is she worth the two hundred ducats I paid for her?"

"I'm not dead, yet, Abdullah," Ahmed spat out. "Somehow you'll be made to pay for your sins. I've not forgotten what you did to my mother. Nor will I forget what you intend for Christa."

"Bah! Your mother was a foreign whore who bewitched our father into naming you his successor."

Enraged, Ahmed jerked loose from the hands restraining him and lunged at Abdullah, knocking him to the floor. When Ahmed attempted to kick out at him with his booted feet, a nearby guard acted instinctively, clubbing him with the broad side of his sword. He dropped like a leaden statue, a small sigh escaping his lips.

"Take him away," Abdullah ordered, pulling himself painfully to his feet. "As soon as he comes to give him ten lashes. And send Hadji to me. The captain has redeemed himself and earned a generous reward."

A long time passed as Christa and Elissa talked quietly, verbally examining all aspects of their surroundings. After what seemed like hours, a small figure dressed in a flowing djellaba entered the bathing room through a door behind them, gazed at the two bent heads for a moment, then approached on silent feet.

"Excuse me, my lady," she said, smiling shyly at Christa. "Abdullah bey sent me to serve you."

Startled by the soft, feminine voice, Christa whirled, pleasant surprise lighting her blue eyes. "Lenore! How glad I am to see you!"

"You know this woman?" Elissa asked with a hint of jealousy, noting that they spoke the same foreign language.

"This is Lenore, a countrywoman of mine," Christa explained in Arabic. "Abdullah sent her to see to my needs on the long journey from Algiers. I lost track of her when the caravan was attacked." To Lenore, she said, "I'm glad you weren't harmed. From now on we will speak Arabic, so my friend Elissa can understand."

Lenore bowed. "As you wish, mistress."

"Don't bow to me, Lenore, and please call me

Christa." Lenore smiled her understanding, but said nothing. "Do you know what is to become of us, Lenore?"

"I know only what I am told, Christa," Lenore offered with a hint of pity. "I was ordered by Abdullah to see that you and your maid are refreshed before you are taken before him."

"Who was that enormous man who met us in the courtyard?" Elissa dared to ask.

Lenore's weary face crinkled in a smile that displayed fine lines radiating from her eyes and lips. "Fedor is the chief eunuch and in charge of the harem. I admit he is quite intimidating, but he will give you no trouble if you follow orders," she advised.

"Wha—what happened to his tongue?" Elissa couldn't help but ask.

Lenore frowned. "It is not for me to say. Please ask me no more questions." She became so agitated that both Christa and Elissa stared at her gapemouthed.

"Surely you can talk to us," Christa confided in a low voice. "If you won't tell us about Fedor, at least tell us why Abdullah's harem appears deserted save for us. Judging from the size of it, scores of women could comfortably be housed within these walls."

"Christa, I . . ." Lenore's grey eyes grew soft and misty with an emotion that appeared to come straight from her heart. Compassion? Pity? Whatever it was seemed finally to unlock her tongue as she spoke in a low, tense voice filled with pain and remembrance.

"When Selim died so suddenly and Abdullah seized power, his first order was to put my lady Emily to death."

"Emily?"

"Prince Ahmed's mother and Selim's beloved

concubine. Abdullah feared Lady Emily's enormous power, astutely aware of her ability to gain support for her son should she be allowed to live. By his order, she was seized and thrown over the walls of the city into the moat. Luckily her younger son, Yazid, escaped before he met the same fate. The rest of Selim's harem was sold to various whoremasters in the city. You are Abdullah's first acquisition. No doubt others will soon follow, for even now agents are scouring the countryside for beautiful young virgins."

"But I am none of those!" cried Christa, frightened by the recounting of Abdullah's cruel nature.

"That may be true, but you possess something equally important in Abdullah's eyes," Lenore answered wisely. "Something that intrigued Abdullah from the moment he heard about you."

"What is that?" Christa asked curiously.

"You are the woman his brother cares about. According to Redbeard, Ahmed holds you in great esteem. Abdullah is so jealous of his brother that he wants to possess or destroy everything Ahmed holds dear. That is why you're here. Besides, he knows you are a great beauty. Barbarossa's description of you was enough to fascinate him, and now that he holds Ahmed captive the bey hopes to intensify his suffering by taunting him with the knowledge that you are submissive to him in all things. That you are his to use and abuse at will."

"Oh, God," groaned Christa, completely shattered by Lenore's latest disclosure. "So Abdullah knows that Ahmed and the Desert Hawk are the same man. I had hoped . . . Has Abdullah harmed him? Oh, please, Lenore, tell me what you know."

"Christa, I know little but what I hear through palace gossip. But I did learn that Abdullah unmasked Ahmed and has him imprisoned someplace in the palace. He has told no one what he intends for his half-brother, but you know it won't be pleasant. He is filled with hate."

Christa fell silent, tears of frustration coursing down her pale cheeks. Was there nothing she could do to help Ahmed? she wondered dismally. What did her own future hold? Was she to be Abdullah's plaything until he tired of her and sold her to a whoremaster? If that was to be her fate, she'd rather die with Ahmed, for she couldn't bear the thought of another man touching her, not after the ecstasy she had experienced in Ahmed's loving arms.

"Do not cry, Christa," Elissa begged, patting her shoulder awkwardly. "We'll think of something. We have to." Somehow her words of encouragement did little to boost Christa's flagging spirits. In her heart she knew that nothing short of a miracle could extricate her from this terrible predicament.

The room assigned to Christa was large and airy, but the furnishings sparse, consisting mainly of a sleeping couch piled high with colorful cushions and hung with sheer pink draperies. The same sheer curtains draped tall arched windows facing the beautiful courtyard through which she had entered earlier. The floor was cool marble strewn with rugs loomed in vivid shades depicting birds and flowers. The walls were tiles etched in delicate gold and turquoise designs. The room conveyed a sense of peace and tranquility, a state Christa was far from feeling.

After her conversation with Lenore she was skillfully disrobed and bathed in the pool, then given a massage by the surprisingly adept servant. When she reached for her soiled robes, she found they had been taken away and in their place she was dressed in sheer violet pantaloons whose golden girdle was studded with pearls and amethysts. The darker violet bolero was also encrusted with jewels,

GET UP TO 4 FREE BOOKS!

You can have the best romance delivered to your door for less than what you'd pay in a bookstore or online. Sign up for one of our book clubs today, and we'll send you **FREE* BOOKS** just for trying it out...**with no obligation to buy, ever!**

HISTORICAL ROMANCE BOOK CLUB

Travel from the Scottish Highlands to the American West, the decadent ballrooms of Regency England to Viking ships. Your shipments will include authors such as CONNIE MASON, CASSIE EDWARDS, LYNSAY SANDS, LEIGH GREENWOOD, and many, many more.

LOVE SPELL BOOK CLUB

Bring a little magic into your life with the romances of Love Spell—fun contemporaries, paranormals, time-travels, futuristics, and more. Your shipments will include authors such as KATIE MacALISTER, SUSAN GRANT, NINA BANGS, SANDRA HILL, and more.

As a book club member you also receive the following special benefits:

- **30% OFF all orders through our website & telecenter!**
  (Plus, you still get 1 book FREE for every 5 books you buy!)

- **Exclusive access to special discounts!**

- **Convenient home delivery and 10 days to return any books you don't want to keep.**

There is no minimum number of books to buy, and you may cancel membership at any time. See back to sign up!

*Please include $2.00 for shipping and handling.

YES! ☐

Sign me up for the **Historical Romance Book Club** and send my TWO FREE BOOKS! If I choose to stay in the club, I will pay only $8.50* each month, a savings of $5.48!

YES! ☐

Sign me up for the **Love Spell Book Club** and send my TWO FREE BOOKS! If I choose to stay in the club, I will pay only $8.50* each month, a savings of $5.48!

NAME: _____

ADDRESS: _____

_____

TELEPHONE: _____

E-MAIL: _____

☐ **I WANT TO PAY BY CREDIT CARD.**

☐ VISA ☐ MasterCard ☐ DISCOVER

ACCOUNT #: _____

EXPIRATION DATE: _____

SIGNATURE: _____

Send this card along with $2.00 shipping & handling for each club you wish to join, to:

Romance Book Clubs
1 Mechanic Street
Norwalk, CT 06850-3431

Or fax (must include credit card information!) to: 610.995.9274.
You can also sign up online at www.dorchesterpub.com.

*Plus $2.00 for shipping. Offer open to residents of the U.S. and Canada only.
Canadian residents please call 1.800.481.9191 for pricing information.
If under 18, a parent or guardian must sign. Terms, prices and conditions subject to change. Subscription subject
to acceptance. Dorchester Publishing reserves the right to reject any order or cancel any subscription.

JOIN NOW!

leaving her midriff bare and breasts scarcely covered. The long, pale veil of her hair was left free to hang at her waist. Elissa was dressed similarly but not nearly so grandly. Afterwards they were fed and allowed to return to their rooms. Elissa's small chamber, suitable for a servant, was but a short distance away. In a voice laced with pity, Lenore advised Christa to rest until Abdullah summoned her. But how was sleep possible when she was soon to meet a man she considered a depraved monster?

The summons, when it came, was almost anticlimactic. It wasn't Lenore who came for her but Fedor, his tongueless mouth wide and grinning. He motioned and Christa followed, her heart pounding until it sounded like thunder in her ears. She was led through numerous corridors and finally into a huge chamber that obviously served as a bedroom. The furnishings in gold and purple were more ornate than any she had ever seen or imagined. She whirled to ask Fedor a question but found him suddenly absent and the door firmly closed behind her. She made to follow, but found the door guarded from the other side by the formidable eunuch who stood like a stone statue, feet spread apart, beefy arms locked across the enormous expanse of his chest. He shoved her back inside and closed the door soundly in her face.

"There is no escape," an amused voice taunted. "I've waited a long time to meet my brother's whore."

At the sound of the voice, Christa swiveled, searching out the dim recesses of the room.

He stepped from the shadows of the window hangings in an oddly awkward gait that Christa found strangely not in keeping with the overall picture he presented. Her first impression was that this pleasant-looking young man couldn't possibly be the ogre she had been led to believe, nor could he be guilty of cold-blooded murder. A year or two older than Ahmed, he was nearly as tall, though not quite so muscular. He definitely could be considered handsome with his light skin and dark hair identifying him as pure Berber. His nose was straight and bold, his eyes dark. But it was the look in those obsidian eyes that gave hint of his true nature. Cold, completely devoid of depth or emotion, they were almost expressionless as they regarded Christa narrowly. And his lips, too narrow and hard, detracted from what could have been an extraordinarily handsome face.

"Are you too frightened to talk?" Abdullah asked in a deceptively gentle voice. "I know you speak Arabic fluently, but if you prefer French I am quite adept in that language."

"Arabic will do," Christa returned sourly.

"We will have to do something about your attitude." Abdullah smiled coldly. "Henceforth you will call me master." He made no move to advance, but remained poised on the opposite side of the room.

Christa refused to reply, thinking it wise to retreat into silence rather than voice her anger and enrage this implacable man who demanded instant obedience.

"Turn around," he commanded, his voice brooking no argument. "Slowly. I want to see what my brother was willing to lay down his life for."

Tilting her chin defiantly, Christa pivoted as a light kindled in Abdullah's black eyes. "Come here," he ordered, pointing to a spot directly in front of him. Reluctantly, Christa advanced until she stood inches from the self-proclaimed bey.

He reached out and touched her hair, letting the silken strands slip slowly from between his fingers before allowing his hand to caress a smooth cheek. Christa cringed, and fury sparked the dark depths of his eyes. He grasped her chin between his thumb and forefinger, bruising the tender flesh as he forced her face upward.

"Do you find my touch repulsive?" he asked tightly. "Was my brother's touch more to your liking?"

"Yes!" Christa shouted, losing all restraint. "You are disgusting. And I definitely prefer Ahmed. What have you done with him?"

"Ah, the English rose has thorns." Abdullah grinned, pleased at the spark he had ignited within her. Christa flinched, recalling that Ahmed had spoken those same words to her months ago in England.

"Your desert sheikh still lives," Abdullah told her. "How long depends on you."

"You—you haven't harmed him?"

"I said he still lives," he repeated cryptically. "Do you love him so much?"

"More than my life."

"Does my worthy brother feel the same about you?"

"I have reason to believe he does."

"Excellent!" Abdullah chortled. "I wondered how best to make him suffer, and now I know it can be accomplished through you. Though I was my father's first born, I was cast aside in favor of Ahmed. His mother was nothing but my father's whore, while mine was a Berber princess, yet it was the foreigner's spawn whom my father named to succeed him. Now it is Ahmed's turn to suffer."

"You would kill your own brother?"

"Did I say I would kill him? What I have in mind for Ahmed far surpasses the quick death I originally planned."

As he spoke, he began slowly circling Christa, and once again she became aware of his lopsided gait. Puzzled, her eyes fell to his feet, and a startled gasp slipped through her lips before she could stifle it.

"So now you know," Abdullah smiled grimly. "Didn't my brother tell you I was a cripple?" Though Abdullah's body at first appeared fit in every respect, his twisted foot kept him from attaining masculine perfection.

"I . . . I'm sorry," murmured Christa, grasping for words.

"Don't be," Abdullah said harshly. "I don't need pity. Not from you and not from my brother. Because of an accident of birth, I was judged unfit to inherit the beylic. My deformity cost me dearly, and in the eyes of my sire I was flawed and valueless."

What Abdullah said was only a half truth. In naming Ahmed over Abdullah, Selim considered carefully the character of his older son before making his final choice. Of course the fact that Ahmed was the son of his beloved swayed his decision, but in truth Abdullah fell far short of Selim's expectations. Even as a child, Abdullah had displayed cruel tendencies that went far beyond mere childish pranks. But Abdullah could see none of that. In his eyes he was despised solely because of his imperfect body. For years he had plotted carefully and tirelessly to wrest power from his brother, and at long last he sat on the throne he had coveted all his life.

Christa stood with her head bowed, trying desperately not to anger the man she now considered mad. Persevere, she schooled herself. Don't show your fear. Live, Christa—live for the day you'll be free of this madman.

"I am told your name is Christa Horton. Were you virgin before my brother bedded you?"

His insolent question shocked her, and though

her mouth worked convulsively, no words issued forth.

"Well?"

Christa nodded at last. "Yes."

"Yes, what?"

She thought for a moment then added insolently, "Yes, master," emphasizing the word master.

"Take off your clothes."

"What?"

"You understand Arabic well enough. If you don't obey me instantly, I'll have my guards do it for you." Then he smiled slyly. "You've heard of the bastinado, haven't you?" When Christa blanched, he continued, "Ah, I see you have. Fedor is particularly adept, though not necessarily gentle with the rod. Should I call him?"

"No . . . master," Christa replied, swallowing her rage as she slowly began to peel off what little clothing she wore. Within minutes she stood before Abdullah clothed in nothing but the silver veil of her hair.

Circling her in his shuffling gait, Abdullah grunted in obvious satisfaction. "You are very beautiful, Christa Horton," he said in a strained voice, as if experiencing difficulty maintaining control. "No wonder my brother desired you. Soon I will lose myself between those white thighs and attain for myself the heaven my brother found so irresistible." Then he did something that shocked her while it eased her fears. He picked up her discarded clothing and handed it back to her, ordering her in precise words to dress herself.

Scrambling into her meager costume, Christa looked longingly toward the door. "May I go . . . master?"

"Don't you want to see your lover?"

Her eyes narrowed suspiciously, finding

Abdullah's offer strangely out of character. "You'd let me see Ahmed?"

"If you wish it, and only under certain— conditions."

"What kind of conditions?" She was painfully aware that nothing Abdullah had to say would please her, but she was determined to agree to almost anything in order to see Ahmed and learn for herself if he had been harmed.

"You may see him, but under no circumstances will you speak or communicate with him in any way. No matter what I say or do, you are to comply with my wishes. Fedor will accompany us and if you so much as open your mouth, he has orders to kill Ahmed on the spot."

"How can you be so heartless?" cried Christa, her hands itching to slap the smirk from his handsome face.

"Don't you think it heartless of my father to look upon me with disfavor because of an accident of birth? Life is cruel, lady. Nothing is as it should be, as you will soon learn. Do you agree to my terms, or don't you care about my brother? It's up to you if he lives or dies."

"I care, damn you, and I agree!" raged Christa, momentarily forgetting she was completely at the mercy of this madman. Her careless words cost her dearly.

Abdullah drew back one hand and slashed her cruelly across the face, sending her sprawling at his feet. "If I did not need you to taunt Ahmed, I would have you thrown from the wall for your insolence. Rest assured I will show you no mercy when you are in my bed. But first things first. We will pay a call upon my brother."

Swiping at the trickle of blood oozing from the corner of her mouth, Christa eased to her feet and followed Abdullah from the room, praying that he would keep his word and allow her to see Ahmed even if she couldn't speak to him.

Fedor fell into step behind them as Abdullah led the way through the palace, across the now dark and deserted courtyard and through a door at the opposite end that lead down a long corridor illuminated by flaming torches stuck into the wall at measured intervals. At length they stopped before a solid wooden door barred from the outside. Fedor lifted the heavy bar, and Christa stumbled as she was thrust into the black interior.

"If you're going to kill me," a voice said, "I suggest you do so quickly, else I fear the rats will deny you the pleasure. They are quite ferocious, you know." Though the voice sounded harsh with pain, it retained a semblance of arrogance and pride, and Abdullah gnashed his teeth in rage.

"A torch, Fedor!" he snapped curtly.

Within minutes the room flooded with light, bringing all the gruesome details into startling clarity. It was not a tiny, airless cell as Christa had first supposed, but a huge chamber bare but for several large bamboo cages lining two walls. In one of these cages huddled Ahmed, unable to stand erect or recline because of the restrictions imposed by its meager confines. He wore the same blood-stained robes she had last seen him in. When he turned slightly she could see that he had more recently been cruelly beaten, for cloth hung in tatters from his savaged back. Her tiny gasp brought Ahmed's haunted eyes in her direction.

"Dog dung!" he flung at his brother when he saw Christa staring at him in a state of shock. "Why do you bring her here?"

"I thought you'd be pleased to see that your woman has been well taken care of. She is delightful, and I've enjoyed her immensely," Abdullah smirked nastily.

"Christa, has he hurt you?" Ahmed asked anxiously. Though she tried to convey her feelings through her eyes, she remained mute. "Christa, my love, please answer me. What has my brother done to you?"

Abdullah chortled with dark humor. "Perhaps she is comparing us and finds you lacking. I am quite adept at lovemaking, you know. We've spent a pleasant afternoon in my private chamber, and now I understand fully your obsession with her. Christa, come here," he commanded, turning his attention from Ahmed to Christa.

Christa obeyed instantly, moving on rubbery legs until she stood at Abdullah's side. A small, inarticulate sound escaped her lips when Abdullah flipped aside the edges of her bolero, exposing her breasts. Idly, he began toying with them, all the while watching Ahmed's face for his reaction.

"Lovely, aren't they, Ahmed? So white and soft." With one finger he stroked a nipple, laughing delightedly as it puckered beneath his caress. "See how responsive she is to my touch after only a few hours under my tutelege?"

A low growl came from somewhere in the depths of Ahmed's soul as he watched Abdullah handle Christa's body intimately. "You depraved bastard!"

"Now you know what it feels like, brother, to want something so badly you ache. Does it hurt to watch someone take what is rightfully yours? I could take your whore right here on the floor and she'd submit willingly, but I don't want to dirty my robes. Perhaps one day soon I'll bring you to my room to observe us." He laughed demonically as Ahmed strained at the thick wooden bars caging him.

"Christa!" he beseeched. "Why won't you speak to me? Tell me what he's done to you."

Unable to bear the pain in Ahmed's green eyes, Christa bowed her head and allowed tears of grief and frustration to slide down her pale cheeks.

"Your woman pleases me well, brother, and the night is still young. You must excuse us if we leave so soon, for as you can see Christa is anxious for us to continue where we left off this afternoon." All the while he spoke he fondled her breasts, and for Ahmed's sake Christa dared not object.

"For the love of Allah, Abdullah, don't do this to her!" implored Ahmed, his pride all but deserting him when he saw Christa bending to the will of his sadistic brother. "Send her back to her family. She is gently bred and little prepared to deal with someone like you."

She deals well enough, Ahmed," smiled Abdullah suggestively. Then he turned to leave. "Sleep well, brother, and pleasant dreams. I'm sure yours won't be nearly as enjoyable as mine."

Lifting her head, Christa's blue eyes blazed into Ahmed's, conveying in that one look all the love she bore him. "Christa!" His agonized cry nearly caused his death as she opened her mouth to answer his tormented plea. From the corner of her eye, she saw Fedor draw the scimitar from his belt and start forward. Seized by panic, Christa whirled on her heel and silently followed Abdullah from the room, Ahmed's hoarse cry drumming in her brain.

Caressing the round softness of Christa's breasts while Ahmed looked on had only served to whet Abdullah's appetite for his silver-haired concubine. He could hardly wait to reach his bedchamber and sample the delights she had to offer. He wished he hadn't been so hasty in getting rid of all his father's women, but he had wanted no reminders of a past regime that had treated him so unfairly. Soon, though, he would have women aplenty to satisfy his special needs. In the meantime he bedded any of the servants who caught his eye. And now he had this proud beauty to satisfy his lust.

The moment she found herself alone with Abdullah, Christa knew exactly what to expect. He would rape her, of course, then force her to submit to his every whim. Not once, but whenever he wanted her. And judging from the paucity of his harem it would be often. Revulsion rose in her throat like bitter bile and Christa knew that the moment he touched her she would react violently.

Abdullah slid his hand down the long sweep of her hair and it came to rest on her breast. He fondled it for a moment, toying with the nipple before dropping to her hip, then to the soft mound between her legs. Christa grew giddy with disgust, making inarticulate sounds of protest deep in her throat. When his lips latched onto a nipple and his hard fingers probed for her warmth, a sickness welled up inside her that could not be quelled. Nor did she try.

It came from the depths of her being, brought forth by the indignities forced upon her. It spewed from her mouth, sour, acrid, and spilled over Abdullah's spotless white robes and onto the price-less carpet beneath their feet. Not even Abdullah's cry of horror could halt the flow of vomit that gushed forth from her throat.

Christa had no way of knowing Abdullah ab-horred sickness of any kind. His mother had been ravaged by a strange debilitating disease, and as a child he had watched the only person he ever loved waste away to mere nothing before she died, trans-formed from a vital, beautiful woman to an old hag before his eyes. He was ever vain in regard to his handsome features, and except for his crippled foot, prided himself on his looks. And he possessed an uncanny ability to remain healthy and disease free.

Now, seeing Christa being sick not only in front of him, but all over him, so terrorized him he shoved her away in abject revulsion.

"Whore!" he screamed hysterically. "Why didn't you tell me you were sick? Fedor!" he yelled, nearly demented with an unnatural fear. "Take this woman from my sight. Have Lenore see to her until she is recovered. Go!" he shrieked, growing more and more frenzied by the minute.

Christa's last sight of Abdullah was one of complete chaos. Like a madman, he had begun tearing off his soiled clothing, calling for the servants to prepare a bath and sterilize his chamber from top to bottom. His obsidian eyes glared at her with extreme disgust, and Christa was grateful to leave his loathsome presence.

14

To Christa's intense relief, she was allowed a week's respite to recuperate. During that time she was spared Abdullah's despised attention, and thanked God for her miraculous deliverance. But her relief did not extend to Ahmed, and she fretted over him constantly, deploring the hell of his existence. She pictured him as she had seen him last, in the cage that was his prison, unable to stand upright or lie flat, bruised, bleeding, his clothes torn and filthy. His hair hung in dirty hanks and he had been denied the barest essentials necessary for survival. His present state was a far cry from the proud, arrogant man who rode his Arabian stallion across the desert as if he had truly been spawned from the bowels of the harsh land he claimed as his own.

Christa had listened in disbelief when Lenore informed her that the cages were a harsh reminder of former times, when beys routinely imprisoned their heirs to keep them from claiming power prematurely from their sires. Perhaps, Christa reflected thoughtfully, Selim would have been well advised to keep Abdullah in one of those cages. But until Ahmed had been imprisoned there, they had remained unused for many years.

Christa's one consolation was that Elissa was allowed to remain near her, and they became inseparable. They spent their days together futilely planning their escape, for each knew such an event was unlikely to occur.

At the end of a week, the dreaded summons came from Abdullah. With a hint of compassion, Lenore told her she was to be brought to his bedchamber that night. Christa was bathed and her body massaged and annointed with fragrant oils and perfumes and dressed in a sheer caftan of pale blue silk the color of her eyes. Though outwardly calm, her mind rebelled, and her stomach roiled dangerously. What would Abdullah do if she became sick all over him again? she worried. Then her pondering came to an abrupt halt as Fedor appeared to take her to Abdullah.

Abdullah lounged on his sleeping couch propped up by pillows, dressed in a white caftan open to his navel. His crippled foot was carefully concealed by the long folds of material, and to all outward appearances there was nothing to detract from his masculine appeal—nothing but his cold, empty eyes.

"I have been informed that you are quite healthy and your body appears free from disease," he remarked, his voice deceptively gentle. "Lenore claims that naught but the strain of your journey ailed you, so I did not summon my physician to treat you. Because you are a foreigner unused to our climes and customs, I will forgive your—er, indiscretion. But now the time has come to use you for the purpose I originally intended. By this time, I suppose Ahmed is nearly demented imagining all the ways in which I am enjoying myself on your body each night. I fully intend to keep him alive— barely—until I present you to him with your belly swelling with my seed. No matter how long it takes."

Christa's horrified expression brought a satisfied smirk to Abdullah's thin lips. "You are evil and corrupt," she gasped, her throat nearly paralyzed with fear.

Abdullah smiled nastily. "Perhaps, but I can be kind and gentle when I want to be. Did you know your hair is like spun gold?" he murmured, letting it ripple through his fingers. "I am experienced in the ways of women and can please you if I so choose. Or I can take you cruelly, without mercy. Which will it be?"

"I'll not submit meekly," Christa warned him.

"Then prepare to suffer the consequences," Abdullah replied as he lunged for her.

Despite his disability he proved surprisingly strong and agile, and Christa found herself lifted bodily and hurled through the air to land on the couch, bouncing once before being pinned to the hard surface. The silken caftan ripped easily from her body and she felt the cruel, hot length of him probe between her thighs.

Without warning, Christa felt her stomach lurch, contracting, relaxing, then expelling its contents in a vile-smelling stream that seemed to go on forever. Jerking back in repulsion, Abdullah began shrieking like a maniac.

"Whore! Bitch! You did it again! Did my brother's touch sicken you as mine does?" Still heaving and retching violently, Christa hadn't the strength to reply.

"Fedor!" Abdullah screamed at the top of his lungs. "Take this bitch away! Then summon my physician to see to her. If there is nothing wrong with her but loathing for me, you are to use the bastinado. Twenty strokes should suffice. I will cure her of this aversion to my touch if it's the last thing I do."

Throwing a cover over Christa's nude form, Fedor hefted her across his wide shoulders and carried her from the room, depositing her roughly in the center of her own narrow bed. Almost instantly Elissa was beside her, bathing her face and offering a soothing drink to settle her stomach.

"What happened, Christa? You were gone such a short time. Did—did Abdullah hurt you?"

Christa shook her head, feeling something halfway between dread and hilarity. She couldn't believe she had vomited on Abdullah for the second time. She was convinced that the only thing that had saved her from death was that the bey needed her for a particular purpose.

"Oh, Elissa, it happened again," she wailed, distraught yet delighted. "The minute he put his hands on me, my stomach gave up its contents. Abdullah was absolutely furious. Perhaps something terrible is wrong with me that even I am not aware of."

"It seems to me you found the only method at your disposal to protect yourself," Elissa said soothingly, more than a little worried herself over Christa's propensity toward illness. "What is Abdullah going to do? Twice now you've thwarted him from his purpose."

"I'm to be seen by his physician, then punished with the bastinado. Twenty strokes," she shuddered. Elissa groaned in sympathy.

A few minutes later the doctor shuffled in and ordered Elissa outside. A kindly old man whose years sat heavily upon his shoulders, Doctor Sayid had served as physician to Selim for many years.

Because of his great knowledge of healing, Abdullah was wise enough to retain the learned man. Truth to tell, Doctor Sayid held little love for the new bey, though he went about his job silently and efficiently. He harbored much compassion in his heart for Ahmed, whom he came to know well during the lad's formative years, and he had asked permission to treat him for his wounds, which Abdullah saw fit to deny. Unwilling to sit back and do nothing, Sayid had secretly bribed a guard to gain access to Ahmed and was appalled by his deplorable condition. There was little he could do to relieve his suffering except to treat his many wounds and leave a vial of liquid to ease the pain.

When Doctor Sayid heard about Christa, his kindly heart filled with pity and he wracked his brain for a way to help the defenseless woman. He didn't fear for himself, for he was old and death held no threat for him. He was told the terrible thing that happened when the bey had attempted to bed his concubine—happened twice, in fact—and he had been ordered to examine Christa for signs of disease. He'd almost rather find her ravaged by some sickness than to see her suffer at Abdullah's cruel hands.

Christa regarded the doctor warily when he sat down beside her and explained his mission. Nodding her understanding, she nonetheless squirmed in embarrassment when he began an internal examination followed by probing, intimate questions. She was still flushed when he finished and sat back, peering at her with great thoughtfulness.

"Your condition is not serious," he finally revealed, "nor life-threatening. I suspect it is your strong aversion for Abdullah that causes you to retch the moment he lays hands on you. I can find no sign of disease or ill health."

Christa shuddered, well aware of her fate once

Abdullah learned of the doctor's findings. "I cannot abide his vile touch."

The doctor studied her a long time before coming to a conclusion. "I want you to think of me as a friend," he confided in a low voice. "I have been taxing my brain for a way to protect you from Abdullah, if that's what you want."

Christa regarded the kindly doctor with suspicion. "Why? Why would you help me?"

"Because I loved and respected Selim, and were he alive I know he would not allow Abdullah to abuse you. Do you love Ahmed?"

Christa nodded slowly. "With all my heart."

His next words did not offend her, though she knew they should. "You were Ahmed's concubine?"

"I . . . we were . . . lovers."

"What I suggest might shock you, but if you agree you will be granted a temporary reprieve from Abdullah's salacious intent."

"Temporary?"

"A few months at the most. But possibly enough time to allow me to convince the bey to petition your family for ransom. Will you hear me out?"

What choice did she have? Christa reflected glumly. So far the elderly doctor had offered the only hope, albeit a temporary one, in her struggle to outwit Abdullah. Anything was preferable to submitting to the bey's base desires. At length, she said, "Tell me, doctor. I'll agree to anything that will save me and help Ahmed."

"Ah, my child, I know not if what I suggest will help Ahmed, but it can do him no harm. As you have learned, Abdullah has an unnatural fear of sickness, no matter what form it takes. Do you follow me, child?"

Wrinkling her brow, Christa replied, "I—I

think so. Will you tell him I have some dread disease?"

"I wish it were that simple. If I did, he wouldn't hesitate to call in another physician to verify my diagnosis."

"Then what . . . ?"

"With your consent I will tell him you are pregnant." He hesitated but a moment when Christa registered shock, then quickly continued. "It is a natural condition, and he trusts me enough to accept my word."

"But what happens when he finds I'm not expecting a child? That is not something so easily hidden."

"Once I advise him of your condition, he's sure to rant and rave for a short time, but knowing Abdullah as I do, he'll soon turn it to his own advantage. He'll also lose interest in you when I tell him you are one of those unfortunate women who must spend most of their time in bed or suffer the consequences. And since he's twice experienced the effects of your illness, he'll shun you like the plague."

"What happens when he finds out the truth? What then? Does your life mean so little to you?"

Doctor Sayid shrugged his frail shoulders. "I am an old man and at the end of my life's cycle. Besides, I have good reason to believe Abdullah will look with favor upon my plea to accept ransom for you. He will not want you while another man's child swells your belly. If you wear concealing clothes he will not suspect our duplicity."

"But what about Ahmed? How can I save myself and leave Ahmed to Abdullah's mercy?"

The doctor's careworn face held a look of pity for Christa. "I will do what I can for the prince, my child, but don't expect miracles. Where Ahmed is concerned, Abdullah is implacable. I am well enough acquainted with Ahmed to know he would want you away from his brother. For his sake you must agree to my plan."

After several long, tense minutes of painful contemplation, Christa acquiesced. "I will do as you say, doctor."

"Then you must promise to tell no one, my child. Of necessity this secret must remain between you and me."

"But Elissa—"

"No. No one. A single slip would prove too costly. Do you agree?"

"If that's the way it must be, Doctor Sayid, then so be it."

"What did you say, old man?" demanded Abdullah, a ferocious scowl darkening his face. "I'll have you flogged if you're lying to me!"

"I am certain, Lord Abdullah," Sayid insisted, bowing low. "The lady Christa is breeding."

"So the bitch is carrying my brother's whelp. You're absolutely certain?" he questioned sharply. "When?"

"I have been a doctor for many years, but as to when I cannot be certain, for the lady conceived only a few weeks ago."

"Leave me! I must think on this," Abdullah ordered curtly. Praising Allah for Abdullah's faith in him, Sayid sidled from the room.

Pacing back and forth in his uneven gait, Abdullah considered carefully all the ramifications of this new development. It would certainly pose no problem, given Sayid's knowledge of medicine, to have her aborted. But was that wise? He could order both her and Ahmed put to death. But if he did, his pleasure would be shortlived. He had hoped to prolong Ahmed's suffering by using Christa; he wanted no quick death for his brother.

Then, with sudden inspiration, the perfect solution came to him. Why not use the lady's pregnancy to his own advantage? How clever of him to think of it. What better way to taunt and torture Ahmed than to cajole him into believing what he, Abdullah, wanted him to believe?

"It should be no time at all before your lady swells with my seed," Abdullah goaded cruelly. Nearly two weeks had passed since he had last seen Ahmed. "I plow her nightly, often more than once, and I have proof my seed is potent. I sired two children on our father's concubines before they were sold to brothels. When she is nicely rounded with my child, I will bring her to you."

Ahmed glared at his brother with intense loathing. Though half-starved, he had not been beaten again. Fending off the rats kept him engaged a good share of the time, but long hours of boredom drove him to the brink of insanity. Thoughts of Christa occupied his mind and his heart. In his mind's eye he pictured her reluctantly submitting to Abdullah, enduring. Pregnant. Allah preserve him! He silently beseeched. How could such an obscenity be visited upon his beloved?

"Have you nothing to say, Ahmed?" Abdullah taunted. "Or do you no longer care about your whore?"

"Never doubt my feelings for Christa," Ahmed grated out, his voice harsh with emotion. "Someday, somehow, you'll pay dearly for your vile deeds. Surely our father is turning in his grave over your despicable conduct."

Abdullah tilted his head back and laughed until tears came to his eyes. Wiping them away with a spotless sleeve, he leveled a look of pure hatred on Ahmed and confessed, "Our estimable father is exactly where I put him. And your slut of a mother followed him in quick order." After delivering that bombshell he turned and left, Ahmed's tortured cry following in his wake.

This scene was to repeat itself nearly every day for the next two months, slowly driving Ahmed out of his mind. When Abdullah sensed his brother could stand no more, he would retreat, only to reappear the next day to continue his verbal torture.

Once Abdullah was made aware of Christa's supposed pregnancy, she awaited the heavy hand of his judgment. When no punishment was forthcoming, she allowed herself a glimmer of hope. Perhaps Doctor Sayid was right, and the bey had forgotten about her. She saw the doctor from time to time and learned he was working tirelessly in her behalf. Already Abdullah was half convinced to write to her family and ask for ransom.

Waited on hand and foot by both Lenore and Elissa, Christa wanted for nothing. Evidently, Abdullah's orders were to cosset and care for her. Stuffed with rich food, groomed and pampered, she never looked better. Her only regret was that she was forced to deceive her friends, especially Elissa. But she trusted Doctor Sayid and would not willingly jeopardize his position or his life. And so the hoax continued, with no one the wiser. But for how long?

Even though her own situation had eased considerably, Christa still worried about Ahmed. From Lenore, her only source of information, she learned that Ahmed still lived and had been moved from the cage to a small cell, which allowed him to move around with slightly more comfort. This concession was insisted upon by Doctor Sayid, who voiced strenuous objections to Ahmed's deplorable living conditions, saying that Ahmed could not possibly survive in such abject misery. Not yet ready for

Ahmed's demise, Abdullah heeded the physician's words and ordered him provided with a room offering meager comforts, though somewhat improved over that which he had previously occupied.

One day Christa was startled to find Abdullah standing in the doorway to her room, his piercing eyes probing beneath her encompassing robe. "Doctor Sayid tells me your pregnancy is progressing well," he said with a hint of mockery.

Warily, Christa nodded. "May I ask what you plan for me?"

"No you may not." Abdullah's eyes roamed her slim figure, seeking beneath her caftan. At length, he ordered, "Take off your robe."

"No! You wouldn't!" she gasped. "Not now!"

"I no longer desire you in that way," he snapped, his lip curling with disgust. "I have found another purpose for you, which I will explain later. All I wish now is to look at my brother's child growing within your womb. Bare yourself."

Well aware of his cruelty when aroused to anger, and quaking in fear lest he discover her deception, Christa complied. Unfastening her single garment she let it drop in a silken puddle at her feet. Abdullah stared at her, frowning uncertainly. "You are far too slim. Aren't you eating? I will have the servants punished for not preparing food to your liking. How can I expect Ahmed to believe you are with child when your belly does not swell?"

"It is so with women in my family," Christa said guardedly. "Our pregnancy is usually far advanced before we show our condition." She held her breath while Abdullah mulled over her answer. A ragged sigh trembled from her lips when he appeared to accept her words.

"Cover yourself," he abruptly ordered as if already bored with the sight of bared flesh. "You don't excite me in that condition. As you already know I now have several women younger and more beautiful than you to fill my needs."

It was true. During the past two months, girls had begun arriving almost daily, all young virgins eager to please their master. Christa and Elissa kept strictly to themselves, mingling little with the new arrivals. If they were curious about Christa or her position in the harem, they were too young and inexperienced to ask.

As Christa waited for Abdullah to leave her room, she saw something in his attitude change, and grew alert. She cared little for the sly, considering way he looked at her. "Would you like to see Ahmed again?"

His words startled her and she went still, all her nerve endings tingling in response. "You'd let me?" Her voice was soft and incredulous.

"Why not, since Ahmed will be with us but a short time longer. I am not so heartless as you seem to think. I will allow him to bid you good-bye."

"Since when have you cared for the feelings of others?" she jeered.

Sliding her a quelling look, Abdullah stipulated, "Of course you must adhere to the same rules as before. You will agree with everything I say and not speak unless I order you to do so."

"But that's cruel! How could you ask that of me?" She vividly recalled Ahmed's stricken eyes when she steadfastly refused to talk to him. Would it hurt more to go to him under the same restrictions, she reflected, or not see him at all? The decision was easy and swift in coming. She had to see Ahmed again. Abruptly she recalled Abdullah's words a moment ago. "What do you mean, Ahmed will not be with us much longer? Are you going to kill him?"

"In good time you will hear my plans for you as well as for Ahmed. Do you agree to my terms? As before, Fedor will stand by in the unlikely event you break your promise."

Oh, God, to see Ahmed and not speak to or touch him would be exquisite torture, Christa agonized. But to not see him at all constituted a torture beyond bearing. She nodded solemnly. "I agree."

"Come along, then, let's get this over with." There was such a satisfied smile on his face that a snake of fear twisted around her heart. It wasn't difficult to imagine what a man like Abdullah had in mind, and more than likely it involved her supposed pregnancy.

Abdullah led her down several corridors, across the courtyard and into another building, but not the same one as before where the cages were kept. He halted before a heavy door and gave Christa an assessing look. "It just occurred to me that my purpose would be better served if I allowed you to speak." A look of incredible joy warmed her face until he added, "But only to add your agreement to everything I say."

"Why should I?" Christa rebelled. "No matter what I do, you will kill Ahmed."

"But you're wrong. I don't intend to kill him at all. See, I'm not such an ogre after all."

"But you said—"

"All I said was that Ahmed wouldn't be with us much longer, not that I intended to end his life. The only thing that will change my mind is your refusal to agree with every word I utter. Then Ahmed will be slain instantly."

"Why should I trust you?"

"You have no choice."

"If I comply with your wishes, you'll spare his life?"

"Yes."

"Does that mean you'll let him go?" Christa asked hopefully.

A look of such cunning crossed Abdullah's face that all Christa's senses reeled in alarm. "You lie! You're going to torture him and let him rot in prison! Knowing Ahmed as I do, he would prefer death to what you plan."

"In a few minutes you'll both know my plans," Abdullah revealed with cold deliberation. "But I assure you, I will neither kill nor torture him, and tomorrow he will be gone."

Christa stared, wanting to put more into his words than he intended. Everything considered, she had no real choice but to obey Abdullah. Ahmed deserved a chance for survival, no matter how slim, no matter what she had to agree to. At length, she nodded her acquiescence and Abdullah moved to the thick door, unlatching it from the outside and swinging it open on rusty hinges. Ahmed sat in a corner, his head buried in crossed arms resting on upraised knees. As the door flung open, his head tilted upward, his eyes blinking rapidly in the unaccustomed light. To Christa those green orbs burned as bright as two flames of emerald fire blazing with hate and defiance.

"What have you come to taunt me with today, Abdullah?" he grated harshly. "Why don't you just put an end to all this?"

"What, and deny me my meager pleasure?" Abdullah laughed cruelly. "Or my revenge?"

At that moment Ahmed spied Christa as she stepped out from behind Abdullah. "Christa! Oh, love, is it really you? Just knowing you are well is a gift I hadn't expected."

"Ahmed!" Christa called out, resisting the urge to run into his outstretched arms as he awkwardly pushed himself to his feet. But a quick glance at Abdullah warned her such an act would prove fatal.

"I knew you'd want to see my concubine one last time so you might bid her good-bye." Abdullah gestured grandly toward Christa. "Just to prove I'm not completely heartless. Needless to say, brother, I never thought to see the day a woman could bring you to your knees. You were always such an arrogant bastard."

Ahmed heard nothing but the word "goodbye." Was there a spark of humanity still alive somewhere in his brother's black heart? "Are you sending Christa back to her family?" he asked, his hopes spiraling, only to have them dashed to the ground by Abdullah's reply.

"Why would I send my favorite away," he asked with mock puzzlement, "when she pleases me so well? She has proved a quick breeder, for already her belly swells with my seed."

"No! No, you lie!" screamed Ahmed, outraged.

Abdullah's answer was to calmly turn and draw Christa to his side, his arm surrounding her possessively. A low growl more animal than human ripped from Ahmed's throat as he lunged forward, his hands going for Abdullah's neck before he was abruptly brought to his knees by the short chain attached to one ankle. Defeat riding him, he lay panting where he fell, head lowered, striking his fists against the filth-littered floor.

"Christa," he begged, his trembling voice filled with a terrible agony, "tell me it isn't true. Please love, tell me Abdullah is lying."

"Tell him," Abdullah ordered, black eyes narrowed in warning as his fingers bit into her tender flesh. "Ease my brother's mind and put him out of his misery."

Christa remained mute, growing faint with the knowledge of the incredible cruelty Abdullah was inflicting upon Ahmed. The man was worse than insane. From the corner of her eye, she saw Fedor look to Abdullah for orders. Recognizing the menace immediately, Christa knew she would agree to anything Abdullah said if it meant preserving Ahmed's life, no matter how much her words might hurt the man she loved.

"It's true, Ahmed," she whispered, her voice low and tremulous in the sudden stillness.

"Louder," Abdullah growled.

"For God's sake, have you no mercy?" Christa implored. "It's true! What more do you want?"

All the blood drained from Ahmed's already pale face, and he drooped dejectedly. Never had he experienced such overwhelming defeat. It was as if all the meaning had gone out of his life. But to his credit, he saw it not as a blight against Christa but as an obscenity forced upon her. When he spoke, his words were devoid of all emotion, for there was none left in him.

"Don't despair, love, it's not your fault. One day Abdullah will pay for his depravity. The only way he'll escape my vengeance is by killing me, for if he doesn't I will find a way to avenge your honor."

"Kill you?" Abdullah laughed harshly. "As I said before, I brought Christa here so you might bid her good-bye."

"For some reason your words bring me little comfort," Ahmed scoffed. "If you don't intend to end my life, I assume you've devised another means of punishment."

"How astute of you, little brother," Abdullah grinned, vastly pleased with himself. "Death is too easily accomplished. What I have in mind is far more subtle, yet knowing you and your love for freedom, a punishment you will view as worse than death.

"Tomorrow at dawn, Captain Hadji, along with fifty Janissaries, will take you to Algiers, where you will be sold to the Spanish as a slave. Think on it, brother. The rest of your life spent digging in some colonial gold mine. But do not fear, Ahmed, I hear few men live lengthy lives under the ghastly conditions imposed by the Spanish, so no doubt your suffering will be of short duration."

"Bastard!" spat Ahmed. "Inhuman bastard! Do you think I will submit meekly to slavery? I will escape, you can count on it. When I do, expect me to return for Christa."

"You'll be wasting your time, Ahmed, for I doubt Christa would return with you in the unlikely event you manage to free yourself. Being the kind of woman she is, she would not leave without her child, and he will be too well guarded for that to happen."

Ahmed regarded Christa uncertainly. Would she love Abdullah's child? The answer came to him in a rush of pain so intense he clutched at his stomach as it rose to meet his heart. The child would be half hers—of course she would love it. Nor would she consent to leave without it.

"Explain your feelings to Ahmed, woman," Abdullah commanded.

Licking her lips, Christa turned stricken eyes on Ahmed. Though she despised deceiving him she did so now to save his life. "I . . . I would not willingly give up my child, Ahmed." She did not add that she would rather die than conceive any child but his.

Consumed by misery and overwhelmed by jealousy, Ahmed could expect no less from her. "I swear I'll escape and come back for you, my love," he promised rashly. "Trust me. I'll not leave your child behind."

"No!" Christa cried, distraught. For him to return for any reason would bring about his death.

"Listen to my woman, Ahmed, for if by some miracle you do escape the Spanish, only death awaits you in Constantine. Christa will be safe as long as she continues to please me. Her son could rule Constantine. If the child is a girl, she will be groomed to warm the bed of one of the nomad sheikhs." A small cry of distress escaped Christa's lips, which went unheeded.

"Christa has proved such an excellent breeder that I fully expect her to produce a child a year. After nine or ten, her beauty will have faded and she will be of no further use to me. By then she will be useful only in the cribs that line the waterfront. Or perhaps," he added slyly, "I might be persuaded to let her go free."

"Do you think I could leave here and put Christa out of my mind?" Ahmed spat contemptuously.

"I should hope not," Abdullah replied, "or my revenge wouldn't be half so pleasurable. I want you to think of her constantly; I want thoughts of her yielding to me consuming your every breath. I want you to suffer the pangs of hell each time she bears me another child, just as I suffered each time our father showed his preference for you."

Straining against the chain that kept him from Abdullah's throat, Ahmed went crazy, exploding in a frenzy of unrelenting fury. But in the end it gained him nothing, for Abdullah merely nodded to Fedor, whose huge fist put a quick end to all Ahmed's struggles. When Christa tried to go to him, Abdullah's restraining hand prevented it, and she began to weep bitter tears.

"If he continued in that manner he would surely hurt himself," Abdullah remarked dispassionately as he gazed at Ahmed's still form. "A quick death for my brother is not what I planned. I want him to live a long, long time under the yoke of slavery. His pride and lust for life will serve him well in years to come, but little by little his spirit will die until he is but a shell of his former self, until he yearns for the release only death can bring him."

"No!" cried Christa vehemently, her eyes dark with loathing. "You don't know Ahmed if you think to destroy him so easily."

"You are mistaken, lady," he contradicted, pleased with his own cunning. "You are the one responsible for his downfall. The moment I discovered Ahmed's love for you, it was only a matter of time before his ultimate destruction. Your lovely body provided the perfect weapon."

15

Later, after telling Elissa all that had transpired, Christa succumbed to the misery that plagued her, as tears flowed in torrents down her pale cheeks. By lying, she had given credit to Abdullah's words and caused Ahmed more pain than he had ever known. Yet, had she blurted out the truth, her love would now be dead. At least this way a slim chance for a miracle existed, and perhaps he would find a way to free himself. She prayed she had been successful in making him realize it would be dangerous and foolish to dwell on her fate. If she could see him one last time, she would still employ all her persuasive powers to prevent him from returning to Constantine for her should the impossible happen and he escape the Spanish.

Christa felt convinced that her own dismal future was just as Abdullah described. But she refused to give up all hope. She would bide her time, persevere, and then when Abdullah least expected it . . .

"Christa, are you asleep?" asked Elissa, bursting into the room, her dark eyes dancing with excitement.

"No, I'm not sleeping, Elissa," Christa replied dully, wiping her hand over her damp cheeks. "I can't sleep. Not after I learned what Abdullah has planned for Ahmed. Not after the way I added to his misery."

"You mustn't cry, Christa, you might do your baby harm."

Christa flushed guiltily. No matter what Doctor Sayid said, she could no longer pretend to her friend that she was carrying Ahmed's child. It just wasn't right. "Elissa, I can no longer lie to you," she confessed. "I am not really pregnant. It was just a ruse devised by Doctor Sayid to keep me out of Abdullah's bed, and it worked. But it won't be long before Abdullah begins to suspect the truth. Unless the doctor convinces him to accept ransom for me."

Elissa's eyes grew round with shock. "I—I never suspected," she gasped. "Of course it did occur to me that you were much too slim. Do you think Doctor Sayid can influence Abdullah in your behalf?"

"I . . . I don't know. I can only hope he does, and soon. But in the meantime we must continue with this deception. No one is to guess otherwise."

"You can trust me," Elissa confided. "We must think positively. Doctor Sayid is an old and wise man who certainly knows what he is about. Besides"—she smiled mysteriously—"I have just the thing to cheer you up." It was obvious she could scarcely contain her exhilaration, and Christa's attention sharpened.

"Have you learned something, Elissa? Something about Ahmed?"

"Well, not exactly, but—oh, Christa, would you like to see Ahmed before he is sent away?"

"See—! Elissa, surely you jest. How is that possible?"

"I bribed the guard," Elissa said evasively, dropping her eyes to study the toe of her slipper.

"With what? You have nothing of value. Nor do I. What could you possibly—oh, no, not that!" Tears flooded her eyes as she suddenly realized the sacrifice Elissa had made in her behalf. "I would never have asked that of you."

"It is done, Christa," Elissa said softly. "It wasn't so bad. Nothing like when the Janissaries . . ." Her voice trailed off. "I'll come for you after midnight. The palace will be sleeping and no one will be expecting you to slip out through the courtyard. Rashid will be waiting for us, but he stipulated you can stay with Ahmed no longer than an hour."

"Rashid?"

"The Janissary I . . . bribed."

"I'm sorry, Elissa."

"I told you, it wasn't so bad," Elissa repeated shortly. "Rest now, Christa. I will come for you when it's time."

Completely shrouded in a dark robe, Christa stepped from the shadows, pausing before the building housing Ahmed. She and Elissa had managed to elude the two guards patroling the courtyard, yet it seemed impossible that her wish to see Ahmed alone was about to be realized. Though deceit was not part of her nature, she had reached the painful decision not to relieve Ahmed of the belief that she carried Abdullah's child. If Ahmed knew the truth, he would stop at nothing to return to Constantine one day, and in so doing sacrifice his life. She couldn't live with the knowledge that she was directly responsible for his death. Elissa had paid dearly for this opportunity, and Christa was determined to convince Ahmed in the short space of an hour to forget her. His very life depended on it.

Suddenly a shadow loomed up before her, and Elissa's frantic whisper set her nerves ajar. "It's Rashid. He will let you in. Remember, one hour."

Slanting Elissa a meaningful look, Rashid opened the door and Christa stepped quietly inside. The sound of the latch clicking into place roused Ahmed from his troubled dreams. Moonlight filtered in through the single barred window high in the wall to paint the dingy interior with a soft glow.

"Did Abdullah send you to torture me before my leaving in the morning?" His haunted voice, hollow and devoid of emotion, tore at her heart. "It matters little. He's already done his worst, there's nothing left save to order my death. The way I feel now, I would welcome it."

"Ahmed." The soft appeal in her voice somehow pierced his misery.

"Allah help me!" he cried, his breath caught on a sob. "Go away, woman! Has my brother devised some new kind of torment? Or am I dreaming?"

"You're not dreaming, my love. I had to see you one last time."

"Christa!" he moaned, jerking to his feet. "How—?"

"Elissa arranged it," she whispered, stepping into his embrace.

"Elissa is in Constantine with you?"

"We've been together all this time. And we've become close friends. I thank God for her."

A low animal sound was torn from the back of his throat as he seized her lips, crushing her fiercely, his mouth moving with exquisite slowness over hers. The longing, the tenderness, the sweetness of his kiss touched Christa deeply, and she gave herself unstintingly, knowing it would be the last time. Each passing minute ticked loudly in her brain, making her increasingly aware that their time together was drastically limited.

"I haven't much time, Ahmed. Please listen carefully," Christa pleaded breathlessly.

"Before you say anything, I want you to know I don't blame you for—for what's happened to you," Ahmed interjected. "Abdullah is insane. Has he been cruel to you? I couldn't bear it if—"

"He hasn't hurt me, Ahmed, truly."

"No, I don't suppose he has," he mused. "Abdullah always had a fine appreciation of beauty. But tonight none of that matters. I want to make love to you. Give me something to take with me, to hold on to for all the lonely tomorrows we are apart."

"Ahmed, I'd like nothing better, but—"

"Are you afraid I'll harm the baby?" Though it hurt him dreadfully to mention Abdullah's child growing beneath her heart, Ahmed forced himself to acknowledge that another man had left his mark on her as he never had.

"No!" Christa cried, anxious to ease his fears. "It's not that. It's just that we have so much to say and so little time before we are separated—perhaps forever."

"Oh, my love," Ahmed murmured, "never doubt that I'll find a way for us to be together. No obstacle is too great, no barrier too high. Don't spoil this brief time together with meaningless words. Let me demonstrate my love in the way we both long for."

Carefully, he laid her down on the pallet of straw, changed daily by order of Doctor Sayid, and undressed her with trembling fingers. It had been so long he felt like an untried boy with his first

woman. Pale moonbeams touched her body with
gold and gilded her hair to shimmering silver. Her
breasts filled his hand to overflowing as he tenderly
kissed her nipples, feeling them grow erect against
his tongue.

Sliding his mouth along her ribcage, he paused
for a heartbreaking moment when he encountered
the nonexistent bulge of her stomach. She was still
so slim, it was hard to believe a child grew inside
her. Inwardly he cringed, his rage at Abdullah so
great it nearly destroyed him. It almost tore him to
shreds to think that his brother possessed at will
the woman he loved.

Sensing his sudden withdrawal, Christa mis-
took his hesitation for revulsion, and struggled to
rise. "No, love, it's not you I'm angry at, it's
Abdullah. I could kill him for what he's done to
you."

Swallowing the urge to blurt out the truth,
Christa found his lips, drowning his sadness in a
kiss that conveyed what mere words failed to do.
His hands slipped lower, caressing the curve of her
hips, the soft skin between her thighs. His mouth
followed, blazing a trail of fire that ignited her
senses and fed her passion with a passion of his
own.

Sliding his fingers upward he encountered the
soft warmth beneath the pale forest nestled at the
union of her thighs. As his fingers worked their way
downward, his lips soon followed. Christa stiffened, crying out softly at the intimate invasion.

Gripping her hips in his hands, he made an
inarticulate sound of uncontrolled passion when
his mouth found her and his tongue possessed her.
Her body writhed and pressed upward, her soft
sounds of pleasure urging him on. Tenderly, lovingly, his tongue worked its magic. And then raw
ecstasy seized her as the contractions began deep in

the pit of her stomach. Still Ahmed did not stop, not until the last rapturous spasm ceased.

"Nothing could change that, sweet siren," Ahmed vowed, breathing raggedly. "Your response to me is unique. Does Abdullah make you cry out in delight as I have just done?" he wanted to know, hating himself for giving voice to his jealousy. Was it truly necessary for him to know how Christa responded to another man? Did he need that kind of subtle torture?

"You are the only one, Ahmed," Christa assured him. "Only you have the power to take me to glory."

"Allah be praised," he whispered, lifting her hips and sliding full and deep inside her, his desire a hard throbbing need of tempered steel sheathed in silk. Christa thrust against him, unaware that he had removed his clothing until bare flesh touched and clung. He groaned in intense pleasure as her moist tightness welcomed him, closing around him in an intimate massage.

"If I died tomorrow, I would go to my reward a happy man," he gasped, sliding nearly all the way out before sheathing himself fully again.

The gentle rocking began as his tongue whispered across her parted lips, skimmed her teeth, then took pleasure in the heady taste of her full lips. She grew dizzy as the bright flame of desire swiftly ignited into a blazing ecstasy, bringing a low moan of rapture to her lips.

Suddenly he was no longer able to control his need as he thrust into her again and again, riding her with a savage urgency that rendered all thought impossible. Logic and reason, the present and future, all ceased to exist. Then he felt the great storm within him break and fill him with shuddering spasms of pleasure. Driven higher and higher by his throbbing thrusts, Christa once again experienced a climax so sublime it bordered on pain, a pain she gladly welcomed.

Slowly regaining her senses, Christa became achingly aware that her time with Ahmed was swiftly drawing to an end and she had yet to tell him what was in her heart. She opened her mouth to speak, but Ahmed shushed her with a tender kiss. "Don't give up hope, my love. Never doubt my ability to find my way back to you."

"No, Ahmed, you musn't!" A look of such incredulity creased his features that she hastily added, "No matter how much I might desire it, you must never return to Constantine."

"Surely you jest. Do you expect me to forget you once I leave here?"

"You'll have trouble enough surviving on that Spanish slaver without having me to worry about. Abdullah won't harm me. Not now. He has no reason to. I want your promise, Ahmed, that even should you somehow manage to escape, you won't return to Constantine."

"Are you out of your mind?" he cried, shocked. "The thought of one day getting you away from Abdullah is all that will keep me from going insane."

Gritting her teeth in frustration, Christa shook her head furiously. "No, no, no! I won't have your death on my conscience! When you leave here, you must not look back. It's for your own good. You must survive, my love, and go to England, where you will be safe. Your grandfather will welcome you, and you can begin life anew. Forget me, my love. Even if Abdullah relents and lets me go free, I will return to my family and marry Brian." Lies! Lies! She could never marry Brian.

Now it was Ahmed's turn to protest, and he did so vigorously. After the storm died, he said, "I have no life without you. Could you forget me so easily?"

"I will never forget you. I will love you forever. I'm giving you back your life, don't you see? If you return for me, my sacrifice will have no meaning. Make your own life, Ahmed, and I will make mine. I release you from any vow made to me concerning our future. Had I been wiser, I would have recognized from the beginning that we had no future together."

"You don't know what you're saying!" Ahmed flung out angrily. "You're hurt and distraught over being made pregnant by my brother."

"Yes, yes," agreed Christa readily, grasping at straws. "I won't leave my child or children behind, no matter who sired them or how they were conceived. So you can see all this talk is useless. I want your promise, Ahmed. If you escape the Spanish, I want you to think only of yourself, forget I exist."

Silence.

"Ahmed, please, your promise! Time grows short, and I want you to love me again before I leave this room. Give me your promise!"

She was becoming so distraught that Ahmed feared for her sanity and decided to agree even if it meant lying. Besides, he had grown hard and throbbing again, swelling instantly with her soft pleas to love her once more. She was perilously close to tears when Ahmed said, "I promise." A bevy of conflicting emotions crossed her face, the strongest of which was relief.

Grasping her by the waist, Ahmed lifted her above him and then slowly sat her astride him. With a sob of joy she lowered herself onto his great length, her nails grazing the taut flesh of his shoulders. Her swollen breasts brushed his lips and he took an exquisitely sensitive nipple in his mouth, sucking vigorously as gasp after gasp sighed from her parted lips. He wanted to make love to her slowly, bring her to shuddering release time after time, but his fierce need commanded his speed. All too soon, urgency overtook him and together they soared to a world where no one dared interfere.

Except for Elissa, whose soft plea called them back to painful reality. "Christa, you must leave now. Your hour is up, and it will go hard on Rashid if we are discovered."

"I'm coming," replied Christa softly, scrambling for her caftan. She dressed swiftly, not daring to look at Ahmed for fear she'd relent and tell him the truth. Should he even suspect she was lying about being pregnant, neither heaven nor hell would keep him from returning to Constantine once he escaped the Spaniards. And it never entered her mind that he wouldn't escape one day.

She turned to him, memorizing the planes and lines of his strong face, the muscular contours of his body, hoping it was enough to last her a lifetime, yet knowing it was not.

"Christa," an urgent voice disrupted her thoughts. "Please hurry!"

Flinging herself into Ahmed's arms, she clung to him a moment longer, their lips reluctant to part. "Remember your promise, my love," she breathed against his mouth. Then she was gone, leaving him bereft, with nothing but the memory of their joining and the taste and smell of her surrounding his senses.

As Christa slipped through the door, she did not hear Ahmed's tortured words. "The day I die will be the day I forget you! Even then your memory will follow me to eternity. We will meet again, my love, for kismet has willed it."

* * *

Lost in the deep depression, Christa lay listlessly in bed. She had reached her room without mishap after seeing Ahmed, but now, as scarlet streams stained the eastern sky, she instinctively knew he was gone. She felt his loss as acutely as if someone had twisted a knife in her heart. All that remained was the memory of his love. Not even Elissa was successful in raising her flagging spirits as the days passed.

When the summons came from Abdullah nearly a week later, Christa knew a fear more terrible than any she'd ever experienced before. Had the bey somehow discovered her secret? Was she destined to suffer an ignominious death away from all her loved ones? Prepared for the worst, Christa dressed in flowing robes and followed Fedor to a room that looked to be a reception area. Squaring her small shoulders she stepped into the room, the sound of the door closing behind her lost in the thumping of her heart.

To her everlasting relief, Abdullah was nowhere in sight. In fact, she assumed she was alone until the tall, slim figure of a man dressed in western attire stepped into view from the patio where evidently he had been waiting. The sunlight behind him prevented her from making out his features, but as he slowly advanced, his face came into focus, and with it instant recognition.

"Brian! Dear Lord, is it really you?"

"Christa, thank God I've found you!" Brian Kent exclaimed as his brown eyes skimmed assessingly over her slim figure concealed beneath her robe. She was more beautiful than ever, he reflected, yet something about her seemed different. She appeared to have matured in a way that enhanced her already spectacular beauty.

Dressed in a flowing caftan of turquoise shot

with silver, her pale gold hair falling nearly to her waist, Brian thought her stunning. Had the bey already made a woman of her? he speculated bitterly. What man wouldn't, given the opportunity. To look at her was to desire her, and the bey looked to be a man with normal male appetites, one who partook freely and extensively of female flesh. And Christa had been his captive many months. Regretfully, Brian could no longer expect her to be virginal.

"Brian, how did you know where to find me?" Christa asked, flinging herself exuberantly into his arms. Seeing Brian here, when she needed him most, was like an answer to a prayer. She was so grateful to behold a familiar face from her former life that she was shaking with joy, laughing and crying at the same time.

"Didn't you know?" Brian asked, puzzled. "Surely Abdullah bey told you he's been negotiating with your father for your release. The ransom demanded for your safe return was quite high, and it's taken your father some time to raise it."

"N . . . no, I had no idea," stammered Christa, clutching at Brian for support. All this came as quite a shock and must have been the direct result of Doctor Sayid's efforts on her behalf, she realized with a surge of gladness. She'd forever bless that kindly, compassionate man.

"Are you all right, my dear?" Brian asked solicitously. "Has the bey hurt you in any way? He swore that you were unharmed and in good health."

"I'm fine, Brian. Abdullah is a cruel man, but he hasn't physically harmed me," Christa assured him, suddenly aware of the calculating look he leveled at her. "Where is my father? Why didn't he come for me? He's all right, isn't he?" she asked anxiously.

"Your father is well, Christa," Brian was quick to respond. "It's your mother who is ill. She hasn't been well since they learned you were taken by pirates, and your father was reluctant to leave her with no one but servants to care for her. I offered to come in his stead. He was torn between duty to your mother and his desire to come to Constantine to deal with Abdullah. I finally persuaded him that his first duty was to his wife and he reluctantly agreed."

Christa began to weep softly when told of her mother's illness, and Brian patted her shoulder awkwardly. "What's wrong with my mother, Brian, do you know?"

"I was told she contracted a debilitating fever while pining for you. Your father said it was heartbreak. None of us expected to see you again, let alone alive and healthy. She began to recover slowly after Abdullah bey's communication arrived. When last I saw her, she was much improved, though still weak and in need of rest."

"Thank God," sighed Christa fervently. "Am I free to leave here with you?"

"Yes, we'll leave in the morning."

"No!" Christa cried out in alarm. She couldn't bear to spend a minute more than necessary in Abdullah's palace. "Now! I want to leave now!"

Brian puzzled over Christa's frantic outburst. He could only assume her forced captivity in Abdullah's harem had been such a shameful experience that she was ready to break under the strain. Did that mean she had been raped by the handsome bey? Most women of her tender sensibilities would have been driven mad, he considered, some even killing themselves after suffering such indignities.

But it had been a long, hot journey from Tunis. Brian looked forward to a day or two of respite, and Abdullah had magnanimously offered one of his concubines to ease and comfort him. Now, looking at Christa's eager face, he decided to forego his own pleasure and humor her.

"All right, Christa," he acquiesced with a hint of disappointment. "The ransom has already changed hands, so it should matter little to the bey when we leave. Go pack your things and meet me back here."

Flashing a grateful smile, Christa turned to leave, then suddenly thought better of it, wheeling to face Brian once more. "I can't leave without Elissa."

"Who in the hell is Elissa?" he asked, his voice laced with impatience.

"My maid—no, my friend. She is of no use to Abdullah, and I won't leave her behind," Christa insisted stubbornly.

"Look here, my dear," Brian cajoled, calling upon all his self-control, "isn't it enough that you're leaving this place behind? It's rarely, if ever, that a woman emerges from a harem alive, so why don't you forget about this Elissa? We will find you a new maid."

"No, I can't leave Elissa, Brian, and that's final." Her eyes grew luminous with determination and her chin assumed a defiant angle, causing Brian to utter a curse and shake his head in vexation. He could tell by the stubborn set to her shoulders that she was adamant in wanting this woman with her. He remembered now that if she had any fault, it was her strong sense of independence and fixity of purpose.

"You win, Christa," he grudgingly conceded. "I'll speak to Abdullah. If it's as you say, he should voice no objection to Elissa's leaving."

"Thank you, Brian," Christa said sweetly. Then she was gone in a swirl of turquoise and silver.

Elissa was elated. Not only for Christa, but for herself. Just when things looked the bleakest, Allah had seen fit to deliver them.

"Will we go to Tunis, Christa?" she asked excitedly as she packed their meager belongings.

Christa went still, a thoughtful look bringing a frown to her face. At length, she said, "Brian didn't say, but I assume that's his intention."

"Who exactly is this man, Christa?" Elissa asked curiously.

"My fiance," Christa explained. "He came in my father's place to negotiate with Abdullah."

"You mean you are to marry that man? But I thought—that is, what about Ahmed? You love each other."

"I will always love Ahmed, but I am convinced we were never meant to be together," Christa said dully. "I—I released him from all vows made to me concerning our future. Should he survive, I hope and pray he will make his life without me."

"You speak brave words, Christa, but life isn't that simple. Can you truly forget Ahmed?"

"Never! Had I known I was to be released, I would never have made Ahmed promise to forget me. But now it is too late. There is nothing left but my prayers that he escape the Spanish and go to England where he will be safe."

"What about you? I know your love runs deep."

"I . . . I don't know. I can't imagine life without Ahmed. If it is our kismet to be together, then kismet will intervene." Brave words, but did she really believe them?

Christa's one regret was having to leave Lenore behind. She had become increasingly fond of the older woman and so had Elissa. Lenore expressed great joy when told of Christa's good fortune, and also a hint of sadness, which Christa suspected was due to her own captivity. By now Lenore was an integral part of the harem, serving as keeper to the many young women being quickly acquired by Abdullah.

Once their few belongings were packed into a wicker trunk, Lenore accompanied them to the room where Brian awaited. She bade the two women a tearful good-bye and would have gone about her business, when she heard Christa ask, "Are we going to Tunis, Brian?" His answer caused Lenore to linger outside the door to listen.

"No, my dear. After careful consideration, your father and I have decided it is in your best interest to send you to England immediately. He realizes, as I do, that this part of the world contains too many painful reminders of your recent captivity.

"We are traveling by caravan to Algiers, where I will book passage aboard the first ship bound for England. Once there, you are to stay with your aunt until your family joins you."

"They are leaving Tunis?"

"Your mother's health demands it, and there is talk of an assignment in London for your father. As soon as my own affairs in Tunis are settled, I will return to London also, and we can finally be married. I am due a leave, and with your father's help I expect to obtain a transfer to a post closer to home. Would you like that?"

This was the first mention Brian had made of their betrothal, and Christa had been more than a little relieved, thinking he no longer meant to honor it. Startled, she stared at him, suddenly at a loss for words.

"I release you from your promise, Brian," she finally said. "I certainly will understand if you no longer want to marry me." She did not add that she could no longer marry him.

"Christa, is there something you're not telling me?" Brian asked, certain that now was as good a time as any to broach the subject of her treatment while in Abdullah's harem. "If there is, I'll understand."

"No, nothing!" She had no intention of revealing her feelings for Ahmed or the love they shared. It was far too precious, the memory of that special love still too painful to voice, to Brian or to anyone, for that matter. Perhaps in time . . . "If it's any consolation, Brian," she added thoughtfully, "I think my father is right. I prefer to go to England. This ordeal had been a traumatic one, and the farther removed I am from the Barbary states the better I'll like it."

"I felt certain you would agree. All the arrangements are made to take us to Algiers. I have only to settle with the merchant whose caravan we are to join. Soon we will be married and all will be well."

Christa's shuttered expression should have alerted Brian to her true feelings, but it did not. The man was too self-centered and labored under the misconception that Christa was still eager to wed him, for surely, he thought, she had been dishonored by the pirates who had captured her. If not, then she had most certainly been used by Abdullah. Privately, he thought Christa lucky that he was willing to take damaged goods. Virgin or not, she was still lovely, still desirable, and by now knowledgeable in the art of love and well trained in pleasing a man in bed. Not to mention her more than adequate dowry, which Brian coveted to advance his career. Besides, her father would be so grateful to him for marrying his daughter despite her damaged reputation that he would be forever in Brian's debt. Sir Wesley had the ear of the king and a good word from him would secure Brian's future in the diplomatic corps. He felt no qualms over taking used goods, so long as it benefited him to do so.

Christa stared intently at Brian, her mind in a turmoil. He was pleasant to look upon, with sandy hair, brown eyes, and broad shoulders, though she knew she would find him lacking in comparison with Ahmed. For some reason his smile struck her as less than genuine, but perhaps she imagined it, for he seemed sincere in his desire to marry her. Yet how could she promise to marry anyone but her own true love? She and Brian would no doubt deal well enough together, but it would be a marriage lacking in warmth and passion.

"Are you certain you still want to marry me, Brian?" she questioned, giving him every chance to demure.

"Of course," he blustered heartily, perhaps too heartily. "Christa, it doesn't matter if you aren't— that is, hell, my dear, I know what you've been through. I'm no innocent."

Christa chewed her lip reflectively. He obviously assumed she had been raped by her captors, and to his credit was willing to overlook it. "I'll think on it, Brian, but I'm not sure marriage is still in our future."

"Nonsense," Brian sputtered. "As I stated before, I have a leave coming. In a few months I'll be in London, and so will your parents. We'll be married just as we planned. With a good word from your father, a transfer to Italy or France is entirely possible." He began to warm the the subject. He had little love for the Barbary states and suspected Christa felt the same.

When Christa remained mute, he continued, adroitly changing the subject, "Abdullah has given us permission to leave immediately. And as you've probably guessed, he has consented to allow Elissa to accompany us."

After listening to the conversation, Lenore silently padded to her tiny room, quickly gathered up her few things, and left the harem through the courtyard door. Being a mere servant, she was allowed freedom to come and go at will and therefore was not stopped or challenged. She waited by the wall until Christa, Brian, and Elissa emerged from the palace; then she stealthily followed, keeping far enough behind to avoid detection in the crowded, narrow streets.

Soon they reached the outer walls of the ancient city, and Brian immediately became engaged in haggling with a merchant he had previously arranged with for a place in his caravan for their small party. Lenore took advantage of Brian's distraction to approach Christa where she waited nearby in the shade of an olive tree.

"My lady," she said softly. At first Christa had no idea who was accosting her, for a concealing yasmak hid all but the person's eyes. Finally she recognized the voice.

"Lenore! What are you doing here?"

"I want to go with you, Lady Christa. I long to see England again. I went back once with Lady Emily, Ahmed's mother, but willingly returned when she did so that I might continue to serve her. I loved her dearly. But now that she is dead, there is nothing here for me."

"What about Abdullah?" Christa asked fearfully. "Surely he'll send his Janissaries after you once he discovers your absence. He's sure to know where you went."

"But he won't, don't you see? He thinks you are going to Tunis, but you're not. I overheard you say you are going to Algiers. It will be a long while before someone reports me missing, and if Abdullah sends someone it will be along the route to Tunis. By then we will be halfway to Algiers."

"Let her come, Christa," Elissa urged, for she held warm feelings for the older woman.

"Yes, yes I'll do it." Christa smiled, pleased at the thought of deceiving Abdullah. "I hold no love for Abdullah and look forward to helping another escape his cruel tyranny."

"What about Brian?" asked Elissa. "Will he agree?"

"No. In fact, he'll probably be livid. As soon as Brian has arranged our transportation, I'll manage somehow to speak privately to the merchant. Keep Lenore hidden until we are well on our way."

"Take this, Lady Christa," Lenore insisted, handing her a bag heavy with coins. "Lady Emily was very generous and I saved everything she gave me. The merchant will demand payment for another to join his caravan. Use what you need. You won't regret this, my lady. I'll serve you faithfully for the rest of my days."

The gold coins paid for Lenore's passage, and just as she had suspected, no one interrupted their journey. Brian was every bit as angry as Christa predicted when he discovered how the three women had conspired against him. But by that time, it was an accomplished fact and out of his hands.

As luck would have it, an English sloop, *Valiant Voyager*, lay anchored in the bay ready to depart when the party reached Algiers some weeks later. Brian had time for little more than a swift kiss on Christa's cheek and a promise that he would join her in a few months — sooner, if possible — before she trudged up the gangplank and into her assigned cabin.

16

Two weeks before Christa's hasty departure from
Constantine, Lady Willow Langtry walked briskly
along the quay, the foul smell and disgusting sights
of the harbor assaulting her delicate sensibilities.
How she hated Algiers and how happy she was to be
leaving this heathenish place! After the *Bon Ami*
was attacked by pirates and Mark presumably lost
overboard, she had continued her journey to Algiers. Thank God, the two French vessels had
chased the corsairs away, leaving the *Bon Ami* in
good enough condition to limp into port. In Algiers
she learned that Mark wasn't dead after all,
that he had been sorely wounded but was rescued
one of the French ships and brought to Algiers
to recuperate. She had been able to learn little
else and often wondered what had become of
him.

Behind Willow trailed a native porter leading a
donkey burdened with her considerable luggage.

Directly ahead, the English frigate, *Lion Heart*, lay anchored in the bay. She hurried her steps.

"Damn Robert for insisting I come to this godless place," she muttered beneath her breath. "And the devil take him for dying and leaving me to fend for myself."

No one had known that Robert Langtry would die of a lung infection when he arrived in Algiers. At the time he thought he suffered from nothing worse than a heavy cold. But after a time the "cold" had worsened and Robert finally consulted a Berber physician, who correctly diagnosed his illness as the last stages of consumption. By that time Willow was already on her way to Algiers, and upon her arrival spent the ensuing months watching Robert slowly die. Having a natural aversion for sickness, she spent as little time as possible with the stricken man, finding her own friends among the English and French colonies in the foreign quarter of Algiers.

The rattle of chains distracted her from her musings and immediately she recognized the shuffling steps of some hapless soul, manacled hand and foot, being led toward a life of slavery, no doubt aboard one of the sad looking Spanish transports anchored in the bay. Willow stepped aside, allowing the small party wide berth. From the corner of her eye she noted that five men made up the group—four uniformed soldiers flanking a man heavily shackled and stumbling along as if in a daze. Every now and then one of the soldiers cruelly prodded the prisoner with the tip of his sword to hurry his faltering steps.

Willow's eyes lingered on the slave, and she thought that at one time he must have been a marvelous specimen, for were he in top physical condition, he certainly would have possessed all the attributes of a well-endowed young male. Sharpening her wandering attention, she allowed her curious gaze further liberties, studying him intently from head to toe.

Dressed in baggy pantaloons, his bare torso had been burnt a deep bronze beneath the relentless sun. His feet were bare, his steps necessarily hobbled by the heavy chain connecting swollen ankles oozing blood where the manacles had rubbed them raw. His hands were bound before him in a similar manner. His neck bore a wide metal collar, the chain held by the lead man, an officer in the Janissaries. Idly, Willow wondered what the man had done to deserve his severe treatment. Was he some dangerous criminal?

Curiously her eyes shifted upward to his face, which was lowered, his features obscured. Suddenly she froze, all her senses reeling in disbelief. What was there about the man that provoked familiarity? His hair, long and unkempt, glowed a dark burnished color beneath the dirt and grime. His sunken cheeks were unshaven, his pallor striking against the deep tan of his torso. Even to Willow's untrained eye, the slave appeared desperately ill. Occasionally a low moan escaped his bloodless lips and sweat beaded his flushed face. As if to support her theory, his body began to shake uncontrollably. Then the slave drew abreast, and Willow gasped aloud when he raised pain-glazed green eyes to stare blankly at her.

Dismay followed by disbelief marched across her face as she cried out his name. "Mark!" Though he was desperately thin, obviously ill and suffering the effects of cruel abuse, she'd recognize those vibrant green eyes anywhere. What had happened these past months to bring him to such a pass? her mind screamed with silent outrage. He was a mere shell of the man she had once known intimately in England and parted from but six months ago. Though Willow hardly qualified for a medal for bravery or was known for her good deeds, nothing could persuade her to abandon Mark Carrington to a life of slavery. His health appeared so precarious that she feared he would succumb within hours if medical attention was denied him. And the Spanish were hardly noted for their mercy.

Prodded by his captors, Mark stumbled forward, his eyes wild and unseeing. Even when he heard Willow cry out, "Wait!" he seemed unable to comprehend what was taking place. "Stop!" Willow called out again, switching to one of the few Arabic words she had bothered to learn.

Glancing back over his shoulder, Captain Hadji frowned at the foreign woman with her face brazenly displayed. Curiously, he paused, waiting for her to state her business.

"Did you wish to speak to me, lady?" he asked in halting English. He had learned a smattering of the language long ago when Selim hired an Englishman to train the Janissaries in modern warfare.

"Where are you taking this man?" Willow asked, grateful to find the imposing Janissary spoke her language.

"The man is a slave and his fate none of your concern."

"I know this man," replied Willow, gesturing at Mark. "Tell me what he has done to deserve this fate."

"The slave, Ahmed, is an enemy of Abdullah, the great bey of Constantine. It is his kismet to serve aboard a Spanish galley. My master has passed judgment and I am but carrying out orders."

"No!" Willow protested vigorously. "Can't you see he's sick? Look at him. His eyes are glazed with fever and his body shaking with ague. He won't last a week chained to an oar. Obviously he's suffered great deprivation and is in need of care."

"The state of the man's health is no concern of mine, lady," Hadji intoned dryly. "My orders are clear, and I must obey them or suffer the consequences. It is not Abdullah's wish that the slave live a long life." Impatiently, he motioned his men forward.

"Wait!" Willow cried, growing desperate. It was not that she was especially heroic or charitable, but something deep inside her would not allow herself to stand helplessly by and watch Mark die an ignominious death aboard a Spanish galley. "I will pay you twice the price offered by the Spaniards if you sell him to me."

Captain Hadji slanted Willow an assessing look, his mind working furiously. Grinning craftily, he saw a way to pocket a small fortune and still discharge his duty to Abdullah. "Abdullah holds a grudge against this particular slave and wants him far from Algerian soil," he clarified with a hint of avarice. He could make no deals until the lady understood his terms. She did.

"I sail for England on the evening tide," Willow revealed, sensing Hadji's capitulation.

"I don't know, lady," Hadji hesitated, pretending mock concern. "For myself, I would do it, but"—he looked somewhat dubiously at his companions—"there are others to consider. Our lives would be worth little should Abdullah learn we did this thing you ask."

Willow snorted derisively. Obviously the man was not as stupid as he looked. "I will take Mark— your prisoner—aboard the *Lion Heart* with me immediately. And"—she emphasized meaningfully—"I will pay you three times what the man is worth as a galley slave. You can split the profit with your men."

Hadji assumed a thoughtful look, carefully mulling over his answer. If he accepted the lady's generous offer, he could easily pick up any one of the beggers inhabiting the waterfront to replace Ahmed, collect a receipt from the Spanish captain to satisfy Abdullah, and give a portion of his profit to his men to salve their conscience. His share would be put to good use, for there was a young girl, no more than thirteen, whom he had spied in the marketplace and thought to buy from her father. His aging wife, worn out from constant child-bearing, no longer held any appeal for him. A second, younger wife would not only ease his wife's burden, but provide a stimulating bed partner.

"You promise to take him far from Algiers, lady?"

"Yes," agreed Willow eagerly, glancing at Mark to see if he understood the terms of his miraculous escape. But his vacant eyes stared straight ahead and his shoulders slumped dejectedly as he swayed dangerously on his feet. Willow strongly suspected he teetered on the verge of collapse, and she wasn't far from the truth.

"Then I agree, lady, for the sum equal to three times the usual amount paid for a healthy galley slave." Hadji stressed the word "healthy," and when he named the amount it would take to free Mark from his fetters, Willow gaped, astounded, but wisely offered no objection. She would gladly beggar herself to set Mark free.

Gesturing to the porter waiting patiently nearby with her baggage, Willow motioned for him to unstrap a small, ornate chest from the donkey's back and set it before her. Taking a key from her reticule she opened the chest, removed a weighted sack and counted out the gold ducats, placing them in Hadji's cupped palms.

Once the required amount lay in his own money pouch, Hadji moved swiftly to unlock the fetters at Mark's wrists, legs and neck, tossing them to his men as they fell free. Fearing she might change her mind, Hadji nodded a curt farewell before barking out an order and herding his Janissaries into the teeming crowds.

Finding himself suddenly bereft of the heavy weights that had been his constant companions for week after hopeless week, Mark held his unfettered hands before him, seemingly unable to cope with sudden freedom.

"Mark!" Willow cried, tears forming in her eyes. "My God, don't you know who I am? It's Willow, and you're free! Do you hear? Free! I'm taking you home to England."

A brief glimmer of understanding crept into those pain-wracked green eyes, but it swiftly disappeared, replaced by a vacant expression that tore at Willow's heart. How she prayed for just a tiny spark of recognition! But any sign of intelligence was quickly snuffed out by the glaze of fever. Just then Mark stumbled and would have fallen if Willow hadn't rushed to place a supporting arm around his narrow waist. His bulk nearly proved too much for her as she staggered beneath it, searching frantically in all directions for help.

Spying the porter still holding the reins of the donkey, Willow entreated, "Help me!"

But the porter stubbornly refused, wanting no part of a man obviously sick and out of his head with fever. In a country where fevers often brought death, the porter's fears were well-founded.

"Coward!" sneered Willow, realizing she would receive no help from that quarter nor from any of the passers-by giving them wide berth. She looked longingly at the *Lion Heart* anchored some distance away and wondered if she dared leave Mark long enough to seek help from the English crew. Surely, she reflected hopefully, a spark of compassion existed in their hearts for a countryman in need of help.

At the end of her tether and reeling under Mark's limp form, Willow nearly wept with relief when a male voice nearby asked, "Can I be of help, lady?" The man spoke English a good deal better than the Janissary captain, and according to custom was covered save for his eyes by a burnous, so Willow had no idea who he might be.

"My friend is ill and I must get him aboard the *Lion Heart* so he may be cared for properly," Willow explained.

"I will carry him for you, lady," the man said, gently lifting Mark in his arms as if he weighed little more than a feather. Only then did Willow notice that the man was huge, and for the space of a breath experienced a pang of fear—until she noted how tenderly he carried Mark.

"Hurry," Willow beseeched, motioning the porter to follow. "I hope to convince the captain to take my friend aboard without too much difficulty."

Omar nodded, for the first time since he had known her grateful to Ahmed's former mistress. He had always thought Willow Langtry a shallow, mercenary creature concerned more with pleasure than weightier matters. Yet somehow she had managed to save Ahmed from a fate worse than death.

Left by Abdullah's Janissaries to die in the desert, Omar had defied the odds by surviving. Abandoned, without food, water or weapons, he and a handful of his tribesmen had managed to stay alive, albeit barely, long enough to be rescued by a caravan traveling from Fez. A kindly Jewish merchant had restored the emaciated men to health, eventually leaving them in Biskra. Several weeks later, fully recovered, Omar had traveled to Constantine hoping to learn the fate of Ahmed, Christa, and Elissa.

In a tavern he had chanced upon a young Janissary named Rashid, whose duty included guarding a special prisoner. Omar's suspicions proved correct when, after plying Rashid with drink, the young man admitted sampling the charms of a dark-eyed beauty in exchange for allowing her mistress an hour with her lover, who was to be taken the next day to Algiers to serve aboard a Spanish slaver. Omar had been beside himself. Ahmed, a slave! It was unthinkable.

Omar winced, knowing Ahmed would prefer death to living under the yoke of slavery. Rashid confided that Ahmed had been beaten viciously by Abdullah before he left for Algiers in the company of Captain Hadji. Omar was able to learn little of Christa or Elissa from Rashid, for he hadn't seen them since.

Omar suffered a frustrating delay of several days before he successfully bargained for a camel and supplies and followed his prince to Algiers. He loved Ahmed like a son and refused to consider abandoning him, hoping to reach Algiers in time to learn the name of the Spanish ship on which Ahmed sailed and set him free.

Driving himself relentlessly, Omar traveled more swiftly than Captain Hadji, entering Algiers only one day later. Fearing he was already too late, he hastened directly to the waterfront, seeking the Spanish vessels anchored in the bay. As luck would have it, he unexpectedly came upon Lady Willow Langtry haggling in a rather unladylike manner with the intimidating Captain Hadji.

At first Omar had not recognized Ahmed standing submissively by, weighted down by shackles and resembling a beggar instead of a proud man of royal birth. Only when the deal was completed and Willow sagged under Ahmed's dead weight did Omar make his presence known and offer assistance.

Lifting Ahmed gently in his arms, Omar was struck by his pallor and the fact that he appeared to have lost considerable flesh. Ahmed's bones stood stark against the skin of his ribcage and his face was all planes and angles. Omar swore beneath his breath, cursing Abdullah for his cruelty and Captain Hadji for affording Ahmed little in the way of comfort on the journey from Constantine to Algiers. "It is good you take him to England, lady," Omar said aloud, shocking Willow. Did he know Mark? she wondered, finding his voice vaguely familiar. But before she found the words to voice her question, they were standing on the gangplank of the *Lion Heart* facing an irate captain. "Lady Willow," he greeted her frostily, looking pointedly at the unconscious man cradled in the arms of a huge Arab. "What is the meaning of this?"

Taking a deep breath, Willow plunged into an explanation, hoping to soften any objection he might offer. It was imperative to make him understand, for Mark's life hung in the balance. "Captain Dexter, this man is Mark Carrington, the future Duke of Marlboro. I found him just moments ago shackled and being led away into slavery aboard a Spanish ship. The man in charge was greedy, else I would not have been so lucky in obtaining his release."

"Good Lord!" exclaimed Captain Dexter, properly shocked. "How could this happen to a man of Carrington's rank? Imagine, an Englishman forced into slavery." Suddenly a wary look came into his eyes and he asked sharply, "You are certain of the man's identity, Lady Willow?"

"Absolutely!" Willow declared with an authority the captain dared not refute. "Mark Carrington and I were—um, well-acquainted in England." Dexter raised shaggy brows, her implication duly noted.

"I'll take your word, Lady Willow. What's wrong with him? He looks ill."

"He has a fever and is obviously suffering from abuse and deprivation. A few weeks' rest and proper care will make all the difference in the world in his condition."

"Fever?" Dexter echoed ominously, his mind rebelling on hearing that dreaded word. "I'm sorry, Lady Willow, but I must think of my passengers and crew. I simply can't allow this man to infect my ship, no matter what his title."

Willow's heart sank, but to her credit she rose admirably to the occasion. "Captain Dexter, my father-in-law is an influential man in England. He is a peer of the realm and claims the king's friendship. Should you refuse Mark Carrington passage, I'm afraid you'll find your career abruptly ended. You have a wife and children, don't you?" she asked sweetly. "And of course there is the Duke of Marlboro to contend with. How do you think he'll react when he learns you've left his grandson to die on foreign soil?"

Captain Dexter had the good grace to flush. His crew and passengers came first, no matter what retributions were heaped upon him, but given the circumstances, he was more than willing to compromise. "Carrington can come aboard only if the ship's surgeon examines him and gives me his word the fever is not contagious."

Willow nodded tersely, anxious to gain help for Mark. "Send the doctor to my cabin. He can examine Mark there." Motioning Omar to follow with his precious burden, Willow brushed past the shocked captain, leaving him little time to protest the unorthodox arrangement.

Omar laid Ahmed gently down in the center of the bed in Willow's roomy cabin. He would have liked to wait to hear the doctor's verdict, but found himself being dismissed as Willow pressed a coin in his hand and urged him toward the door. He had no choice but to leave the room, but he did not leave the ship. Instead, he sought out the first mate.

Moments later Doctor Stanley bustled in, dismissed Willow with a curt nod and turned his attention to his patient. He worked swiftly and efficiently, opening the door once to order cold water and towels and a short time later calling for hot water. An hour elapsed before he stepped wearily from the cabin, closing the door softly behind him and rolling down his sleeves.

"Well?" Captain Dexter asked shortly. "Is the man contagious?"

"Carrington appears to be stricken with malaria," the doctor revealed crisply. "He is suffering a rather severe attack, and his treatment these past weeks has done little to improve his condition. He is not contagious and should recover, given time and proper care. Now if you'll excuse me, I have duties elsewhere."

"Doctor, wait!" Willow entreated, placing a restraining hand on his arm. "What kind of care does he require? He has yet to recognize me and has uttered not one word. How soon will he gain his senses?"

Recognizing Willow's genuine distress, Doctor Stanley softened his gruff manner considerably. "Force liquids down him, Lady Willow, and bathe him with cold water when his fever rises. I will send an infusion of quinine, which should ease him considerably, but other than that just keep him comfortable. I'll wager that in a few days he will come around and be eternally grateful for your timely intervention. But for you, the man would surely have died." Nodding to the captain, he turned and strode away.

"Doctor Stanley's word is good enough for me," Captain Dexter informed Willow. "I'll arrange another cabin for Carrington."

"That won't be necessary, Captain," Willow demurred. "There is ample room in my cabin."

"Lady Willow!" Dexter blustered, aghast. "That is hardly proper. Think of your reputation. You are but newly widowed, and extremely vulnerable at this sad time of your life."

"Nevertheless, Mark will share my cabin," Willow persisted defiantly. "You heard the good doctor say he needed constant care. As long as I am willing to provide that care, you have no business questioning my motives or my reputation."

Bowing to her logic, Captain Dexter reluctantly concurred. Truth to tell, he was too short-handed this trip to spare even one man to play nursemaid to an English lord. Though deep lines of disapproval wrinkled his brow, he gave grudging approval.

"Christa!" Mark's anguished cry awakened Willow, who had been sleeping on a cot placed nearby so as not to disturb his rest. Besides, his wild thrashings took him from one side of the bed to the other.

It was not the first time he had cried out that woman's name. Willow grimaced, displeasure evident on her beautiful face. The last she'd seen of Christa Horton was of her being carried off by pirates. How had Mark found her? And where?

Until he regained his wits, conjecture was all she was allowed.

To Willow's credit, she proved a competent nurse and cared for Mark devotedly, forcing food and liquids down his throat even though delirium drove him to reject her tender ministrations. Two days later, when Doctor Stanley looked in on his patient, his pleased look told Willow there had been a marked improvement in his condition. He left more of the quinine mixture and promised to return.

Mark opened his eyes and blinked through a haze of blue-grey mist at a form taking shape before him. A cup was held to his parched lips and he drank greedily, gratefully. He sputtered, coughed, then grimaced, rejecting the rest of the bitter brew remaining in the cup.

"Drink it all, darling, the doctor says it will cure your fever."

"Christa?" Mark asked, cursing the fuzziness that blurred his vision.

"It's Willow, Mark. Willow Langtry."

"Willow?" It took several minutes before his mind cleared so he could put a face to the name. By then his sight improved enough to make out the face peering down on him with such tender concern. "Where am I?"

"Aboard the *Lion Heart* on your way to England," Willow told him.

Sweeping the room through wary eyes, Mark was aware enough to recognize the cramped confines of a ship's passenger cabin, though Willow's was larger than most. The gentle rocking of the sea and the creakings of a ship in motion were other indications that Willow spoke the truth. "How?" he asked, frowning from his effort to remember.

"Do you recall nothing?" Mark shook his head.

"Are you up to listening?" Willow tried not to notice that his hands shook or that his eyes were still too bright.

"Yes, please," Mark implored. "I'd rest easier knowing what happened."

As concisely as possible, Willow repeated how she had found him and in what condition. She ended by relating how she had brazenly bargained for his freedom and argued with the captain to allow him passage.

"I owe you my life," Mark whispered hoarsely, viewing Willow in a different light. "How can I ever repay you? You'll get your money back, but that is hardly recompense for a man's life." After so much effort, exhaustion claimed him before he heard Willow's reply and he drifted off to sleep.

"I'll find a way, my darling," Willow murmured, smoothing his brow lovingly. "In fact, becoming Lady Marlboro is the only reward I'll accept."

That day marked the beginning of Mark's recovery. The following day he explained to Willow how Abdullah had captured, then imprisoned him, finally sending him to Algiers to live a life of slavery in the Spanish colonies. He made no mention of Christa, for the pain of her loss was still too raw, his heartbreak too recent. In return, Willow revealed the circumstances of her husband's death and how she happened to book passage on the *Lion Heart* and be on the docks the day she found him.

"You'll soon be in England where you belong, darling," Willow stated. "Forget Constantine, forget Abdullah. Your grandfather will be happy to have you back."

"Forget Abdullah? Never! Not after what he did to my parents. Someday, somehow, I will see him in hell!" When he spoke so fervently, his thoughts were of Christa, mentally calculating the time it would take him to regain his strength to return to Constantine and claim the woman he loved.

Suddenly, he recalled his hasty promise to Christa, a promise he had no intention of honoring. Though it might hasten his death, it was preferable to leaving Christa to serve as slave to a man like Abdullah. All this he kept to himself, sharing nothing with Willow of his love for Christa or his determination to return to Algiers.

The next day the fever left Mark's body and did not reappear. Cautiously he began moving about the cabin in an effort to regain his strength. But his illness and long weeks of captivity, combined with the frequent beatings and other deprivations, made Mark all too aware that his recuperation would be lengthier than originally anticipated.

One thing happened shortly before the *Lion Heart* came within sight of the English shoreline that raised Mark's spirits considerably. The doctor suggested that he take short strolls in the brisk air, and Mark gladly complied, leaving the stifling confines of the cabin and Willow's cloying attentions with a light heart. Though Allah knew he owed Willow his life, it rankled to have her fluttering constantly at his side now that he had begun to recover. Yet, he couldn't bring himself to voice his objection, for his debt to her was too great.

To Mark's delight, his stroll gained him more than mere exercise. Chancing to glance up into the rigging he idly noted that one man working on the ropes looked oddly familiar. His huge body, bared to the waist, moved with unusual dexterity for one his size. Mark continued to watch as the man descended to the deck, nimbly jumping the last few feet with the grace of a cat. As he turned to face

Mark, a look of intense joy suffused his features and was reflected in Mark's incredulous countenance.

"Omar!" Mark cried as the big man came bounding up to him. "Allah be praised! Do you have any idea how happy I am to see you alive and well?"

"Perhaps as delighted as I am to see you," Omar replied, grinning foolishly. "Though you are pale and far too thin, I can see for myself that you will recover. Allah has answered my prayers. It appears Lady Willow has taken good care of you."

"Without Willow's timely intervention, I would be dead," Mark ventured. "But tell me how you happen to be aboard the *Lion Heart*."

Omar explained the small part he had played in saving Mark's life and his fervent wish to remain with his prince. "I inquired of the first mate and learned there was a berth available, which I immediately applied for. I want only to remain by your side to protect you and fulfill your father's wish."

"Thank you, my friend," Mark said sincerely. "Are you certain you want to return to England with me? What of your tribe?"

"Abdullah's army succeeded in wiping out nearly all of my tribe. Those who survive joined with another clan and no longer need me. You are my prince; my kismet lies with you. I gave my word to your father, and as long as you have need of me I will not leave you."

"Your devotion humbles me, Omar," Mark said, a mysterious moisture gathering in his eyes. "We will talk further when time permits. There is much to tell you."

"Wait—Prince Ahmed, what of Christa? And Elissa? You have not spoken of them."

A look of intense pain crossed Mark's features,

making Omar wish he had not asked. "I—not now, Omar. That must wait, too. If it will ease your mind, know that both women were alive and well when last I saw them. Though Allah forgive me for saying so, I would rather Christa were dead." Without another word of explanation, he turned on his heel, leaving a confused Omar to ponder his words.

17

Chafing under the restrictions placed upon her by Mark's illness, Willow longed to share his bed, but she realized he was far too weak to satisfy her body's demands. Each night she retired to her solitary cot, dreaming of how it would be once he regained his former robust health. She recalled with vivid yearning how tender and caring a lover he could be, striving to give her as much satisfaction as he received. Under the cover of darkness she smiled contentedly, thinking of the huge debt he owed her. A man of Mark's honor would naturally insist on doing all in his power to repay that debt.

Mark was well aware of his obligation to Willow, even more so when he happened to overhear a conversation between two seamen discussing the sleeping arrangement insisted upon by Willow.

"I heard the doctor tell the captain that it was the lady's business if she wanted to ruin her reputation," one of the seamen revealed.

"Now that Carrington is nearly recovered, you'd think he'd ask for separate quarters," ventured the second man. "I wonder if he's well enough to keep the lady satisfied."

The first man snickered knowingly. "Do you think he'll marry her? I hear the Langtry's a rich widow." Then they moved off, leaving Mark thoughtful.

Before eavesdropping on the two men, he hadn't considered the consequences of sharing Willow's room. He was aware that for the first few days of the voyage he had required constant care, and he appreciated Willow's efforts on his behalf. Stupidly he failed to realize how his presence in her room compromised Willow's reputation, such as it was, now that he was ambulatory and able to request more suitable arrangements. Now, with England within sight, it hardly seemed worthwhile to ask the captain to provide another cabin for his use. But if it preserved Willow's reputation, he would do so immediately.

The thought of marrying Willow never entered his mind. Though Christa might be lost to him forever, spending a lifetime with another woman still seemed abhorrent to him.

Still pale and shaky from his debilitating illness, Mark walked down the gangplank, stepping onto English soil with Willow clinging possessively to his arm. Though it had been a mere half year since he left these shores, he recalled with fondness those happy years spent in the company of his beloved grandfather. With a prick of trepidation, Mark wondered how the old duke fared, for his health had been far from robust when they parted. Truth to tell, he would be happy to see the old gentleman again. His one regret, besides the obvious heartache over Christa, had to do with the fact that his brother Yazid was still missing. He was ever a resourceful rogue, and Mark held high hopes that he had found a safe haven far from Abdullah's reach.

"Mark, must you rush off to Marlboro Manor so soon?" Willow pouted sullenly. "Stay in London with me, at my townhouse. I'd like to be more to you than mere nurse, darling, much more. Surely you can recuperate as well in London as you can in the country." She was still miffed over Mark's request to be moved to another cabin once he was well enough to care for himself.

Mark had no difficulty deciphering Willow's meaning. "I'm anxious to see my grandfather, Willow. Besides, I'll be weeks regaining my former health and you'd be bored to tears tied down by an invalid."

"You won't forget me, will you, Mark?" she begged coyly.

"Forget you? My angel of mercy? Impossible," Mark teased with something akin to the old sparkle in his eyes. "Seriously, Willow," he said, turning sober, "you have been more than a friend to me, done more than I've a right to expect. If I can ever do anything for you, you've only to ask. And I certainly shan't forget you. When I return to London, you will be the first to know. You can depend on it."

Appeased for the moment, Willow flashed him a brilliant smile. She was astute enough to realize he'd need time to recover from his illness, and she was not yet ready to retire to the country after all those months in Algiers and weeks caring for Mark. Besides, she had some pressing matters to attend to. A duty call upon her bereaved in-laws was expected, and she hadn't the courage to go against polite society despite the fact that she held little love for the Langtrys. Another reason to confront her husband's parents had to do with Robert's inheritance. She meant to make damn certain she received all that was due her.

Ransoming Mark had nearly beggared her, and though he promised to repay her the moment he acquired the funds from his grandfather, Willow's hunger for wealth was as insatiable as her need for sexual gratification. Deep in her heart dwelt the dream of becoming the Duchess of Marlboro, but until that time arrived, or at least until she shared Mark's bed again, she would seek her pleasure as discreetly as possible.

The passion in Willow's farewell kiss did not go unnoted by Mark, but he considered it little enough payment for her indispensable help and tireless care. With a sense of relief, he saw her off to her townhouse, then waited for Omar to join him. They planned to travel together to his grandfather's country estate, far from the hustle and bustle of London, aware that the old gentleman left his hearth less and less of late. Never in his wildest imagination did Mark anticipate the surprise waiting for him there.

Christa walked down the gangplank, Lenore and Elissa trailing behind. Tears filled Lenore's eyes, for she had nearly forgotten her beloved England and the sights and sounds of London. And she owed her deliverance from slavery to Christa, whom she had come to love dearly.

Elissa's dark eyes grew round as saucers when confronted with the huge city and its strange inhabitants. Everyone seemed in a hurry, the pace nothing like her own country's, where indolence so often prevailed. Stranger still were the women who walked about brazenly with their faces uncovered for all to see. Christa had convinced her that it was proper to appear unveiled in public, and though she had followed her friend's example she felt far from comfortable—almost wicked, in fact.

Already Christa could feel the promise of winter in the chill autumn wind and automatically pulled her cloak closer about her shivering form, noticing as she did that both Elissa and Lenore quickly responded to the cold air in the same manner. Using some of the coins Brian had given her, Christa hired a carriage for them and their meager baggage and gave her aunt's address, wondering if the poor woman expected her or if she would faint to find herself invaded by three travel-weary women without a decent set of clothing among them. One consolation was the letter of credit her father had given Brian for her use. Thoughtful man that he was, he had wanted her to purchase whatever she needed to insure her comfort in England without burdening her aunt.

As the carriage turned into her aunt's street, Christa could hardly wait to see the woman she held nearly as dear as her parents. As they neared the house, Christa became aware of the uncommon commotion taking place in front of the fashionable townhouse belonging to her aunt. Halting before the door, Christa noted another conveyance piled high with luggage parked in the street directly in front of the house. Try though she might, she did not recognize the coat of arms emblazoned on the carriage door. Before she was able to get out of the carriage, a man and a woman hurried out the door toward the waiting conveyance. So intent were they on their purpose that they seemed not to notice Christa hanging out the window of her own carriage, stunned and puzzled by all the activity.

"Aunt Mary!" Christa cried as the small woman was being helped into the carriage by a stately, distinguished man with graying hair.

Turning in the direction of the voice, Mary

Stewart gasped, and if the man behind her hadn't placed a steadying arm about her plump waist, she would have fallen. "Christa? Dear Lord, what are you doing here? You're supposed to be in Tunis." So severe was her shock she had nearly forgotten her great hurry of only a few moments before.

"I—I've come back, Aunt Mary, if you'll have me," Christa said hesitantly. "Didn't Father write you?"

"Dear child, you are always welcome here," Mary replied sincerely. "But I've not heard from Wesley since before you left London months and months ago. Has something happened?" By now Mary stood before Christa, the gray-haired man following, a puzzled frown furrowing his dignified brow.

"Mary," he reminded her gently. "We must leave, else our ship will sail without us."

"You're leaving?" Christa asked, dismayed.

"Oh, my dear," Mary wailed, her mind a quandary of indecision. "Had I but known you were coming . . . you see, much has happened in the months since you left. I met Charles"—she smiled lovingly at the man beside her—"and it was love at first sight for the both of us. Given our age—well, we decided to wed immediately. Charles is taking me to Spain and Italy for our honeymoon, and we intend to remain abroad for a year or more."

"I'm Sir Charles Whitelaw," the man said, smiling broadly as he filled in the gaps left out in Mary's excited telling. "Ours was indeed a whirlwind courtship and marriage. But your aunt stole my heart the first time I laid eyes on her. I've been a widower for some years with no children to ease my loneliness."

"Yes," agreed Mary, soft brown eyes lingering lovingly on her husband. Never having married, she considered herself beyond the age until she met

Charles. "Charles rarely attended parties or left his estates in Kent, but destiny must have guided him when he made an appearance at the Jordons' ball, where we met."

"I'm so happy for you, Aunt Mary," Christa said, wiping away a tear. "And also for you, Sir Charles. Now you are off on a grand tour."

"Exactly." Sir Charles nodded, suddenly recalling their need for haste. "And if we don't hurry, my love," he addressed Mary, "we will be too late. Unless, of course, you wish to cancel now that your niece is here."

His disappointment was so clearly evident that Christa protested. "No! you musn't change your plans because of me. Please don't let me spoil your honeymoon."

For a moment, doubt assailed Mary, until Charles remarked, "Have you forgotten, Mary, that this house now belongs to your niece?"

"What!" exclaimed Christa, thoroughly perplexed.

"Oh dear, oh dear," Mary moaned. "All this rush and the shock of seeing Christa has addled my brain. From now on my home will be with Charles in Kent. For our infrequent visits to London, we'll use his townhouse, so I've deeded this house to you, Christa," she explained breathlessly. "My lawyer has all the details, you must consult him. I've also made you my beneficiary."

"Me? Oh, Aunt, how generous," Christa exclaimed, touched by her aunt's thoughtfulness. "How can I ever thank you?"

"By coming to visit us in Kent," Charles beamed, answering for his wife.

"Of course." Christa laughed, taking an immediate liking to the older gentleman.

"But—but it isn't right that I leave you alone." Mary suddenly shook her head. "What am I thinking of? You'll need a proper chaperone, and—and I've dismissed the servants. Oh dear," she lamented, turning to Charles with a helpless shrug.

Suddenly Christa grinned, opening the door to the carriage and stepping down, motioning for Elissa and Lenore to follow. "As you can see, I did not come alone. Lenore"—she pointed, indicating the older woman—"is perfectly capable of acting as chaperone, and Elissa"—placing an arm about the young girl—"is my maid and companion. The three of us will do nicely on our own until my family arrives."

Mary glanced hopefully at Charles. "Do . . . do you think we dare?" She had so looked forward to this year abroad with Charles.

Charles slanted Christa a measuring look, then shifted his glance to include Lenore and Elissa. At length he said, "Christa looks to be a responsible young woman. And if your brother trusted her to travel with Lenore and Elissa, then we can do no less than extend the same courtesy to her. The house is already Christa's to do with as she wants. I see no harm in continuing with our plans. When will your parents arrive, my dear?" He addressed his question to Christa. "You talk as if it will be soon."

"Yes, very soon. In fact, they may already be on their way." On the spur of the moment she wisely decided to withhold any mention of her mother's illness for her aunt was ever one to worry. "He's been given a post in England and I—I wanted to come ahead."

"What of your marriage?" Mary interjected. "I thought you and Brian were to wed in Tunis?"

"Because of Father's sudden transfer, our plans have been postponed indefinitely," Christa replied. "I'll be fine, Aunt Mary, truly. I insist you continue with your plans. I am perfectly capable of caring for myself until my family joins me."

"Well . . . if you're sure," wavered Mary, still not entirely convinced.

"I'm positive," Christa repeated firmly.

"I'm sorry, my love, but we must leave now," Sir Charles interrupted, fidgeting nervously.

Throwing her arms around Christa, Mary hugged her furiously. "If I had but known," she apologized, torn between duty to her niece and love of her husband. Then she was literally torn from Christa's embrace by Charles and hurried toward their own waiting carriage, barely given time to thrust the key to the house into Christa's hand.

"I have accounts in every store in London, my dear," Charles threw over his shoulder. "I'd feel better about taking your aunt off like this if you'd charge anything you need to me. Hang the expense! Redecorate the whole house, hire servants, whatever pleases you." Then he lifted Mary into the carriage and soon they were hurtling down the street at breakneck speed, her aunt leaning out the window blowing kisses.

"Fate works in mysterious ways," Elissa said cryptically, looking toward the deserted house that now belonged to Christa.

Christa sagged in exhaustion. The trip had been long and fraught with sadness and anxiety over Ahmed's fate. With the end of her journey came total fatigue and a feeling of intense melancholy.

"You're tired," Lenore said crisply, guiding Christa toward the front entrance. During the past weeks she had been told the truth about Christa's pregnancy, and though she had been disappointed she still behaved like a mother hen protecting her chick. "There will be nothing in the house to eat, so

I will go to the market while Elissa makes you comfortable.''

After much conferring between the women, it was decided not to hire extra servants for the time being. With only Christa living in the house, Lenore took over the kitchen duties and Elissa the chores. They ate all their meals in the kitchen and sat together quietly in the evenings reminiscing, until Christa realized it did them little good to dwell constantly on the past.

Using the letter of credit, they purchased adequate wardrobes and filled the cupboards with food. As for Christa, she rarely ventured out of the house and gardens, except for the visit to Aunt Mary's lawyer to sign the papers making her legal heir to her aunt, using the time until her parents' arrival to heal her mind and heart. Because she spoke English, Lenore took over the shopping chores while Elissa spent long hours attempting to distract Christa from her raging grief. But much to her chagrin, she found the task nearly impossible.

At night, Christa's dreams turned into nightmares as she pictured Ahmed slaving deep in some airless mine, his smooth, brown back bearing the mark of the lash. Was he still alive? Or had he miraculously escaped? If he had, she fervently prayed his promise to her would prevent him from returning to Constantine with false hopes of rescuing her from Abdullah. At their last meeting, she had striven desperately to convince him of the danger should he show himself in Constantine. If he were caught again, Abdullah would not hesitate this time to put him to death.

The weeks slid one into another and Christa received a letter from her father. Their departure had been somewhat delayed by a slight worsening in her mother's condition, but they hoped to leave very soon. He counted on Aunt Mary to keep her from becoming too lonely and eagerly anticipated their reunion. Enclosed were letters from her brother and sister that brought on a bout of tears as Christa recalled vividly their dear faces and youthful antics. In the same packet was a letter from Brian.

In it he renewed his promise be with her soon to claim her for his bride. Truth to tell, Brian occupied but a small part of Christa's mind. Her thoughts of Ahmed and the love they shared left little room for another man. At night, she imagined herself being held next to Ahmed's heart, experiencing the full measure of his love in all the exciting ways he had taught her. Night after night, she woke gasping with the sensations his hands and mouth had evoked, only to find herself alone. Her sobs of disappointment often brought Elissa into her room, and the young girl soothed her back to sleep with soft words and warm milk.

Then one day Christa was plunged into a situation she would have given anything to postpone. Brian Kent appeared at her door. Though not entirely unexpected, his visit nevertheless came as a shock, for she had expected her family to return first.

"It's good to see you, my dear," Brian said with an enthusiasm Christa found curiously stilted.

His cool gaze raked her slim figure, thinking how beautiful she looked despite her sullied past. He had nearly forgotten it was her enticing beauty that had drawn him to her in the beginning. Having her in his bed would be pleasant, and idly he wondered what tricks her captors had taught her, and if she had taken a lover since her return to London. That last thought brought a fierce scowl to his face. Though he might overlook her being used against her will, taking a lover of her own choosing was more than he would countenance. He would find out soon enough if there was gossip circulating about her when he made the rounds of the clubs to drink and gamble.

"Brian!" Christa started, her legs turning to rubber beneath her skirt. "I—I hadn't expected you so soon."

"I told you I'd not be long in arriving," he replied.

"Yes, you did." Christa nodded, feeling foolish as well as at a loss for words. Somewhat reluctantly, she invited him inside, flushing when he seated himself beside her on the sofa.

Brian smiled, exerting considerable charm to make Christa aware of what had inspired her to accept his proposal months ago. Any woman would consider Brian attractive and charming. "Surely your betrothed deserves a warmer greeting than that," he teased her in an affectionate manner reminiscent of their former relationship.

Christa could not help but smile in response, delivering a swift kiss to his cheek. But Brian wanted more than a brief peck; she was no longer a shy virgin whose sensibilities must be considered. No doubt she possessed the experience of a practiced whore and needed what he could give her, now that she was newly awakened to passion. Reaching for her, he pulled her roughly into his arms, pressing the length of her body into the curve of his, seizing her lips and forcing his tongue between her teeth into the moist warmth of her mouth. Too shocked to resist, Christa remained mute until she felt his hands cup the soft mounds of her buttocks and squeeze. Only then did she struggle to free herself, pushing and shoving against his chest in an effort to escape his unwanted attentions.

Abruptly, Brian released her, studying her

through narrowed eyes. Actually, he hadn't expected her to object so strongly. Wasn't it only right that she give willing to her fiance what others had taken by force? What should he do? Apologize? Or force her to his will in order to impress upon her that he was fully aware of her altered state. He had almost settled on the latter when he thought of Sir Wesley and his love for his daughter no matter what horrors had been visited upon her. He needed Sir Wesley's good will to further his career and if that meant coddling his daughter, then coddle he would —until they were safely wed. Then he would demonstrate by deed that he meant to use her to serve his every need, in every way possible.

"I'm sorry, Christa," he apologized insincerely. "We've been separated far too long, and when I saw you looking so—so damned desirable I couldn't help myself. Betrothed couples are allowed moments of passion, you know."

Christa glared at him belligerently, preparing to give vent to her anger when his next words forestalled her. "I have a message for you."

"Message?" He now had her complete attention.

"Your family will be in London in time for our wedding. The doctor has finally given your mother permission to travel, and they will arrive soon. I promised we'd wait until their arrival to celebrate our marriage, so they might attend the ceremony. Though it will be difficult to wait after so long a delay, I nevertheless agreed. Besides, you'll need time to plan the affair. I want it to be a grand event, Christa. Your aunt can help you."

Christa flushed. She had deliberately neglected to mention that Aunt Mary had left on an extended honeymoon with her new husband the day she arrived in London. "Aunt Mary is not in England," she revealed. There was no sense in keeping it from Brian, for he'd find out soon enough anyway.

"What! You've been living here by yourself?"

"Of course not," she retorted defensively. "Lenore and Elissa are still with me."

"I'm certain your father wouldn't have been quite so willing to send you to England had he known you'd be left to fend for yourself."

"That's why I failed to mention it in my letters," Christa confessed guardedly. She had written regularly to her family since her arrival in London.

Brian scowled. "Now that I'm here, I'll see to your welfare. Once we're married, I'll take care of you properly."

Christa swallowed a laugh. How did he think she had managed all these months without his help? She was no child in need of protecting. In the past months she had experienced more of life than any woman her age should have to. She certainly didn't need Brian to look after her.

"Brian—" Christa began in a rush of words. Suddenly it was imperative that he know about her love for another man, for she could never marry him. "Before you go any further with your plans there is something you should know. Something you won't like."

Brian prided himself on being nobody's fool, and he knew exactly what Christa was referring to. Didn't she realize he had already guessed what the pirates and Abdullah had done to her? Somehow he must try to convince her it didn't matter. Sir Wesley had already spoken to him at length concerning her ordeal, and they had agreed she couldn't have escaped unscathed. Swallowing his disgust, Brian had assured Sir Wesley that it made little difference to him; the wedding would take place on schedule. A grateful Sir Wesley had then promised to speak directly to the king about Brian's promising future, virtually assuring him of reaching the pinnacle of his career in the shortest time possible. All the power and wealth he coveted would soon be his.

"There's no need to tell me a thing, my dear," Brian responded knowingly.

"You — you know?"

"Did you think I wouldn't? I've lived long enough in the Barbary states to realize what happens to beautiful women captured by corsairs and sold into slavery. I seriously doubt you escaped ravishment by those unspeakable villains, but if by some miracle you did, then the bey most certainly used you. But I've agreed to overlook the fact that you are no longer a virgin," he offered generously. "Now that that's settled, there should be no more argument."

Stunned, Christa was left momentarily speechless. Of course Brian would think she had been ravished! Her father and mother probably suffered under the same misapprehension. It was true she was no longer a virgin but she had freely given up her innocence long before the *Bon Ami* was attacked by pirates. It was time to disabuse Brian of the notion that they would soon wed.

"You don't understand, Brian," Christa patiently explained. "I don't love you. There is — or was — another man."

Brian's face grew red with indignation. "Another man! Abdullah? Surely not him!"

"No, not Abdullah. I — I fell in love with a man I met aboard the *Bon Ami*." There was no need for Brian to know Mark's name or anything else about him.

"Where is this man you love? Why aren't you

together? I find all this hard to believe, Christa. Certainly this man doesn't love you, or he'd be with you now."

"He was sold into slavery just as I was and now serves in the Spanish colonies."

"Then he is as good as lost to you," Brian assured her. "Besides, he might not be as understanding as I am in regard to your sullied past. Most men demand innocence in a wife."

"I willingly gave my innocence to my lover," Christa admitted.

"You what!" Red dots of rage exploded in his brain. "You did this while still engaged to me?" he sputtered angrily. Christa nodded, hoping she had at last discouraged him, only to learn otherwise.

"Your lover will surely die under the yoke of slavery. As you well know, few escape the Spanish. I am still your fiance, and once we are married you will please only me. We will marry just as your father intended. Now I must go. I want to get settled in at my club and spend the next hours soaking in a tub that isn't filled with salt water. I'll call on you tomorrow. We need each other, my dear. With your questionable reputation, you have little hope of marrying well should you be unwise enough to turn me down. As for myself, I need your father's backing to reach my goals in life."

Christa stood gaping at Brian's departing back. It appeared he had their lives all planned. Despite her confession of loving another man and losing her innocence to him, Brian adamantly insisted on going through with their marriage. And he had finally admitted he needed her, that love wasn't his primary reason for wanting her. Were her parents really so set on her wedding him? Were they worried about her reputation and the fact that no man save Brian was likely to ask for her? Perhaps, she considered bleakly, she should honor her promise to him and become his wife. No doubt she could do much worse, and she had no wish to become a burden to her parents.

Though she loved Ahmed with all her heart and soul, she felt there was little chance they would ever meet again. She had told him—nay, begged him—to forget her and make a life without her. Had she the courage to follow her own advice?

Silent as a wraith, Elissa appeared at her side. "Do you intend to marry that man?" she asked with cautious concern.

"I don't know," said Christa truthfully. "It does seem to be one choice."

"But is it the right one? Perhaps Ahmed . . ."

"No, I've learned to live with the fact that I'll never see Ahmed again. Should he escape slavery, as I know he will, he most certainly will return to Constantine and seize the beylic from Abdullah. He will either succeed or die trying. I truly believe it is his kismet to become ruler of Constantine. I can rightly occupy no place in his life, for we are worlds apart despite his English heritage." Noticing Elissa's deep frown, she gave the girl a sharp glance and asked, "You don't like Brian, do you?"

Elissa shrugged, her eyes carefully hooded. She had nothing on which to base her feelings and so kept her misgivings to herself. "I want your happiness, Christa. I think only of you."

"You and Lenore are part of my life now. You will remain with me no matter what," Christa said, hoping to ease her mind.

"I know," Elissa replied, tightlipped. "Still, I can't help but wonder . . ."

"Enough, Elissa," Christa scolded, suddenly weary of the subject. "I have weeks in which to decide. Perhaps in that time Brian will discover that he no longer wants to be saddled with me for life, although my parents are counting on this wedding, and I'd hate to disappoint them. I haven't been much of a daughter to them of late.''

Reluctantly acquiescing, Elissa turned and left the room, praying that Christa knew what she was doing, for there was something about Brian Kent she neither liked nor trusted.

18

Christa pivoted slowly before the long mirror, carefully scrutinizing her face and form. Though she felt years older, she was shocked to discover that she looked much the same as she had less than a year ago. Her rounded breasts stood proud and firm, her waist tiny in comparison. Trim hips and long supple legs added to the overall picture of seductive beauty and femininity.

Try though she might, Christa could find no fault with her face or hair. In honor of the occasion her pale blond tresses were arranged artfully atop her shapely head in a mass of riotous curls. Her gown, finished just today by the best dressmaker in town, was fashioned of lavender silk. Ruffled underskirts in pale pink and deep violet created a dazzling display where the skirt was gathered up and held in place by small bouquets of violets. Her smooth shoulders were bare but for tiny sleeves resting low on her arms. Though Christa decided

she looked as pretty as she ever had, in truth she
had never looked more entrancing or sensually
desirable.

When Brian informed her two weeks ago that
he had secured an invitation to a ball given by Sir
Peter Trenton in honor of the new Duke of Marlboro, Christa had been struck dumb. She had heard
that the old duke died shortly after Mark left
England and wondered vaguely who would inherit
now that his grandson was lost to him. Evidently
they had found another relative to assume the title
and estates.

At first Christa adamantly refused to attend
with Brian, remembering with a painful lurch Sir
Peter's party months ago, where she had first met
and lost her heart to Mark Carrington, her Berber
prince. But Brian wheedled and cajoled until she
finally acquiesced. Brian, he told her, had met Sir
Peter at his club and had somehow snagged an
invitation despite the fact that they were hardly
social equals, until he let slip that he was engaged to
Christa Horton. It pleased him to think of all the
opportunities opening to him as the future son-in-
law of Sir Wesley Horton, which he certainly would
be if Christa could be convinced that marriage to
him was the only course open to her now that her
reputation lay in ruins.

To humor Brian, as well as to reintroduce
herself into society in style, Christa visited the
dressmaker, resulting in the violet silk she now
wore. She had become so much of a recluse since
her return to England that going out again in public
offered an exciting change. After all, no one knew
what had happened to her in Algiers. Unless . . .
But, no, she wouldn't think of that, not tonight.

Since her return, she had seen no one but Elissa
and Lenore until Brian had arrived two weeks ago

and convinced her to take the plunge into polite society. The one thing that miffed her was that Brian still insisted that they would marry soon and was set upon claiming her as his fiance despite her protests to the contrary.

Startled from her revery by the loud clatter at the door announcing Brian's arrival, Christa gave herself one last glance in the mirror before turning and quietly leaving the room. Brian waited at the bottom of the stairs, a thoughtful look on his face as he stared at the creamy smoothness of rounded flesh visible above the deep décolletage of her gown.

"You're exquisite," he said shakily, reaching for her hand and kissing her fingertips before running his tongue intimately over her palm. Suppressing a shudder, Christa quickly drew her hand away, surprised at the repulsion his touch evoked.

Brian appeared mesmerized by the delicate color spreading across the high cheekbones and lengthy column of her neck. Seeing her like this, Brian wondered if he could wait the long weeks before their wedding to possess her. She was no innocent, after all. Perhaps she would let him . . . The direction along which his thoughts had wandered was abruptly halted when Elissa entered the foyer carrying Christa's new purple velvet cloak. Until now, Brian had paid little heed to the young girl except to note she was quite pleasant to look upon. But in the new clothes fashioned especially for her vivid coloring and diminutive figure, long black hair swirling free about a miniscule waist, Brian suddenly realized that she was not merely lovely, but breathtaking, as exciting in her own way as Christa was in hers. Dark thoughts formed unbidden in the farthest recesses of his mind. Surely Elissa had no one in England to look to for protection except Christa, he reflected deviously. Surely a young, beautiful girl would soon fall victim to unscrupulous men, should Christa cut her adrift once they were married. Wouldn't she be eternally grateful to him for allowing her to remain with Christa after the wedding? Grateful enough, perhaps, to let him bed her?

"I won't be but a moment," Brian heard Christa say as he reluctantly dragged his thoughts from Elissa's exotic beauty.

"What did you say?" he asked distractedly.

"I said I forgot something upstairs, but I won't be a minute," Christa repeated, wondering where Brian's thoughts had fled.

"Hurry along, my dear," Brian smiled blandly as he watched Christa disappear up the stairs. From the corner of his eye he saw Elissa edge from the room and flung out an arm to stop her. "I'd like a word with you, Elissa," he informed the startled girl.

"Yes sir," answered Elissa in English. Thanks to Christa's efforts, she now had a working command of the language. She stood before Brian, realizing that the more she saw of him the less she liked him, although she had nothing on which to base her judgment. Now, his bold look and leering smile gave her good reason to believe she would soon learn his true nature.

"How old are you, Elissa?"

"Sixteen," she answered warily.

"So young? You're very beautiful, you know."

Elissa frowned, wondering exactly what Brian had on his mind. She didn't have long to wait. "I expect you to be suitably grateful for my allowing you to remain in Christa's service once we are married. She seems to dote on you and I'll indulge her as long as it pleases me. Or," he hinted broadly, "as long as you please me."

Pretending to misunderstand, Elissa assumed an innocent look and replied, "I'll try my best, sir."

"I'm certain your best is very good, indeed." The grip on her arm tightened, causing Elissa to wince painfully. "Don't pretend ignorance, my dear," he warned when she continued to stare blankly at him. "You are no wide-eyed innocent. You have the look of an enchantress about you and your eyes promise knowledge far beyond your years. You will please me well, my dear, very well indeed."

Elissa blanched. It was far worse than she thought. Brian Kent expected her to share his bed on a regular basis if he married Christa. Thankfully, Christa had yet to agree to the marriage, and if Elissa had anything to say about it, Christa never would.

"I see you are shocked," Brian said with a nasty laugh. "Though I'm surprised one of your—er, calling should be shocked at anything. I intend to get Christa with child as soon as possible and then I'll have need of your delectable body. You'll find me not ungrateful."

Before Elissa could spit out a scathing retort, Christa's footsteps sounded at the top of the stairs and she pulled away from his loathsome grasp, rubbing the bruised flesh of her upper arm. When he turned his charming smile in Christa's direction, Elissa made good her escape, wondering if Christa was fully aware of Brian Kent's despicable nature. If not, she was in for a rude awakening.

Most of the English nobility attended the lavish affair given by Sir Peter Trenton. Rumor had it that even the king was expected to make an appearance. For the first half hour or so, Christa walked sedately around the room on Brian's arm, greeting friends of her aunt and those she had met on her previous stay in London, as well as old friends of her father's. When she introduced Brian, whose normal circle of friends was far removed from her own station in life, he was quick to offer the information that he was Christa's betrothed. Though his words and proprietary manner nettled Christa, rather than make a scene she did nothing to correct him. Besides, she had yet to resolve the dilemma in her own mind. If her parents wished for her to marry Brian, perhaps she should honor their wishes. Her abduction had caused them so much grief, she knew it would please them to see her settled.

A short time later, when Christa sat in front of the mirror in the powder room staring at her reflection and wondering what she was doing there with Brian, a man she did not love, she overheard the end of a curious conversation between two women as they prepared to leave.

"They say announcement of their engagement is just a formality, that they will wed before summer's end," the thin blonde revealed.

"I'll believe it when I see it," scoffed the voluptuous brunette. "It'll be quite a feather in her cap, should she pull it off."

"They've been inseparable these past months," sighed the blonde wistfully. "He's so handsome and mysterious."

"Gossip has it that she saved his life, and he hasn't gotten over being grateful," the brunette remarked.

"Grateful enough to marry her?" the blonde replied, rolling her eyes suggestively. "You'd think he'd be satisfied to bed her."

They laughed, then left the room, instilling in Christa a strange foreboding, though she hadn't the vaguest idea to whom they were referring.

Mark stood across the room, a bored expression etching his handsome brow. Lady Willow Langtry, stunningly gowned in crimson that should have clashed with her red hair but in truth enhanced it, clung to his arm. His skin appeared pale beneath his fading tan, but few were aware of the circumstances of his recent life. None but his closest friends knew of his near brush with death, nor of Willow's role in his rescue. But during the long months of his convalescence in the country, Willow had discreetly revealed to several acquaintances the story of Mark Carrington's narrow escape from life-long slavery, as well as embellishing her own role in his miraculous liberation. She also hinted that the new duke would soon make her his duchess.

The new Duke of Marlboro's boredom was due to the brash young man, a year or two older than his own twenty-eight years, to whom he had just been introduced. Though obviously not of the nobility, he appeared to have high-placed friends as well as a fiancée of noble birth whom the duke had yet to meet—not that he had any desire to do so, for no doubt the lady would prove as tiresome as her betrothed.

"Would you like to meet her, your grace?" Brian asked, spying Christa just entering the ballroom.

The name Brian Kent seemed only remotely familiar to Mark. Idly he recalled that Christa's fiancé was named Brian, but as far as he knew he had never heard the last name spoken. And Brian was a common name.

To Mark's chagrin, his recovery from malaria had taken the better part of the winter. Returning to find his beloved grandfather dead had not aided his recuperation. But the surprise that awaited him at Marlboro House more than made up for the pain caused by the old duke's death. Even now a smile curved his lips when he recalled his initial shock . . .

"Mark, darling," Willow prodded, "Mr. Kent asked if you'd like to meet his fiancée. Whatever are you thinking about?"

Coming out of his revery, Mark felt the force of her presence long before he saw her. Some power greater than the life beating within him impelled him to glance across the room to the ethereal, violet-clad vision floating toward him on a cloud of dreams. She couldn't be real! Mark blinked, amazed that he could want Christa so badly that he had conjured up her image at a time when she was thousands of miles away.

True, it wasn't the first time memories of Christa had invaded his thoughts or appeared as a vision before him, but never had she seemed so vividly alive, so gorgeously attired, like the fairy princess of his dreams. If he was dreaming, he never wanted to return to reality.

The tawny fringe of golden lashes fluttered like dancing butterflies as Christa stared in disbelief. Ahmed! Here! Impossible! The virile substance of him filled her senses and she drifted forward without awareness of ever moving her feet. Her throat convulsed as she fought for breath, wondering if she had wished for him so desperately that she had summoned him from out of the depths of despair.

No! There was no mistaking the devastatingly handsome face, proud and lean, and those high cheekbones and full, generous lips. The arresting green eyes set below dark, slashing brows, and his strong and gracefully noble nose emphasized the hawkish leanness of his beloved countenance.

Christa felt her body tense and shudder, as a cry of joy that could not be contained rippled from her throat. People standing nearby looked at her strangely, but for her no one existed but Ahmed.

No—Mark, for obviously he was no longer her desert prince, but the Duke of Marlboro.

Suddenly they stood just inches apart, her legs weak and trembling, the wild nobility in his dark features touching her soul and warming her heart. Unconsciously she reached out, only to have her hands captured by Brian, who had mistaken her intention, thinking the love suffusing her face was meant for him.

"Ah, here is my fiancée now, your grace." Brian beamed, slipping an arm about Christa's tiny waist. "My dear, this is—"

"Mark," breathed Christa on a sigh, using the English name his mother gave him. She felt herself struggling through a heavy blanket of memories into the blinding light of reality.

"Christa," Mark said, the word more like a caress than a spoken sound, causing Willow to bristle with jealousy.

"You two know each other?" Brian asked, suddenly wary.

"Only too well," murmured Willow spitefully.

"We—we met aboard the *Bon Ami*," Christa replied, searching desperately for composure.

"Then you know about . . ." Brian faltered. He had hoped to keep Christa's shameful past a secret, for he wanted nothing to interfere with his career.

"We both know," Willow crowed maliciously. "I saw Christa being taken aboard the pirate ship. You see, I was also a passenger on the *Bon Ami*. If you ask me, Christa offered little resistance to her captors."

"Willow!" reprimanded Mark sharply, giving her a quelling look. "I am well acquainted with Miss Horton, Mr. Kent. You say she's your fiancée? I seem to recall her mentioning you in one of our conversations."

Willow snorted derisively but said nothing,

fearing Mark's anger. Silently she wondered what indignities Christa had endured before returning in England, and wished the younger woman had remained in Algiers. She couldn't help but notice the look of intense longing in Mark's eyes when he saw Christa coming toward him, and she cringed inwardly, recalling how he had felt about her at one time. Her one consolation lay in the fact that Christa had surely been ravished by her captors and was hardly worthy of a duke. Nothing! Absolutely nothing, Willow vowed, would interfere with her plans to marry Mark and become a duchess.

"Come along, Mark, I want to dance," Willow said plaintively, pulling on his arm.

Annoyed, but unable to refuse gracefully, Mark frowned as Willow led him onto the dance floor. There were so many unanswered questions he needed to ask, so much to tell Christa. How did she come to be in England? Why was the man with her calling himself her betrothed? Why had Abdullah freed her? Without meaning to, his eyes lingered on the flat expanse of her stomach and he wondered what had happened to Abdullah's babe.

Sensing the thoughts that whirled in his mind, Christa knew that she had to remove herself from his disturbing presence or break down completely before Brian and Mark's fiancée, for she now knew who it was the two women she had heard earlier had been talking about. Willow and Mark were either already engaged or about to be. She had no right to interfere with his life now. Everything had changed. What they once meant to each other no longer existed. Their lives had taken different courses.

She needed to escape, to recover from the great emotional shock she had just sustained. She said in a voice bordering on hysteria, "I'd like to dance, too, Brian. After all, this is my first ball in months."

His suspicions momentarily laid to rest by Christa's words, Brian smiled. "Of course, my dear, I didn't mean to keep Lord Marlboro from his own party. By all means, let's dance."

Mark watched them walk away, the frown never leaving his face. "Why the dark looks, Mark?" Willow demanded petulantly. "Surely you've gotten over that little slut by now. After all this time, every pirate on the Barbary coast will have had her."

"Why must you be so damned spiteful, Willow, when you know nothing?" Mark snapped, his voice tinged with contempt. "You have no idea what Christa has been through and no reason to speak of her in such a manner. Where is your compassion?"

Caught in the snare of her own words, Willow floundered, aware that she still had much to fear from Christa Horton, despite her engagement to the boorish Brian Kent. "I'm sorry, my love," Willow apologized prettily, though inwardly she smoldered with hatred and contempt for the woman who possessed the power to deny her her heart's desire. "Let's dance. I need to feel your arms around me."

Willow's words brought another scowl to Mark's face, for during the past weeks she had tried every opportunity to get him into her bed. Thus far he had persevered, but Allah only knew how much longer he could have resisted her subtle seduction. He was only a man, one who hadn't tasted a woman's flesh since he had last lain in love with Christa in Constantine.

These past weeks had been a living hell for Mark. Finally in possession of his health after a long, slow recuperation, he had traveled to London purposely to hire a ship to take him to Algiers—and to Christa, knowing full well it might cost him his life. After considering long and hard his hasty promise given Christa in a moment of weakness, he still floundered on the horns of dilemma. Only the advice of another he held dear kept him in London this long.

Though Mark was quick to admit that Willow had helped ease the loneliness and pain he suffered at Christa's loss, he knew that she was waiting patiently for his proposal, hinting time and again at her expectations of becoming his duchess. Yet how could he wed another, when a sweet siren with bluebell eyes and hair the color of spun silver possessed his heart? Even should Christa be lost to him forever, he still had no intention of proposing marriage to Willow, despite the fact he owed her his very existence. Rescuing Christa from Abdullah's harem had occupied his heart and mind, leaving room for nothing else. Now, through some miracle, Christa was close enough to take into his arms.

Unable to think of an acceptable reason to deny Willow's request, Mark led her out on the dance floor, straining his eyes to find the object of his desire in the press of bodies. If Brian Kent could be believed, and he had no reason to doubt him, Christa would soon become his bride. How could she marry that man? Mark wondered distractedly —until he remembered that she had obviously had no idea he had escaped slavery and fled to London. No doubt she thought never to see him again and sought only to attain some sense of normalcy in the shambles of her life. But no longer was there a need for Christa to cling to Brian Kent for protection. And before this night was over Mark fully intended to claim what was his.

Christa lost sight of Mark the moment she set foot on the dance floor and was forced to turn her reluctant attention to Brian's rapid-fire questions

concerning her past association with the Duke of
Marlboro. Hoping her brief replies eased Brian's
suspicions, Christa suddenly grew weary of being
interrogated while still in a highly emotional state.
So when the dance ended she feigned thirst, re-
questing Brian to fetch her a glass of punch, knowing the crush around the refreshment table would
likely cause a considerable delay and give her
enough time to slip out the door and gather her
shattered wits.

Still encumbered by Willow's cloying possessiveness, Mark brightened when a handsome young
man threaded his way through the crowd to stand
beside him. "Allen!" Mark greeted him, enthusias-
tically. "I'm afraid I'm not as well as I thought, and
Willow is eager to dance. Why don't you lead her
out for the next set while I recoup my strength."

Allen slanted Mark an anxious look, but a
surreptitious wink laid the younger man's anxiety
to rest. Evidently Mark had grown weary of Willow's domination and wished to escape for a time.

Actually, Mark had seen Christa slip out the
side door alone and ached to follow. They had so
much to talk about, so much to reveal to each other.
He hoped Allen would take the hint and keep
Willow occupied for some time. Before easing out
the door into the night, he stopped Peter and slyly
suggested he detain Brian Kent for at least an hour,
using whatever means necessary.

He found her standing before the maze staring
pensively into the darkness, as if remembering that
time months ago when they first met—and shared
a kiss. Even then he knew she was his kismet.

So stealthily did Mark approach that Christa
assumed she was alone until two steely arms surrounded her, pulling her into the curve of a hard,
lean frame. Soft lips nuzzled the back of her neck,
inhaling the special fragrance that clung to her,

sending his senses reeling with desire. It was always thus when they came together, their passion explosive and all consuming.

"Christa, my love," Mark murmured into the pink shell of her ear. "I don't know what miracle brought you to me, but never again will I scoff at fate."

The moment he touched her, Christa knew it was Mark's arms that embraced her, Mark's lips that brushed the soft skin of her neck. She had lain in his arms too often not to recognize the virile scent of him, a blend of soap, tobacco, a mixture of spices, and his own natural masculine odor. Slowly she turned in his embrace, their eyes meeting beneath the brilliant moonlight, and Christa found herself lost in deep pools of emerald green.

"Ahmed . . . Mark, I . . ."

The words died in her throat as his lips descended to devour her mouth in a demanding kiss that seemed to go on forever, conjuring up memories of how she felt in his arms, all warm and soft and writhing with passion. What they shared transcended the body and joined the souls. This was the man responsible for leading her across the threshold to womanhood, the man who had tutored her in the art of love, taught her what it meant to express her sensuality and demand love in return.

His caresses were exquisite torture; his nearness, touch and smell drove her wild, and for a moment all sense of reality deserted her. Nothing mattered but the knowledge that she rested in Mark's arms, where she belonged.

"Christa, my love, we need to talk," he said, reluctantly breaking off the kiss. "Come." Grasping her hand, he led her into the maze where he knew they would not be disturbed. Blindly, she followed, until they came to a bench and he pulled her down beside him. Drawing her breath in sharply, Christa could only gaze into those green eyes holding her captive with their bold, seductive promise.

"Mark." His name tasted warm and sweet on her tongue.

"Christa, my love, do you know how I've agonized over your circumstances these past months? Just the thought of you forced to Abdullah's bed, bearing the child that should have been mine, drove me to the brink of despair. All those weeks I lay sick, I suffered pain far greater than any inflicted upon my body."

Abruptly Mark realized what he had said about the babe, and his eyes lowered to Christa's flat stomach. According to his calculations she should be huge with child. "What happened to the child? Did you lose it?"

Christa froze, realizing the time had come to reveal the truth. "Mark, there is no child. There never was. My pregnancy was something Doctor Sayid invented to keep me out of Abdullah's bed."

Mark frowned in confusion. "I—I don't understand. You mean Abdullah never . . . that you never . . . How could such a thing happen? It doesn't sound like Abdullah."

"I'll try to explain," Christa said slowly. "It's simple, really. Each time Abdullah tried to take me, I became so upset I—I was sick all over him."

"You were sick in Abdullah's presence?" Mark laughed, well aware of Abdullah's abhorrence of illness of any kind. "That's rich! Surely Allah guided your path."

"Perhaps," Christa granted. "When it happened more than once, Abdullah sent Doctor Sayid to examine me. The good doctor held little love for your brother, and when he suggested a method of keeping me out of Abdullah's bed I quickly agreed. He told Abdullah I was pregnant, and since he hadn't bedded me, the child could only belong to you. My bouts of nausea infuriated Abdullah, especially when Doctor Sayid predicted that the pregnancy would be a difficult one and my bouts of illness likely to continue indefinitely. As the doctor predicted, your brother quickly lost interest in me."

Mark grew thoughtful. "Why didn't you tell me all this when you had the chance? Why did you deliberately lie to me?"

"At first I was forced to agree with Abdullah. He threatened to kill you instantly if I objected to anything he told you. I'd rather hurt you than cause your death."

"Yet you continued to perpetrate the lie when we were alone later," Mark accused her.

"I had no choice. At the time, I had no idea Abdullah meant to release me for ransom. Had I but known, I would have been truthful. Please understand," Christa pleaded, "that I feared you would one day make your way back to Constantine if you knew the truth. I value your life too much to cause your death. Returning to Constantine would be akin to committing suicide. I knew Abdullah would learn soon enough I wasn't pregnant, and I probably would have killed myself rather than go to his bed willingly. That's why I extracted your promise to make a life without me, and I see you have followed my advice."

Was there any merit to the gossip that had Mark and Willow engaged? Christa wondered. Evidently Mark had taken her advice to forget her, and she closed her eyes against the sudden thrust of pain that thought brought her.

"I have no life without you, Christa," he said, his voice suspiciously hoarse. "I never intended to keep that promise. But tell me, what happened after I left Constantine with the Janissaries?"

"After Abdullah sent you away, he had no further use for me. I was nothing more than an instrument of his revenge. And by that time his harem was quite full of young virgins, many of them younger and more beautiful than I. My usefulness came to an end when he no longer needed me to taunt you. Nor did he desire me, since he thought I was carrying a child. Thank God Doctor Sayid convinced him to write to my father and demand ransom for my safe return."

"Did your father go to Constantine to get you? Did he take you to Tunis before returning to England?"

"No, Father didn't go to Constantine. Mother was ill, so he sent Brian in his stead. And I came directly to England."

"So Brian has been here in London with you all this time," Mark said, tight-lipped with jealousy.

"No," Christa said. "Father thought I should leave the Barbary states and all sad memories behind as quickly as possible, so Brian took me to Algiers where I booked passage to England. Then he returned to Tunis. He only arrived in London recently."

"And you are soon to marry your fiancée."

"It's what my parents expect."

"No! I won't allow it. You love me. We belong together."

Christa flushed, unable to deny his words. Instead, she said, "You mentioned you were ill. Tell me how you escaped the Spanish and how you came to England."

"I owe my escape and my life to Willow," Mark revealed, launching into the tale of how Willow found him sick and out of his head and bought his freedom. "I was suffering from malaria and single-handedly she nursed me back to health. She brought me to England, and I've been months recuperating from my illness. I owe her more than I can ever repay."

His words made Christa sadly aware of Willow's strong hold on Mark. A hold that would have eventually led to marriage had Christa not reappeared to alter his life. "There . . . there is talk of an engagement between you and Willow," she remarked cautiously.

"I won't deny it didn't enter my mind," Mark disclosed, his eyes burning into hers. "But most of the rumors were Willow's doing. Before I continued with my life, I intended to return to Constantine."

"You were going back to Constantine?" gasped Christa. "Knowing it might mean your death?"

"Yes. I wanted desperately to return. It grieved me deeply to think of Abdullah possessing all that is rightfully mine. He destroyed all I loved and held dear and he must be made to pay for his evil deeds."

The thought that Mark would risk his life for her sent her heart leaping for joy. "I'm glad you didn't go to Constantine," she confessed. "Forget Abdullah. Your life is here in England."

"You're wrong, Christa. One day I will return, I swear it by all I hold holy. Abdullah will not escape punishment for causing the death of my parents, for I since learned that he is responsible for my father's death as well as my mother's."

Christa's heart sank. As long as Mark insisted upon seeking revenge there was no future for them. She could not bear the agony of losing him again now that he had returned to her life. Somehow she had to dissuade him.

"If you are so set upon this course, Mark, I wish you luck," she said sadly.

"You sound as if this is the last time we'll see each other," Mark accused her sharply.

"Your life lies in another direction," she responded brokenly. "With Willow, perhaps, to whom you owe your life. My future lies . . . with Brian," she lied. "We are to be married soon."

"No!" asserted Mark defiantly. "We belong together! Willow understands that gratitude is all I feel for her. She knows I don't love her. What about you? Can you truthfully say you love Brian?"

"I . . . I'm fond of him," she hedged. "Our marriage was planned long before I met you. My parents want this match and . . . and I feel obligated to honor their wishes."

"Obligation be damned!" Mark thundered, scowling darkly. "You're mine. If you have any doubts, I'll soon change your mind."

19

Confusion and anger warred within Mark as his hand cupped Christa's chin, tilting her head upward, his eyes probing mercilessly into the deep blue depths of hers. And when words failed him, he captured her lips, his hungry kiss possessing her utterly, demanding capitulation. Denying her feelings, her head rolled from side to side and she breathed erratically as his mouth feasted upon hers, his tongue stabbing relentlessly into the moist depths. Through the thin silk of her gown she felt the insatiable, demanding hardness of him as he drew her onto his lap.

"Would you deny this, sweet siren?" he whispered hoarsely as she felt her breasts swell with desire beneath his questing hands. "We were made for each other. Allah has brought us together, and nothing else matters."

"It—it's different now, Mark," Christa insisted. "Many things have changed. We are no longer

the same people. You now have Willow to consider.
Your debt to her cannot be so easily dismissed. And
what about Brian?''

"Hang Willow!" Mark exclaimed, his anger
bordering on violence. "You're mine and I'll have
you, Willow and Brian be damned!"

Tugging down the neckline of her low-cut
bodice, Mark freed her breasts before a protest
formed in her throat, the cool night air
honeycombing her nipples, which to Christa's chagrin grew erect beneath his burning gaze. He
chuckled appreciatively as the rosy buds peaked
and hardened to almost painful sensitivity. She was
all that was passion, he thought with pride, his
sweet, wild siren, all that was woman, and he would
never let her go.

As his fingers worked their magic on her helpless, tingling breasts, a languid heat built inside
her, until hot flames danced along her defenseless
flesh, threatening to consume her completely. And
then she felt the warmth of his mouth capture a
sensitive nipple, his tongue wet and rough as he
licked and suckled, his teeth nipping gently. Suddenly the pulsing between Christa's thighs became
a roaring throb, and she clung to his broad shoulders lest she drown in the whirlpool of her passion.

"Mark, no! Not here," she pleaded, fearing
that either Willow or Brian would burst upon them
at any moment.

But her words fell on deaf ears as his fingers
lifted the hem of her gown and she felt the warm
brush of his hand against the sensitive flesh of her
inner thigh. Then he found the moist warmth
nestled between her legs, and Christa gasped at the
blissful sensations his touch brought her. His
smooth, honeyed caress lured her to the brink of
ecstasy and held her there, suspended, as his fingers
worked magic on her swollen flesh.

"I want to give you pleasure, my love," Mark breathed into her ear. "Come, don't hold back. It pleases me to bring you joy."

The renewed pressure of his fingers dancing in and out of that place that yearned for his possession brought her exquisite rapture. The cry of surrender that broke unbidden from her lips was stifled by Mark's mouth, leaving her breathless and shaken. Christa's passion sparked Mark's, as he hastily unfastened his trousers, desperate to ease his own driving need. He shifted her on his lap, flexed his hips, and Christa felt the hard, throbbing length of him probe the tender opening. But his intentions were thwarted by the sound of approaching footsteps crunching on gravel, driving them apart.

"Mark, where are you?" a petulant voice demanded.

"Damn!" Mark cursed bitterly, setting Christa aside and hastily arranging his clothes into some semblance of order before helping Christa with hers.

"Mark," Willow repeated reproachfully. "I know you're in there, though Allen tried to convince me otherwise. Are you alone?"

"You may as well answer," Christa sighed regretfully. "I hope you have a good explanation for your—er, Willow."

"I owe her no explanation," Mark snapped crossly. Given a few more minutes he would have possessed fully the woman he had yearned for, the woman he had dreamed about for months. But that precious moment now lay shattered at his feet, and nothing remained but the wild desire pounding in his blood. Christa was his, damn it, and if it took force to make her realize that marriage to Brian Kent was not her kismet, he wouldn't hesitate to use it.

Grasping her elbow, Mark led Christa through

the winding paths of the maze, his face still flushed with suppressed passion, a passion no one but Christa could assuage. When they reached the entrance, Christa saw that Willow was not alone. Beside Willow stood a handsome young man who stared fixedly at Christa, as if seeing a ghost.

"I'm sorry, Mark." The young man shrugged. "I tried, but—"

"It doesn't matter, Allen," Mark maintained, clasping him on the shoulder. Turning to Christa and ignoring Willow's glowering expression when she recognized Christa as the woman monopolizing Mark, he said, "Christa, this is my brother Allen. Allen, this is Miss Christa Horton."

"Yazid," breathed Christa, her eyes enormous. "But I thought—"

"Allen," the young man corrected gently. "It is the name my mother chose for me. Of course you had no idea I arrived in England about the same time, ah—Mark left. The Duke was still alive then."

"I'll admit it came as quite a shock to find myself welcomed home by Allen," Mark interjected, his love for his brother clearly evident. "I feared I might never see him again."

"But how—?"

"Let Allen tell you," Willow rudely interrupted, understanding none of the conversation and feeling left out. "I've hardly seen Mark all evening and since he is *my* escort, I intend to monopolize him the rest of the night."

Though his face tautened in displeasure, Mark allowed Willow to grasp his arm and lead him toward the house. He would certainly be lacking in manners if he purposely ignored Willow, for he had indeed escorted her to the ball and courtesy demanded he attend her. Flinging an apologetic look over his shoulder, a look that promised Christa their next meeting would prove more satisfactory, he said, "Please see that Christa gets safely inside, brother."

Christa watched them walk off toward the beckoning lights of the house, Willow's plaintive voice drifting back to her. "What in the world were you doing with that woman in the maze? Once everyone knows what she is, she'll be too ashamed to show her face in public." Mark's sharp retort was lost, but whatever he said effectively cut off Willow's insults.

In the filtered moonlight Allen saw the deep flush spreading across Christa's face and wanted to break Willow's slim neck. Of course he knew all about Christa and Mark, for he had spent long hours with his brother during the course of his illness and heard over and over the story of their ill-fated love.

"Pay no attention to Willow, Christa," he urged, his voice tinged with compassion. "She's vicious as well as jealous. I know for a fact that you're the only woman my brother loves."

"You . . . you know about us?"

"Please don't be alarmed. Mark and I are very close. During his long convalescence he confided in me. I know all about you."

Christa lowered her head, unable to look Allen in the eyes—green eyes very much like his brother's. In fact, he resembled Mark a great deal. Tall, whip-cord lean, with a proud profile. Only his blue-black hair differed from Mark's burnished locks.

"Christa, there's no shame in what you feel for my brother. Don't deny that love."

"You don't understand, Allen," Christa sought to explain. "I tried to tell Mark that we are no longer the same people. There are other things involved now, other feelings to consider. Mark is . . . He owes Willow his life and she expects him to—to make her his wife."

"Did Mark tell you he was committed to Willow?" Allen asked sharply.

"Not exactly," Christa hedged, "but everyone is talking about it. It's obvious they belong together."

"Obvious to you, maybe, but not to me, or to Mark. My brother loves you. Did he tell you I had to forcibly restrain him from rushing off to Constantine long before he was physically able? Did he reveal how I discouraged him from facing Abdullah when he hadn't a chance of returning alive?"

"You know that Abdullah held me captive?"

"I told you, Mark told me everything. Everything," he repeated, staring at her fixedly.

"Oh," Christa said in a small voice. So Mark had told him about her supposed pregnancy. No wonder Allen discouraged his brother from pursuing a woman he assumed had become Abdullah's whore. It was on the tip of her tongue to reveal the truth, but at the last moment she decided to leave the telling to Mark, adroitly changing the subject. "Tell me how you came to be in London, Allen. How did you escape Abdullah?"

"The Grand Vizier learned of Abdullah's plot to seize the beylic after Father's death and sent word to me. I was away at the time hawking in the desert and living with the Tuaregs.

"I returned to the city at once, hoping to bring Mother to safety, but it was already too late. Abdullah had put her to death."

Filled with compassion, Christa placed a soothing hand on his arm when his voice cracked with emotion. Clearing his throat, Allen continued, "I knew it was foolish to retaliate without Mark's help, so I fled Constantine while I was able, expecting to find Mark still in England. But evidently the

Grand Vizier's message reached him before I did, for I found him already gone. Thankfully I arrived in time to see the old duke alive. He died shortly afterwards, leaving his title and estates to Mark."

"And you've been in England ever since?" Christa questioned.

"I had no idea where to find Mark. I felt if I waited long enough, he would send me word where to join him. The Grand Vizier knew where I was, of course, but Mark told me he was put to death shortly after I left Algiers. Abdullah wanted no reminders of Father's regime."

By now they had reached the house and the noise from the party came out to greet them. So did Brian. "Where have you been, Christa?" he asked sharply, eyeing Allen warily. "I've looked everywhere for you."

"No need for worry, Brian, I merely stepped outside for air," Christa explained. "And the duke's brother was kind enough to keep me company. Have you met Lord Allen?"

Smiling obsequiously, Brian turned his attention to the young man standing beside his betrothed. "I've not had the pleasure. It's good to meet you, my lord. I am Brian Kent, Miss Horton's fiance."

Allen nodded curtly, wondering how Christa could have ever promised herself to such an obnoxious boor. "Mr. Kent, Miss Horton, good to have met you both." His green eyes pierced Christa's composure as they effectively conveyed his sentiments in regard to her fiance.

As if in a daze Christa danced, smiled, and made appropriate replies the rest of the evening, from time to time her eyes searching out Mark and Willow as they flirted and talked together like close friends—or lovers. Then suddenly Allen was beside them, inviting Brian into the library for something stronger than punch. His eyes glowing with pride at having been singled out by the duke's brother, Brian accepted with alacrity, leaving Christa to her own devices without a backward glance.

The moment they disappeared through the door, strong arms claimed Christa and swept her onto the dance floor. When she raised her eyes, Mark's mischievous grin smiled down on her. "That was rather underhanded of you," she accused him, suppressing a surge of joy.

"The man doesn't love you, Christa," Mark remarked boldly. "I took special note of the fact that he left you without a thought for your welfare. He's merely using you to further his career." Mark prided himself on his ability to judge a person's character and his competence in recognizing a man in love when he saw one. Under no circumstances could Brian Kent be described as being besotted by love.

"You don't know that," Christa retorted shortly. Although she couldn't deny the truth of his words, it hurt too much to admit that Brian held her in little regard.

"Nor do you love him."

"Mark, please don't confuse me. I'm not right for you. If word got out about—about my past, I'd be shunned by society. I'm not good enough for you. Besides, one day you will return to Constantine and—"

"If you marry me, Christa, I might be persuaded to remain in England," Mark revealed, stunning her with his surprising disclosure.

"I don't believe you, Mark. You will never be content until Abdullah is punished and you seize the beylic."

"Perhaps," Mark admitted somewhat guiltily. "But even if that were so, I'd change the law so you could become my wife—my only wife."

"If that were possible, your father would have done so long before now," scoffed Christa.

"Father was of the old teaching, while I intend to seek reform if given the power to do so. I want you, Christa, and I'll have you, Brian be damned!"

Though they spoke in low tones, Mark's last sentence was heard by Willow who had manipulated her dancing partner to within hearing distance of Mark and Christa. But they were so engrossed in each other that neither saw Willow or the crafty look that crossed her face upon hearing Mark's declaration. With a flash of cunning, Willow instantly contrived a way to thrust Christa to the outer edges of society and at the same time to provide London with delicious scandal. Once Christa became an outcast, Mark would realize just how unsuitable a wife she would make. Flashing a malicious smile, she raised her head and whispered into the ear of her partner, a notorious rake and gossip, who slanted a startled look at Christa, then bent his head again so as not to miss a word of Willow's scintillating gossip.

"Please, Mark, don't stare at me so intently," Christa pleaded. "People are beginning to wonder."

Through a fringe of dark lashes, Mark noted that they had indeed become the center of attention. Even those standing on the sidelines exhibited uncommon interest in them. "Ignore them," he advised, hoping Christa hadn't noticed Willow standing in a group of people, all looking at her with something akin to revulsion. Had Willow deliberately revealed facts about Christa's captivity in Constantine after he told her to keep her knowledge to herself? Immediately he sought to divert Christa. "Where are you staying?"

"In my aunt's house," Christa answered. "She has remarried and left her home to me. Aunt Mary and her new husband are on their honeymoon."

"And you're staying there alone? With no one but servants in attendance?" It annoyed him to think that Brian Kent had free access to the woman he loved.

"Elissa and Lenore are with me."

"Lenore? Mother's woman?" Christa nodded. "And Elissa, too? You brought that little slut to London?"

Christa bristled indignantly. "She's changed, Mark. She's not the same person you once knew. I told you before, we've become close. She's suffered much since you saw her last and has been a great comfort to me."

Mark shook his head doubtfully, but he was willing to give Elissa another chance for Christa's sake. "Omar will be glad to hear Elissa is safe. Though he is a stern father, he worried constantly over her fate."

"Omar is here with you?"

"He found me in Algiers shortly after Willow bought my freedom. He obtained a berth on the same ship and arrived in England with us. He would not leave me."

Suddenly the music ended and they left the dance floor, aware of the curious stares directed at them. Seeing Brian nowhere in sight, Christa quickly excused herself and was fleeing toward the withdrawing room when she saw Willow swiftly closing in on Mark.

Primping in the mirror and making minor repairs to her hair, Christa gave little heed to the two bejeweled matrons who entered just behind her, their frosty glances sweeping her with barely disguised contempt.

"I can't imagine Sir Peter inviting someone like

her to his party honoring the Duke of Marlboro,"
sniffed one of the women, casting a disparaging
glance in Christa's direction.

"Imagine! Willingly consorting with corsairs,
agreeing to become their—their whore!" They
spoke as if Christa were invisible. "What must Sir
Peter be thinking of? And that fiance of hers. What
kind of man would saddle himself with a woman
whose reputation could do him no good? I wonder
how many pirates she bedded?" The second woman
shivered delicately.

"Someone ought to speak with his grace. I saw
them dancing and he appeared quite entranced
with her. Had he realized what she is, I'm certain he
would have avoided all contact with such a notorious woman."

Having completed their toilette, the two matrons swept haughtily from the room, lifting their
skirts aside as they brushed past a stunned Christa.

"Oh, God," she sobbed, covering her face with
her hands. "Who would . . . ?" And then the answer came to her. No one but Willow would spread
evil lies about her. Consumed by jealousy, she had
grotesquely distorted the truth until nothing was
left of Christa's reputation but mutilated shreds.

Wanting only to escape an intolerable situation, Christa fled the room, searching frantically
for Brian, painfully aware of the derisive looks and
scathing remarks that followed in her wake. Breathing a sigh of relief, she saw him just entering the
ballroom with Allen, blissfully unaware of the
malicious rumors spread by Willow.

Rushing to his side, she beseeched him, "Brian,
I want to leave. Now! Please."

"Leave? Now?" Brian repeated stupidly. "But
I'm having such a grand time."

"Please, Brian, I—I'm ill."

"Well, in that case, my dear, of course we'll leave," he allowed grudgingly.

Puzzled, Allen watched their departure before going off in search of Mark. If something had happened to hasten Christa's departure, he intended to find out what it was.

Still abed despite the late hour, Christa lacked the will to rise and begin the day. Last evening had been a nightmare. Though finding Mark alive and well was like a dream come true, discovering Willow so enmeshed in Mark's life plunged her into the depths of dispair. She should have realized, given Willow's intense jealousy where Mark was concerned, that the woman wouldn't hesitate to ruin her reputation at the first opportunity. If Willow meant to ridicule and embarrass her in public and belittle her in Mark's eyes, then she had succeeded admirably.

"Christa, are you unwell?" Christa was so immersed in misery that she failed to hear Elissa enter. "It isn't like you to lie abed so late. I heard you return last night, and it was still quite early. Didn't you have a good time?"

"If you only knew," groaned Christa, recalling the hateful remarks directed at her by the two matrons.

"What happened? Did Brian—"

"It's nothing Brian did, Elissa. Sit down, dear, for what I'm about to tell you will surely come as a shock." She sat up, allowing Elissa to fluff the pillows before the younger girl settled down beside her.

"Ahmed is alive and well and living in England."

"Prince Ahmed alive?" squealed Elissa incredulously. "How do you know? Oh," she said, comprehension dawning, "You saw him at the party. Ahmed is the new Duke of Marlboro!"

"Exactly," Christa confirmed with a tight smile. "You can well imagine my shock when we came face to face last evening."

"I imagine his shock was nearly as great as yours," Elissa commented wryly. "Were you able to speak with him privately?"

"Yes," sighed Christa wistfully. "You see, a— lady bought his freedom before he was sold to the Spanish. A lady he knew previously. His mistress, in fact. He was ill and she brought him to England."

"Oh," said Elissa, uncertain how to respond. "Did you tell Ahmed the truth about your pregnancy?"

"He is called Mark now, and yes, I told him everything. Thankfully, he understood and held me blameless. But it made little difference. I still urged him to make a life without me. A woman of my soiled reputation has no place in his future."

"Christa, what are you talking about? That's ridiculous."

"You haven't heard everything."

"There's more?"

"Willow Langtry, the woman who bought Mark's freedom, was aboard the *Bon Ami* when Redbeard launched his attack. She knows nothing of what happened after I was abducted, but she deliberately spread vile gossip about me. She told everyone at the ball that I was—that I willingly played whore to my captors. Of course the tale spread like wildfire and I became an instant outcast, looked upon with loathing and contempt. If Willow hoped to debase me in order to make me unacceptable to Mark, she succeeded admirably. I couldn't get out of there fast enough."

"The bitch!" Elissa spat. "Surely Mark is wise

enough to disregard the woman's vile tongue. He is one of the few who knows the truth."

"He's a duke now, Elissa. Taking up with me would harm his reputation and place him outside polite society. Even Allen understands my dilemma."

"Allen?"

"Oh, of course you don't know. Mark's brother Yazid is in England. He is called Allen now. He arrived about the same time Mark left. I know Mark was greatly relieved to find his brother safe, for he worried constantly about his fate. There is something else you don't know," Christa beamed, eyes dancing mischievously. "Omar is with Mark."

"My father? He is alive and in England?" Elissa exclaimed happily. "I nearly convinced myself he hadn't survived the ordeal of being abandoned in the desert by Abdullah's men."

"Your father is not an easy man to kill," remarked Christa, recalling the huge man who had proved his devotion to Mark many times over.

"I can hardly wait to tell Lenore about Ahmed—I mean, about Mark and Father. She'll be as happy as we are." Suddenly a sobering thought brought a frown to her face. "What do you intend to do, Christa? About Brian, I mean. He expects to marry you soon."

"I don't know," Christa pondered. "I need time to think. I want to do what's best where my parents are concerned but . . ."

"What about yourself? Doesn't your happiness count?"

Christa shook her head. "My own desires are not important."

"Mark loves you. I know he does."

"And I love him, but too much is involved here

to take up where we left off. How long will it be before he leaves me and returns to Constantine to deal with Abdullah? I'm afraid, Elissa. Afraid to follow my heart. But it would kill me to lose him again.''

20

Christa exhibited little shock when Mark appeared at the door the next afternoon. What did surprise her was finding Allen with his brother. Mark's face wore an inscrutable mask as he charged into the house, daring anyone to stop him.

"Mark, what are you doing here?"

"I told you we needed to talk." When her gaze shifted to Allen, Mark added, "Allen came along to take Elissa to see her father. Would you please call her?"

"Why didn't you bring Omar here?" Christa asked curiously.

Mark smiled, his teeth a white slash across his tanned face. "I want no interruptions while we are . . . talking. Lenore will accompany them. Will you call them or shall I?"

Christa bristled. "This is my house and I—"

"Elissa!" Mark bellowed. "Lenore!"

Christa looked to Allen for help, but the young man met her silent plea with amusement.

Elissa appeared almost instantly. "Prince Ahmed," she greeted him somewhat shamefacedly, recalling her brazen behavior that night she had tried to seduce him and earned his anger.

"Seeing how fond Christa is of you, Elissa, you may call me Mark, the name I am known by in England," he informed her coolly. That he held no fond feelings for the girl was evident. "This is my brother Allen, who is here to take you to visit your father. Lenore is to accompany you."

Schooled by years of being taught her master's wish was to be instantly obeyed, Elissa did not question his authority, but nodded her acquiescence. Stealing a shy look at Allen through a fringe of heavy dark lashes, Elissa was clearly intrigued by Mark's younger brother. She thought Allen just as handsome as Mark, with his swarthy features and green eyes, and from that moment her heart was hopelessly lost.

Allen appeared nearly as smitten as Elissa. Next to Christa, he thought Elissa the most exquisite creature he had ever seen. Her facial bones were delicately carved, her lips full and red. High, well-defined cheekbones lent an air of mystery to her exotic features. Smooth, silken skin glowed warmly with gold undertones, and her curtain of dark hair swung loose to her tiny waist, which flared into rounded hips. She was petite and flowerlike with firm, high breasts that held Allen's sparkling eyes captive. Such was Christa and Mark's absorption in one another that neither noticed Allen's preoccupation with the beautiful Berber girl.

"You don't have to go if you don't want to, Elissa," Christa declared, annoyed. "You are no servant to be ordered about."

"I'd like to see my father, Christa," Elissa replied, glancing up at Allen with a coy expression. "I'll get Lenore."

Lenore chose that moment to come bustling in, wiping her hands on her apron. "Did someone call?" Then her eyes lit on Mark and Allen, and she squealed in delight, throwing herself into first Mark's arms and then Allen's. When the boys were growing up, she had helped Lady Emily care for them and had become quite attached to her two charges. Abruptly remembering that they were no longer children but grown men, she drew back in embarrassment.

But neither Mark nor Allen seemed to mind Lenore's exuberant greeting. Both recalled with fondness her devotion to their mother as well as her care of them as children. When asked to accompany Allen and Elissa, she agreed without hesitation, which served only to fuel Christa's vexation. She cared little for Mark's intrusion into her private life or his ordering her two friends around as if he had the right to do so. But what good would it do to protest, she wondered, when already Allen was herding the two women out of the door? He murmured a hasty good-bye to Christa and bent his brother a meaningful look, causing Christa to blush furiously. She had little difficulty deciphering his silent message. Whether she liked it or not, in a matter of minutes she was alone with Mark.

Glancing around at the various doors leading from the foyer, Mark grasped her hand, allowing her no time to protest as he led her into the sitting room, carefully closing the door behind him. Turning to face her, he asked, "Why did you leave the party so abruptly last night?"

Tilting her chin at a defiant angle, Christa replied, "You know very well I couldn't face those

horrible things being said about me. How do you
think they found out? Certainly not from Brian,
whose greatest fear is having everyone learn about
my sordid past. Did you tell them?''

"What! Christa, you know I'd never do such a
thing!" Mark declared, aghast.

"There's only one other who knows about me
and—and what happened on the *Bon Ami*.''

"Surely you don't think Willow—ah, I can see
you do. I don't believe she would do such a thing. I
realize she can be—er, unpleasant when things
don't go her way, but spreading gossip about you is
downright cruel."

"Willow would go to any lengths to help her
cause. Can you deny she expects you to offer
marriage?" she challenged.

Mark had the grace to flush. "I must admit the
thought did cross my mind but I never seriously—"

"Perhaps not, but Willow certainly is serious
about becoming a duchess," Christa interrupted
rudely.

"I owe Willow my life, Christa. I can't very
well ignore her. Besides, this conversation is getting
us nowhere. I didn't come here to talk about
Willow, I came to speak about us.''

"There is no 'us,' Mark. Our lives have taken
different courses. Willow wants to be your wife and
I can see no reason to deny her that honor."

"It's you I love, Christa. Have you forgotten so
soon the love we shared? I want no other woman in
my bed but you."

"I've . . . forgotten nothing," Christa choked,
quailing beneath the heat of those stabbing green
eyes that pierced her soul and turned her body to
quivering jelly.

"Perhaps you need reminding," he said sharply, angered by her foolish resistance to the inevitable.

Tenderly he fingered a stray tendril of hair curling on her cheek, then touched her trembling lips with one finger. Scattering her firm resolve like leaves before the wind, he traced the line of her cheekbone and chin, his touch sending rivers of fire racing along her spine.

His hands felt warm and strong as they lingered on her collarbone, moving downward to her bare arm which he massaged in a circular motion, sending erotic messages to her brain—messages she tried hard to ignore.

Then he pulled her roughly, amost violently, to him his hand locking against her spine. "Sweet siren," he whispered seductively, "you drive me wild with wanting."

Burying her face against his throat, inhaling his special male scent, Christa knew that she was fashioned only for this man; no other would do. Surrendering to the whirlwind of passion his touch created, her arms slid around his neck. His hands dropped to the hollow of her back, then lower, to cup the smooth mounds of her buttocks, clasping her into the hardness of his body until she felt the virile proof of his desire throbbing against her stomach.

"I've not had a woman since the last time we made love in that dismal cell in Constantine," Mark admitted, groaning as the soft curves of her body molded intimately with his own.

Christa drew back, astounded. Could it be true? Surely not, she scoffed. Not with a desirable and accomplished woman like Willow eager to grant his every desire. "But—what about Willow?" she asked, giving voice to her doubt.

Mark shook his head in denial. "At first I was

too ill. And later, I . . . couldn't. For the love of Allah, Christa, how could another woman appeal to me after knowing the pleasure of your love? No other woman would do, though Allah knows I've had plenty of opportunity."

"Surely you would have married Willow if I hadn't returned to complicate your life," Christa stated reproachfully.

"I seriously doubt I would have gone so far. I probably would have forsworn marriage and left it to Allen to provide an heir for the Marlboro estates and title."

Weary of words, Mark seized her in a crushing embrace, driving the breath from her as he captured her mouth, devouring its softness, outlining the full contours with his tongue before delving inside. Coherent thought fled as she met his kiss with wild abandon, opening her mouth wider to accept the homage of his tongue.

Without breaking contact, his nimble fingers moved to the fastenings on her dress, working each button, each lacing, with gentle impatience until piece by piece all her clothing lay in a careless heap at her feet. Anxious now to join her flesh to his, Christa helped him peel off the constricting layers of his own clothes. Delight seized her when she felt the warm texture of his bare skin beneath her fingertips. As with one accord they sank to the thickly carpeted floor, stretching out side by side, breasts, hips and thighs molded together, lips clinging.

With maddening deliberation, his mouth slid downward, tracing a trail of fire along one cheek, delicate chin and white throat, coming to rest on an erect nipple, his tongue darting out to caress the sensitive, swollen bud. His hands skittered across her silken belly and onto her thigh as the hot, moist tugging at her nipple sent a thrill of excitement surging through her body.

Wishing to bring him as much pleasure as he was giving her, Christa's small hands explored with tantalizing slowness. She felt the muscles along his broad back tense and shudder beneath her fingertips and his buttocks tauten as she outlined the tight mounds. Creeping forward, her wondering fingers closed around the hard, unyielding ridge of his staff, and he bucked upward, a cry leaping from his throat.

She was surprised when his hand grasped hers, tugging it away. "Sweet, sweet, siren, if you continue, I'll not be able to control myself. I have been too long without a woman and I want to give you pleasure," he said, smiling.

Before she realized his intent he moved downward, and when his lips found the velvet dip of her pelvis, planting erotic kisses there, she arched her hips, writhing against him. Lower and lower his lips trailed, until she felt him drawing her legs over his shoulders, and then his head disappeared.

A searing flame jolted through her body, settling in the moist cleft of her womanhood as intense pleasure radiated from the tiny spear of flesh upon which his mouth feasted. Skillfully he plied his tongue and fingers to intensify her pleasure until her head was tossing from side to side and her hips jerked and twisted. When he reached beneath her to grasp her buttocks, the firestorm of ecstasy swept her up and carried her away. Bursting into a million tiny fragments, she slowly floated to earth, piece by piece, to find Mark staring lovingly into her eyes.

"I love to watch your face when I bring you pleasure," he whispered, nipping her ear. "My happiness will be complete when I feel myself deep inside you with your tight muscles closing around me. I want to stroke your insides and send us to paradise together."

Christa cried out as the long, throbbing length of him thrust into her, sheathed completely by her silken walls. A hoarse moan burst from Mark's throat, making him realize how desperately he needed and wanted to feel his flesh inside her, joined together as Allah meant them to be. His hands grasped her from behind as he plunged deeper, feeling waves of ecstasy undulate from his groin to all parts of his body. He felt her golden sheath surround him and pull him deeper into her welcoming warmth, and his stroking grew frenzied.

Christa felt him grow huge inside her as their loving assumed an urgent, wild rhythm. He rode her with swift, savage joy that sparked her own passion with devouring flames that threatened to turn her to ash. Again and again he thrust into her until Christa thought she would die from the pleasure. But she did not die. Instead, she climbed to the highest mountain, her body vibrating, wailing like a banshee as she leapt off into space.

At the same time the tremors began in Mark's own muscular body as he spiraled upward to join Christa in her descent from those lofty places he had taken them. Still joined, Christa stared into his sparkling eyes, marveling at his power to control and manipulate her violent response. Twice, within minutes, he had taken her to rapture's summit and still she yearned for more.

"After what we just shared, can you still deny kismet meant us to be together?" he challenged confidently. "Do you think Brian Kent has the power to satisfy you as I do?"

Mutely, Christa shook her head. She could deny nothing. Nor did she want to. Suddenly her eyes grew wide when she felt Mark still inside her, hard, virile and throbbing with life. "Mark!" she gasped, astounded. "You're still—I mean—" A deep flush turned her cheeks rosy.

"Do you find it odd that I still want you?" He laughed softly. "It's been so long, my love, and you're more beautiful than I remember," he said, raking her with an appreciative glance. "Your body is perfect in every respect." He ran his hands familiarly over her curves, causing a shudder to slither across her skin.

"I love your breasts. Your legs are long and supple. My two hands could easily span your waist. You're incredible, my love, and I want you again. Give yourself to me."

"Do I have a choice?" she asked with mild reproof.

"The choice is not yours to make," Mark smiled, confident of his prowess. Then he thrust slowly forward. The bold proof of his desire caused the blood to tingle warmly in her veins, and her blue eyes leaped to shimmering life. "You are warm and damp and inviting," he groaned as he stroked into her softness. His erotic words stoked her ardor into leaping flames as her hips jerked upward to meet his thrust.

The muscles of her legs quivered as she felt his passion ignite and burn out of control. He felt her legs tense, felt the shuddering of her slender body as she neared her climax, and when she cried out he took her keening cries into his mouth, reveling in his ability to please her so thoroughly. And then he knew no more as he reached for the stars and found them.

"Christa, I don't want to hear another word about you marrying Brian Kent, is that clear?" Mark said sternly after they were both dressed and seated together on the sofa.

Twisting her hands in her lap, Christa nodded. "I don't think I could have gone through with it anyway, or allowed him to—to—"

"I understand, love," Mark assured her, a gentle smile curving his lips.

"But, Mark, I'm not good enough for you," she persisted doggedly. "You heard the rumors. They spread like wildfire. You're a duke and—"

"Let me work it out, Christa. Just tell Brian you can't marry him and let me handle the rest."

"Mark, about Abdullah," Christa began hesitantly. "Will you be content to remain in England? Or will this vendetta against your half-brother eventually lead to your death? I couldn't bear the thought of losing you again."

His jaw hardening, Mark's eyes grew distant. Then just as swiftly the look softened. "I'll never leave you for long, my love, can't you understand that? Nor can I forget what Abdullah did to my parents or what he tried to do to you. It's not so much the beylic I want, but revenge. And as Allah is my witness, I'll have it!"

Christa stared at him from beneath shuttered lids. Her proud prince. Would she have him otherwise? No, she decided in a burst of insight. She would not change him, but she would have his promise to let the past go and look to their future together.

She opened her mouth to form the words, but the moment passed when the front door opened and voices alerted them to the fact that Allen had returned with Elissa and Lenore. Sensing Christa was about to say something of importance, Mark mouthed the word, "Later," as a timid knock sounded on the sitting room door.

"He's wonderful," Elissa sighed after the men had left.

"Who?" asked Christa distractedly, her thoughts still on Mark. "Your father?"

"No," Elissa giggled, "although he's fine, too. At least Lenore thought so. I meant Allen. He's every bit as handsome as his brother." She sighed wistfully and Christa gave her an amused look.

"From your obvious adoration, I assume you've lost your heart to the young man. And if my instincts are correct, I'd say you weren't the only one smitten."

Elissa's dark eyes glowed happily. "What happened between you and Mark, Christa? Have you settled your differences?"

"I . . . more or less." She shrugged, flushing. "There was so little time."

"No time! But we were gone for hours. What did you—? Oh." Elissa grinned cheekily. "Then I assume everything is right between you. What about Brian?"

"I can't marry Brian. Even if I don't marry Mark, I could never give myself to Brian, or any other man."

"I'm glad," Elissa confessed. "Brian Kent is not the man for you." She decided against telling Christa about Brian's outrageous behavior with her the day before. "Do you think Mark will return one day to Constantine? Allen feels strongly that Mark should remain in England."

"Not nearly as strongly as I feel about it," Christa muttered dryly.

"Dammit, Willow, I don't want to hurt you, but you know how I feel about Christa," Mark stated, threading long fingers through his hair as he stood before Willow in her richly appointed sitting room.

"How could you, Mark?" Willow accused him,

affronted. "Christa isn't right for you. Her reputation is far from pristine and she could only hurt you if you make her your wife. Besides," she hinted slyly, "you owe me a great debt. If not for me, you would be rotting at the bottom of the sea."

Mark flushed, fully aware of the considerable debt he owed Willow. Short of offering marriage, he was willing to give her anything she wanted. At length he said, "It wouldn't work between us, Willow. I don't love you, and I certainly never mentioned marriage. If I did so while delirious, you can hardly hold me accountable. Ask anything of me but that."

"Marriage is all I want, darling," Willow smiled seductively. "I think you've forgotten how good we are together. At one time you were happy to share my bed. If you give us a chance we could recapture that magic."

During the course of the conversation Willow had sidled so close to Mark that her full breasts brushed his chest. Bewildered by his lack of response, she pressed herself full length against his hard form, reveling in the virile bulge of his masculinity straining against his trousers even at rest. No other man had ever come close to matching Mark's skill in bed, and she'd do anything, employ every subterfuge, to win him. After all she'd done for him he owed her more than mere gratitude.

"I'm sorry, Willow," Mark replied, setting her aside with firm resolved. "I won't give up Christa. Not for you, not for anyone. I'll find a way to repay you, but marriage is definitely not it."

"What about Christa's fiance?" she asked slyly. "Does he know about you and Christa? Do you think he'll give her up so easily?"

"He doesn't love her," Mark said tightly. "He wants her only for what her father can do for his career."

"Then this is good-bye?"

"I'll always think of you as a friend, Willow. And if ever—"

"I know," Willow sneered. "If ever I need anything I have only to ask you. Thank you so much, but what I want you refuse to offer. Get out, Mark. Don't come back until you come to your senses and realize your mistake. When you do, I'll be here waiting."

Aware that his attempts at placating the fiery redhead were failing miserably, Mark shrugged and let himself out the door. It was difficult to remember that at one time her delectable body had given him great pleasure. Exploding in fury, Willow seized the nearest object, a priceless crystal vase, and flung it at the closed door. Feeling somewhat better for the outburst, Willow began searching her mind furiously, conjuring up all manner of mischief she might visit upon the woman Mark claimed he loved.

She thought back over those endless days and nights at sea when she had tirelessly and selflessly nursed him during his life-threatening fever, recalling all the delirious rantings she had listened to but paid little heed to at the time. And now, like a bolt from out of the blue, a good portion of what he said began to make sense. And from it evolved a method of ridding herself of the blond vixen who had robbed her of the only man who could make her happy.

Later that day Willow stood facing Christa, having been shown into the sitting room by a disapproving Elissa.

"Hello, Willow," Christa greeted her warily. "Elissa said you wished to speak with me."

"Don't pretend innocence with me, Christa," Willow fumed, tossing her head of flaming hair. "You've set your sights too high, my dear. Snaring a duke is quite an accomplishment for a mere diplomat's daughter. It didn't take you long to dump a nobody like Brian Kent once Mark entered your life again. Haven't you already done him enough harm?"

Christa bristled indignantly. "I've done him no harm. I love him and surely you must know by now that he loves me."

"Love, bah! You've bewitched him! Why didn't you stay in Constantine where you belong? Or weren't you woman enough to please Abdullah? How many corsairs bedded you before they sold you to the bey?"

"What! How—how do you know about Abdullah? What did Mark tell you?"

"You forget I sat beside Mark night and day listening to his feverish ravings," explained Willow smugly. "What he failed to tell me during his more lucid moments were revealed during his delirium. Did you bring the bey's babe back to England with you?" she asked slyly.

"You—you're mistaken," Christa stuttered, thoroughly dismayed.

"I think not," Willow said. "And if you insist on going through with this marriage to Mark, I'll make all of London aware that you were not only whore to Barbary pirates, but concubine to the bey of Constantine. You'll never be accepted in polite society. Your ostracism will extend to Mark should he be foolish enough to marry you." She paused for breath, giving her words time to settle. Christa quickly jumped into the void.

"There is no child," she insisted, waiting for Willow's reaction. There was none. "There never was. It's a long story, Willow, one I won't bore you with, but suffice it to say I have no child by Abdullah, or anyone."

"I don't believe you," scoffed Willow. "Nor will anyone else. Perhaps you left the child in Constantine. Or maybe it died. But I'm convinced you carried the bey's child. So is Mark. Think what the revelation of that fact will do to Mark once the gossips start in on him. Or to your parents."

Christa's heart sank. Was Willow capable of such deviousness? Of course, came the emphatic reply. Especially if she thought it would gain her Mark's love. The lie that had spared her the horror of Abdullah's bed had come back to haunt her. What would happen if she disregarded Willow's threats?

"I see you're giving the matter serious thought," Willow gloated. "You'd be wise to do so. Besides, Mark owes me an enormous debt and his pride demands he honor it. I wield considerable influence over him, whether he realizes it or not. As long as that debt remains unpaid, I have him just where I want him."

"I realize Mark owes you his life, and rightfully so. But you don't own him. Do you think he would be content to sit back and allow you to spread lies about me?"

"Lies? I think not." Willow smiled complacently. "Were you not Abdullah's slave? Did you not live in his harem?"

Christa flushed, unable to deny the accusations Willow flung at her. "What do you want of me, Willow?" she ground out. "Yes, I was Abdullah's slave! Yes, I lived in his harem! But he never took me to his bed, nor did I bear him a child. My God, you're heartless!"

Willow's brittle laugh brought Christa little comfort. "Heartless, perhaps," she granted, "but also practical. You were never meant to be a duchess, while I was made for the role. I want you to tell

Mark you don't love him and then go away. Marry
Mr. Kent, do what you want, but stay out of our
lives."

"And if I refuse?" asked Christa belligerently.

"You'll find yourself despised and ridiculed by
all of London. Your disgrace will be broadcast far
and wide until you are too shamed to show your
face in public. Leave Mark to me. I know exactly
how to comfort him."

"You're mad! I won't do it. Mark is perfectly
capable of countering anything you do to discredit
me." She'd be damned if she'd allow Willow to
drive her away with lies and deceit. After all she'd
endured, she deserved a chance at happiness.

"What must I do to convince you that I will
always come first with Mark no matter what he
feels for you?" Willow asked, exasperated by
Christa's stubbornness. "How can I prove that my
influence over Mark's life far surpasses your own
hold on him?"

"Words are cheap," Christa challenged, her
chin set at a defiant angle. "Can you prove that?"

"It is done," Willow accepted, gloating inwardly. "And if I succeed I'll expect you to release
your hold over Mark."

Christa hesitated. What had she just done?
Surely Willow was bragging, wasn't she? No one
could be more important to Mark than the woman
he loved. But what if—what if Willow was correct?
Could she go through life knowing that Mark's
indebtedness to Willow came first with him? Had
she known the lie concocted by Doctor Sayid would
have such far-reaching consequences, she would
never have agreed to it.

"If you can prove to me that you come first
with Mark no matter what, I—I promise to think
about all you've told me," Christa temporized.

"That's all I ask." Willow smiled deviously.

"Don't bother to show me out. I know the way."
She whirled past Christa in a swirl of silk, leaving
the cloying scent of jasmine in her wake.

The next day Christa's confrontation with Brian went as expected. It was far from pleasant. By
now Brian had heard the gossip spread by Willow
and was beginning to have second thoughts about
marrying a woman whose tarnished reputation had
followed her to England. Certainly she could do
little to enhance his career, he decided. It was
doubtful now that even Sir Wesley's influence was
considerable enough to suppress the notoriety connected to his daughter. Still uncertain about his
decision concerning Christa, he was chagrined to
learn the choice was no longer his to make. Christa
would not have him for a husband no matter what
his decision might have been.

"I'm sorry, Brian, but I don't love you," she
said, hoping his disappointment wasn't too great.
She need not have worried, for Brian was more than
a little relieved by her announcement, though his
pride was stung by the fact that he wasn't the one to
make it. "I'm going to marry someone else."

"What!" Brian asked, miffed. "Who is he?
When did all this take place?"

"I . . . the Duke of Marlboro. I've always loved
him. He's the man I told you about. I doubt if I
could ever have married you, even if Mark hadn't
come along when he did."

"The Duke of Marlboro! I thought you were
just casual acquaintances."

"More than casual friends," Christa admitted,
blushing. "We were lovers. Mark has asked me to
marry him, and I don't see how I can refuse."

"All this has come about since your meeting
two nights ago?" Brian said, amazed.

"I don't want to go into the details, Brian, but
this isn't something that happened overnight."

"If I were a duke, perhaps you'd feel differently about me," Brian accused her bitterly.

"Brian, that's not fair!" cried Christa, stung. "I love Mark. We fell in love almost from the moment we met. Fate worked to keep us apart, but now we are reunited."

"Well, my dear, I'm not all that disappointed," Brian confessed. "I began having second thoughts about taking a whore to wife. Obviously the duke was but one of your many lovers besides the bey. I count myself too fastidious to accept damaged goods."

Christa gasped, clutching her throat. "How dare you! Do you care nothing for me?"

"I cared for what I thought your father could do for my career," Brian divulged with a hint of sarcasm. "I wouldn't have you now if you begged me."

"Get out, Brian!" Christa ordered crisply. After her encounter with Willow, trading insults with Brian was more than she needed.

"I'm leaving, my dear," he smiled, clamping on his hat. "But should you find yourself suddenly abandoned by the duke once your—er, rather colorful past catches up with you, don't expect me to take you back. Unless," he added slyly, "that little maid of yours comes along with the bargain. Life would be far from dull with both of you sharing my bed."

"Get out, damn you! You're despicable!" Christa screamed, finally recognizing Brian's true nature. Chuckling to himself, Brian sketched a mocking bow and left.

Collapsing into a chair, Christa thanked her lucky stars that fate had saved her from a lifetime of marriage to Brian Kent. How could she have so badly misjudged his calculating nature? Had her parents known, they would never have consented to their engagement in the first place.

Suddenly she recalled Willow and her surprise visit the day before, and new fears plagued her. How did Willow intend to demonstrate her influence over Mark? There was no way, she convinced herself, that she could. Mark loved her. She had to trust him.

21

Because of pressing business regarding his grandfather's estate, Mark did not return to see Christa until late in the same day that he and Willow had their confrontation. And though his day was filled with activity, thoughts of Christa consumed his mind—how she seemed to fit him so marvelously, the feel of him sheathed tightly in her velvet moistness, the taste and smell of her. He loved her! More than he thought possible to love another human being. Just gazing into her beautiful face lifted his spirits and fed his soul.

"Mark, oh Mark!" Christa exclaimed, flinging herself into his welcoming arms. "I'm so glad to see you."

Breaking into an irresistibly devastating grin, Mark admitted wryly, "I thought the day would never end. Countless meetings with solicitors, endless papers to sign—when all I wanted was to hold you in my arms and make love to you over and over.

Being without you all these months has been sheer torture."

"For me, too, my love," Christa replied shakily. "These last two days have turned my life around completely."

"Did you tell Brian?" Christa nodded. "How did he take it?"

She snorted derisively. "I don't believe his heart is broken."

Eyeing her curiously, Mark asked, "What is that supposed to mean?"

"Forget Brian, Mark. I don't want to talk about him. Suffice it to say, Brian Kent is no longer part of my life and is not particularly disappointed to be left out. Soon my parents will be in England, and once I explain I'm certain they'll understand."

"Where is Elissa?" Mark asked, glancing about.

"With Allen." Christa smiled. "Your brother seems quite taken with her."

"I hope he knows what he's doing," he remarked cryptically. "Where is Lenore?"

"Abed."

"Then we're alone. Christa, I want to make love to you. I've waited all day for this moment." A lazy smile hung on one corner of his mouth.

The answer in her eyes contained a sensual flame. With one finger she traced the strong lines creasing his forehead and the dimples that dived into his cheeks and deepened the cleft in his chin when he smiled. Crisp, wavy hair framed his face and a fringe of thick lashes surrounded large green eyes alive with fire that staggered her. She wanted him as much as he did her, and no words were needed to convey that message.

"Don't look at me like that, sweet siren, else I'm tempted to take you here on the floor," Mark said, his voice a husky whisper as he drew her into the hard contour of his body. Melting into his embrace, she surrendered to the pulsing warmth his lips induced when they captured hers.

His hands freely roamed her body as their kiss deepened, and through the impediment of their clothing she felt the accelerated beat of his heart. A pleasurable ache began in the pit of her stomach and settled in her loins, and she wanted him with a fierceness that matched Mark's own burning desire.

"Come, love," she answered quickly over her choking, beating heart. Grasping his hand firmly, she intended to lead him to her bedroom, seriously doubting if either Lenore or Elissa would be shocked to find Mark in her bed.

Suddenly a loud banging on the door interrupted their flight, and Mark made an inarticulate sound that was half unrequited passion and half anger at having their privacy disrupted.

"Elissa?" he asked in a grudging voice.

"I don't think so. She has a key." The clatter continued and in dazed aggravation she moved off to investigate.

"Don't answer it," Mark urged, a premonition of dread chilling his flesh.

Christa paused, something in Mark's tone nearly convincing her to heed his plea—until she recognized the voice calling to them through the closed panel.

"Mark! Christa! I know you're inside. Please open the door. It's urgent."

"Willow!" Mark groaned. "What the hell does she want?"

"Mark, please, I need your help!"

Evidently she used the right words, for Mark responded instantly. "Let her in, Christa. She must be in trouble to come here for me."

More than a little annoyed by Willow's unwanted interference, Christa moved to obey. The

moment the door opened, Willow flung herself at
Mark, forcing him to grasp her voluptuous form to
keep them from falling. Cursing beneath his
breath, he slanted an apologetic look at Christa,
then carefully set Willow aside. "What is this all
about, Willow?"

"I am in desperate need of help, Mark."

"At this time of night? How did you know
where to find me?"

"I went to your townhouse, and after much
cajoling Omar finally told me where to find you."

"All right, Willow, what's so damn important
that you felt the need to track me down?"

"Can we talk alone?" Willow asked, casting a
surreptitious glance at Christa.

"I have no secrets from Christa," Mark said,
his voice courteous but patronizing.

Willow shrugged. "If you say so. Do you recall
my telling you that Robert's father was trying to
take my husband's inheritance from me?" Mark
nodded. "That vile man contends that since Robert
had no heir, the money and lands in Cornwall left
to him by his grandmother should revert to Robert's younger brother. Mark, I need those lands. All
my money comes from them. Without that income,
I would be destitute. The Langtrys have always
hated me."

"What do you expect me to do, Willow?"

"I have no one, Mark, not one person to stand
up for me. I received notice today that a court
hearing is to be held in Cornwall in one week. If
you don't help me, I'll lose everything. Besides, you
are more than a little responsible for my predicament."

Unconsciously his brows furrowed, realizing
the truth of Willow's charge. It was only after the
Langtrys learned of his involvement with their
daughter-in-law during her husband's absence that

Willow earned their hatred. "I have no legal knowledge, Willow. What is it you want of me?"

"Come to Cornwall with me. Help me fight this."

"I know of a solicitor in Cornwall who could help you. A man I met in school. I'll write him a note and you can—"

"No!" Willow declared, glaring at him with reproachful eyes. "It won't do! I need you, Mark. Have you forgotten so soon what I did for you?"

Fury almost choked Christa. Leave it to Willow to appeal to Mark's sense of honor in order to gain his compliance. She didn't deceive Christa for a minute, for she was aware of the devils that drove the woman. Surely Mark wasn't so gullible as to be taken in by her ploy. Or was he? The answer came almost immediately, stunning her.

"When are you leaving, Willow?"

"Now! Immediately! There's no time to lose. London is along way from Cornwall."

"Wait in the coach," he ordered. He sounded curt, abstracted. "I want to talk to Christa alone."

"Of course," Willow smirked, triumphant. "I'm sorry if this comes at a bad time, Mark." Though her words were contrite, her eyes glowed with satisfaction.

"It doesn't matter, Willow. Just wait outside please." The moment Willow closed the door, Mark gathered Christa in his arms. "I can't refuse, my love. If not for Willow, we wouldn't be together now."

"I'm begging you, Mark, don't go," she pleaded, her eyes luminous with unshed tears. "I don't trust Willow. She'd go to any lengths to part us." Deliberately she refrained from telling him about Willow's recent visit, for she wanted nothing to influence his decision but his love for her.

"Surely you realize that I don't want to go, but

I have no choice. Once my debt to Willow no longer hangs over my head, I will be free of her. You have nothing to fear from her, my love. Nothing she could do would entice me away from you. Wait for me. The moment I return, we'll be married. It is our kismet to be together."

"Mark, I'm asking you—no, begging you—not to go. Let us be done with separations once and for all."

"I must go, Christa," he stated firmly, steeling himself to resist her soft pleas. He felt torn, wavering between love and duty. And duty won. The least he could do for Willow was see her through her troubles. He had a lifetime to devote to Christa.

"I'll be back as soon as I can, my love. You'll wait for me?"

"I . . . suppose." Vividly she recalled Willow's confidence with regard to Mark's feelings, and her own rash promise to consider leaving Mark should the redhead succeed in luring him to her side. In a matter of minutes Willow had proven where Mark's loyalty lay, she thought bitterly.

"I know you are angry now, my love, but . . ."

The door opened and Willow poked her head inside. "Whatever is keeping you, Mark?"

At the end of his patience, Mark said for Christa's ears alone, "A week, two at the most, and I'll be back. Allen will be here to look after you." Then he was gone after a wild kiss that left her breathless and shaken.

"Never fear, I'll take good care of Mark," Willow threw over her shoulder.

"I'm sure you will," muttered Christa bitingly, slamming the door behind them. They did not see her lean against the portal, or hear her heartrending sobs.

* * *

During Mark's absence, Allen's frequent visits led Christa to believe more than mere infatuation existed between him and Elissa. Thus it came as no surprise when Elissa shyly revealed that she had told Allen all about her past, and he loved her despite it. Christa had no idea if Mark would be pleased by this turn of events, but Allen was old enough to make his own decisions in life.

Serving to complicate matters, Lenore timidly confessed to holding a certain fondness for Omar. Where it would all lead, Christa hadn't the least idea, for her own relationship with Mark was in grave trouble. Against her will, she gave considerable thought to Willow's words. And though she did not doubt Mark's love, she did question his misplaced loyalty, so much so that it threatened the very foundation of their future. What kind of life faced them with Willow a constant bone of contention between them? Her dilemma did not improve when she received word through Allen that Mark's homecoming would be delayed indefinitely. No reason was given for the change of plans. Nor did Mark write to her directly.

After Mark's departure the entire structure of her life had fallen apart, Christa reflected despondently as she sat across from the thin, bespeckled man who nervously twisted his hat in his hands. She had recognized him immediately as Silas Fargate, her aunt's solicitor. The distressing news he delivered brought a rush of tears to Christa's blue eyes.

"I'm sorry, Miss Horton, to be the bearer of such sad tidings," the little man lamented. "But as you are the sole beneficiary of your aunt's will, I felt obliged to tell you the manner in which your aunt and her new husband met their deaths."

"An accident, you said," Christa gulped on a sob.

"Yes, in Italy. Their carriage overturned into a deep ravine on a narrow mountain road. Tragic, just tragic," Fargate shook his head woefully.

"But my aunt couldn't have left much of an estate," Christa insisted, puzzled. "She lived comfortably but was far from wealthy. Didn't you say she left me an heiress? I—I don't understand."

"You will once I explain, Miss Horton," said the solicitor, suddenly business-like. "You see, Sir Charles, your aunt's husband, preceded her in death by several days. He was killed outright in the accident, while your aunt lingered a few days before succumbing to her injuries.

"According to Sir Charles's will, all his worldly goods went to your aunt upon his death, while your aunt's will named you as sole beneficiary. Since Sir Charles died first, everything is now yours."

"But what about Sir Charles's heirs?" Christa asked, finding all this difficult to believe.

"There are none. The influenza epidemic some years back wiped out nearly every living member of his family. Not even a distant cousin remains to claim his wealth. So you, my dear girl, have inherited vast wealth through your aunt, God rest her soul."

"I . . . I am overwhelmed."

"I have here a paper listing all monies, stocks, investments, lands and estates. There is even a chateau in southern France you might like to visit one day."

Gingerly Christa grasped the report, staring blankly at the printed words that so far meant little to her. "I'll . . . I'll study this later," she said, stunned, "after all this has time to sink in."

"As you wish, Miss Horton," said Fargate. "I'll be happy to continue serving you in any capacity. Your aunt trusted me to handle her affairs, and I can do no less for her niece."

"Yes, please, Mr. Fargate. I know my aunt depended on you and so shall I. I'll write to you later, after I've had time to mourn my aunt properly."

"I understand." The lawyer nodded gravely. "One more thing. Your father has been notified, and from what I gather he'll soon be in England. He's also been sent a complete listing of your holdings so he might help you with your investments once he arrives."

"Thank you. You've been more than helpful, Mr. Fargate, and I appreciate your kindness."

Later, in the privacy of her room, Christa mourned her aunt's senseless death, never realizing until now just how much that good woman must have loved her. She regretted the fact that her life with Sir Charles was cut short, but knew the few months they did share had brought them both happiness.

The next day Christa received another shock, this in the form of a message from Willow Langtry delivered by a coachman from her Cornwall estate. It was very short and concise. It said: "Mark will remain here with me as long as I decide to keep him. What more proof do you need? If you aren't gone by the time we return, I will see that no one in England will receive you socially." There was no signature; none was needed.

Crumpling the message in her clenched fist, Christa flung it at the door, seething with impotent rage. As one day drifted into another, she began to better understand the hold Willow had on Mark— one far greater than the love he bore her. When Allen came to call on Elissa that evening, she questioned him closely.

"Have you heard from Mark?"

Allen flushed, annoyed at his brother for going away with Willow and hurting Christa with his behavior. In the short time he had known Willow, he had come to recognize her as the devious woman she was. That she wanted Mark was patently evident. And even though his brother loved Christa, Willow's tenacity was incredible.

"Not since the last message announcing his unavoidable delay."

Christa bit her lip, worrying it between small, white teeth. "I . . . I hope he'll return soon."

"Look, Christa, Mark loves you," the young man declared stoutly. "This debt he owes Willow has nothing to do with his feelings for you."

"I wish I could believe that," she said with a watery smile, "but every day that Mark is gone brings new doubts to my mind."

"Christa, I'm certain—"

"No, Allen, don't make excuses for him. I know Mark loves me, but I'm not stupid enough to underestimate Willow's power over him. As long as Willow chooses to interfere in our lives, I doubt we could ever find true happiness together. She is determined to sabotage our marriage plans. At this point I'm inclined to believe she can do it."

"Has Willow threatened you?" Allen asked sharply.

She was saved from answering by the appearance of Elissa, who captured Allen's rapt attention the moment she entered the room. Christa took the opportunity to slip quietly away. There was much she had to think about.

Brian stood poised on the threshold, one hand on the knocker, the other holding a letter. He was somewhat surprised when Christa herself appeared to answer his summons, but quickly regained his aplomb. God, she was beautiful, he thought, his eyes lingering on her breasts that rose and fell in agitation upon finding him on her doorstep. Too late he realized his hastiness in allowing her to escape him so easily—especially since he had learned that she had unexpectedly inherited great wealth. If there was a way to win her back, he would not hesitate to employ it.

"What are you doing here, Brian?" Christa asked with cool authority. She had not forgotten his verbal abuse of her the last time they had spoken.

"A letter from your father came in the diplomatic pouch, and since it also bears my name I decided to deliver it myself." Without waiting for an invitation, he slipped inside, closing the door behind him.

"You read it?" asked Christa, snatching the letter from his hand.

"Of course. My name is on the envelope. Your father still thinks we are to be wed."

Quickly perusing the missive, Christa let out a gasp of dismay. "They know about Aunt Mary and are now in southern France. After they landed in Marseilles, mother's health worsened and they decided to go directly to the chateau I inherited from Sir Charles rather than risk the overland journey through France and across the channel by ship at this time," she recited worriedly.

"I know," Brian smiled smugly. "They want us to join them at the chateau and be married there."

"I will write immediately and explain," Christa said, disappointment coloring her words. "I had so looked forward to seeing them."

"What about the duke? I haven't seen him about of late. No one has, it seems. Has he grown tired of you so soon? Word has it he is off somewhere in Cornwall with Willow Langtry. There is even talk of an elopement."

Of course, Christa thought bitterly, Willow would find a way to make it look as if Mark had run off with her. There had been little time before he left with Willow for anyone to be made aware of his feelings for Christa.

"Mark did accompany Willow to Cornwall. It was strictly business," she responded sharply, more than a little irritated by his mocking tone. "Is there anything else you wished to say?" she ripped out impatiently. "If not, I'd like you to leave."

Brian eyed her narrowly. Perhaps he'd been too hasty in renouncing her, he considered cunningly. Evidently she had slipped considerably in the duke's high regard during these past weeks, or he would not have gone off with the delicious Lady Willow.

"Will you be going to France to join your parents?" Brian asked as he reluctantly prepared to leave.

"I . . . perhaps," she reconsidered.

"If you do, let me know," Brian informed her importantly. "I'll gladly arrange passage for you. Your father's high position in the diplomatic corps virtually guarantees you and your servants passage aboard a government packet."

"I'll think about it, Brian," Christa said coolly.

When she appeared unbending in her condemnation, Brian was moved to confess, "I wish you would forgive me, Christa, for all the nasty things I said to you. I was angry. You must admit I had good reason to be. You could have told me from the beginning that you didn't love me instead of leading me on. I was willing to overlook everything and marry you no matter what. Say you forgive me, my dear, please," begged Brian, smiling obsequiously.

"All right, Brian," Christa sighed wearily. Anything to be rid of him so she might read her letter in private.

"And you'll let me know if I can help you in any way?"

"Yes, yes, I will. Please go now, Brian. I'm tired."

Brian lingered a few moments outside the door, gloating over his incredible luck. Perhaps all wasn't lost after all. It would be quite pleasant to have all the money one wanted, as well as the social standing that accompanied such wealth. Having Christa in bed wouldn't be too difficult to accept either, once he got past the revulsion of imagining her in the arms of all those other men. And then there was the little slut, Elissa. . . .

Two more weeks passed with still no word from Mark. After much soul-searching Christa came to the heartrending conclusion that she would never mean more to him than Willow did. If he truly loved her, he would have found time to send one message in all these weeks, or at least a brief word of explanation for his long delay. The longer she pondered his silence, the clearer the reason for it became. Willow had won the prize she sought. Suddenly Christa knew what she must do, especially if what she suspected was true.

Upon arising these past mornings, a terrible nausea had sent her racing for the chamberpot. Not only that, but her woman's time had failed to arrive. Worried, she had consulted Elissa, who confirmed that the lie she'd told Abdullah for her own protection had become fact. She truly did carry Mark's child—conceived, no doubt, that first time they came together nearly six weeks ago.

As time went on, it became increasingly evident that Mark did not want her, leaving her but one alternative. She would travel to France to join her family. Originally she had hoped to take Mark with her to meet them, but now she would go alone.

After giving the matter considerable thought,

she decided to accept Brian's offer and let him arrange passage for her. According to her wishes, he booked rooms for three women aboard the *King Henry*, privately gloating over the fact that no mention was made of the Duke of Marlboro or his intention to accompany them. If Christa had known that Brian also arranged his own passage on the same ship, she would have flown into a rage. But the message he relayed only informed her of the time and date of departure and his willingness to come for her in his carriage.

Elissa squealed in delight and Lenore's joy could hardly be contained when she learned of Christa's pregnancy, happily looking forward to holding Lady Emily's grandchild in her arms. But when they learned Christa intended to sail for France, both women expressed dismay, insisting she remain in England until Mark returned. Stubbornly, Christa refused, citing Mark's delay of nearly six weeks and the fact that she had heard nothing from him in all that time. Besides, she longed to see her parents and worried constantly over her mother's health. When she suggested that either woman or both might remain behind if they so chose, they protested vigorously. Though Elissa was madly in love with Allen, she could not easily forget all Christa had done for her. Lenore was of the same mind, so the tedious job of packing began.

Mark charged through the countryside at breakneck speed, his clothes splattered with mud and a blue stubble darkening his lean jaw. Omar trailed not far behind. The day before, Mark had received a disturbing message from Allen urging him to return posthaste. He accused Mark of neglecting all he held dear for a woman who used his honor as an excuse to keep him at her side. His brother's harsh words rankled, for Mark had written Christa several times but received no answer, although Willow assured him her coachman had waited for a reply, and when none was forthcoming returned home as directed.

If only the damn hearing involving Willow's property hadn't been so long delayed, he silently fumed. If he didn't know better, he would have sworn most of the delays were contrived. His first disappointment occured when he found his solicitor friend on holiday in France and was forced to select another to represent Willow. And truth to tell, he liked the fellow little. Though his work could not be faulted, Mark did not trust him. And when questioned about the maddening delays, the man refused to look him in the eye, blaming all manner of circumstances.

As his horse thundered into the outskirts of London, Mark cursed Willow beneath his breath for attempting to seduce him every day he remained in Cornwall. In self-defense he had moved out of her house to a nearby inn, but still she demanded his nearly constant attention, reminding him daily—nay, hourly—that she had saved his life and demanded he do no less for her. For to Willow, being cast adrift virtually penniless was tantamount to death.

For the hundredth time he wondered why Christa hadn't answered his letters or even mentioned to Allen that he had written. When he received Allen's message, he had no idea what to make of it, but the serious tone convinced him to rush immediately back to London, and Willow be damned. As far as he was concerned, these past weeks more than repaid the debt he owed her.

As he neared his townhouse, Mark grew anxious. Was Christa well? he wondered distractedly. Why had Allen summoned him home with words that both mystified and angered him? Why hadn't Christa answered his letters? Soon, soon, all his questions would be answered. Soon he would hold her lithe form in his arms and tell her in person how much he cared. How could she doubt him? Nearly overcome by weariness, he halted in front of his house just as the door unexpectedly flung open.

"Mark, damn I'm glad to see you!" exclaimed Allen, taking note of his brother's stubbled chin, blurry eyes and badly soiled clothing. "You look as if you haven't slept or changed clothes in days. At least you took my letter seriously."

"You're right," Mark grumbled. "I've neither slept nor taken off my clothes in days. After I received your message, I stopped for nothing except to toss a few essentials into a saddlebag and borrow horses along the route. What's wrong, Allen? Do you know why Christa hasn't answered my letters?"

"You've written her?"

"More than once."

"She never mentioned hearing from you," Allen said thoughtfully. "In fact, she asked me nearly every day if I'd received word from you. Perhaps she never received your letters."

"I gave them to Willow, who entrusted them herself to her coachman. He seemed reliable enough." Allen said nothing, but stared in an odd manner at his remarkably naive brother.

"Where are you off to?" Mark asked, eyeing his brother's elegant attire.

"To see Elissa," replied the smitten young man with a grin.

"Give me time to scrape the beard off my face, bathe and change clothes and I'll join you. We can get to the bottom of this together."

"Fine," agreed Allen, following Mark into the

house, Omar close on their heels. "I forgot to ask, how did Willow's hearing turn out? It certainly took long enough."

Mark gave a disgusted snort. "It's still not settled, but there is nothing more I can do for her other than hold her hand and commiserate with her. I left her in competent hands, and I'm certain it will be settled as soon as those damn delays are dispensed with."

"What did Willow think of your leaving?"

"She screamed like bloody hell. Accused me of abandoning her. After weeks of catering to her, I felt I had more than paid my debt. I intend to devote the rest of my life to Christa."

"It's about time you came to your senses."

Less than an hour later their coach, driven by an exhausted Omar, ground to a halt before Christa's house. The two younger men headed for the front door, while Omar drove around to the back where he knew Lenore would be puttering in the kitchen. Allen and Mark reached the door at the same time that Brian Kent came bustling into view.

"Why, your grace," Brian said insolently. "Fancy meeting you here."

Mark's brows rose inquiringly. "I might say the same of you, Kent. I thought Christa told you about us. You no longer have any reason to come calling on her."

"I heard that you were in Cornwall with Lady Willow," Brian taunted, ignoring Mark's remark.

"As you can see, I'm back," Mark informed him coolly. "What exactly is your business with Christa?" His eyes glittered like green chips of ice, and Brian took an involuntary step backwards. "Well?" Mark demanded impatiently.

Brian swallowed convulsively. "I've come to inform Christa that all arrangements are complete for our journey to France."

"What!" Allen's and Mark's incredulous voices joined together in protest.

Allen turned to Mark. "I know nothing of this, brother. The man is obviously lying. Why would Christa go to France with him?"

"Why, indeed," Mark replied tersely, struggling to maintain a tight rein on his temper. "I intend to find out shortly. Allen," he said, turning to his brother, "see that Mr. Kent reaches his club safely."

"I won't go without—" Brian's words stuttered to a halt. The rage on Mark's glowering features reminded him of a hawk about to strike, and Brian fled willingly before becoming the predator's prey.

22

The insistent knocking brought Elissa immediately to the door, hoping it was Allen calling on her. She would desperately miss the man she had come to love, but right now Christa needed her more. Besides, in her heart she knew she was not good enough for Allen, whose royal heritage placed him out of her reach despite his protests to the contrary. Their stations in life were too different. It would be best if she left now, for the more she saw of him the more difficult it would be to part from him when the time came for him to choose a wife. With a wistful sadness, Elissa answered the door, and was more than a little surprised to find not Allen, but his brother Mark poised on the threshhold.

"Mark, you're back! Allah be praised! Christa will be so happy."

Mark considered the small girl standing before him with more friendliness than he had since those long months ago in the desert when she tried to seduce him. She had proved a good friend to Christa, and his brother had become more than a little fond of the young woman.

"Where is Christa?" Mark asked, stepping inside.

Twisting her hands nervously and glancing toward the stairs, Elissa replied, "I'll get her for you. She—she's resting." She turned to make a hasty exit.

"Wait!" Mark ordered in a voice brooking no argument. "I'll go myself."

Elissa froze, her eyes wide with fright as she watched Mark slowly ascend the stairs. She knew Christa had been feeling ill all day and had spent most of the time bent over the chamber pot. She hated for Mark to see her that way. And she wasn't all that certain Christa wanted to tell Mark about the baby yet.

Poised on the horns of dilemma, she sought to forestall him. "Please, Mark, perhaps it's best if I go up first."

Mark bent her a frosty glare. "Is there some reason why I shouldn't go myself?"

"N . . . no," she stammered, at a loss for words.

"Then I suggest you wait here for Allen. He'll be arriving any minute," he replied dismissively as he continued up the stairs. "Which is Christa's room?"

Unable to prevent Mark from doing exactly as he pleased, she replied, "First door on the left."

Mark stood before Christa's door wondering whether to knock or burst in unannounced. Good manners won out, and he rapped lightly.

"Come in, Elissa," Christa called out, thinking it was Elissa bringing her supper, although the mere thought of food caused her stomach to lurch dangerously. She gagged, bending over the chamber pot and discharging the contents of her stomach until nothing remained but dry heaves shaking her body.

The sounds coming from within sent Mark's heart hammering in his veins, and the sight that met his eyes as he rushed inside frightened ten years off his life. Christa, looking weak and pale, lay in bed with her head hanging over the side as she emptied the meager contents of her stomach.

"Christa, you're ill! Oh, my love, is that why you failed to answer my letters? Had I known, I'd have returned immediately. Allen was remiss in not telling me you were sick."

With difficulty, Christa found her voice. "I received no letters, Mark, else I would have answered them. Why did you stay away so long?" she asked reproachfully.

"Darling, there must be some misunderstanding. I did write. How long have you been ill? Have you seen a doctor?"

"It's nothing," insisted Christa. "Just a temporary upset. Certainly not serious enough to consult a doctor."

Mark looked dubious but found no reason to question her words. Gingerly, he perched on the edge of the bed, searching the pale contours of her face as he suddenly recalled Brian Kent and his claim that he and Christa were leaving England together.

"It appears I returned just in time. What's this nonsense about you traveling to France with Kent? I don't understand how you could do this, Christa. You promised to wait for me."

"How long was I supposed to wait?" Christa bit out.

"My letters explained everything."

"I received no letters."

"You must have. Willow assured me her coachman put them directly into your hand," Mark insisted.

"Willow!" spat Christa derisively. "When will you see her for what she is? She's done everything in her power to separate us."

Mark scowled. "I'll admit Willow is a bit overbearing, but you have nothing to fear from her. She knows I love only you. She . . . ." He paused, finally aware that Willow was indeed devious enough to divert his messages to Christa and lie about it. "My love, forget about Willow. She's not important. Tell me about Brian Kent. Is it true you were running off with him?"

To Christa it appeared his words excused Willow of any wrongdoing. "Believe what you want but I'm not going *with* Brian," Christa snorted, exasperated. Why should she explain when he refused to discuss Willow?

"Kent believes otherwise."

"Well he's wrong. Brian merely booked passage to France as a favor to me. My parents are in France staying at my aunt's chateau—my chateau now. My mother is ill and resting there until she improves enough to continue her journey to England."

"You own a chateau in France?"

Christa nodded and told him of her aunt's tragic death in Italy and of the considerable estate she had inherited.

"Why couldn't you have waited for me? I would gladly have taken you to France," Mark said with a hint of disapproval. "You needn't have gone running to Kent for help." Intense jealousy made his words harsher than he intended. He should have been the one to help her, not Brian Kent.

"I wasn't sure you would return at all," Christa admitted doubtfully.

"But my letters . . . Well, never mind. I'm here

now and we'll leave together. I'm eager to meet your parents. And I'm sorry about your mother—and your aunt," he said somewhat belatedly.

"Mark, I'm—" Whatever she intended to say was lost when she turned sickly green and made a desperate lunge for the chamber pot.

"Christa, I'm going for the doctor immediately!"

"Mark, no! I didn't want to tell you until I was certain Willow hadn't poisoned you against me. You were gone so long I—I began to doubt your feelings for me."

"Tell me what, Christa? You're not making sense. How could you doubt my love, and what has that to do with your illness?"

"I'm pregnant, Mark. Although I've yet to consult a doctor, I'm certain I'm carrying a child."

"Pregnant!" Intense joy surged upward through his veins, but the shout of happiness died in his throat as a terrible thought reared its ugly head and cast doubt into his mind. If Christa was carrying *his* child, why was she going off with Brian Kent? Injudiciously, he voiced his qualms. "Is it my child? Or did you bed Kent before we were reunited?"

"My God, Mark, what a horrible thing to say! I don't believe you ever truly cared for me. If you did, such a thought would never enter your mind. Go away and leave me alone. I don't need you. I'm perfectly capable of raising my child alone."

"Christa, I have to know. Why were you running away with Kent if it's not his child you carry?"

"Have you heard nothing I've said? It no longer matters what you think. Whether you like it or not, I'm going to France. Alone. Not with Brian and certainly not with you. Go back to Willow. She's the one who deserves your loyalty. Thanks to my aunt, I'm wealthy enough to provide for myself and my child. I don't need a man to complicate my life."

Mark's fragile temper exploded. "Judging from your answer, I assume you still refuse to divulge the paternity of your child. Did you know you were pregnant when I made love to you?" Why was he saying these terrible things? he wondered distractedly. Hadn't Allen told him that one day his temper would be his undoing?

"Go to hell, Mark!" Christa screamed, stifling the urge to jump from the bed and strangle him. Balancing on the edge of hysteria, she lay back against the pillows, panting, stubbornly refusing to either look at Mark or acknowledge his presence.

Maintaining a tenuous hold on his temper, Mark knew he had to leave or beat some sense into the little vixen. All he wanted was for her to admit the child she carried was his. Was that too much to ask? Deep in his heart he relinquished the absurd notion that she had bedded a man like Kent. But his stupid accusation had enraged her, and her refusal to admit the truth in turn stoked his own anger. He freely admitted he had acted purely out of insane jealousy and things had gotten swiftly out of hand.

Abruptly he rose, yearning to placate her but unable to control his temper long enough to do so. She looked so ill, he hated himself for deliberately provoking her, thus adding to her distress. "I'm leaving, Christa." There was no answer. It was as if she was struck deaf and dumb. "Dammit! Until you tell me the truth, we have nothing more to discuss. I warn you, don't leave London until this matter is settled," he tossed over his shoulder as he yanked open the door.

"Mark, what's wrong?" Allen asked, nearly colliding with his brother as he stormed from the room.

"Ask Christa!" he returned tightly, refusing to discuss the matter as he rushed past.

Peeping from behind Allen, Elissa stared at Mark's departing back, then at Christa's partially opened door. It didn't take much imagination to realize what had happened. Why was Mark so angry? Didn't he want a child? If that were so, then Christa must be devastated.

"Christa needs me," she said, scampering past Allen.

"What is this all about, Elissa? What could have made Mark so angry?"

Allen followed Elissa inside, then stopped dead in his tracks when he saw Christa lying abed looking more dead than alive. "For the love of Allah, what has Mark done to you?" he cried out, thoroughly shaken.

Mark rushed out the door, angry at himself for allowing his jealousy to rule his head, and at Christa for deliberately provoking him. Eventually it would pass, but until it did he presented a menace both to himself and to Christa. Considering his foul mood, he decided to find a place where he could be alone until his anger cooled. Dammit, why did Christa have to be so stubborn when all he wanted from her was a simple answer? What he really craved was a drink—no, dammit, a bottle!

Mark was relieved that Omar was not waiting outside in the carriage as he rushed headlong down the street, the approaching darkness and fog all but swallowing him up. In his frame of mind he had no need of a nursemaid. With no destination in mind, his angry steps took him far from Christa's fashionable neighborhood into the stews of London, where men were known to disappear forever.

The revelry coming from the dingy inn caught his attention and Mark directed his footsteps into the brightly lit room just beginning to spring to life as darkness descended. Rarely had Mark visited such a shabby establishment, but tonight it fit his mood perfectly. In a place such as this he would have little difficulty blending in with the crowd to become just another anonymous face. As long as he could afford the price of a bottle, he expected to be served with no questions asked.

Counting the coins in his pocket, Mark waited until the saucy barmaid sidled up to take his order. It was seldom, if ever, that so handsome and fashionably attired a man entered the Singed Goose and the girl could not help but ogle him, tugging her bodice down a notch to attract his attention. The wealthy seldom frequented so humble an inn unless slumming in groups of three or four for safety's sake.

"What'll ye have, sir?" the girl asked. "Me name's Sophie and I'll be more than happy to oblige ye in any way I can," she said, rolling her eyes suggestively.

Ignoring her blatant invitation, Mark slapped a handful of coins on the table. "Take one for yourself, Sophie, and use the rest to supply me with drink until I either pass out or tell you otherwise."

Sophie's eyes bulged and her tight blond curls bobbed up and down as she gaped at the sizeable stack of coins. "Gor, sir, are ye daft? That's enough to keep you drunk for a week!"

"Perhaps I am daft, Sophie," Mark admitted wryly. "Just see that I get the good stuff, not that poison the innkeeper calls brandy. Understand?"

"Aye, sir," Sophie said, corkscrew curls bobbing against her white shoulders and breasts visible above the low-necked blouse. "And should ye be needin' anythin' else—anythin' at all—just ask Sophie." Then she scurried away, returning soon after with a dusty bottle and a dirt-clouded glass. She lingered a few minutes longer, but when Mark paid her little heed, she shrugged and moved on to a more responsive customer.

Allen dogged Mark's footsteps by mere minutes, but by the time he had received an explanation from Christa concerning Mark's uncharacteristic behavior, his brother had already disappeared into the swirling fog. "Damn," he cursed, peering into the darkness. Where in the hell could he have gone? Retracing his steps, he found Omar in the kitchen with Lenore and explained, to the best of his meager knowledge, what had happened.

"You know his habits better than I, Omar. Where would Mark have gone, given his frame of mind?" Allen asked worriedly.

"Someplace where he could drink without drawing attention to himself," Omar replied thoughtfully.

"That could be any number of places in a city the size of London," groaned Allen. "Well, come on, Omar, it looks as if we have our work cut out for us. I warned my brother his temper would be his undoing."

Though Allen and Omar searched far into the night, they failed to find even the smallest trace of Mark. Only when exhaustion claimed them did they give up the search and return home for a few hours of much needed rest before continuing the next day. And the next. How could Mark have disappeared so thoroughly? Allen asked himself, amazed.

At first the steady drinking had little effect on Mark, save to intensify his anger, his mind his worst enemy as he recalled his exasperating conversation with Christa. The longer he thought about it, the more he blamed himself for their senseless argument. He should have never voiced his doubt.

No one but he could possibly be the father of Christa's child. Allah forgive him for being so pigheaded.

Did he want his child to be born a bastard? Bastard! The word stuck in his throat. As long as he lived to draw a breath, no one would call his child a bastard. Nor any of the other children he and Christa might produce. As soon as his terrible anger abated, he would go to her and beg her forgiveness. With a child on the way, she had no choice but to marry him immediately. Were he in Constantine, Christa could be nothing but his concubine, as his mother was to his father. But as long as he lived in England, he would gladly conform to English law, making it possible for Christa to become his wife and his children to bear his name.

The more Mark drank, the deeper his thinking became as the obliging Sophie provided a seemingly endless supply of brandy. Occasionally he was persuaded to eat a bite, but he professed little appetite for food, preferring instead to feed his despair with strong drink.

If anyone thought it odd that the well-dressed man sat alone hour after hour with a bottle before him, no one mentioned it, for none among them hadn't at one time or other wished to drown his sorrow in drink. Sometime that next day, Mark reached the saturation point; his brain no longer functioned rationally and his body lost the ability to consume another drop. When he finally slumped over the table in blessed oblivion, he had Sophie to thank for using his remaining coins to rent him a room behind the kitchen.

Grateful for her assistance, he tumbled into bed, falling almost immediately into a stupor. Listening to his drunken mutterings, Sophie wondered what ghosts haunted his past. She could understand it of the low types who normally frequented the inn, relying on liquor to dull the pain of their mundane lives, but this was a man of obvious breeding and wealth. Little did she know that once Mark began to drink, it was not only thoughts of Christa that fed his thirst, but all the pent-up emotions that had begun with the death of his parents and grown with the cruel punishment Abdullah inflicted on his own body and mind. After months of suppression, brandy had provided the outlet he had thus far denied himself. Shrugging philosophically, Sophie tiptoed from the room, laughing at her caution, for she seriously doubted that a cavalry brigade parading through the room could awaken the man.

Mark's continued absence added fuel to Christa's resentment. He had no cause to act in such a despicable manner, she fumed silently. She had expected him to return long before now, contrite and seeking forgiveness. Where was he? He was not with Willow, for Allen had already investigated that possibility. In fact, he and Omar had searched nearly everywhere. It wasn't like Mark to behave so foolishly, and she began to worry that something terrible had happened to him.

After three days of waiting and wondering, Christa's patience came to an abrupt end. Why should she worry over him when he obviously felt little concern for her? In view of the circumstances, her original plan of joining her parents in France became more attractive in her eyes. Should Mark by chance inquire, Allen knew where to find her. But when she told Allen of her decision to leave, he protested violently.

"Christa, I know my brother won't like it if you leave now. Give him a little more time. You carry his child, and he's sure to come to his senses soon."

"You know where to find me, Allen, and I want to see my parents. They are expecting me. I explained all this to Mark, but he refused to understand. Is it unreasonable to expect him to trust me? I trusted him when he went away with Willow. Could he do any less for me?"

"Christa, I know Mark acted unwisely, but he's been through so much that he couldn't bear the thought of another man touching you. Your refusal to tell him the truth didn't help matters any. As soon as he comes to grips with his feelings he'll be back."

"In the meantime I'm supposed to sit and wait like an obedient wife," she remarked coolly. "We're not even married and not likely to be. I'm leaving for France tomorrow as planned, whether Mark returns or not."

Allen watched Christa storm from the room, disappointed that he had failed miserably to change her mind. He was annoyed not only with Christa, but with his brother, who should have realized his mistake by now and come rushing back to claim the woman who carried his child. Just then Elissa entered the room and he brightened considerably. In the short time he had known the beautiful Berber girl, he had experienced feelings quite foreign to him. But Allen was much wiser than his hotheaded brother. He meant to claim Elissa for his own.

Though Allen had been in England several months, he had never felt as comfortable with its mores and customs as did his brother. In his heart he yearned for the vast sandy expanses, brilliant blue sky, and soft purple nights of the desert. Desperately he missed riding his Arabian stallion across the dunes and hawking with his friends. Elissa, with her dark sultry beauty, brought him closer to all he had loved and lost. Not only that, but the girl herself had somehow captured his heart.

"Allen, what is it?" Elissa asked when Allen continued to stare at her with a strange yearning. "Were you able to convince Christa to remain in London?"

"That lady has a mind of her own." Allen shook his head regretfully, though secretly admiring her spirit. "My brother has finally met his match. Their union, once it's made permanent, will be anything but tranquil."

Elissa smiled, recalling how Christa had valiantly protected her from the second attack by Abdullah's Janissaries. Had they had their way, she would certainly be dead by now from their terrible abuse. Only Christa's intervention had saved her. "Christa does what she has to do."

Allen's eyes gentled. "I . . . I don't want you to leave, Elissa. I'll miss you dreadfully. Let Christa go if she must, but stay here with me. I'll take care of you."

Elissa's heart swelled with love and her dark eyes grew misty. Surely Allen must love her if he wanted to take care of her. Did he want her for his mistress? If so, she wouldn't object, for she knew she was too far beneath him to marry. In order to remain close to him, she was prepared to agree to any kind of relationship.

"I can't leave Christa now," she said regretfully. "I owe her my loyalty. If she's determined to go to France, then I will go with her."

"Elissa, I think you know by how much I care for you. I won't give you up easily. As soon as Mark returns, I'll come to France for you. And—and when I do, I'll have something to ask you."

Reaching out, he pulled her close, molding her tiny, voluptuous form to his. Strong hands pressed against her spine until she felt his manhood rise hard and throbbing against her softness. And then his lips claimed hers. Though he had kissed her many times before, it was nothing like this fierce kiss plundering her mouth. His tongue probed and tasted, drawing, sucking, rendering her without will or reason. She wanted it to go on forever, even though she feared her ability to respond fully to a man after suffering so much abuse. But Allen soon dispelled that doubt as his passion caused hers to ignite and burst into flame. When she thought she would disappear in a puff of white smoke, he abruptly released her and she stumbled, only his strong arms holding her upright.

"If I don't stop now, I'll take you right here on the floor," he murmured raggedly, struggling to maintain his fragile composure. "You are so lovely, you try a man's patience. Soon, Elissa, soon I will claim you. You do care for me, don't you?"

Elissa gazed lovingly into his green eyes, wanting to blurt out that she loved him beyond reason, beyond life. But habit made her cautious. "No other man makes me feel as you do, Allen."

Evidently her answer satisfied him, for he hugged her briefly before setting her aside. "I must leave, love, if I'm to find Mark before you and Christa sail. But should I fail, I'll come for you later. My brother might make a shambles of his own life, but he'll not interfere with mine." Then he was gone, leaving a starry-eyed Elissa staring at his departing back.

Christa was packed and ready when the hired carriage ground to a halt in front of the house. After much grumbling by the coachman as he struggled with mounds of luggage, they departed in a flurry of swishing skirts as the ladies settled themselves inside. At the last minute, Elissa couldn't help but glance over her shoulder in the hope that Allen might still appear to bid her farewell. Even Lenore showed disappointment when Omar failed to arrive.

Upon reaching the dock, Christa was angered to find Brian waiting for her aboard the packet *King Henry*. He fidgeted nervously as the ladies made their way forward, glancing after them with anxious eyes.

"Brian, what are you doing here?" Christa questioned sharply.

Too cowardly to openly defy Mark's instructions to keep away from Christa, he had chanced to show up today in the hopes that Christa still planned on leaving London to join her parents without the duke. Besides, it was all over town that he had mysteriously disappeared several days ago. If something had happened between Christa and her lover, he intended to take advantage of the estrangement.

"I'm a fellow passenger," Brian revealed cautiously. "My leave is up, and I'm traveling to Marseilles and then to Tunis. Mayhap you've forgotten I work for a living. Not all of us are born to wealth."

Christa bristled beneath his mild rebuke but chose to ignore it. "Are you alone?" Brian continued, his eyes searching the wharf.

"As you can see, Elissa and Lenore are with me," she returned brusquely.

"Where is your—the duke?"

"He's delayed."

Brian smirked knowingly. Delayed, indeed! Perhaps all was not lost after all. He had days in which to convince Christa that Mark could not be trusted, and that he, Brian, was a more likely match for her than the fickle duke.

"Come, my dear," he said, grasping her elbow

in a proprietory manner, "let me see you to your cabin."

So much time had elapsed that Allen despaired of finding Mark safe and well before Christa left English soil. If Mark was anywhere within reach, he'd gladly strangle him for causing everyone so much grief these past three days. But with the passage of time, he began to consider the possibility that his brother had suffered some mishap to prevent him from returning long before now.

On the day of Christa's departure, he and Omar found themselves in a less than respectable section of London, a part of the city they had failed to explore in their previous searches. They decided to split up, Omar going in one direction and Allen taking another. Thus it was that Allen found himself standing before the Singed Goose.

Once inside the dark, dismal inn, he nearly turned on his heel and fled, certain his brother wouldn't dream of venturing into such an appalling place, no matter what his mood or inclination. Before he made good his hasty exit, however, Sophie approached, brashly making her presence known.

"Would ye like a table, sir?" she asked, appraising the richness of his clothes as well as his good looks, thinking this man was every bit as handsome as the one who had stumbled into the inn the other night.

"I don't think . . ." Allen protested, then shrugged, abruptly changing his mind. Why not? He was thirsty and perhaps this buxom maid had seen Mark. He nodded and Sophie led him to a small table in the deserted room nearly devoid of customers at this time of day.

"Ale," Allen requested, watching the swish of Sophie's skirt beneath her rolling hips as she hurried off. She returned shortly, setting a brimming mug before him.

Curious, Sophie lingered a few minutes, staring at Allen strangely. Somehow he reminded her of the other gentleman sleeping peacefully in a room behind the kitchen. So immersed was Allen in his own thoughts that he was unaware of her scrutiny until he chanced to glance up and encounter her questioning brown eyes. His brow rose questioningly.

"Gor, sir," Sophie stammered, flustered by those probing emerald eyes. "I don't mean to be rude, but it's not often two fine gentlemen show up at the Singed Goose in the same week." Embarrassed, she turned on her heel, preparing to flee.

Her words struck Allen with profound impact, and without warning he reached out, stopping her flight as his hand closed on her wrist. "Another gentleman was in here, you say? What did he look like?" In his excitement he tightened his hold on Sophie's wrist.

"Please, sir, you're hurting me," Sophie whined, suddenly frightened.

"I'm sorry, miss," he apologized, relaxing his grip. "I didn't mean to frighten you. What's your name?"

"Sophie, sir," replied the shaken girl, wondering what she had said to anger the young man.

"Well, Sophie, I want information and am willing to make it worth your while."

"I'll gladly help if I can," gulped Sophie, fingering her apron nervously.

"You mentioned another man a moment ago." Allen smiled beguilingly, bringing a blush to Sophie's rosy cheeks. "Describe him to me. When did you see him last? Do you know where he went?"

* * *

Mark groaned, coming awake slowly. His head felt like a balloon about to burst and foul-tasting cotton filled his mouth. A single shaft of light filtering through a dirty window pane provided him with a glimpse of his strange surroundings. Attempting to sit up, he grasped his head in pain. Where in the hell was he?

The room tilted crazily, and when it finally stopped he grimaced at the filthy cubbyhole that served as a sleeping chamber. The narrow bed he rested upon boasted a straw mattress covered by a dingy gray sheet of some rough material and a torn blanket. A lopsided nightstand with a broken leg stood askew beside the cot. Against the other wall sat a squat chest of drawers holding a badly cracked bowl and pitcher.

Stumbling to his feet, Mark carefully made his way to the chest sighing in gratitude when he saw the pitcher was filled with fresh water. Dispensing with the dirty glass sitting beside it, he gulped thirstily from the pitcher. When he had drunk his fill, he bent over the bowl and poured the remaining water over his tousled head. When he straightened he felt almost human—almost, but not quite.

Moving with slow deliberation, he sat down on the bed, allowing his mind time to clear enough for lucid thought. And when it came, he cursed himself for a thousand fools. Whatever possessed him to run off as he had he ruminated with self-loathing. He was going to be a father! The woman he loved was with child—his child! And how did he react to that startling news? He had gone off in a fit of anger to drink himself senseless. Christa must despise him. He prayed her love for him was strong enough to survive what he had put her through. Could she forgive his despicable behavior?

Only one thought burned in his brain. He must

go to her immediately and beg forgiveness. He had needed these days—how many was it?—to come to grips with all that had happened to him since Abdullah had murdered his parents and seized the beylic. And now all his ghosts lay behind him, and nothing remained but his pressing need to make Christa legally his and claim his child.

His mind clearer than it had been in months, Mark stood on shaky legs, smoothing his stained and rumpled clothing into some semblance of order. He supposed he had Sophie to thank for the room and planned to reward the girl generously for finding him a safe haven to sleep off his drunk. But for her, he might have been thrown out into the alley for thugs to rob and perhaps murder. Tunneling long fingers through his thick, burnished locks, he reached for the doorknob.

23

"What! My brother is here?" cried Allen, excitement coloring his words. His chair crashed to the floor as he leaped to his feet. "Allah be praised! Why didn't you tell me sooner?"

Astounded by Allen's reaction to her words, Sophie could only stare, mouth agape. If the young man could be believed, and she had no reason to doubt him, the two green-eyed men were brothers. "Gor, sir, I had no idea until you told me. I saw to him meself when he passed out. Put him in a room next to the kitchen, where you'll probably find him now, sleeping like a babe."

"Sophie, I could kiss you!" Allen exclaimed, smacking her cheek to Sophie's intense delight. Then he cleaned out his pockets, removing every single coin he found there and placing them in the startled maid's hand. It added up to a small fortune, more money than she had seen in her life, even enough to leave the Singed Goose and return to the small village where she had been born. There was a boy there—no, a man now, who held fond feelings for her. . . .

Thanking Allen profusely, Sophie pocketed the coins before he could change his mind, remaining only long enough to point toward the narrow door just visible beyond the public room.

Reaching for the doorknob at the same time that Mark exerted pressure from the other side, Allen was hurled forward by his brother's forceful exit. "Allen!" Mark exclaimed, steadying his brother as he stumbled against him. "What in the hell are you doing here?"

"I might ask the same of you, brother," Allen returned crossly. "You look terrible," he added, running a critical eye over Mark's stubbled chin and disheveled clothing. "Are you ready to return to Christa now?" His tone hinted eloquently of his strong disapproval, and a guilty flush stained upwards from Mark's neck.

"More than ready, Allen. I only hope Christa will forgive me for acting the jealous fool. I love that woman more than my own life. Even more now that she carries my child. I'm going to ask her to marry me, and I'd like you to be my groomsman."

"That happy event is unlikely to take place if we don't hurry," came Allen's ominous reply.

"What do you mean?" Mark questioned sharply.

"Christa, Elissa, and Lenore are leaving London for France within the hour. She's disappointed in you, Mark, and I can't rightly say I blame her."

"Within the hour," Mark repeated blankly. Suddenly Allen's words penetrated his muddled brain, spurring him into action. "No!"

"I'm afraid so, brother, and if we don't hasten it will be too late."

Allen's words produced the magic to release Mark's frozen senses. "Let's go! I'd be a fool to let Christa get away from me again. I love her too much to lose her. But first I want to reward the barmaid."

"I've already taken care of the girl," Allen threw over his shoulder as he led the way out the door. "And if I'm not mistaken, that's her hurrying down the street now. I hope she'll find a better life for herself."

Omar met them just outside the Singed Goose and shouted with joy at the sight of Mark, thoroughly rumpled but apparently unharmed. He listened to an abbreviated explanation before all three broke into a run, their destination the docks, thankfully situated but a short distance away.

Out of breath and panting from their exertions, they reached the river in good time. Asking directions, they headed to where the *King Henry* was berthed, only to find its sails unfurled and gently filling with a fresh breeze as it eased away from the quay. White-clad sailors scurried to and fro manning the ropes and were far too busy to heed Mark's frantic shouts and gesturing. He stared in dismay at the ship's billowing canvas as she slipped farther and farther away.

"No!" he cried out in protest. "I won't allow it!"

Allen thought him crazed when he raised his arms and dove into the water, unaware of what he intended until it was too late to stop him. Executing a graceful arc, Mark split the murky depths, coming up sputtering as his strong strokes carried him to the line he had spied dangling from the stern of the *King Henry*.

Shocked, Allen and Omar looked at each other in consternation, then nodded in mutual agreement as they followed Mark's daring descent by mere seconds, miraculously catching hold of the same line. "Fools!" Mark shouted above the roar of rushing water.

Grinning with devilish delight, Allen mutely agreed while Omar tilted his head and roared with laughter, the thrill of adventure coursing through his veins. Suddenly a hue and cry sounded from above, where several sailors gathered at the rail to stare down at them with utter amazement. After several fruitless attempts, certain that their arms would leave their sockets, the three were slowly hoisted upwards. Mark landed on deck first, followed by Allen, with Omar close behind. At length, all three stood in the center of a widening circle of sea water, grinning foolishly and slapping each other's backs.

"What is the meaning of this?" blustered a stout man dressed in a spotless uniform sporting shiny gold buttons.

"I wish to book passage to Marseilles for a party of three," Mark said with as much aplomb as he could muster while standing soaking wet in a pool of water.

"Are you insane, man? This is no passenger ship. The *King Henry* is a government packet engaged in the king's business. You will be put ashore immediately in a longboat. I've never seen anyone board in such an unorthodox manner."

He barked out a crisp order, sending men scurrying to obey. Within seconds the sails slowly rolled downwards, bringing the ship to a shuddering standstill, water gently slapping against the hull as she rode the waves.

"Captain," Mark implored in a conciliatory tone, "it's imperative you allow me to remain aboard. I'll recompense you handsomely for your consideration."

"Marlboro, what are you doing here?"

Mark whirled, glowering menacingly as Brian Kent stepped forward.

"Do you know this man, Mr. Kent?" Captain Ashton asked.

Rendered nearly speechless at the sight of Mark, dripping sea water yet somehow managing to maintain his poise, he stammered, "This man is Mark Carrington, Duke of Marlboro. The two with him are his brother and servant."

"The Duke of Marlboro!" Had Brian realized to what extent his words helped Mark's cause he would have bitten his tongue through rather than utter them. Captain Ashton had heard of Marlboro. Who hadn't? "Your grandfather was friend to the king, was he not?"

"A privilege which I continue to enjoy," Mark lied convincingly. Though he had met the king on occasion, he did not enjoy the warm relationship with him shared by his grandfather. But the captain need not know that.

"Well," blustered Ashton, a man clearly in awe of the nobility, "in view of your rank, your grace, I might find room for your party aboard my ship. I am Captain Ashton."

"Now look here!" sputtered Brian loudly, finally gaining his wits. "I demand you put these men ashore."

"You demand?" sneered Mark, looking down his hawk-like nose at the thoroughly flustered Brian. "Didn't I warn you to stay away from Christa? You are forcing me to violence, and I assure you it won't be pleasant."

"I don't know what this is all about, your grace, but I have a ship to run," Captain Ashton commented dryly. "This appears to be a private matter, so I'll leave you to settle it between yourselves." He snapped out several concise orders, and the sailors standing around gaping at them with interest quickly scattered to perform their duties. Amidst a flurry of activity the sails unfurled again, waiting for that first gust of air to fill them.

"What are you doing aboard the *King Henry*, Kent?" Mark asked with quiet menace.

"I heard that you disappeared and your brother was quite worried," he explained cautiously. "I assumed you had changed your mind about Christa. Surely you can't blame a man for moving quickly to take your place. She is a desirable woman. As long as you have no intention of marrying her, why shouldn't I occupy your place in her bed? If used goods were good enough for a duke, why should I find fault with them?"

Brian's careless words brought a groan to Allen's lips, for he was only too aware of his brother's penchant for violence when roused to anger.

"I think you've said enough, Kent," Mark said tightly.

Emboldened, Brian shrugged. "I'd be happy to take Christa off your hands, Marlboro. You're aware, of course, that God only knows how many men bedded her. A woman of Christa's vast experience scarce deserves your illustrious name. Lady Willow would be a far better choice for you," he remarked, warming to the subject. Little did he realize that from the moment he uttered his first word, his fate was sealed.

"What does Christa think about your generous offer?"

"With the right kind of coaxing, she'll soon agree. She needs a husband and I was her parents' choice. If you hadn't happened along, we'd be married by now, perhaps even have a child. Given her tainted reputation, offers for her hand are virtually nonexistent."

Red dots of rage exploded behind Mark's brain

as he lunged at Brian. Unprepared for Mark's ferocious attack, Brian reeled backwards, falling heavily to the deck. In a matter of seconds Mark was all over him.

"Christa is too good for the likes of you, you bastard!" he ground out, his pounding fists giving emphasis to his words.

Though Brian stood nearly as tall as Mark, his flabby muscles rendered him easy prey for Mark's superbly disciplined body. The beleaguered Brian was hard put to deflect more than one or two of Mark's well-aimed blows, let alone administer any of his own. When it became obvious to Allen that Brian could endure little more of his brother's punishment, he motioned to Omar and together they struggled to pull Mark away.

"He's had enough, brother," Allen admonished as Mark fought to free himself.

Omar helped Brian to his feet. Bruised and battered, he staggered to the rail, grasping it to support his sagging weight. But Mark was not finished by half. Shrugging off Allen's restraining hands he leaped for Brian. Yelping in fear, Brian found himself suspended in air for a horrifying instant before being plummeted down to meet the swirling water below. It all happened so fast that neither Allen nor Omar could prevent Mark's swift justice. They could do little more than watch helplessly as Brian hit the water with a splash and struggled to the surface.

Hearing Brian's terrified scream and the loud splash, Captain Ashton came running, peering over the side just as Brian's head bobbed to the surface. "What is the meaning of this, your grace?" he demanded to know, more than a little upset over the turn of events. "What happened to Mr. Kent?"

"Mr. Kent suddenly decided he no longer wished to sail aboard your ship, Captain," drawled

Mark, highly amused despite the captain's scowl of disapproval. "Look," he pointed downward. "He's already been hauled aboard one of those scows that troll the river for fish."

Sure enough, Brian appeared unharmed as he stomped angrily about the deck of a small fishing boat, wringing the water out of his clothes and waving a fist at the *King Henry*, whose sails suddenly filled and scudded before the wind.

"This is highly irregular, your grace," Captain Ashton blustered, completely unsettled. Never had anything like this happened aboard his ship. Only Mark's title and claim to friendship with the king kept Ashton from clapping him in irons. But as long as nothing but Kent's pride was hurt, Ashton decided to overlook the duke's highhanded method of ridding himself of someone he obviously disliked. He wasn't too fond of the man himself.

"You'll be amply rewarded for any delay in your schedule, Captain," Mark promised, hoping to sooth the man's ruffled feathers. "Once we reach Marseilles, sufficient funds will be available to me to buy our passage as well as provide recompense for your trouble."

Somewhat mollified, Captain Ashton replied. "We have few passenger cabins aboard the *King Henry*. I have already vacated my quarters to a lady, but I'm sure my officers won't mind doubling up to accommodate your party. Wait here while I make the necessary arrangements." He turned to leave.

"Captain, wait!" Mark exclaimed, swiftly catching up to the puzzled Ashton, whose eyebrows quirked askance. They rose even higher as he listened intently to Mark's astonishing request.

At first he demurred, but as Mark continued to talk his expression grew thoughtful; then he grinned, nodding his head in vigorous agreement as he strode off chuckling to himself. This trip would provide many hours of gossip once he returned to London.

Alone in her cabin, Christa hadn't the slightest idea of what was taking place on deck. After seeing that Lenore and Elissa were settled, she sought her own spacious cabin, one that the captain had graciously vacated for her use. It was located in the bow of the ship and Christa especially appreciated the two long windows opening onto the narrow ledge guarded by a railing where she could step out and view the wide expanse of sea rushing by. She stood there now, contemplating her life and the blows dealt her by fate. She heard neither the door opening nor the soft footsteps falling upon the carpeted deck.

When a pair of strong arms encircled her slender waist, dragging her against a hard body, she gasped in indignation. Still angered over Brian's presumption that she would be happy to see him aboard the *King Henry*, Christa's temper flared, assuming he had taken it upon himself to enter her room unbidden. Didn't he realize there was no hope for him, that she could never accept him as a husband, even if Mark didn't want her?

"Damnit, Brian, what are you—?"

Her words fluttered to a halt as the arms around her tensed, nearly squeezing the breath from her lungs. Whipping around, her startled eyes met the scowling glare of emerald green.

"I'm sorry to disappoint you," Mark snarled tightly, "but your friend is no longer a passenger aboard the *King Henry*."

"No longer . . ." Suddenly, unaccountably, she giggled. "What did you do, throw him overboard?"

"Exactly." Mark grinned wickedly, relaxing his grip on her waist. "Are you sorry, Christa? He has no right to steal what is mine."

"Am I, Mark? Am I yours? Or do you want me

only when it serves your purpose?" she asked resentfully.

"You have every right to be angry, my love, but you must admit you provoked me into acting as I did. Why are you leaving London when I expressly asked you not to?"

"Did you expect me to wait around for you to come to your senses? I feel as if I've been to hell and back. I knew you would return once you realized no one but you could have fathered my child, but I never thought you'd remain away so long. I began to suspect you had returned to Willow. That's when I decided I didn't need you, or any man. I'm rich enough to support our child without your help."

"Are you certain you don't need me, love?" he asked, his gaze bold and assessing. "Do you think I'd let you deprive me of my child?"

Her heart jolted and her pulse pounded, and she struggled to fight her overwhelming need to be close to him. But she'd be damned if she'd allow him the satisfaction of knowing how easily she'd fall into his arms despite his contemptible behavior. "If you cared a fig about your child, you would have rejoiced instead of expressing doubt," Christa said with bitter emphasis.

"I apologize for that, Christa, but please try to understand my feelings. I was consumed with the terrible thought that you were pregnant and leaving with Kent. If the child was mine, you wouldn't have considered such a thing. I became so angry I couldn't trust myself to remain in the same room with you. I became self-destructive and went on a colossal drunk.

"Even before I reached the inn, I realized my mistake and cursed my insane jealousy. I had hurt you dreadfully and prayed you would forgive me. But by then all manner of devils drove me—my parents' senseless deaths, Abdullah, losing the beylic—until it became a sickness within me whose only cure lay at the bottom of a bottle. Eventually I passed out and came to my senses only today, when Allen found me. To my horror, I learned you were sailing for France within the hour."

"You deserted me, Mark," Christa accused him sullenly. "I'm not certain I can forgive you. I'm even less sure that I—I still want you." She was being less than truthful, but Mark was far too confident of her love for her to acknowledge it. It would do him good to suffer the same doubts he inflicted on her.

"Oh, you want me, sweet siren, as much as I want you," he murmured lazily. His eyes swept over her with fiery warmth. Like sipping fine brandy, it was highly intoxicating. The sight of her whetted the palate and left him hungry and wanting.

With slow deliberation his mouth met hers, his kiss savage, fierce, impatient. His insistent lips pushed hers apart as his tongue probed forcefully inside the welcoming warmth, claiming and extracting from her responses she tried to withhold but was powerless to prevent. The kiss went on and on. Just when she feared she would faint from lack of breath, he drew away, his piercing gaze probing intently. A breathless expectancy settled over them, as sultry and heavy with promise as the warm, scented wind that blew from the sea. As their eyes met and clung, Christa's anger melted into desire; the love she bore this special man brought with it a deep, profound hunger and the urge to throw herself into his arms and remain there forever.

Mark needed no prodding as his nimble fingers found the lacings at the back of her dress, and like magic the bodice fell away, revealing smooth shoulders and the tops of creamy breasts. A flip of the wrist released the ties holding her chemise together and Mark's impatient hands brushed it neatly aside.

The warm, tempting flesh brought a groan to his lips, and he cupped the soft coral-tipped mounds to bring them to his mouth, feasting hungrily on one nipple, then the other. Not satisfied with so meager a meal, wanting her completely naked in his arms so he might devour every inch of her delectable flesh, he swiftly divested her of her remaining clothing.

Eager to feel the warm surface of his skin beneath her fingertips, Christa tore at his shirt, noting distractedly that he was dripping wet. "Mark, you're soaked! How—?"

"Later, my love," he breathed raggedly, shrugging off his clinging trousers and shirt. "It's been so long I can't wait to love you."

Standing proud and nude before her, he made Christa quail before the onslaught of such overt masculinity and sleek strength, her glance sliding across broad shoulders, down narrow waist to lean flanks. A thick forest of curling hair furred his chest and tapered to his loins where his manhood rose immense and throbbing with life.

The look of awe she bestowed on him brought a chuckle to his lips, for he was no less inspired by her own nude beauty. Poised on the balls of her feet, back arched, the tips of her breasts brushing his chest, she was the answer to all his dreams and desires. Drawn like a moth to flame, his eyes settled on the silvery triangle crowning her thighs, and his loins swelled in avid anticipation.

Scooping her up in his arms, he carefully placed her in the center of the captain's oversized bed, falling to his knees beside her. Uttering a soft sigh, his lips seized hers, his tongue thrusting deep inside, probing, tasting, drawing on her sweetness. Abruptly he left that tantalizing territory as her breasts beckoned him to more erotic exploration. With lips and hands he teased and titillated, drawing the nipples deeply into his mouth and laving the sensitive tips with the roughness of his tongue.

A moan broke from her throat as his mouth drifted lower, blazing a fiery trail over flat stomach and rounded hips, then between shapely thighs until he found the hidden treasure he sought. She gasped as she felt his probing tongue invade her moist warmth in an intimate caress. When he gently pushed her legs apart, she eagerly obeyed his unspoken command, allowing him to pleasure her in any way he wished. One splendorous sensation after another cascaded over her as she writhed and moaned beneath his loving onslaught. And then she was there, somewhere beyond the moon, half-way to the stars. Her mind went blank, her body became a mass of quivering emotion.

Still reeling from Mark's special loving, she felt him slide upward, his mouth on her lips, drawing from her a sense of wonder and peace and plunging her recklessly into renewed turbulence. The taste of herself on his lips excited her beyond reason and she clutched at the hard mounds of his buttocks, drawing him closer still, until his massive staff probed relentlessly at that place where she ached for him most.

Holding his own passion in tight rein, Mark slowly, with great patience and amazing fortitude, kindled Christa's until she begged for release. "Not yet, my love," he whispered, kissing her until her whole body tingled and burned.

But Christa could not tolerate another moment of this exquisite torture as she sought to bring it to a pleasurable end. Grasping his manhood she urged him forward and his restraint quickly fled with her soft, teasing touch. They came together with wild, explosive abandon that nothing could contain. She clutched at him frantically as he drove into her, appeasing at last the sweet ache that coiled in the very core of her. His loving was expert and pervasive as she felt him hard and erect inside her, and she squeezed her muscles tight, wanting all he had to offer. She wasn't disappointed as he filled her completely, driving relentlessly into her soft flesh, stroking her to completion.

"Mark, I love you!" Christa cried out, clasping him tightly in the cradle of her thighs as the world and all in it spun out of orbit.

"You're mine, sweet siren," Mark groaned in response. "Don't ever think of leaving me again." Then words failed him as he felt the contractions racking her slim form, her violent release triggering his own as he plunged upward one last time, then shuddered, caught up in the throes of his own thundering climax.

24

Lying nude atop the thoroughly rumpled bed, arms and legs entwined, the reunited lovers succumbed to exhaustion. Nearly an hour later, Mark was the first to awaken, staring down at Christa with a tenderness he had never felt before in his life. Not only was Christa the woman he loved, but she carried his child, making her even more precious in his eyes. With anxious concern his gaze drifted downward to her stomach, fearing that their furious loving might have hurt the child.

Her body was still so slim that it seemed impossible that a baby grew inside her. With gentle awe Mark placed a hand on the slight swell of her belly, marveling at the exciting prospect of becoming a father. Son or daughter, it made little difference, as long as Christa and his child survived the ordeal.

Christa's eyes flew open with a start, surprised to find Mark gazing at her with something akin to wonder, his hand massaging the place where his seed grew and was nurtured. Moistening her lips, she said, "When you left the way you did I thought —that is I assumed—"

"That I didn't want a child?" Mark finished. "It was a natural assumption given the way I allowed my jealous temper to cloud my thinking. But I hope I was able to explain everything to your satisfaction. I know it is my child you carry and I couldn't be happier."

Though his words went a long way in easing her doubts, Christa grew thoughtful. It suddenly occurred to her that Mark had said nothing about marriage. Did he intend to keep her for a mistress? He seemed not to notice her pensive mood as he continued stroking her stomach, a silly grin turning up the corners of his mouth.

Just then a discreet knock interrupted Mark's pleasant musings. "Who is it?" Christa called out, smiling at Mark's frown at having been disturbed.

"It's Elissa. Allen said to tell Mark he's found a set of clothes for him. He's waiting in the first mate's cabin."

"Clothes? Where in the world did he come by clothes to fit me?" Mark asked. "Certainly not from the captain, who's a good six inches shorter than I am."

"I believe Mr. Kent left his trunk full of clothes when he left so—er, abruptly," Elissa replied, choking on her laughter.

"Allen is aboard the *King Henry*, too?" Christa asked, astounded. "However did you two get aboard? I remained on deck until the gangplank was drawn up and saw no one." Abruptly she recalled Mark's wet clothing. "Mark! You didn't! Surely you and Allen didn't jump into the Thames!"

"My love, not only did Allen and I swim out to catch the *King Henry*, but Omar succumbed to the same folly that drove us. Now you know to what lengths I'd go to claim what is mine."

"Mark, you're mad, but I love you anyway."

Grinning foolishly, he turned toward the door and called to Elissa, who still stood on the other side of the panel, "Tell Allen I'll join him directly. Then inform the captain we'll meet him on deck as soon as I'm properly dressed."

Puzzled, Christa asked, "What are you up to, Mark? What is this all about?"

Flashing a winsome smile, Mark replied, "I'll send Lenore in to help you dress. Wear your prettiest gown."

"What are you talking about? Why should I wear my prettiest dress?"

"You want to look your best for our wedding, don't you? I've arranged for Captain Ashton to perform the ceremony. Hurry, darling. I can't wait until you are legally mine."

"You—you want to marry me? Now?"

Exasperated he asked, "Didn't I just say so?"

"But I thought . . . I wasn't certain what you intended."

"My intention all along was to have you for my wife. No one will call my child a bastard."

Dressed in shimmering blue silk that enhanced the blue of her eyes, ash-blond hair gleaming like newly minted silver in the sunlight, Christa stood beside Mark, who was equally resplendent in Brian Kent's finest clothing. Clustered about them stood Allen, Elissa, Omar, Lenore and most of the crew of the *King Henry*. Decked out in his finest uniform, prayer book in hand, Captain Ashton read the brief words that united them forever.

If anyone thought it strange that the happy

couple were so anxious to wed that they couldn't
wait until they reached Marseilles, no one gave any
sign of it. Not only Mark's exulted rank, but the
couple's obvious joy in each other prevented anyone from giving voice to such an opinion. The
entire ship had been in an uproar since the Duke of
Marlboro had been hauled aboard the *King Henry*
and the wedding ceremony was the culmination of
the day devoted to surprises.

A loud shout rent the air as Mark bent down to
kiss his blushing bride, for he delivered not the
customary peck, but an exuberant, lusty kiss full
on the mouth that lasted nearly a minute. When he
reluctantly relinquished his wife, the captain
claimed his right, bestowing a chaste buzz on her
cheek. Allen was not so circumspect, claiming her
lips briefly after flicking a mischievous grin at his
scowling brother. Before members of the crew were
given the opportunity to request the same privilege, Mark quickly whisked Christa away to the
saloon, where a sumptuous supper was set out for
the bridal party.

Darkness had descended before the newlyweds
escaped to the privacy of their own cabin. Throughout the festive celebration and countless toasts,
Mark had displayed an indecent interest in his
blushing bride, his barely contained desire a cause
for merriment among their companions. Thus it
came as no surprise when he rose abruptly, grasped
Christa's hand, and led her off with hardly a word
of explanation—not that any was needed.

Finally alone with the man she loved, a man she
had never expected to become her husband, Christa
turned unaccountably shy, fidgeting nervously
with the tiny buttons at the back of her dress.
"Here, let me help, my love," Mark said, brushing
her fingers aside. "I think I'll enjoy providing maid
service until we reach Marseilles. I've waited so

long for this day, I don't want to share you with
anyone."

Beneath his experienced hands, the top of her
dress fell away, and he cupped her breasts, drawing
her into the hard contour of his body. The only
light in the cabin came from the lantern swinging
from the ceiling and the brilliant moonlight filtering through the two long windows, turning her hair
into a living flame. "I love you," Mark whispered
tenderly, his warm breath fanning her cheek. "I
have from the first moment I set eyes on you. You
please me in every way."

"And I love you," Christa responded, a familiar shiver of arousal sweeping her from head to toe.
In the half-light, her eyes appeared dark, mysterious, utterly captivating. "I will love you until death
parts us and even beyond."

Tenderly, lingeringly, they undressed each
other, touching, caressing, as if they were newly
awakened to love. Gently he lowered her to the bed.
"I want to be inside you so bad it hurts," he
groaned hoarsely.

Instinctively his fingers found the velvet of her
inner thigh and stroked upward as a warm wetness
began in her sensitive core. She felt him probe
inward, his every movement setting off turbulent
waves of grinding pulsations inside her. Using his
mouth he suckled and tugged at the peaks of her
breasts, and she could feel his long, swollen shaft
pressing hot and hard against her thigh.

"You drive me to distraction, sweet siren,"
Mark panted. "No other woman could satisfy me
as you do."

They touched, kissed and mingled bodies until
all restraint fled. The flame in Christa burned hotly,
fed by Mark's passion, his needs a perfect match for
hers. He flexed his hips and in that single, practiced
motion the hot length of him slid inside her wel-

coming warmth. Inside, she felt like a torch flaming out of control, searing with exquisite agony all those wanton parts of her womanhood. Their coupling was swift and urgent, as passion drove them. He rode her with a fierce, savage joy that ended with a wild crescendo of brilliant lights and exploding ecstasy. Afterwards, they slept, but only for a short time, for once again their insatiable passion for each other brought them together with dazzling need. This time Christa took the initiative, loving him with her hands and lips as her mouth found him, surrounded him, and tasted deeply.

Before the night faded into dawn they came together once more in mutual need. When the sun was again a fiery ball high in the sky, their need for food finally drove them from their nuptial bed.

A few days later, much to Christa's delight and Mark's mixed feelings, Captain Ashton was called upon to perform another ceremony, this one a double service uniting in marriage Elissa to Allen and Lenore to Omar. Forever afterwards, the bemused captain was to think of this trip as a honeymoon voyage instead of his usually boring run between London and Marseilles. It was an experience he was not likely to forget and one he could brag about for years to come.

The chateau in southern France, near the village of Miramas, lay but a half day's journey from Marseilles. While Mark made arrangements with the bank to pay Captain Ashton and provide himself with funds, Allen hired a carriage for the women, horses for the men, and a dray to follow with their considerable baggage. Before they departed Marseilles, a shopping spree was called for to provide much-needed clothing for the men as well as several new ensembles for the women. At

last the entourage left the city for Miramas, and
Christa became more than a little anxious at the
prospect of presenting her parents with a son-in-
law other than the one they expected.

They arrived at dusk, descending upon the
unsuspecting chateau with much trepidation, at
least on Christa's part. But she needn't have worried, for her welcome couldn't have been more
exuberant. Amid a flurry of excitement, Christa
learned that her mother had recovered from her
illness, aided in part by the temperate climate of
southern France. There existed only slight evidence
of lingering weakness as she greeted her daughter
with tears in her eyes. A tiny woman, and frail,
Lady Horton possessed a strength of character that
she had passed on to her daughter.

When Christa ran into the arms of her still
handsome father, he broke into a wide smile that
softened his rather imposing features. Despite Sir
Wesley's military bearing, he exhibited nothing but
tenderness toward his family. No one was more
aware of it than Christa, as he enfolded her in his
strong arms and hugged her close to his large,
rawboned frame.

Not to be outdone, Christa's younger brother
and sister clamored for attention. Will, at twelve,
was a tall and lanky lad, all arms, legs and elbows.
He whooped with joy as he hugged his much-loved
older sister. Little Cora was eight and a darling with
long blond curls and mischievous blue eyes much
like Christa's. Her greeting showed slightly more
restraint, though no less happiness than her rowdy
brother's.

Disentangling herself from the loving embrace
of her family, Christa turned to the group waiting
in the background while her parents looked on with
polite expectancy. One by one Christa introduced

her friends, deliberately saving Mark for last.
Drawing him to her side, she said tenderly, "And
this, Mama and Papa, is my husband, Mark
Carrington, Duke of Marlboro."

"Your—your husband!" blustered Sir Wesley.
"How could that be? What happened to Brian Kent?
I thought your marriage to him was all but an
accomplished fact?"

"Oh, Christa," wailed Lady Horton, "what
have you done?"

"I've done nothing but marry the man I love,"
Christa explained, gazing at Mark with so much
love that the older couple looked at each other with
raised eyebrows.

It didn't escape Mark's notice that Sir Wesley
was slow to acknowledge him, preferring to withhold judgment until he had learned more about
their hasty marriage. The hand Mark offered was
politely accepted, but with little enthusiasm. Mark
hoped his cool reception would change once an
adequate explanation was given.

"You deserve to know all the details, Mama
and Papa, and Mark and I will gladly oblige. But
later, when the excitement of our arrival has passed
and our guests are settled in. If that's all right with
you."

Nodding curtly, all the while eyeing Mark with
distinct suspicion, Sir Wesley herded the group
inside the large, sprawling chateau nestled against
the quaint setting of thickly wooded hills and lush,
grassy valleys.

"Christa, when Brian returned to Tunis after
your release, he hinted that you had been—er, that
the pirates and Abdullah had . . ." Lady Horton
floundered helplessly. At last everyone had been
assigned rooms, leaving Christa, Mark and her
parents alone. Christa had already explained how

she and Mark had met and all that had happened during the intervening year.

"Brian was wrong, Mama," she refuted sharply. "No one touched me in—in that way. I already told you that Mark is Prince Ahmed, rightful ruler of Constantine. My usefulness to Abdullah existed only to the extent that it brought about Mark's downfall and increased his suffering. I served him only as a means to an end." She hoped her rather simplified explanation satisfied them. "I—I have something else to tell you. I'm expecting Mark's child."

"This is all highly irregular," blustered Sir Wesley. "Your mother and I did our best to raise you properly. First you admit to being married only a few days ago aboard ship, then you calmly announce you are pregnant. This is all rather sudden, isn't it? I don't wonder that Kent called off your marriage. What in the world possessed you?"

Though his disapproving words were addressed to his daughter, his baleful glance settled on Mark. It was obvious that he held his new son-in-law responsible for leading his daughter astray.

"If you must blame anyone, Sir Wesley, blame me," Mark quickly leaped to Christa's defense. "I'm afraid I was rather persistent."

"Harumph!" Sir Wesley sputtered, clearing his throat as his face turned vivid red. Though he had been married for years, he wasn't so old that he couldn't remember how it was to be young and impulsive.

"I for one am glad we're finally reunited," Lady Horton sighed. "And you do seem happy with the duke."

"I love your daughter, ma'am," Mark volunteered. "Christa and my child mean more to me than my life. I hope you and Sir Wesley will find it in your hearts to accept me into your family."

"Gladly." Lady Alice smiled. "All we've ever wanted is Christa's happiness, isn't that true, Wesley?" she added, jabbing him in the ribs.

"Umph!" Sir Wesley winced, giving his wife an affronted look. "Of course, of course," he allowed generously. "If Christa is satisfied, then so am I. The choice was always hers to make. Welcome, your grace—er, Mark."

"I can't believe I'm soon to become a grandmother," gushed Lady Horton.

Even Sir Wesley smiled benignly when reminded of Christa's condition. As for Mark, Christa certainly could have done no better than a duke. Though he liked Kent, he would never have forced Christa into a marriage she didn't want. He loved his daughter far too much for that.

"Papa, I love you so much!" Christa exclaimed, throwing herself into his arms. "And you, too, Mama. Never doubt my happiness. As long as Mark is with me, I am content. He is my life."

The months spent at the chateau were among the happiest in Christa's young life. She was reunited with her parents and siblings, she had her friends, and best of all, Mark was with her. Often alone, sometimes with Allen and Elissa, they went on picnics, toured Marseilles and the surrounding countryside, and even attended fairs along with the country folk of the area. And they made love— occasionally in the fragrant grass beside a bubbling brook, but mostly in the big bed in the privacy of their room. When Christa began to swell with child, their loving assumed a gentle nature, yet was more satisfying in a way it had never been before. To Christa it seemed as if nothing could mar those golden days or destroy their happiness.

But one day Sir Wesley received a summons

from the king. If Lady Horton had recovered from her illness, Sir Wesley's presence was requested in London as soon as possible. An important post in England had been found for him, one he could not refuse despite his earlier resolve to retire. Being far from wealthy and nearly beggared by the ransom demanded by Abdullah was one reason for Sir Wesley's quick compliance. The other was that he was still a vital man, eager to serve his country. And since Lady Horton's health had drastically improved, he felt strongly about doing his duty.

Plans were made to leave within a fortnight, much to Lady Horton's dismay. She had hoped to be on hand when her grandchild was born. The babe was due in two months, but Christa insisted that Lenore was perfectly capable of delivering her child. Besides, Mark was there and she needed no one else, though her mother's presence would have been welcome. Confident that her daughter would be in good hands, Lady Horton gave reluctant agreement to leave with her husband, since Mark had revealed that he and Christa would return to London as soon as the baby was able to travel.

Shortly after the Hortons' departure, Mark, accompanied by Allen and Omar, made a hasty trip to Marseilles. Their main purpose was to visit the bank, but Mark also wanted to pick up a thick gold wedding band he had ordered for Christa weeks earlier. But all his plans scattered like ashes before the wind when he spied an Algerian vessel berthed in the harbor. On a sudden whim, he decided to board her and speak with the captain. It had been months since he heard any news from his own country. Eagerly, Allen voiced agreement, as did Omar.

Of the three, Allen missed his homeland the most, not having had the experience of living many years in England as his brother had. As for Omar, he seemed perfectly content to follow his prince.

Captain Hamid greeted them cordially, especially after learning their identities. He invited them to share his meal, and what they learned over the sumptuous repast changed not only their immediate plans but possibly their future. When they left hours later, grim-faced and tense, all thought of gifts fled. After a brief stop at the bank, they returned directly to the chateau. By the time they arrived darkness covered the land and the household had already retired for the night.

The warmth was welcome, Christa decided, glad that she had ordered a fire built in the hearth. There was a definite chill in the air now that winter was almost upon them. Summer had passed so swiftly, she silently complained, that she had been scarcely aware of its passing, so content was she in her own little world. It was as if nothing or no one existed but her own family, and her love for Mark. In somber moments she often thought her happiness too perfect to last.

Moving to the French doors, now closed to shut out the chill, she peered into the darkness, thinking that Mark should have returned from Marseilles long ago. Absently, she splayed her hands across her swollen abdomen, feeling the child move strongly in her womb. She smiled, loving the sensation almost as much as the feeling of his father's maleness filling her. She nearly always referred to the babe as male, for the feeling persisted that she would give Mark a son.

Little did she know as she stood poised in the flickering firelight, every delicious curve of her body outlined beneath the thin silk of her nightgown, that Mark was already mounting the stairs. The door slid open silently beneath his touch and he stepped inside, his eyes finding her immediately. Hearing the telltale click of the latch, Christa turned from her contemplation and smiled in welcome.

"I've been waiting." Her voice was a husky purr that sent his senses reeling. If he lived to be a hundred Mark would never forget the way Christa looked as she turned to greet him. The diaphanous gown hid nothing of her charms from his eager eyes. Her added bulk served only to enhance her beauty in his eyes. Though he knew her body intimately, had thoroughly explored and tasted every inch of her delectable flesh, he would never tire of looking at her, of wanting her, of loving her. Her nipples, enlarged by pregnancy and thrusting against the soft material of her gown, begged to be fondled, her flesh hungered for his caress, the pale triangle between her thighs pleaded for his possession. Head thrown back, long neck exposed to his ardent perusal, Christa's glorious hair caressed her back like a silver curtain. How could he ever leave her? he asked himself despondently as he moved forward to meet his kismet.

"You're so beautiful it hurts to look at you," he choked out, hating himself for what he must do.

"Come, my love," Christa urged, so attuned to his mood she sensed immediately that something troubled him. "Come to bed."

"Nothing would please me more than to make love to you, my darling," Mark breathed raggedly, "but I don't want to hurt you or our child. Are you certain it's all right?"

"Even if this is to be the last time before our baby is born," she said prophetically, "I want you. I'm far from fragile, and our babe is too firmly entrenched in my womb to do it any harm. Surely one more time can't hurt."

Mark could deny her nothing, vowing to make this night memorable, for it was their last for many nights to come. Their lips meshed, clung, the kiss deepening until a fierce, hungry need seized them. Drawing away, Mark swiftly undressed, his smoldering gaze never leaving the woman he loved beyond all reason. Mesmerized, Christa watched. Orange light from the hearth played over him in dancing patterns, highlighting his burnished hair and bronzed features. The beauty and symmetry of his virile form never ceased to amaze her. She was totally consumed by his maleness and wanted him with a fierceness that was a dagger in her body.

Clothed in a mantle of masculine beauty, Mark flipped his wrist and the wisp of material that served as a nightgown left her body. She moved effortlessly into his embrace. Through a fringe of lashes she smiled up at him as he lowered her gently onto the surface of the bed.

What transpired next went beyond mere pleasure. No part of her body was sacrosanct as Mark plied his tongue, hands and mouth with equal dexterity, bringing her again and again to the shuddering brink, filling her being with dazzling sunbursts of delight. He loved her in every conceivable way, gasp after gasp sighing from her parted lips as his glossy head nestled between her thighs. Moments later wrenching ecstasy carried her to its stabbing climax. Wanting to bring him the same pleasure, Christa recriprocated in the same thrilling way, his groans like haunting strains of music to her ears. Unable to stand another minute of such exquisite torture, Mark lifted her from her pleasurable task, moaning her name over and over, signaling the end of his endurance. Slowly, with great tenderness, he lowered her to the hard pillar of marble and Christa made no effort to hold back a shriek of elation as he filled her with the essence of his maleness. She rode him wantonly, demanding his all, receiving nothing less. Later, it occurred to Mark that should he die tomorrow, he would leave the world content, for he had been privileged to experience what most men searched all their lives to attain. He had found perfect love.

25

"I'm leaving tomorrow," Mark said quietly, feeling Christa stiffen in his arms. "I want you to return to England immediately to be near your parents."

"Oh God, no!" wailed Christa, clinging to him with a desperation that nearly destroyed his resolve. "I knew the moment you stepped into the room tonight that something was wrong. Why? Why must you leave me?"

"I don't want to, but I must," came his anguished reply. "I learned today that Constantine is in turmoil. Abdullah has openly defied the dey of Algiers. He has taxed the residents of Constantine and a rebellion is in the making. He has cruelly and methodically destroyed all who disobey him. A delegation of citizens petitioned the dey of Algiers to end Abdullah's tyranny. When the dey publicly chastised Abdullah, he retaliated by attacking the dey's caravans and confiscating valuable merchandise meant for the dey's cotters. Abdullah must be mad to attempt such folly."

"But I don't see what all this has to do with you!" Christa complained bitterly. "I thought the beylic was no longer your concern. You are Duke of Marlboro. Your life is in England with me and our child."

"I learned from the captain of an Algerian vessel berthed in Marseilles that the dey is preparing to strike against Abdullah. Previously, the dey had refused to interfere with internal strife between brothers. Now, with the dey's backing, I will finally see the end of Abdullah's reign. My honor demands that I see this to its conclusion. Once this is settled, my parents' deaths will be avenged. Allen and Omar are to accompany me. We sail tomorrow with Captain Hamid. It is all arranged."

"Just like that? You're leaving just like that?" she cried, her voice growing increasingly shrill. "What guarantee do I have that you'll return? There'll be great pressure on you to take over the reins of government and remain in Constantine as their bey."

"Our child is your assurance that I will return," Mark replied, stunned to think that she would doubt him. "Are you so doubting of our love that you no longer trust me? I naturally assumed it was strong enough to survive a short separation."

"Our entire relationship consists of one separation after another," Christa accused him with bitter emphasis. "And how could Allen possibly leave Elissa now that she's expecting his child?"

"That's between my brother and his wife, my love," he contended. "What concerns me is you and my child. Do you prefer to live in the London house your aunt left you, or in my townhouse?"

"I gave my house to my parents," Christa informed him coolly.

"Then go to my townhouse. The staff there will look after you until I return. Before I leave, I'll write some letters to pave your way into society."

"I care nothing about that. Mark, I'm afraid. So afraid. What if—"

"Don't do this to yourself, darling. Nothing short of death will prevent me from returning to you. You are my kismet. It is our destiny to grow old together."

"Is it also your kismet to become bey of Constantine? Where will I fit into your new life? Do you intend to take Abdullah's place once he is disposed of? Tell me, Mark," she challenged him, "tell me you have no ambition to fulfill your father's wishes."

A long, tense silence sent all Christa's hopes and dreams for the future plummeting. At length, Mark replied, "I can't tell you exactly what will happen when I reach Constantine, for I don't know myself." His words promised nothing. "But if I am certain of one thing in my life, it is that my love for you will never die. Should my kismet be to rule Constantine, I will still return, if only to take you back with me. Right now I can't think beyond the fact that Abdullah is close to being punished for the cruel murder of my parents and that I must, *I must*," he repeated forcefully, "be there. And Allen is in complete agreement. Omar, of course, goes where I go."

"I understand your feelings, Mark, truly I do," Christa allowed grudgingly, bowing to the inevitable. "It's just that I fear for you. How long will you be gone?"

"A month, my love. Six weeks at the most. I should be back in plenty of time to see our child born. After this is settled, we'll never be parted again."

It was not exactly what Christa would have wanted, but no one had ever told her life would be easy. Kismet had brought them together when she thought never to see Mark again, and she could do no less than trust to fate one more time. But at the moment, she was where she belonged, in the arms of the man she loved. The remaining hours of the night lay before them. Perhaps, if they tried hard enough, they could wish away the dawn.

"Mark, love me again. Don't give me time to think, only to feel."

Covering her with his body, he gave her all she wished for, all she desired, until dawn intruded and the spell was broken.

Just before Mark left the next day, Christa received a surprise she wasn't expecting. Somehow Elissa had cajoled Allen into taking her to Algiers with him. Thoroughly insensed, Christa didn't hesitate to voice her protest.

"Why should Elissa be allowed to accompany you when I cannot? Nor Lenore?" she challenged, blue eyes blazing defiantly.

"Elissa is Algerian," Allen explained patiently. "Though she's not complained, she misses her homeland as much as I do. She has relatives in Algiers and will be safe enough in their home. You are a foreigner and the danger too great to yourself, as well as to your child."

"Elissa is pregnant, also."

"Elissa won't deliver for months, while our child will be born soon," Mark intervened, eyeing her growing bulk with some misgiving.

"I wanted to have my baby in Algeria," Elissa explained wistfully. "Don't be angry with me, Christa. I've never had a friend like you and, Allah willing, we will see each other again."

"Oh, Elissa, I'm not angry with you," Christa

countered, hugging her friend. "I'll miss you desperately. "It's just that—"

"My love, think of our child. You wouldn't want to have him in Algeria where danger and intrigue lurks at every turn, would you? It would ease my mind greatly if I knew you were safe in England. Omar has agreed that Lenore should remain behind to care for you."

Then he was kissing her and Christa knew a desolation she hadn't experienced since Abdullah had sentenced Mark to a lifetime of slavery.

London was dreary in winter, but the first month of her return to the city was not too difficult for Christa to bear. As Mark promised, he had written a letter to Mrs. Benton, his housekeeper, delivered by Christa, which assured her of a warm welcome. In fact, the entire staff couldn't have been more gracious or helpful. In addition, she saw her parents and siblings often enough to keep loneliness at bay.

Lady Horton was especially happy to have Christa where she could attend the birth of her grandchild. Sir Wesley had been rewarded by the king with a post in London, which greatly pleased his wife, for she had spent many years away from her beloved country.

Another letter written by Mark was delivered to Sir Peter Brent. In it he announced his marriage to Christa and asked his good friend to make certain she received the recognition and respect due a duchess. Sir Peter took his duty seriously, calling upon Christa immediately. A warm friendship developed and soon Christa began receiving calls and invitations from her peers, few of which she accepted due to her advanced state of pregnancy. But Mark's foresight had paved the road to her painless re-entry into society. Despite previous gossip, Christa's new rank virtually assured her acceptance.

Upon her arrival in London, she feared Willow Langtry might try again to destroy her, but she soon learned that Willow no longer presented a threat to her or to Mark. Peter told her the lady's petition to receive her late husband's inheritance had been denied. Unable to live within her modest means, she had married an aging earl who immediately whisked her away to the country, where she lived in virtual seclusion. Christa could well imagine Willow's desperation and almost felt sorry for her. She knew the woman abhorred the quiet life she was forced to lead and no doubt yearned for the gaiety of London. Christa considered it a just reward for all Willow's evil machinations and could find little pity in her heart for her predicament.

At the end of six weeks, Christa and Lenore waited and watched for the return of their men. The sound of carriage wheels or horses' hooves sent them flying for the windows. It was a dismal time of year in more ways than one.

At the end of two months, Christa grew frantic, certain that something dreadful had happened to Mark to keep him from returning to her. If not for the imminent birth of her child, she would have left immediately to search for him. Both Lenore and the Hortons did their best to lift Christa's spirits, but they were unable to shake her from her despondency.

On a blustery February day, Michael Mark Carrington, the future Duke of Marlboro, emerged into the world screaming at the top of his well-developed lungs. In attendance were Lenore, Lady Horton, and Mrs. Benton. He tipped the scale at seven pounds. Michael's cap of fuzz promised to be the same color as his father's burnished locks, while his dark blue eyes resembled those of any other newborn babe.

Christa fared well during the delivery, her suffering greatly eased by Lenore's knowledge of herbs and medicine acquired during her years of captivity. Thankfully Michael wasn't unduly large, for had he been the outcome might not have been so pleasant. But Christa tolerated childbearing exceptionally well, given her small-boned frame. Her one sorrow was that Mark did not appear to witness the happy event. Did his promise mean nothing to him?

The harsh winter warmed into a gentle spring, and Michael began to develop a personality all his own. Christa could not help but think of how much Mark was missing. He had been gone four months. Did he even care about his child or her anxious wait for him?

Peter was a constant visitor, coaxing Christa out of her doldrums by making her laugh. But his tales of Mark and their college pranks were brief diversions, and the moment he left she surrendered once again to depression.

It took little imagination on Christa's part to realize what had happened. Once Abdullah was removed from the beylic, Mark would have slipped naturally into the role of Prince Ahmed, bey of Constantine. With the passage of time, it became increasingly obvious that Mark never meant to return. All his promises were nothing but empty words. Evidently, resuming his life as Ahmed bey meant more to him than his wife and child. And why not? No doubt Abdullah's harem consisted of young virgins far more beautiful than she.

When the weather turned warm, Christa yearned for the countryside where Michael might breath clean, fresh air and learn to walk barefoot in

the grass. After confiding in her parents, she left the
London townhouse for the Marlboro country estate
located a half day's journey from the city.

She threw herself wholeheartedly into opening
the huge mansion, cleaning and refurbishing it, and
somehow the days slipped by with boring regulari-
ty. Peter came to call, and left cursing Mark for
putting Christa through such anguish. When he
left, Christa returned to her own little world, where
nothing or no one existed but her son. If she
couldn't have Mark, she wanted no one. She would
content herself to live out her days in the country
with her own little family. She had enough of love
to last all of her days. Love only hurt.

Relaxing beneath an apple tree, Christa thought
the orchard a perfect place to laze away an hour or
two on such a golden day. A country lass named
Maggie had been hired to help care for Michael,
though Christa insisted on nursing her child herself, so that she could occasionally steal away for an
hour or two of solitude.

As so often happened when Christa was alone,
her thoughts turned to Mark and all they had
shared before fate tore them apart. A hopeless
gloom settled over her and a lump as large as a
boulder lodged in her throat, too dry, too painful to
swallow. She had only to close her eyes to conjure
up his beloved image—the wild nobility of his
sun-darkened face, the green eyes as clear and
sparkling as emeralds, the panther-like grace of his
slim body when he moved. And the way he loved
her, with a consummate passion that fired her body
and warmed her soul. The dimple in his chin when
he smiled at her danced upon her mind, as did the
deep timbre of his voice when he whispered love
words in her ear. In her state of half awareness, she

imagined that resonant voice speaking to her, rich, caressing, bringing back memories of the way she felt in his arms, all warm and soft and writhing with passion.

Defying all logic that voice beckoned to her even in her sleep. "Wake up, my love."

No! A scream of denial was torn upward from her heart and died stillborn on her lips. It wasn't right that she should suffer his loss even in her dreams.

"Christa, I nearly went out of my mind when I found you gone from the townhouse, until Mrs. Benton told me you were in the country."

Slowly Christa opened her eyes, fearing he would disappear if she made a sudden move. "Mark?" she whispered as astonishment followed disbelief across her face. "Is it really you?"

Mark knelt at her side, his eyes roaming freely over her petite form, still perfect after childbirth, marveling at her beauty and the subtle grace with which she moved.

"Didn't I tell you I'd return, love?" he chided gently. "I'm sorry it took so long, but it couldn't be helped."

Flinging herself into his arms, Christa sent them both sprawling to the soft grass beneath them, laughing, crying, murmuring his name over and over. "I thought you had forgotten us."

"Forgotten you and my son?" Mark scolded her sternly. "How could you think such a thing? I never make promises I don't intend to keep. I saw our son, you know. I stopped at the house and Lenore presented him to me. He's perfect in every way. I think his eyes are going to be blue, like yours."

"More like blue-green," Christa corrected. "I'm glad you approve of him. I named him Michael as we discussed before you left."

"I wanted to be here," he said sadly. "Was it terrible?"

Christa shrugged. "No more than I expected, though I don't know if I could have endured it without Lenore and her herbs. The pleasure I receive from Michael more than compensates for the pain I suffered."

"You're a marvel," he murmured, green eyes shining with admiration.

He moved to take her into his arms but Christa turned aside, the question she yearned to ask burning the tip of her tongue. "It's been over four months, Mark. What happened to keep you so long? I nearly drove myself mad imagining all sorts of things."

Mark sat up, leaning against the tree and pulling her into his arms despite her mild protest. "I may as well start from the beginning, for I can see you won't be satisfied until you hear every detail."

Christa studied his beloved features while he made himself comfortable. The sun had darkened his handsome face and the forces of nature had eroded and hardened the laugh lines that strayed from the corners of his vibrant green eyes, cutting deep slashes through his cheeks. But instead of detracting from his looks, they only enhanced his attractiveness.

"We reached Algiers in time to lead the dey's forces to Constantine," he explained. "Abdullah's Janissaries were well trained, but they weren't our only obstacle. The city of Constantine is nearly impregnable. The high walls, deep moat and guarded drawbridges leading into the city were Abdullah's protection and salvation. Or so he thought.

"His Janissaries would ride out, strike at one of the dey's caravans, then withdraw quickly to their citadel. There was no way to get to Abdullah, and the dey was on the verge of admitting defeat, until Allen and I convinced him otherwise."

"Allen! Where is he?" asked Christa with a hint of fear. "And Omar and Elissa! Are they with you?"

"All in good time, my love, all in good time," Mark teased her. "Now where was I? Oh yes. Both Allen and I knew of a secret entrance into the city that our father showed us long ago. There are four natural arches of stone leading into the city, but Allen and I knew of a fifth, one cut into the stone by the River Rummel. Years ago Father had the passage cleared for just such an emergency. You have to dive beneath the water to get to it, but soon the water gives way to a steep rise eventually leading to a tunnel beneath the castle. Time had blocked the passage with debris and it took weeks to clear it."

"To make a long story short, we finally entered the city through the secret passage late one night and spread rumors that the dey was expecting a rich caravan from Tunis to pass this way. Just as we hoped, the rumors reached Abdullah's ears and he immediately dispatched all but a handful of Janissaries to intercept it. We had only to wait until the men rode out and then, under cover of darkness, we overpowered the guards and opened the gate. The fight was fierce, but of short duration. Constantine was soon ours."

"What happened to Abdullah?" asked Christa breathlessly. "Did you—is he—"

"Yes, my love, he's dead. Only it didn't happen the way you might think. In the end, Abdullah wasn't slain by one of his own flesh and blood, which is as it should be."

"How did he die?"

"Abdullah was no coward, I'll give him that," Mark admitted wryly. "When his palace was invaded he seized a scimitar and attempted to defend himself. Of course he recognized the uniforms of the dey's army, but when he saw me he exploded into a fury of insane rage, so certain was he that he had gotten rid of me long ago. He rushed forward to end my life as he should have done when I was his prisoner, and forgot his lame leg. He tripped on the hem of his caftan and fell on his own sword. It pierced his heart, killing him instantly."

"How horrible!" Christa shuddered, recalling vividly the handsome young man whose mind was warped by jealousy.

"It's no worse than the fate the dey had planned for him," Mark said. "And probably more humane. His death would not have been so quick nor so clean had he been taken alive."

"So it's over." Christa sighed with intense relief. "And now the beylic is yours. I'm surprised you came back for me and Michael. Didn't any of the young women in Abdullah's harem please you?"

"I didn't bother to investigate," Mark countered, suppressing an amused grin.

"I thought perhaps that's what detained you. Dallying with Abdullah's women could keep a man of your appetites occupied for months," she hinted sullenly.

A suspicious twitch drew up the corner of Mark's mouth. "Jealous, my love?"

"I certainly am! Where is Elissa? If you won't tell me the truth I'm certain she'll—"

"The truth is, I fell ill before I could return to England."

"Ill? What happened?"

"Malaria. The same illness I suffered before. It seems the moment I set foot in that part of the world, it strikes with a vengeance. I'm sorry, love. I would have returned to you sooner were I able. It appears as if Constantine will have to survive without Ahmed bey."

"I can't believe you mean it, Mark." Christa gasped in delight. "It's what your father wanted for you. Are you certain you're willing to give up your heritage for me and our son?"

"I think Father would be pleased with my decision," Mark replied cryptically. "All I want or need is right here in England. Constantine has a bey. One who will rule it wisely, with much love and compassion for his people."

"Who! Who could possibly rule in your place?"

"Yazid bey."

"Yazid? Your brother Allen?"

Mark nodded. "I abdicated in my brother's favor. The dey of Algiers agreed that Yazid should take my place. The love he bears the land of his birth runs deep, with a dedication I failed to attain. I am my mother's son, with roots in England. Duke of Marlboro is the only title I aspire to. In addition to father and husband, of course."

"Is Elissa happy with Allen's decision?" Christa asked. "There are many things she'll have to accept. Not all of them pleasant."

"If you're referring to the keeping of a harem, don't worry. Allen swore to Elissa that all the women now in residence in the serai will be released or married to good men. As long as he is bey, he will take but one wife, as I would have done. Elissa's children will be his only heirs."

"Then it's truly over," Christa sighed gratefully.

"No, it's only the beginning, my love. The beginning of the rest of our lives. And now, dear wife, how about a kiss of welcome for your husband?"

Christa needed no further urging as she threw

her arms around his neck, meeting his lips with a hunger that matched his own. She kissed him lingeringly, savoring every moment as his hands explored the soft, inviting curves of her body. Her breasts swelled beneath his touch, nipples tautening to hard, stabbing points of sensation.

So enraptured was Christa by his drugging kisses that her dress left her body without her knowledge. Nor did she know when Mark rid her of petticoat and chemise. Her figure needed no corset to mold it to slim proportions.

"How would you like another child?" Mark asked teasingly, nuzzling her flat stomach.

"Do I have a choice?" Christa smiled mischievously. "My husband is a most virile man. I'd venture to guess that one day the mansion will be bursting at the seams with offspring, unless you learn to control yourself."

"It's impossible to control myself with a temptress in my arms," he teased her. "Best you prepare yourself for a houseful of children." He became serious for a moment. "My love, I'm sorry I missed Michael's birth. I would have given anything to see him slide into the world. I promise to be here for our future children."

"I understand. You are too honorable a man to allow Allen and Omar to fight your battles." Mark said nothing, his silence adding mute agreement to her words. "You were obliged to see this to the end."

"But I left you to have our child alone," he said guiltily. "I should have been with you, even if I had to crawl from a sick bed to do so."

"You're here, my darling. That's all that matters."

"How you must have suffered all those months, thinking I wouldn't return. You've borne much for my sake, but never again. I'm here to stay.

From now on, I intend to shoulder my responsibilities. You and our children will want for nothing. Nothing or no one will separate us again. When our next child is born, I'll be right there beside you."

"If you don't stop talking and make love to me, there never will be another child," Christa protested cheekily, tearing at his clothes.

"Ah, sweet siren, I don't deserve you," Mark groaned, swiftly shedding his clothing.

"Mark, wait," Christa cried, suddenly thinking of Lenore. "Did Omar return with you or did he remain with Allen?"

"Omar did not wish to leave me. But I suspect it was Lenore who brought him back. Now will you be quiet so I can love you properly?"

And in that orchard with the sun hot upon their naked bodies, they imagined themselves lying on the shifting desert sands, the handsome sheikh and his beautiful silver-haired captive. In each other's arms they recaptured the glorious passion that belonged solely to them, and transported their desert ecstasy to verdant green pastures, where it soared in waves of rapture that bound them together for all time.

Connie Mason

Highland Warrior

She is far too shapely to be a seasoned warrior, but she is just as deadly. As she engages him on the battlefield, Ross knows her for a MacKay, longtime enemies of his clan. Soon this flame-haired virago will be his wife, given to him by her father in a desperate effort to end generations of feuding. Of all her family, Gillian MacKay is the least willing to make peace. Her fiery temper challenges Ross's mastery while her lush body taunts his masculinity. Both politics and pride demand that he tame her, but he will do it his way—with a scorching seduction that will sweep away her defenses and win her heart.

Dorchester Publishing Co., Inc.
P.O. Box 6640
Wayne, PA 19087-8640

_____5744-1
$6.99 US/$8.99 CAN

CONNIE MASON

To Tempt A Rogue

Kitty O'Shay has been living outside the law for years. Dressed as a boy, she joined the notorious Barton gang, robbing banks and stealing horses with no one the wiser of her true identity. Except their newest member: Ryan Delaney. He is the only one who sees through her charade.

Ryan has infiltrated the Barton gang, hoping to find some information on a dying man's missing illegitimate daughter. Little does Ryan know he'll find her *within* the group. Stealing Kitty away is easy; controlling his desire for the maddening vixen is not. Ryan thought his biggest problem would be convincing Kitty to visit the father she'd never known—until he realized he was in danger of losing his heart to the beauty.

A Taste of Paradise

CONNIE MASON

When lovely Sophia Carlisle stows away on a ship bound for Jamaica, she hardly expects to find Christian Radcliff at the helm. She and the captain have a turbulent history, which involves the breaking of her heart and the death by duel of his best friend. Now they will be forced to share a cabin, and if Christian has it his way, a bed. But Sophia finds herself forgetting the past and giving in to temptation. No man can arouse her senses as the swashbuckling captain does, and she has no use for prudence or propriety when in his kiss she can find...*A Taste of Paradise.*